August 20

Dear Nena & John —
I hope you enjoy
my wacky first novel.
It was fun to write.
All the best,
Bill

LONG PIG

A FANTASY CONCERNING CANNIBALS,
COURTS AND OTHER CONSUMERS

WILLIAM C. MILLER

LOST〰
COAST
PRESS
Fort Bragg
California

LONG PIG
A Fantasy Concerning Cannibals, Courts and Other Consumers
Copyright © 2002 by William C. Miller

DISCLAIMER
All persons in this story are fictional, and any resemblance to any person living or dead is purely accidental. All companies are fictional and any resemblance to real companies is purely accidental.

Cover Design: Gopa Illustration and Design

Library of Congress Cataloging-in-Publication Data

Miller, William C., 1930-
    Long pig: a fantasy concerning cannibals, courts and
    other consumers / William C. Miller.
p. cm.
LCCN 2001099079
ISBN 1-882897-68-4

    1. San Francisco (Calif) -- Politics and government-
    Fiction. 2. San Francisco (Calif) -- Social life and
    customs --Fiction. 3. Cannibalism--Fiction. 4. Courts-
    Fiction. 1. Title.

PS3613.1593L56 2002   813'.6
    QB133-220

2   4   6   8   9   7   5   3   1

TO MY WIFE,

Hannelore Steinbeck Miller

PART I

SAVAGES

1. EAST AND WEST

THE YOUNGER OF THE TWO MEN carrying the beheaded male corpse stopped at the border of the roasting pit and looked at the red-hot coals. "Shouldn't we put him down and do the spitting here on the ground?"

His older companion was decisive. "Absolutely not. The spit always remains over the coals, and the long pig must be brought there and placed on it. That is the traditional way."

This was the younger man's first time as a long-pig skewerer, a great honor, but daunting. "But how do we get him pushed onto the spit? He is very heavy."

"We just take a little run at it. He will go right on. Just be careful not to drop him. That happened once, and there was trouble."

The two backed off a few paces, and then, holding their cargo in a horizontal plane, hurried it toward the sharp end of the spit.

It was a late winter afternoon on Nova Cannes, an island near New Guinea. The temperature was ninety-six degrees Fahrenheit, and the relative humidity ninety-nine percent. Water from the earlier rain dripped off the branches and leaves of lofty trees onto the tribespeople gathered around the big open hearth. The spitting of the body successfully accomplished, the expectant diners were now watching the evening meal roasting, indifferent to the weather. It was always hot and wet on Nova Cannes, but meals were not always as good as this one promised to be. A successful war party had brought back a captive male from another tribe. Now, his spirit long since flown from his body, the latter was being turned slowly over the hearth. The most common roast meal on the island was pig. Pigs were spitted lengthwise and barbecued. Enemy tribesmen were prepared for consumption the same way, except the head was cut off for addition to the tribe's skull collection. A human thus barbecued was called "long pig."

After capture, the victim had been put on trial and convicted of bearing arms against the tribe. In the memory of the tribe, no captured enemy had ever been acquitted of this offense. All had been eaten. In this case, the trial proceedings and the beheading had taken less than an hour. Preparation of the deceased for consumption took longer, but by late afternoon he was almost done, basted from time to time by the principal chef. "Is he ready yet?" a boy in his early teens inquired of the elder who was basting the roast.

"Not yet. Here, have one of these sweet potatoes."

"Thank you," the boy replied and began to bite into the hot tuber. Then he asked, "Are the white people coming to the feast?"

"No. They do not like long pig."

"That is very funny. The white people are very funny."

"Indeed, but you must not say so. That is not polite."

"They cannot hear. They are way over there." He pointed in the direction of the two tents where the anthropologists had their camp.

"That is no matter. It is nevertheless impolite." The chef spoke firmly, while applying more sugary vegetable sauce to the turning body. It was almost ready, and the sight and odor made the boy's mouth water.

"The last time we had long pig, Malu got sick," said the boy.

The chef snorted. "That was not my cooking. Malu was drinking koda, and he is too young to drink koda."

"I am old enough to drink koda," said the boy, pulling himself up to as great a height as possible.

The elder laughed. "Yes, and you are young enough to get sick from it, too." But the boy did not respond. He had seen some of his friends taking swigs from a gourd filled with koda, the local tipple, and ran to join them.

The adult males in the crowd were naked except for flute-shaped, wooden devices that fit around and projected beyond their penises. These were raised to a forty-five-degree angle and secured by a cord around the waist, so that the wearer appeared to have a permanent and profound erection. The women wore short, front and rear half-aprons made of leaves, which hung from a waist cord. Their upper bodies were bare. The children wore nothing.

The adults had been consuming lots of koda. A long-pig feast was always accompanied by appropriate sexual license, and koda helped ensure the proper mood. The teasing, pinching and other romantic foreplay had already started. Children and some of the younger males ran about swinging bullroarers. These were flat slabs of stone or wood with a hole in one end to which a cord was attached and the object whirled overhead to produce a roaring noise. Others in the crowd, both sexes participating, stomped their feet rhythmically. Around the margins of this activity, elderly males sat beating drums and drinking koda. Somewhere to the west, beyond the dense rain forest, the sun was going down into the ocean.

The roasting pit lay some twenty yards from the tribe's long house, a large rectangular structure of wood and leaves that was the principal center of communal activities. At twice that distance from the other side of the long house was the camp of the two foreigners, which had been established six months earlier as a base for anthropological study of the island's natives. From the camp came loud, terrible music out of a black box possessed by the newly arrived white man who was called Dipper Edwards. This competed with the drum, foot stomping and bullroarer sounds of the tribe's long-pig music and was very annoying. Before the new white man came there had been no such terrible noises. They did not like him. They wished that he had not replaced the other white man, Peter Walker, who had had to go back across the water because of family troubles. Their tribal leader had told them that Peter's sister was on trial for murder in a place called San Francisco.

The white woman on the island, Ellen Ross, also did not like the new white man. They could see that she was very unhappy with the change. Some of the people thought that she did not like them either, but this was not clear — it might be that she just did not like Nova Cannes. Whites were fussy about the heat, the mosquitoes and the leeches. What was clear was that she did not like the fact that they made long pig. Yet man was the highest order of creature, and should, therefore, be the most valuable thing to eat. Any objection to eating people stood the situation on its head.

It was important, however, to be tolerant of the opinions of others. Big Mouth, the principal deity of the tribe, had so laid it down long ago in his First Principles. But the new white man was difficult to tolerate. Even now, with the pleasures of the long-pig feast before them, there was grumbling by some of the men to do something about it. Another of the tribesmen, taller than the rest, urged them to ignore the situation. "Do not trouble yourselves over him or his noise. He will be gone soon, and Peter will return."

This man's name translated into English as *Tallfellow,* and he and his ancestors had been tribal leaders and priests of Big Mouth for sixteen generations. Since whites had first come to the island six years earlier, he had begun thinking that he must bring the teachings of Big Mouth to the foreigners. They were in need of spiritual guidance. Very few whites, however, had come to the island. He knew that most of them lived across the water. Peter had been teaching him the white man's language, and when he had mastered it he would somehow get across the water and undertake the mission.

For tonight, however, the great thing was not to let this Dipper person ruin a good time. "Pay him no heed," he urged his companions. "The man has no brains, and tonight we shall have plenty of koda, lovemaking and long pig."

ACROSS THE PACIFIC in San Francisco it was a foggy, late-summer morning with the temperature at fifty degrees. In the Civic Center Park near city hall a large crowd of street people and demonstrators were gathered. Most of the latter were professionals retained by commercial organizations that mounted protests for paying clients. In recent months there had been demonstrations every day in the park and on the steps of the nearby City Hall. Media representatives, the demonstrators' symbiotic partners, were always in evidence. There had, however, never been a media presence like that which the trial of Peter Walker's sister, Penny Hill, had attracted.

A rich and beautiful woman of forty, Penny Hill was charged with shooting a street person who had called himself "Smoking Mother." The alleged crime occurred during a hotly contested race for the mayor's office. Soon after her arrest, the incumbent mayor, Waylon Homer, had called a press conference to announce that there would be a vigorous prosecution. "In our city," he stressed, framing the issue so as to give it political energy, "the rich must not go about taking the lives of the poor."

On the fourth floor of City Hall, in the courtroom of Judge Potter B. Flex, the trial was now in progress. Television people and equipment were everywhere. Judge Flex had ruled that the trial would be televised live, following assurances from the media that he would be provided certain television professionals. A makeup man prepared the judge prior to each day's proceedings and accompanied him to chambers for touch-ups. The judge's normally pinkish-gray face now continuously displayed a glowing, youthful tan. In addition, a camera director was seated beside the judge's law clerk. From that position he could direct the cameras so as to obtain favorable shots of His Honor. Judge Flex had advised this individual that he wanted plenty of close-ups, particularly when he was ruling, and to be careful they didn't get any shots of the court, say, scratching itself or picking its nose.

The early days of the trial had been consumed with motions and selecting a jury. After the jury had been selected and received some preliminary instructions, Judge Flex directed the lead prosecutor to make his opening statement. The prosecution had two lawyers at its table. The lead prosecutor was Tremorgan Davies, III, some of whose male ancestors had labored in the coal mines of Wales. His more immediate forebears had prospered in America. His father and his father's father had been lawyers and, like the third of their line, were given in the presence of a jury to asserting kinship with the working man by invoking their forefathers' exertions in the pits of the old country. Tremorgan was a skilled player of populist themes. He knew how to snarl at the "big boys," the "vested interests," and the "elite," and how to appeal to commonly held prejudices.

He was in his early fifties, just above average height, with a powerful upper body and neck. A sharp, hook-like nose of good size dominated his face. He had small black eyes, his skin smooth and toward olive in color. He was nearly bald; what hair he had was thin and dark and lay straight back upon his domed, strongly formed skull. Despite this array of features, more suggestive of a large predatory bird than a charmer, Davies came across to juries as the latter. In a courtroom, he had a grace on his feet and manner that beguiled jurors. These characteristics, coupled with a voice that could, as occasion demanded, crack like a whip or soothe like a mother's whisper, had made him the most successful prosecutor in the state.

Davies' assistant was Sonia Taft, a woman of thirty-five with several years' trial experience. She and Davies wore black armbands on which, in white letters, appeared the words "The People." When first displayed, this device had provoked a stirring objection from the defense. It did not, however, move Judge Flex, who was not at all troubled by the armbands. "The jury", he assured the defense, "will decide the case on the evidence, not on the armbands." He added that if the defense wished to wear armbands labeled "The Accused" he would allow it. The defense declined. On television the presentation of this episode ended with a zoom-in shot of the judge's wife seated in the first row behind the bar, her face flushed as if with pride at her husband's administration of justice.

The defense table had three persons seated at it: the defendant, Penny Hill, and two lawyers. One of the lawyers was Hamilton Sayer, of Blunt, Hammer and Tuggle, a firm that had represented Penny in business matters prior to her arrest. Sayer had brought in as the principal trial counsel a criminal defense specialist named Barton Playchek, whose chief claim to fame was his successful use of the defense of "diminished capacity," a species of the insanity defense. At one time this defense had been abolished in California, but it had been reinstated through the efforts of then Governor Harry Lovebird, primarily remembered for his belief that crime would be reduced if criminals were given more respect. Playchek was the first lawyer to successfully employ the defense after its rebirth.

In that trial, which became known as the "Don Quixote case," Playchek had persuaded a jury that his client's capacity to tell right from wrong had been so diminished by listening to and watching talk shows — as Quixote's mind had been warped by reading romances — that he should not be held responsible for shooting his daughter's boyfriend three times in the head. The result was severely criticized in legal circles, even more so by talk show hosts. Nevertheless, it enabled Playchek to more than double his usual retainer and hourly rates.

Playchek was in his late forties. The son of immigrants from Eastern Europe, he had become a lawyer after a moderately successful career as a musician. He played several instruments well and had written a song that had been recorded by another artist and became a hit. With the royalties as a reserve he entered law school. He was of medium height and build. His hair was dark, starting to go gray, his face dominated by heavy beard shadow despite close shaving. His eyes were blue and friendly. Big, widespread ears framed his face. He had been married, briefly, and remained on good terms with his former mate. He was a likeable man.

Penny Hill turned in her chair to look back at her brother, Peter Walker, the anthropologist, who was seated three rows behind the bar. He had recently returned from an island near New Guinea to be with his sister during the trial. She tried to catch his eye, but he was gazing fixedly at the prosecution table.

Prosecutor Davies stood up and turned toward the jury box, chest expanded, shoulders squared as if about to be measured during a physical examination. His face carefully expressed the seriousness of the occasion. For good luck, he carried in a breast pocket a letter from his mother encouraging him about the case. His mother always wrote to him about his cases, and he had, at times, fantasized reading one of his mother's letters to a jury. The rules of evidence presented a formidable obstacle to such a performance, but perhaps, he had mused, with Judge Flex on the bench ... But that had to wait, for now he must deliver, as if they were simply a guide to the evidence to come, the precisely constructed arguments he had been preparing for almost a month.

He began, "On the day of his death, ladies and gentlemen, this gentle soul called Smoking Mother by his many friends and other homeless persons, whose vile murder brings us here today, this young, innocent victim rose with expectation, with hope ... "

2. Smoking Mother Rises

Standing in the portal of the New Reality Homeless Shelter, Thorson Grebe, also known as "Smoking Mother," stretched himself awake and surveyed the foggy San Francisco morning. It was almost a rain, a cold, early-summer fog. A nearby clock showed 7:45 A.M. Across the street, in sparse garments, shivered the day's first hooker. He quickly ducked back into the shelter. It was the same whore whose purse he had snatched three days ago, a profitless crime as it turned out. The purse contained no money, only makeup articles, condoms, padded handcuffs, a short leather whip and a pair of panties. He had tried to pawn the cuffs and whip without success. He waited for her to move on, then re-emerged.

Smoking Mother was twenty-three and had been on the street in San Francisco for nine months, attracted to the city by the social programs of a former mayor, John Lint, including a recently discontinued municipal food stamp program that included beer and wine in its coverage. When he had arrived he had only his real name. But he had read in a newspaper that smoking was especially bad for pregnant women. Later he was drinking wine with a pregnant street girl who was a heavy smoker, and to bug her he told her that pregnant women should not smoke; that smoking mothers were bad for their babies. She rounded on him drunkenly, "You're a shmokin' mother." He liked the sound of that. "Me Smoking Mother," he declared with feeling, and began to introduce himself that way on the street. It was distinctive and had a nice Indian warrior ring to it. His blonde hair and blue eyes defied the association, but he took to wearing a beaded headband with a feather stuck in it.

Smoking Mother was big and strong and was proud of his size, which was useful in bullying people. He had two cigarettes left from the night before and lit one. A black male of small stature appeared magically from a doorway. "Hey, man. How about a smoke?" Smoking Mother moved quickly toward him and kicked him hard in the leg. The smaller man shrieked, "Hey you prick! What you do that for?" But Smoking Mother was already striding away, his immediate destination a small news and coffee shop in the next block.

The Asian proprietor did not want his sidewalk swept in exchange for coffee and a roll. "It's already clean. I swept it." So Smoking Mother sat down on the sidewalk directly in front of the shop and took off his shoes, exposing filthy, ragged socks and dirty feet. "OK. You sweep it again. I'll give you coffee and a roll but don't come back." Smoking Mother smiled. It would be awhile before he came back. There were plenty of similar shops to hit the same way.

He took his breakfast to the Civic Center Park, which was bounded by City Hall, the library and other government buildings. It was a large rectangular area, mostly concrete, with central fountain, a shallow pool, some low trees and grassy areas. There were many benches. An elderly man was sleeping on the bench Smoking Mother wanted. He shook him hard. "Get off my bench," Smoking Mother shouted in the sleeper's ear. The man shuffled off, muttering darkly. Smoking Mother seated himself and took the lid off his coffee cup, spilling some of the hot, creamy liquid on his already filthy pants. "Son of a bitch gave me a bad cup," he cursed.

Nearby, the professional demonstrators who came to the park each day, like working men to a union hall, were beginning to gather. Smoking Mother had tried without success to get hired as a demonstrator. It was, he believed, the state of his clothes. This Saturday there would be another clothing distribution at the Reality Shelter, but he always had trouble finding anything large enough for his frame. Why didn't big men give away their clothing? It was a fucking shame, he thought. He decided to try again to get hired. His breakfast finished, he tossed the cup on the ground, in preference to the waste receptacle near at hand, and walked toward the assortment of would-be demonstrators.

A slim, neatly dressed young man with a clipboard was recruiting for a morning performance. This was Martin Blender of Strident Students, Inc., a professional protest organization. He saw a huge, dirty man with a beaded headband, a broken feather stuck in it, and attempted — to no avail — to avoid Smoking Mother. "Hey. I like demonstrating. I'm good at it. Put me down." Martin was as much offended by Smoking Mother's smell as by his appearance. He could not say he had all the demonstrators he needed because he was manifestly still hiring. There was no way out but the truth.

"I'm sorry, sir. You just would not do."

"Why not?" asked Smoking Mother, trying to look appealing behind a wide smile, through which the fumes of last night's wine escaped.

"I said, 'I'm sorry,'" Martin responded, and turned his back to Smoking Mother, counting on the nearby crowd of recruits to deter the big man from offering violence.

"Motherfuckin' little pansy," shouted Smoking Mother and turned away. He would go over by the library. It would open soon, and there might be a purse to snatch. He had scored a good one there a month ago. Given his distinctive size and appearance, he knew it was only a matter of time before he was identified and apprehended. It was a game he was playing with the authorities. He was a man of courage and feared no jail. There would be amusing publicity: "Giant Purse Snatcher Named Smoking Mother Caught." He would send the news items to his mother back in St. Paul. That'll give the bitch something to think about, he mused happily.

HIGH ABOVE CIVIC CENTER PARK and the library-bound Smoking Mother, Waylon Homer, mayor of San Francisco, stood at his office window and looked down at the firemen hosing the occupants of the City Hall steps. The sight made him gloomy, a poor mood for a professional officeholder. The firemen did this three times a day, but the occupiers always came back. When in place they blocked access to City Hall from the park side. The step sitters had formed to protest the demise of former Mayor John Lint's municipal food stamp program and called themselves "No Stamps, No Steps."

The walls of the mayoral office bore portraits of its prior occupants, including the benign face of Mayor Lint, Homer's predecessor. Before becoming mayor, Lint had been in the state legislature and had served on then Governor Harry Lovebird's Crime Reduction Panel. The panel had issued a report concluding that crime could be most effectively reduced, statistically, by reducing the number of arrests. In aid of that objective, Lint had championed adoption by the legislature of the Lint Law Enforcement Control Act. He described this bill as "providing much-needed obstacles to law enforcement."

The act was aimed at police, and its core provision made the enforcement of any law "in bad faith" a felony. The offender was also subject to civil suit for damages. "Bad faith" was not defined in the act, which left that up to the sentiment of judge and jury. The real beauty of the act, however, lay in the fact that it denied reimbursement of the costs of defense, even if the defendant prevailed. This provided truly effective deterrence to law enforcement by police. It was left to Judge Flex to hold that any use of physical force by a policeman was tantamount to "bad faith." Homer had turned to the fire department and its hoses to maintain access to City Hall, because no policeman would venture to lay hands on the occupants of the steps.

Mayor Lint's defunct stamp program had been supplementary to state welfare benefits, and was to be financed by an occupancy tax on businesses employing more than four persons. The program was at once attacked in court by the businesses to be so taxed. Judge Flex upheld the tax at the trial-court level, but was reversed on appeal on the grounds that the tax scheme violated both state and federal constitutions. During a press conference called by Mayor Lint to denounce this miscarriage of justice, Lint suffered a fatal attack of apoplexy.

In accordance with provisions of the city charter, Waylon Homer, as chairperson of the board of supervisors, succeeded Lint as interim mayor, pending a new mayoral election. But the stamp program's popularity survived its legal defeat and the death of its creator. In aid of that survival, Judge Flex advised the media that he was "perplexed" by the order reversing him and that elimination of the stamp program was "against his conscience." From that foundation sprang "No Stamps, No Steps," and as he looked down on its members, already regrouping from the last hosing, Mayor Homer thought how unfair it all was to him.

Homer had been running for office most of his adult life. He was presently engaged in the election campaign for the mayor's office required by Mayor Lint's death, a position sought by three other candidates. Anything that could cost him votes offended his sense of fairness. He was a lifelong populist and wanted to be considered a follower in Lint's footsteps, a supporter of measures like the stamp program. Yet as mayor he had to maintain access to City Hall, even though many of the city's voters looked upon hosing away the demonstrators as a species of atrocity. It made him appear to be an antagonist to the stamp program and a foe of the needy. The media were playing those tunes. There had to be a way to divorce himself from this wolfish role and restore his traditional image as a champion of the downtrodden. He went to the phone and called his principal campaign consultant, R. "Doc" Wayward.

IN CIVIC CENTER PARK at the demonstrator recruiting area, Martin Blender was still furious over Smoking Mother's shouted insult. The Strident Students program director, Maria Cantu, was trying to calm him. "Listen, Maria, did you hear what that filthy savage called me? We ought to have police protection against these bums. Look, there are cops all over, and none of them ever does anything to help. They just stand around and smile."

"Never mind, Martin. He's gone, and I've got to get things going. On the first one today I'll need a few Mid-eastern types. It's for 'Families Against U.S. Gulf Aggression.' That's the Iraqi oil consortium. Let's see your clipboard." Maria examined the list of recruits. There was a dismal lack of Arabic or other suitable names. "All right. Here. Use Perez, Gonzalez and Maldonado. The order is for thirty demonstrators, so mix them up. I don't want the three of them in a bunch. Here's the chant. It goes like the old 'Ho, Ho, Ho Chi Minh.'"

Martin looked at the paper Maria had handed him, which bore the marching song:

14

Sad, Sad, Saddam Hussein,
U.S. aggression down the drain.
Sad, Sad, Saddam Hussein
Bush-Clinton criminals, Saddam still reign.

But the words did not register with Martin. He was still seeing Smoking Mother and hearing his foul remarks. "Filthy savage," Martin repeated aloud.

3. Penny Hill Rises

WHILE MARTIN BLENDER WAS VENTING his rage, Penny Hill was still asleep in her San Francisco home. Penny was Peter Walker's half-sister, the only offspring of her father's first marriage, as Peter was of the second. Although they did not meet often, they had been fond of each other since childhood. Penny was good-looking and had married and divorced well. She had plenty of money and no regular employment. She lived in San Francisco with her only child, an adopted daughter, April, now nineteen, whose primary activity was body building; April could bench press two hundred pounds.

At the moment, Penny was tossing about in her bed, legs struggling with the covers, in the throes of a dream inspired by her brother's last letter. This had contained a detailed account of Nova Cannes, its natives and their habits. In the dream she crouched naked, beset by leeches and mosquitoes, behind a tree in the Nova Cannes forest, watching the native men prepare an enemy tribesman for dinner. Their enhanced penises bobbed mischievously. If they saw her, there was no telling what they would do. Then one turned and saw her, pointed, and a roar arose. They were coming. She started to run and tripped over a vine. Penny half woke. Yes, her foot was caught. Woke all the way. Caught in the bedclothes. Dreaming. Good grief! The room was light. She looked at her bedside clock. It was late.

She sat up in bed facing the life-sized oil painting of her that leaned against a wall. For the last several months Penny had been pursued ardently but unsuccessfully by a painter and sculptor, Eric Krane, fifteen years her junior. The artistic result of his infatuation stood in her bedroom. He had achieved a good general likeness of her face and figure, but in details of expression and bearing the work fulfilled Eric's vision of a wished-for Penny rather than representing her as she had ever appeared. He had seen her one day in riding habit and begged her to pose for him so attired. His explanation of why he wanted her to do so was unsatisfactory, but she was curious and granted his request.

He had produced a luminous, sharply outlined standing figure against a dark green and brown background. She stood booted and spurred in jodhpurs, feet set well apart, holding a riding crop across her midsection. Eric had managed to give her face a threatening yet provocative expression. On top of that, his aroused hand and eye had converted the modest white blouse she had posed in into a virtually transparent one, so that the form of her brassiere-covered breasts loomed erotically above the brandished crop. Penny could see where things were heading from the first sketches, but continued to indulge Eric's sublimated passion because she liked him. Besides, she was intrigued by his skillful depiction of her as an S & M mistress, even though she had no desire to be one.

Eric had, she assumed, intended to keep the painting for himself. She was surprised when he insisted on giving it to her. "But where can I put it? I can't have it hanging around the living room. It's — "

Eric had a solution. "Keep it in your bedroom," he suggested. Her mind took off on this proposal: to scare off potential bedmates, or magically inspire her to emulate the painting? But she didn't want to hurt his feelings by insisting that he take it away.

"All right," she agreed, "but I'm not promising it'll stay there." As time passed, however, she had grown used to it. Now it was a fixture in the bedroom, and she said hello to it in the morning,

as a child does to a stuffed animal. Her friendship with Eric remained platonic.

Penny walked past the portrait and went to and opened a north
facing window. Below it on the roof stood a large bag of birdseed.
Steller's blue jays raucously greeted the opening window like Pav-
lov's dogs responding to the bell. Penny tossed several handfuls of
seed onto the roof. It was very foggy, the bay invisible beneath the
thick white cover, the Golden Gate Bridge towers visible only at
their tops. She shut the window and began to dress. She was late,
and there were a lot of things she wanted to do today. She meant
to get to the library. She had been putting that off, but Peter was
coming on leave to stay with her soon, and she wanted to be prepared to discuss his work on the island. She wanted to obtain library
books and learn more about Nova Cannes and its part of the world.

As she dressed, Penny thought about the bad dream, recalling
it vividly. Why was she naked in a place like that, for God's sake?
But then she thought how she had often had dreams of being
naked, and in only one or two instances had nudity been appropriate. She finished dressing in haste. Grabbing the purse she had
used the day before, she stuck her hand inside to be sure her
wallet and other things she needed were there. Her fingers touched
the pistol. This ancient single-action revolver had been her father's. She had kept it, along with a box of cartridges, which she
found among his things after his death. Although she knew nothing
about firearms, she thought it might come in handy one day. For
several years she had carried it along whenever she had to drive
any distance on the freeways. It afforded some protection in case
of a breakdown, or so she believed. Shortly after finding the weapon
she had fired it three times into a sand dune south of San Francisco. It worked. Since then it had not been fired or even oiled.
She kept it — loaded — in a small safe in her bedroom closet. Yesterday she had driven to Sacramento and back, and had taken it
along. She never took it just driving around town, but she didn't
want to take the time to put it back in the safe. Taking the bag,
she started downstairs.

As she approached the lower floor, a grunting noise came from behind the closed door of what had been a second parlor and was now her daughter April's "fitness room." Penny knocked before opening the door. There was another young girl working out in the room with April. Each wore gym shorts of dramatic snugness and a five-inch band of elastic material around the chest, sort of a bosom girdle. Fitness, Penny had earlier concluded, seemed to require highlighting the crotch and buttocks while flattening the breasts. The two were perspiring heavily from their exertions. "Close the door, mother, there's a draft," April shouted between intakes of air from where she lay benched on her back. She was tall like her mother, but her long limbs were layered with much more muscle. She grimaced, pushing a large barbell upward. Penny closed the door.

"April, I'm going downtown right after breakfast, and I'll be gone most of the day." There was no response from the girl, who firmly re-elevated the barbell. Penny looked at her straining daughter, whose sweat ran down her face and neck, darkening the mysterious breast band, her elasticized bottom pulsing muscularly. It was not, she thought, an appealing sight. Then she left for her breakfast.

4. SAVAGE PRACTICES

AS PENNY PROCEEDED TOWARD BREAKFAST in San Francisco, a column of savages came down the mountain trail toward their village on Nova Cannes. They were all males, and their wooden penis sheaths jiggled prominently as they walked. Such ornaments were similar to those of other Pacific island aboriginal cultures, abandoned elsewhere under civilizing influences. But here on Nova Cannes the practice had survived the missionaries who had come and departed. Now the only whites on the island were the two American anthropologists, Peter Walker and Ellen Ross, who stood in their camp on the outskirts of the village watching the men approach.

Nova Cannes had been thought to be uninhabited until six years before Peter and Ellen's arrival. The island had no harbors or beaches, and was surrounded by an impenetrable mangrove swamp. From the air, the dense tree cover blocked evidence of life. Smoke from the inhabitants' fires dissipated in the humid air, the lofty vegetation. World War II, which saw neighboring islands beset by Americans and Japanese, had passed it by. Then, against all odds, a fire started in the ever-wet forest, attracting the attention of a plane from Port Moresby. Some of the inhabitants were seen in the burnt-away area. In due course, the island was elevated from uninhabited to the status of a United Nations tribal territory.

Peter saw Tallfellow striding in the van of the approaching tribesmen. He had become quite proficient in English, and Peter regarded him as his best informant as to the culture of the Trumani tribes, the natives of the island. In the middle of the column, two unfortunates, Trumani of another tribe, their penises defrocked, walked hands bound and with ropes around their necks. Soon, Peter knew, the captives would lose their heads, which would be de-fleshed, polished, and placed on display in the tribe's skull collection. Their bodies would be barbecued and eaten. Long pig. Peter turned to his colleague who was staring gravely at the procession. "It looks like our side won, Ellen."

"Are they going to eat those two?" she asked.

"I'm sure they are, from what Farrington told us."

David Farrington, an Australian employed by the United Nations' tribal territory organization, had briefed them in Port Moresby on Trumani customs before they came to Nova Cannes. Cannibalism was one of them. "It was," Farrington had said, savoring the subject, "an acquired taste. But," he added, looking meaningfully at Ellen, "they never eat the fairer sex." Now, faced with the immediate prospect of this acquired taste being indulged before her eyes, Ellen declared, "It's horrible."

"They'll do it over behind the long house. They know we don't like it," said Peter in a soothing voice.

Ellen was not consoled. "I don't care. It's horrible. And it's not just eating people. This whole place. It's just awful."

As she spoke, the women of the village began to congregate around the procession, verbally abusing the captives, while the children ran about hooting. It was beginning to rain again, as it had each day for about a month, a steady hot drip from the lofty trees. Peter and Ellen were identically clothed: their bodies were shrouded in mosquito netting, long pants tucked into boots and long-sleeved shirts held around the wrists with rubber bands. Despite the frightful heat and humidity, such arrangements were necessary to minimize the success of insects and leeches.

The crowd was now joined by several elderly men holding aloft a man-sized effigy of the god Big Mouth. Big Mouth possessed the body of a man, including penis and sheath, but his head, while somewhat human in form, was primarily that of a crocodile. Fierce-toothed jaws projected from the lower face. "Big Mouth eat more," the bearers of the effigy chanted over and over.

Peter had learned of Big Mouth from Tallfellow. A male deity, considered the primary source of Trumani moral principles, Big Mouth was, nevertheless, generally invoked in connection with his principal activity, consumption of food. Big Mouth was, in fact, especially revered because he "eat more." Peter had inquired why, hoping not to offend but too curious to forego the risk. Tallfellow replied amiably, "He eat more than other gods. Big Mouth eat more." But why was that important, Peter wanted to know. "Eating very important. Big Mouth eat more." Further attempts to penetrate this reasoning produced equally circular responses. Tallfellow, however, expressed himself as keen to acquaint Peter with Big Mouth's views on various subjects. "When my English get good," he promised.

Later Peter explained to Ellen. "Big Mouth heads the pantheon because he eats more than the other gods, and that's that. It's like our God and Heaven are above us, and hell and the devil below — it's that way because it's that way."

Peter and Ellen had learned a lot about Nova Cannes and the Trumani since their arrival six months earlier. In some ways it was a most fortunate place for the natives to live. It had plenty of food sources and apparently nothing of value to interest the rest of the world. Hence, after preliminary surveys had established this fact, the Trumani were left to the attention of scientists and, briefly, missionaries. The latter had found the Trumani a tough nut to crack. The Trumani, in turn, had tolerated these disciples of foreign gods without in the least adopting their religious principles. For one thing, the powerful Christian image of the virgin birth of Jesus was lost on the Trumani. They had no concept of physical paternity, and attempts by the missionaries to explain it had been rejected as preposterous. Pregnancy, they knew, was caused by the decision of an ancestral spirit to be born again. It would enter a woman's abdomen and in due course emerge a child. The woman's mate played no part in this process. Mary's virginity was thus beside the point. The Trumani enjoyed plenty of sex but were spared dynastic concerns. Indeed, when a Swiss missionary, charmed by a Trumani girl, fathered a light-colored child, the pigmentation error was attributed to the white flour of the foreigner, which the girl had been eating. In time all the missionaries had departed.

In other respects the island was less fortunate. The vegetation that had shielded the people from earlier discovery blocked much of the sun's light from reaching them and inhibited air circulation. The dominant species of tree, a dark, dense-grained hardwood, grew to enormous height. Its topmost leaves spread laterally, filling the sky and forming a forest roof. The Trumani had no metal industry of any kind, but even metal axe heads would not have been adequate to the task of felling these tall, hard-grained trees. Tribespeople simply sited their villages in places where such trees were not as thickly grouped. Soon after Peter had arrived, he had considered the value metal axes and saws would have to the Trumani for clearing living space and building accommodations. The missionaries and other visitors had not introduced them. Had they concluded that the Trumani would surely use them to sever each other's heads more efficiently? Did they fear destruction of the forests? Then he discovered that the wood of the tall trees was so hard that even his metal tools could not fell them. Logging was not an environmental threat to Nova Cannes.

The village was sited on a slow-moving river that had the coppery tea color of the leaves that fell into it. Bathing in the river was possible but dangerous. The tribe had constructed a rude log fence in the river shallows as a crocodile barrier, but Peter had seen a large crocodile surmount the barrier and come within a foot of dining on a woman and her child. Some of these beasts were twenty feet long. They huddled together, tails and heads draped willy-nilly over each other, on the bank opposite the one on which the village was sited, ponderous, patient. When they moved it was usually at a languid, almost awkward pace, but if something edible appeared in the water they would move with incredible speed to prize it.

The Trumani subsisted on fruit, vegetables, roots, fish, and, on special occasions, swine and themselves. There were some dozen tribes on the island, which was roughly one hundred miles long by forty-five miles wide. All the natives were of the same Melanesian race and constantly at war with each other. The sole object of war was the capture of enemy males, so that their heads could become tribal trophies and their bodies long pig. Women were never long pig. This distinction inevitably contributed to an excess of women. Tribal territory was treated as sacrosanct and never disputed.

Apart from the animals regularly hunted as food, snakes and other small reptiles were common, some of them poisonous. There were other, more exotic, animals: flying squirrels that barked, a fish that could walk on its fins from waterhole to waterhole, and three species of multi-colored birds of the parrot family, which flourished in great numbers. These animals and birds were revered as totemic icons by the Trumani and never eaten.

Peter and Ellen had arrived on Nova Cannes under United Nations tribal territory auspices, but funded by a grant from an American university. Neither had any experience in the field with Pacific island aborigines. It had been difficult, however, to recruit for Nova Cannes work. The discomforts and hazards of the island were well known in the anthropological community. Accordingly, the grant went to Peter, in whose family field research under hazardous and uncomfortable conditions ran in the male line.

His father and paternal grandfather were scientists and explorers whose careers had been undistinguished except for the number of harrowing and unpleasant assignments they had undertaken. His father, as the climax of a long career in the field, had been successfully stalked and eaten by a polar bear while attempting to survey the ring-necked seal population of an Arctic island. His grandfather met his end recovering artifacts from an ancient well in Belize when the apparatus securing him to the top of the well broke. He fell into its depths. The natives accompanying him had not attempted a rescue. They were, in fact, fond of the old man, but had been reluctant to risk offense to the god of the well, to whose intervention they attributed the fall. Or so Peter's father had concluded after an investigation of the matter. Thus, Peter was equipped by heredity, or at least by family tradition, for a posting like Nova Cannes.

Ellen's story was quite different. She was on a lower rung of the academic ladder, needed field work to advance her career, and was attracted to Peter. When he suggested she join him she consented without regard to the expected conditions of life on the island. She was not lacking in courage. It was her tolerance for native customs and the discomforts of Nova Cannes that both had overestimated.

Both were in their thirties. Neither had been married. Women usually considered Peter attractive. When twelve years old, Ellen had heard herself described by her mother as "a plain girl but with several good points." Her mother had not been one for making much over the children and had never identified the good points. Ellen remained uncertain what they were, but felt she had a good brain and figure. Her confidence, however, had suffered since her arrival on Nova Cannes. A closer relationship with Peter had not developed.

This was made all the more distressing by the fact that Peter had early on explained to Tallfellow that he and Ellen were not mated. They had separate tents, he pointed out. In fact, Tallfellow found this pronouncement unworthy of belief, assuming that for unexplained reasons it was important to whites to lie about their sexual habits. He remembered some peculiar ideas of the departed missionaries. Ellen, however, became convinced that the natives were looking down on her in her separate tent, that she was perceived as a woman scorned by her fellow tribesman even when she was the only tribeswoman available. This belief added greatly to her general discomfort, and she saw no way to broach the matter with Peter without further embarrassment.

Peter was oblivious to the torment caused by his disavowal of any romantic activity, but he perceived correctly that Ellen's disaffection for the assignment was gathering force. They were due to return to the United States on long leave in two months, and he hoped the prospect would forestall a blowup. It was likely, however, that Ellen would be unwilling to return to Nova Cannes. Despite her reactions to the assignment, Peter was hoping for a change of mood on her part. He did not want a new colleague on his return. He liked Ellen, and at times he had even had sexual thoughts about her. These fantasies had been suppressed by the reasonable conclusion that assaying sex on Nova Cannes would be a chancy thing. Apart from inhibitions presented by the climate, there were the mosquitoes, the mosquito netting itself and other natural obstacles to effective performance. Similar thinking, abetted by a libido whose demands had never been excessive, had seen him chastely through earlier professional temptations.

The Trumani were now mostly gone behind the long house. Already the crackling sound of fire came from that direction. Long pig coming up, thought Peter. It would be a loud night. Lots of koda, lots of shouting and squealing. He got a bottle of vodka and two glasses from his tent. Ellen held up her palm. "I don't want any, Peter. I can't bear to think what's going on back there."

He put his arm around her shoulders. "Come on, Ellen. You'll sleep better. It's going to be noisy." Unaccountably to him, she burst into tears. "Oh Peter," she cried, and then the tears stopped as suddenly as they had arrived. "All right, give me a drink," she said with determination. He poured two stiff ones, and they sat down in their camp chairs, wrapped in mosquito netting, like furniture covered for the season. "Well, in two months we'll be heading home for a spell," he declared cheerfully.

"I don't know if I'll be coming back here, Peter."

"Ellen, when you've had a break it won't seem so bad."

"It's not just that," she offered without explanation, sipping her vodka beneath the netting. "Are you still going to San Francisco to your sister's?"

"Yes."

"And you want to spend your whole leave with her?"

"Yes. Very much so." He could tell at once that it was the wrong way to have put it.

5. A POOR START TO THE DAY

HAVING ADVISED HER DAUGHTER of her plans for the day, Penny proceeded to the kitchen to get breakfast. The room was empty. This was one of the days of the week that Millie, the help, did not come. On the table was a flattened bakery bag. Written large upon it was, "Mother, we ate the croissants. Sorry." Penny had bought eight of them. She stared at the empty bag and muttered, "Fitness; they're supposed to eat fruits and nuts." She fixed some coffee and toasted raisin bread.

At 10:30 A.M. she backed her car out of the garage onto her driveway. There was an awful, crunching sound followed by the screams of a child. She put on the hand brake and jumped out of the car. A boy of eight or nine stood by the rear wheels. "You busted my wagon," he screamed. It was true. Beneath a rear wheel lay a toy wagon, totaled, it appeared to Penny. "You ran over my wagon. I hate you."

"Why did you leave it in my driveway, Harold?" The hatred was reciprocal. Harold had been caught earlier in the week ripping flowers from Penny's front garden. The child lived across the street. Penny looked that way and saw an adult male figure, half hidden behind curtained French doors, watching the tableau. It was the boy's father. Why didn't he come out?

"You busted it. You ran over it," Harold screamed.

Penny got back in her car and pulled forward, releasing the wagon. Then she got out again and looked at the toy. It was finished. She sighed and handed the screaming boy a twenty-dollar bill. "Get another but keep it off my property." Harold seized the bill quickly, without ceasing his lamentations, and gathering up the stricken toy ran toward his house. Penny looked after him. The father was still standing there looking at her, his face expressionless. She felt an urge to give him the finger, a gesture she had not performed since high school. Earlier that week she had tried to reach Harold's parents about the rape of her flowers, but had not gotten past an answering machine, and her call was not returned.

She got back into her car and turned the ignition key. At first nothing happened, then there was a funny noise; finally the engine turned over, but it sounded sick. "First that dingbat kid, and now the car is acting up," she exclaimed. The day was off to a poor start. She would have to leave the car at the repair place and take a cab to the library from there. She backed into the street and turned on the radio.

The California news was in progress. Governor Pelton Throwback, who had recently been elected following a campaign that had promised "an end to all these unwelcome changes," was speaking. He was, he said, pleased that drive-by pregnancies in the greater Los Angeles area were sharply down from the record-setting prior year. He also applauded the conclusions of a report showing an increased use by teenagers of condoms and low-fat drugs. "We are on the right track with our programs," he congratulated himself.

The news was followed by a pitch for a new kind of doll, Huggie Bedwetter, which, depending on how you manipulated a switch imbedded in its rump, was alternately a girl or a boy. The spokesman for Huggie vowed that this was the first opportunity the world had had to obtain a doll that was both anatomically and politically correct: "This lovable, gender-bending doll assures that your child will view the sexes as totally interchangeable. Huggie Bedwetter nips politically incorrect, sexist thinking in the bud, and your child will love her/him. Call this toll-free number and — " The radio's offerings were not improving Penny's frame of mind, and she turned it off. There was one more stop she wanted to make before turning the car over to the repair shop, and she trusted to luck that it would not quit on her. Most of the time Penny was lucky.

6. LADIES' MUD WRESTLING

"DISGUSTING," MUTTERED ELLEN.

"Not so loud." said Peter. "That's one word they're sure to understand." Before them in an open muddy space between the long house and the anthropologists' camp, two naked young women were wrestling. They were slick with mud and encircled by a cheering mob of their fellow tribespeople, male and female, who shouted and swung bullroarers. The two women grunted mightily as they strove to get the upper hand in the slippery contest.

Ellen groaned. "I know, Peter. I'm not supposed to react like this. I'm a professional and all that. I ought to love up to all these weird practices, but I can't. It's disgusting."

"Please, Ellen," whispered Peter uneasily.

"All right. I'll shut up. But at least they could wear something," added Ellen. "They usually cover their crotches."

"Yes, but with wrestling it would make it easier for the opponent to get a hold on them," Peter explained, without being at all sure that was the reason why the wrestlers had discarded their aprons.

A roar arose from the spectators. One girl had managed to mount the back of the other and was ardently pressing the latter's face in the mud. A cry of capitulation came from the beleaguered head. The victor rose, followed slowly by the crestfallen loser. A young male stepped from the crowd and gripped the winner's muddy arm, leering at large, and further alarming Ellen that they might couple on the spot. To her relief, he led his champion away.

Peter and Ellen had been briefed on Trumani female wrestling by Farrington in Port Moresby. The shortage of young males due to tribal warfare required competition among females to acquire mates. The Trumani solution was female wrestling, which had the added advantage of entertaining the rest of the tribe. But like so much else Farrington had told them about Nova Cannes, the reality exceeded the description.

At the time Peter had thought Farrington was laying it on rather thick to amuse himself at Ellen's expense. In fact, his briefing had presented a fundamentally conservative and positive view of Trumani activities. "They're completely unreformed cannibals, y'know," he declared with satisfaction. "Sensible practice for them — nutritious and helps control the population. Call the feast 'long pig.' See, they roast swine and humans the same way. Spit them end to end and turn them nicely over a wood fire. Only difference is they leave the pig's head on."

"I see," said Peter. Ellen sat silenced by the appalling account.

Farrington continued. "Now we don't want to interfere with their feeding habits. We'd lose their trust, you see. And after all there are only a few places left in the world where cannibalism is practiced. It's an acquired taste and quite rare. Mustn't have it go the way of the passenger pigeon, eh?"

"It's like an endangered species," Peter inquired?

"Something like that. Nothing to worry. They won't eat whites. Don't like how we smell." He sucked on his pipe, his muse gathering force. "And when you think of it, the things we civilized blokes do to each other. Make meals of each other in different ways. It's just on Nova Cannes there's no poppycock about it." He paused as if waiting for applause, proud of these sonorous platitudes.

"I see what you mean," said Peter obligingly.

Ellen groaned at the turn the conversation had taken, but Farrington, evidently encouraged by Peter's response, returned gleefully to his theme. "Mind you, it's a bit rough when you first see it, and the smell. Not exactly your usual bit of barbecue — Oh! I'm sorry, Miss. I shouldn't have said that." Ellen was bent over, retching on Farrington's floor. It was the first sign that she might present a problem.

Her discomfiture suppressed Farrington's muse, and the remainder of the briefing had been restrained. He explained about the female wrestling, for example, with no attempt to be even mildly amusing, omitting the fact that the women went at their competition naked.

The wrestling over, the crowd dispersed. Ellen watched them do so uneasily. "Peter. Six more weeks! I don't know if I can take it that long."

Peter sought to cheer her. "Look, Tallfellow says he can safely visit the other tribes with us, a sort of truce. If we get out of the village for a while and collect some material from the other tribes — "

She cut him off. "Peter, they'll all be the same, do the same things. We know that," but she added, "I'm sorry. Let's have a drink." Somewhere beyond the impenetrable trees the sun was going down, and recently Ellen had regularly joined him in a sundown drink.

"A good idea," Peter declared, pleased, although it seemed to him later that Ellen had gotten a little tipsy that evening.

7. MEN JUST DON'T GET IT

THE NEXT DAY PETER WAS SEATED PLACIDLY on his camp chair when he heard Ellen swear loudly and looked up to see her coming toward him, her face grimacing beneath its mosquito-net veil. An attractive young Trumani woman, whom Peter had often seen of late near their campground, was striding away, having evidently been the object or the cause of Ellen's oath. Concerned that she was the former, he rose to meet his colleague, his face betraying his anxiety. Ellen looked at him with annoyance. "Don't worry, I didn't curse her. I was just cursing at large. This is the most ridiculous thing yet."

"The most ridiculous thing —"

"Do you know what she wanted, the slinky little trull? She wanted to wrestle me."

"Wrestle you! Whatever for?"

"For you, of course, what else? They all think I'm a would-be suitor for your marriage bed. So she's a rival and wants to bring the matter to a head. Perfectly reasonable when you think about it, but it kind of ticked me off."

Peter was relieved. The news was not as bad as he had anticipated; it was amusing actually, and the Trumani girl was rather pretty. But Ellen would react differently, of course. He tried to patch up the situation. "Yes. It is unfortunate. I tried to explain our situation to Tallfellow, but he just didn't seem to understand."

Ellen's voice rose a notch. "You don't understand our situation either ... " and became louder ... "What you told Tallfellow about the two tents, that was bad enough. It made me sound like a woman scorned. But this takes the cake. I mean if there'd even been a failed attempt, but nothing ... I'd be ashamed to wrestle. Wrestling would be like living a lie," she declared, her voice rising to a summit of indignation. But Peter's perplexed expression showed the point was lost on him, and she was loath to carry it further. The man simply did not get it. It made her want to be sarcastic. "Don't worry,

Peter. I won't let her get near you, even though I refuse to wrestle. I'll brain her before she gets a hand on you. Unless maybe that's what you want?"

"Ellen. Good God!"

"I'm not serious, Peter. Calm yourself." She smiled. "There, you see? I'm all calm now too. I'm just damn glad I only have a few weeks more to spend on this female wrestling ground."

Peter could see it was no time to raise any questions about Ellen's post-leave return, but he felt a pang. He was going to lose her. Her last statement left no room to expect her back, and despite her antipathy to Nova Cannes his own desire for her company had been growing. He looked at her with admiration rather than anger. She was really witty, and he found more and more that he enjoyed looking at her. Even with the mosquito netting and all, she was graceful, nice to look at.

Ellen noticed the fixity of his gaze but misread it. "Come on, snap out of it. Your admirer's gone for good. She'll not be back." Ellen looked at her watch. "Anyway, it's time for a drink." Peter snapped out of it and got the bottle.

They were no sooner seated, glasses in hand beneath the netting, when two Trumani males, walking together, appeared on the path down which the would-be wrestler had departed. Peter waved at them and they returned the salutation.

"You know," said one to the other, "that's another thing. All that arm wagging when they see you. It's very odd."

"They all do it. The missionaries did it. They're all damn odd."

"Yes. I often wonder what they think about with their blank, pale faces."

"Truly. They seem to lack the light of human intelligence. They are like animals. Hardly human."

"It's pathetic really. I respect Tallfellow's judgment, but I think he's gone a bit overboard on these two, even as to the Peter one."

"My sentiment exactly. Tallfellow is captivated by the language lessons. But it is like learning how to bark. This Peter is just an animal too. Of what use is it to learn how to bark like him?"

They both laughed. It was a good joke. "I must say," said the first speaker, "I was entertained by that story the missionaries had about The Virgin Mary, but they got a bit stiff when we were amused. They actually take that mumbo-jumbo seriously."

"Yes. And on the other hand, foreigners simply have no grasp of normal human behavior. As, for example, what Lima was just telling us: the woman, the Ellen person, refused to wrestle. Of course, I cannot understand what Lima sees in this Peter. She must be a bit desperate."

"Perhaps it is because she is too slender to be a good wrestler and would lose to our other girls. I suppose she felt she could handle the Ellen woman fairly easily."

"Doubtless that is the explanation. But if I were a woman I would not want that man's pale body covering me. They are the color of the sago palm beetle's grubs, these whites." They laughed again.

"It is difficult to understand women."

"Even so, brother. Very difficult."

Ellen watched the men pass out of sight behind some trees. "Peter, I'm sure I heard them using our names, but I can't understand them unless they speak slowly."

"Neither can I, but it's very likely they do talk about us. That would be expected."

"Something tells me they were talking about my aborted wrestling match. I think I heard them say 'Lima,' and that's the girl's name. Unless there are two women with the same name."

"Not likely." Peter paused. "That's a pretty name, Lima."

Ellen snapped back. "Yes. And she's got a pretty figure too, doesn't she?"

Peter took a big swallow of vodka. "Ellen, please don't be sarcastic." Why did she get upset just because he thought the girl's name sounded nice? It was difficult to understand women.

8. A FURIOUS RACE

MEANWHILE, IN SAN FRANCISCO, Penny, en route to the library via the car repair shop, had first driven to the former Soviet, now Russian, consulate building. She parked her car in front of it and tooted her horn. A small woman carrying a paper bag appeared from a side door. Penny got out of her car and shook hands with the woman. The latter handed over the bag, and Penny gave her some money. The bag contained tins of caviar. The woman, with Penny's money in hand, re-entered the consulate premises through the gate in the high, spiked fence that encircled the grounds. Penny drove off with the caviar.

At the corner she saw a Casper Bell campaign poster. Across a kind of Liberty Bell graphic ran the legend RING IN A NEW MAYOR. Bell was a rare bird for San Francisco politics, where any candidate not having at least the appearance of labor or liberal credentials was at a great disadvantage. Bell had neither; the best he could manage, image-wise, was middle of the road. He had, however, parlayed a leonine head and a kind, grandfatherly expression — with pious comments about the aged and the poor — into a successful supervisorial campaign. He was, at heart, a lifelong fascist who had had to suppress his natural inclinations in order to participate successfully in local politics. He often, for example, daydreamed of being able to blast "welfare abuses," a pigeonhole within which he included, without distinguishing in his mind which was the greater "abuse," everything from outright fraud to people on welfare having children.

The Cockerel, the principal San Francisco newspaper, widely referred to as "The Cock and Bull," or simply as "The Cock," had described the race for the mayor's office as "furious." Waylon Homer, as good Mayor Lint's successor, had been the first to throw in his hat. Bell had followed. Then came Sybil Watch, a child psychiatrist in her forties who was new to politics, and who presented herself as professionally the most qualified to understand the problems of the city and its inhabitants. Finally, James Blake, an African-American lawyer Penny's age, became a candidate. Political analysts gave him little chance. He had no real financial backing and seemed to lack the necessary political instincts, often expressing opinions without regard to their attractiveness to voters. He had, for example, taken aim at the Lint Law Enforcement Control Act, calling it nonsensical and harmful to the poor. But polls showed that the poor were by no means of a single mind on the issue. Blake's chief appeal lay in the fact that he was neither an established politician nor a psychiatrist.

Recent polls showed a close race among Homer, Bell and Watch, with Watch surprisingly in the lead and Blake well behind. Mayor Homer had gotten off to a relatively rocky start. He appeared to devote almost twenty-four hours a day to his job as mayor, which application to duty should have redounded to his credit. *The Cockerel,* however, saw an issue to be made of such devotion, citing it as evidence that he was "often inattentive as a father and husband." A tearful denial by Homer's spouse and children that he was ever inattentive was readily discounted by *The Cockerel* on grounds of family bias. Homer's handling of "No Stamps, No Steps" was also on trial. As Penny drove toward Civic Center, Mayor Homer was closeted there in his office with his campaign consultant, R. "Doc" Wayward.

WAYWARD HAD SERVED AS CONSULTANT on dozens of campaigns in California, both those where individuals were seeking election to office and on changes in the law that required voter approval. Now in his late fifties, these struggles had neither exhausted his interest in the sport nor left him cynical about the process. He remained a lover of gathering votes. Each campaign was a new romance, even though, as with other forms of romance, there were more elements in common to each of them than there were novelties. He had already decided upon a basic theme to re-energize Mayor Homer's campaign, and now sat opposite his client explaining what must be done.

"The voters will want to make the race as interesting a matter as possible. They want issues like the ones they see on TV. That is why campaigns can never be waged successfully on what is really at stake." He took a gulp of mineral water. "Now, to get to the point, since you are inheriting the Lint stamp tax issue, our pitch has to be rich versus poor, privileged versus underprivileged, with you, naturally, on the side of the downtrodden. Right now, unfortunately, because of the 'No Stamps, No Steps' sit-ins and the hosing, you're being thought of as on the side of the wealthy taxpayers. Sybil's campaign is making hay on that. We've got to turn the situation around and get you identified with the 'have-nots' by taking some position that bashes the 'haves.'"

He took another drink and leaned back in his chair. "Naturally," and Wayward's rich voice deepened as it came to the matter of money, "on fundraising we'll need the continued support of the wealthy, so the privileged bashing has to be nicely tailored. And the businesses, they've got to have assurance you won't try to revive that occupancy tax — "

"Well, Doc, you know I sort of said I'd support the stamp program back when John Lint died, if it could be done legally."

"Stamps, yes. Tax, no."

"You mean we can draw a distinction?"

"Not exactly draw one, Mr. Mayor. Rather, we'll blur the distinction."

"I'm not sure I understand, but anyway, attacking the rich, Doc, that's not very novel."

"Of course it isn't, Waylon; we want to win, not get a patent on the campaign. It's an issue that's been working since Roman days."

"They had election campaigns in Rome?"

"You bet. Big ones. All the bells and whistles. Sometimes I wish I could have been ... " His voice trailed off as his mind's eye caressed the subject. He saw his tall, ample form in a purple-bordered toga standing in the forum. Homer broke the reverie.

"Well, how do we bash the rich while enlisting their financial support?"

"Yes, exactly. My approach is, we've first got to defuse the 'No Stamps, No Steps' issue. The problem arises from you using law enforcement, albeit the firemen, against the have-nots. At least, that's how it comes across when you have the steps hosed. So what I have in mind is demonstrating that you believe in using law enforcement against the privileged. We need some sort of campaign issue that sets you against white-collar crime or against crimes by the well-to-do, something of that kind. I'm meeting with Frank Lavelle in an hour."

"The district attorney's office? Is it wise to involve them?"

"We have to. They're the first to determine there's a crime to prosecute. I want Lavelle to alert us pronto if a live one turns up. It's essential in establishing issues of this kind that you be very prompt in collaring the media, and make a big splash in which you assure the public there will be a vigorous prosecution of the fat cat. If another candidate gets in ahead of you, you won't come across as the driving force for justice."

"Have there been any white-collar crimes recently?"

"No. They're hard to come by. That's why we need vigilance in Lavelle's office. Anyway, it doesn't really have to be a classic white-collar crime situation. All we need is a rich defendant."

There was a sudden increase in the noise level from the City Hall steps that drew their attention. From the window they saw a pudgy, middle-aged man in a T-shirt that bore the words "Sybil Loves You" handing out portable electronic megaphones to the step dwellers. "Damn," Homer cursed, "that's Wagner Watch, Sybil's husband. The son of a bitch." Now the chanting began to assume a greatly elevated, orchestral magnitude. "Doc, can't we at least stop that sort of thing?"

"Freedom of speech, Mr. Mayor. Can't be viewed as rocking that boat."

"I guess not. But the megaphones, it's disgusting."

"Never mind, Waylon. Looking at those stamp program sit-ins just gave me another idea. You'll take the position that you're all for the stamps, but that more creative means of funding the program must be found. Then we'll appoint a blue-ribbon committee of about twenty-five popular citizens to explore the funding issue. If we pick the right people, the election will be over before the committee members even finish the nominating speeches for chairperson. That's the way troublesome issues of this kind are usually handled, particularly in an election year."

"Doc, that's inspired. You really understand politics."

"Mr. Mayor, the city needs the best man to win."

"Thank you, Doc, and I know how you feel. I felt a tremendous sense of responsibility when I realized I was what the city needed."

PART II
LAW AND DISORDER

9. THE DEATH OF SMOKING MOTHER

THE CAB DROPPED PENNY AT THE LIBRARY, and she ran up the steps. Out of the corner of her eye she saw a big blonde man sitting on one of them, wearing a beaded headband with a broken feather sticking out of it. Penny went by so quickly that Smoking Mother could not react to her or her purse, but he immediately determined to be ready when she left the library. Penny was dressed in clothing that looked expensive to him. This was the first wealthy-looking prospect he had seen that morning, and she carried her large purse loosely from a strap on her arm. It would be an easy snatch. He adjusted his position so as to watch the library doors for her reappearance.

A moment later an intoxicated, older man of shabby appearance came to the steps and, ascending two of them, stared at Smoking Mother and his feathered headband. He came closer, lifted his right hand toward Heaven and, in a booze-timbered voice, declaimed, "Once plains dark with buffalo. White man come. Kill buffalo. Bring firewater. Screw squaw." Then he laughed uproariously, his red eyes tearing in his glee. He was unable to dodge Smoking Mother's big fist, which hit him in the abdomen knocking out his wind and landing him hard on his buttocks.

"Mock me, will you," cried Smoking Mother, who was feeling in the downed man's pockets for money while pretending to raise him to his feet. The search produced two one-dollar bills and some change. Becoming aware of the theft, the victim cried, "Hey you're robbing — "

Smoking Mother hit him again, and he went down in a heap, where he remained motionless. Smoking Mother went back to his seat on the steps. The other inhabitants of the area who had paid heed to the encounter now feigned disinterest. They wanted no part of the big man's wrath.

Presently, Penny appeared at the top of the steps, holding a load of books up to her chin, which she was using to steady them as she descended. Her purse dangled from her left arm. Smoking Mother spotted her and gathered himself. At the proper moment he closed, seized the purse strap and pulled it toward the end of its bearer's arm. Penny felt what was happening and screamed. Books and purse fell to the stone steps. The revolver inside the purse discharged. The bullet entered Smoking Mother's forehead, killing him instantly.

Penny's scream and the report of the pistol drew a crowd, mostly of street denizens. "He grabbed my purse," Penny shouted, looking at the unmoving form at her feet, the small hole in his forehead, the seeping blood. She thought, "Oh God! The gun in my purse, it went off," and she shouted, "Call 911, an ambulance. Somebody call them." Then she turned to the nearest members of the crowd. "Did you see him do it? Snatch my purse?"

A man replied "Nah. I just heard the shot."

She turned to a different sector of the crowd. "Which of you saw him snatch my purse?" There was no response. "Please, didn't anyone see him snatch my purse?"

Then a young male spoke up. "I'll get a cop, lady. There's always a lot of them over near City Hall. I'll have them call an ambulance."

"Yes, please hurry. Maybe he's not dead."

The young man ran off, but an older man who was looking down at Smoking Mother said, "He sure looks dead. What a shot! Got him right in the middle of the forehead."

Alarmed, Penny turned on the man: "Don't say something like

that. I didn't shoot him. It was an accident."

A scruffy, middle-aged woman bent over Smoking Mother's face and looked in his mouth. "He's dead. I used to be a nurse. I know a goner when I see one."

This pronouncement was followed by a younger female voice raised in anger. "He's so young. Why did you have to shoot him?"

Penny's heart leapt. "I didn't shoot him. I told you that. He snatched my purse, and the gun was in my purse. It went off somehow. I never touched it."

"I don't believe you," responded the young female, who had moved into the inner circle of the crowd. The woman was about twenty-five, with unkempt dark hair. She wore a spacious poncho-like blanket over dirty blue jeans. "You can't shoot people in the head just because they try to take your purse." There was an ominous mutter from the crowd suggesting general agreement with this principle.

Penny stared at her accuser and spoke with a level voice. "Of course not, and I didn't. He knocked my purse to the ground. It must have made the gun go off." Then Penny had an idea: get the purse from the ground and find the hole the bullet would have made. As she bent toward it, however, she saw that the muzzle of the weapon protruded from the open mouth of the purse. There would be no hole; no proof the gun had gone off inside the purse.

The young woman reacted with prosecutorial fury. "Hey! You can't touch that. It's evidence." Intimidated by this assault and set back by the lack of a bullet hole in her purse, Penny obeyed. "Besides," continued the woman, emboldened by Penny's compliance, "your story doesn't sound right to me. Guns don't just go off like that. I think you figured it's just some street bum stealing from you, so you cooled him."

Penny rose to the challenge. "I'm telling the truth. You're not. You're just getting your kicks out of accusing me of murder in front of all these people."

"Calm down, lady." It was the man who had admired the shot. "Here's the police."

A paramedic vehicle accompanied them. Two white-coated individuals sprang from the car and ran up the steps to where Smoking Mother lay. They examined him. "He's dead," said one. They photographed the body.

Penny approached them. "May I explain what happened?"

"Not to us, lady. We're just interested in if the victim's dead or alive." Without another word they went back to their vehicle and drove off, leaving the two police officers who had come with them.

One of these officers was a fine-featured, powerfully built, but deaf and mute white male, the other a tall, good-looking Asian female. She spoke very little English. The two made their way through the crowd to the corpse. Arrived there, the female, speaking at large, said something in a language not apparently understood by anyone else present.

The officer then turned to her colleague and hand signaled something. He began to write on a large pad he was holding. When he had finished, he held it up for all to see. The note read, "Who shot this corpse?"

The young woman who had accused Penny immediately pointed at her and shouted, "She did!"

The officer wrote another note on his pad, tore out the page and handed it to Penny. It read, "Did you shoot the corpse?"

"No," said Penny.

The female officer understood the word "no" and asked, "Who shoot man?"

Penny explained. "No one shot him. He was snatching my purse, and the gun I had in it went off accidentally." But this was too much English for the female officer and could not be heard by the male. Penny began to grasp the communication problem and, pointing at the pad, said slowly and distinctly, "Let me write it for you."

The female officer reacted enthusiastically to this suggestion, took her colleague's pad, and gave it to Penny, saying "OK. You write." Then she spoke with sudden, thrilling emphasis. "Confess now! Write confess paper!" It was her first homicide case, but she knew from early training in the land of her birth what to do. She must maintain correct thoughts and struggle against criminal elements. The teachings of the Great Helmsman came back to her. She jabbed her finger at Penny. "You confess now!"

The young woman who had accused Penny approved. "Yes. Confess, you rich bitch."

A male voice followed this from the back of the crowd. "Lynch her! Coming down here and shooting at us." Then he laughed loudly.

Penny finished writing on the pad and handed it to the male officer. The note read, "My purse was being snatched by the dead man. I had a gun in the purse for protection. When he pulled the purse it fell on the steps, and the gun went off. It was an accident."

The officer read the note, then, using a handkerchief, picked up the purse and appeared to examine it for a bullet hole. Finding none, he removed the weapon and looked at it.

"It was my father's," Penny said absently. "It's very old."

The officer put the revolver back into the purse, tore off the page on which Penny had written, stuck it in his pocket, and wrote on a new page, "You will have to come with us to the station." He handed Penny the note and put the purse back on the steps.

The female officer turned her attention to the crowd and began passing out sheets of paper. "Witness write name, address, everything. Make statement," she said loudly and handed a sheet to the nearest onlooker, the young man who had summoned the police. He looked at it a moment and, without writing, handed the sheet to a man next to him who quickly handed it off to the young woman who had accused Penny. She signed up. Her name was Wendy Papp, and she gave the New Reality Homeless Shelter as her address. Eventually, five more people in the crowd signed statements. One of them, a man, wrote that he recognized the deceased as a street person who called himself Smoking Mother.

A siren signaled the arrival of other authorities. These were police department specialists in crime scene investigation. Two men emerged from an ambulance-like vehicle and approached the crowd. Their attempts to engage the earlier-arrived officers in conversation failed, but the deaf mute gave one of them a note. The recipient turned to his companion. "He can't hear or talk, and his buddy don't speak English. They're taking the suspect to the station."

Penny, hearing English spoken by a policeman, took heart and spoke to the newcomer. "May I explain what happened here, officer?"

"No, lady. We can't talk to suspects. We're only interested in the crime site and the corpse."

"But these officers. There's no way to talk to them."

"Yeah. I see that. No matter, there are some officers who can speak English at the station." He turned from Penny and began to draw a chalk outline around Smoking Mother's form.

The deaf mute officer now approached Penny and presented her with a printed paper the size and texture of a playing card. This contained a Miranda warning, a formalized summary of the requirements laid down in a famous criminal case as to what the arresting authorities must tell the person being arrested. If the suspect is not so warned, the arrest or subsequent prosecution may be flawed. She had a right to remain silent, it said. She pondered that; it appeared useless to talk anyway. She read further. She had a right to be represented by counsel. Penny turned toward her purse, which was lying near the feet of the female officer, bent down and put out her hand toward it. The policewoman put her foot on the purse.

"My purse," said Penny. "My lawyers' number is in it." The policewoman's face became angry, and she brandished her baton, an officer as yet not intimidated by the Lint Law Enforcement Control Act. "Oh, God," said Penny, at her wits' end, "I just want the lawyer's number. I won't keep the purse."

"Purse evidence. Go 'way from," said the policewoman firmly.

Penny pulled back her hand. Then, moving too quickly for the female officer's satisfaction, she attempted to go over to the other policeman so as to write a note on his pad. The policewoman intercepted her and pushed her back with her nightstick. "You try escape! No escape," she said angrily. Penny burst into tears.

"That cryin' won't get you anywhere. You and your fancy clothes," declared Wendy Papp. "You're goin' to the slammer." And as if on cue, the paddy wagon arrived.

"You come. No try escape again," said the policewoman, her nightstick poised menacingly near Penny's head. Penny went. Wendy Papp and a few others in the crowd hooted. Across the park, the noise from the steps of City Hall could be heard more clearly as the rising afternoon wind blew the chant, "No stamps, No steps" eastward toward the library. The fog had come in with the wind, and Penny felt the cold as she was marched to the paddy wagon.

"Could we stop and pick up a cup of coffee?" she asked vaguely, forgetting for the moment that neither of the police could understand what she said. "It's three, and I haven't had anything to eat or drink since breakfast."

"You suspect. Talk too much," declared the policewoman as they climbed into the wagon.

10. THE HALLS OF JUSTICE

ON THEIR WAY TO THE STATION, the policewoman took her colleague's pad and pen and handed them to Penny. She was undaunted by her prior failure to obtain a confession. One had to continuously maintain correct thoughts in struggling against criminal elements. "You guilty. Already try escape. Write confess paper!" It was an English-language *tour de force* for the determined officer. Penny stared at the woman, who kept jabbing at the pad and nodding her head.

Penny wrote, "My lawyer's phone number is in the wallet in my purse. May I please have it? Your partner is crazy." She handed the pad to its owner before the female officer could intercept it.

He nodded, rummaged in the purse, and gave Penny her wallet. This act of seeming indulgence aroused the policewoman to fury. "Evidence escape," she shouted, and lunged for Penny, who managed to fend her off until she had extracted the lawyer's card and returned the wallet to the male officer. Frustrated, the policewoman grabbed Penny's wrist and attempted to handcuff her. Penny resisted successfully. "Resist arrest," yelled the woman, and receiving no help from her colleague promptly hunkered down in a sulk that endured for the rest of the ride.

Arrived at the station, the policewoman's sense of mission returned. She blocked Penny from getting to a public phone and hustled her toward a counter behind which a white-haired sergeant sat reading the *Wall Street Journal*. At the counter the policewoman took charge, leaving her partner standing idly behind them. Pointing at Penny, she declared, "Shoot man dead, already try escape." The sergeant seemed quite at ease despite this lurid description of Penny's conduct, and, encouraged by his reaction, Penny said calmly, "She's lying. I didn't shoot the dead man and I didn't try to escape. She's a cop, but she's nuts."

"Lady, I'm not the judge. I'm just here to book you."

"But before I'm booked shouldn't someone hear from me? These officers can't be talked to. And all she does is keep demanding that I 'write confess paper.' It's like a Chinese communist opera where the landlords are forced to confess, like the Cultural Revolution."

"Now, lady, don't get racist. She's just new on the job and excitable."

The new and excitable officer intervened. "Shoot man dead. Book murder, assault, weapon deadly, everything."

"OK. Anything else for the booking?"

"Hide loaded gun. Try escape. Resist arrest."

"That sounds like enough to get her to the Hall of Justice." He began to type on a computer keyboard. "What's your name, lady?"

"Penny Hill."

"Address and phone?"

Penny gave them.

The sergeant turned to the policewoman. "Where's the material evidence?"

"Say again?"

He repeated the question, and Penny responded, "The gun's in my purse." She gestured toward the deaf mute officer. "He has it. The dead man was snatching my purse. It fell, and the gun went off. I didn't shoot it."

"You shut mouth," said the female officer, raising her baton.

The blood of ancestors who had climbed sheer cliffs and stared down charging rhinos roared in Penny's veins. She made a fist of her right hand and landed it on her tormentor's nose. She was quickly restrained by the deaf mute, who also prevented his partner from retaliating. The women remained poised for combat, each ready to strike the other.

"Come on, come on," said the sergeant, and, lacking sensitivity training, added, "This ain't no place for a hen fight."

"Sergeant, I don't want to fight," said Penny, delighted to see that she had bloodied her opponent's nose. "I just want this crazy woman off my back. I want to call my lawyer and tell my story to someone."

"Well, you're going right over to the Hall of Justice, and you can call your lawyer from there. You'll be interrogated by the inspector over there, too, so you can tell him your story. The magistrate," the sergeant looked at his watch, "he'll be gone in ten minutes, but you can tell him all about it tomorrow."

"Tomorrow? Can I go home tonight?"

"Lady, you're under arrest."

"What about bail?"

"Well, the magistrate has to set that."

"You mean I have to stay in custody overnight?"

"Unless you can find a magistrate. The only one who's going to be there in the evening is in Department 33; that's sex offenses, and it's the rush hour for them, but these aren't the kind of charges Department 33 sets bail on. It would have to be a special case."

"How do I get someone to consider whether I'm a special case?"

"Well, ask your lawyer when you get him." The policewoman's nose was now bleeding profusely; she was holding a handkerchief up to it. "You sure gave her a good whack. I tell you what — I'm not going to add that to the charges. It would just muddy things up anyway."

"Will she be coming with me?" asked Penny, gesturing at her hated adversary.

"Yeah. The inspector will want to talk to her too. But no more fighting, or they'll put the cuffs on you."

"They ought to muzzle her, with her 'confess' and 'shut up' talk. She's crazy!"

"Yeah, but like you say, lady, she's a cop."

AT THE HALL OF JUSTICE, Penny was fingerprinted and photographed. Then she was taken into a small room along with the policewoman where an inspector sat before a computer terminal. "Did you get the Miranda warning?" he asked, without looking up from the witness statements that were in a pile on the keyboard.

"You mean the playing card that says I can remain silent and call a lawyer?"

"Yeah. Do you want to remain silent?"

"No. I didn't do anything wrong. I want to get my story in the record."

"Do you want to call your lawyer first?"

Penny's frustration precluded deferring her story any further. "No. I want to get this over with. I'll call them after."

"That's fine with me, Ms. Hill. Tell me what happened."

Penny told him, while the policewoman from time to time commented adversely. When Penny was done, the inspector typed a statement, printed it, and handed it to Penny. "Is that a fair statement of what you told me?"

She read it. It was a fair statement of what she had told him. "Yes."

"There's a place for your signature." He handed Penny a pen, and she signed the paper.

"Write confess paper?" A note of jealousy filtered through the policewoman's stuffed-up nose.

"No. It's just her statement. Ms. Hill, you can go in that room and call your lawyer now if you want."

Penny departed, the policewoman on her heels. When they were gone, the inspector reread the witness statements and his notes of the interview. Then he typed a report summarizing the data, which was printed out at another terminal on a different floor, one occupied by deputies of the district attorney's office. Two young men, so-called "rebooking deputies," looked it over. Their role was to evaluate, on the basis of the report and the data from the booking sergeant, whether to revise the charges under which a suspect had been booked.

They both reviewed the data. One of them shook his head and said, "This is really weird. I mean, after that talk we got today from the chief. He must be psychic."

"Yeah? How?"

"Well, this murder charge. It's against a Penny Hill who lives in Pacific Heights. That's gotta be the Penny Hill that gets in the social pages."

"I never read social pages."

"She's wealthy, divorced. She rides horses. Her picture's in the paper a lot."

"Oh. You mean Lavelle coming on about being alert to white-collar crime and offenses by the upper crust? I just drew a blank on that. I think everybody did. I never heard him talk like that before."

"Well I don't know what got into him either, but here's one of the nobility in the net. We better tell Sonia." The speaker dialed a number. A senior assistant district attorney, Sonia Taft, answered.

"Sonia, we got a homicide and related charges against a Penny

Hill who lives in Pacific Heights. I think she's a high-society type, and it brought to mind the chief's speech today."

"Right. Tell me about it."

The rebooking deputy told her.

"What about witnesses to the shooting?"

"Well, that may be a problem. According to this report, there were a lot of people at the scene who heard the shot, and one woman who swears up and down that the suspect must have shot the victim — "

Sonia interrupted. "Must have?"

"Yeah. She didn't see Hill using the weapon. It's her opinion Hill shot the guy."

"Based on what?"

"You can't tell from the statements or the report."

"Oh, for Christ's sake. No one saw the suspect shoot the victim?"

"Evidently not. And the weapon, it's an old, single-action revolver. The inspector says those things can discharge if they're dropped. Hill claims the victim was snatching her purse, and it fell, and the gun went off when the purse hit the ground. Maybe she's telling the truth about the purse snatching. She may just be a misdemeanor candidate for carrying a concealed and loaded weapon."

"Did anyone see the purse being snatched?"

"As far as we can tell, that wasn't witnessed either."

Sonia pondered the situation. "Well, that's interesting. It's kind of a standoff."

"A standoff?"

"Just send the file up to me. I'll handle any rebooking, if necessary, when I've seen it."

THE SMALL ROOM INTO WHICH PENNY was conducted in order to phone her lawyer contained nothing but a pay phone. There was a glass window in the door, and the policewoman stood outside and peered in while Penny went to the phone carrying her lawyer's card. She placed the card on the phone sill while rehearsing her credit card number in her head before dialing. The lawyer whose number she intended to dial had prepared her will. His name was Boyd Evans, and he was a partner in the firm of Blunt, Hammer and Tuggle. Doubtless he did not handle criminal matters, but she assumed he could direct her to some lawyer who did. She began to dial. Many digits later, a female voice thanked her for using the credit card and the number began to ring.

After four rings, another female voice began to speak: "You have reached the voice mail of Boyd Evans of Blunt, Hammer and Tuggle. Mr. Evans is unable to take your call at this time. Please leave a detailed message after the tone, or, if you prefer, press 0 now and you will be connected to the firm's central switchboard." Penny pressed 0 and got an immediate response: "Thank you for calling Blunt, Hammer and Tuggle. You have been connected to our fully automated legal service directory. Please listen carefully to the following menu and make your selection. If you are an existing client of the firm and desire to speak to one of our lawyers with whom you have had prior contact, press 1 now, followed by the initials of the lawyer's name using the numerical keys associated with the alphabetic units. Penny pressed 1 and B-E for Boyd Evans. She got an immediate response: "We are sorry, but you have entered an unacceptable alpha-numeric value. Please be sure you have entered the correct initials of the lawyer with whom you wish to speak."

"Oh, God," Penny exclaimed," I forgot to put in his middle initial." She tried again. It worked, sort of: "You have reached the voice mail of Boyd Evans. Mr. Evans is ... " Pondering her next move,

Penny let the message run its course. Now began a pounding on the glass door of the phone room. It was the policewoman. "You time up," she was shouting. Desperately, Penny pressed O again. She was back with the central switchboard, which thanked her again. Now, she thought, trying to keep calm, the great thing is not to select the first option. I've got to listen to all of them. The menu was sounding the second option: "If you are not a client of the firm, but seek our legal services, press 2 now.

No. She was a client. "If you are a client of the firm and have a new matter to present to us that may not be within the expertise of lawyers with whom you have previously dealt, press 3 now." That was it. She pressed 3, and as she did, she noticed that another officer had joined the dreaded policewoman at the door. She was getting a response to her menu selection, and she ignored the two at the door. "Thank you for bringing a new matter to Blunt, Hammer and Tuggle. If you know your client number, enter it now. If you do not, spell your last name, followed by the initial letter of your first name, using the numerical keys associated with the alphabetic units." She did it. The voice advised her that the computer was searching the client files. Then, "Thank you. You are Penny Hill, client number 123786. To confirm, press 1 now." Penny pressed 1, but at the same time, the door was thrust open and the new officer said, "Come on, lady. Your arresting officer says you've been in here twenty minutes."

But there was a god at Blunt, Hammer and Tuggle after all, for the voice in her ear now said, "Please leave a short message describing the nature of the work that will require our services." Before the policeman could part her from the phone, Penny shouted into it, "I'm charged with murder at the Hall of Justice. I need a lawyer to get me out on bail. Please come soon." She hung up the phone.

Penny then went quietly, and as soon as they had exited from the phone room the policewoman left them. "Is she gone for good?" Penny asked this of the other officer, a robust black man with two gold earrings.

"She's just now off duty. You won't see her anymore tonight.

You don't like her company?"

"I don't even know her name, but I hate her, and she hates me. She kept after me to confess, and I hit her on the nose. It was awful."

"Ms. Hill, I'm Sergeant Floyd, and I don't give a damn about confessions, so don't hit me, but I got to put you in a holding cell now."

"Sergeant, I've got a nineteen-year-old daughter at home who doesn't know I'm in custody. Do you let me call her, or do I scream and roll around on the floor until you have to call a psychiatrist?"

"It's a deal. Make a quick call."

Although spared another encounter with voice mail, all Penny got was her own answering machine asking her to leave a short message. She left one: "April, don't worry, but I'm in custody for murder at the Hall of Justice. A man got killed by accident with my gun. Try to reach someone at Blunt, Hammer and Tuggle to come here and bail me out." Penny turned to Sergeant Floyd. "She wasn't there. I left a message."

"I'll make a note in your file. What's your daughter's name?" Penny told him. "OK, we've got to get your shoes checked and some things signed before you can go to the cell."

"Sergeant, how do I get bailed out of here?"

"Ms. Hill, it's after six o'clock. There's no judge here except in Department 33, the Sex Court, and he usually won't set bail except for prostitutes."

"Can't we try?"

"That's not my place. I can't ask the judge to give you a bail hearing."

Penny decided it was a good time to cry. A stream of tears flowed down her face. "But if no one tries, there's no way to know if he'd set my bail. Please, officer. Would you want your mother to spend the night here?"

Sergeant Floyd looked at the weeping woman and pictured his mother in the slammer. He was taken with an impulse to help her. "Look, I'll tell his clerk. Maybe she'll take the file."

"Oh, thank you so much. I really didn't shoot that man, and I'm afraid of spending the night here."

Later, Sergeant Floyd approached Irma Fong, the clerk of Department 33, and explained about Penny and that she had not been able to reach her lawyer. "Irma, I looked at her file. She ain't gonna skip. She's never been in custody before, and she's scared of overnighting here. Any chance he'll set bail for her?"

Irma had just become a grandmother for the first time and was feeling generally warmhearted. "No lawyer? She'll have to use one of our regulars. Counselor Fulmen is here as usual. Let me have the file. I'll slip it in with the others and tell Fulmen. He looks pretty sober tonight."

Sergeant Floyd left the courtroom feeling better. Ms. Hill had seemed like a nice person, especially when she was crying. He had felt bad about putting her in a holding cell with those whores.

THE OTHER OCCUPANTS OF THE CELL into which Sergeant Floyd led Penny stared at her as at a curiosity. They were young women detained earlier that day on charges of soliciting acts of prostitution. One, a lanky black girl in purple hot pants and tank top, was fascinated by Penny's suit. "How can you work in clothes like that?" she asked.

"Work?" Penny responded hesitantly, uncertain what to expect from her new companions. "I wasn't really working."

The two girls laughed. "We all say that," said the other of the two, a pale-skinned redhead clad in black leather vest and skirt. All three women wore fluffy white slippers of imitation rabbit fur with pink-ribbon trim depicting a bunny's face and ears. This departure from the drab, shuffling slippers for which prisoners had been required to exchange their shoes was one of Mayor Lint's jail reforms. He had announced with pride that the new footwear was the creation of a Hollywood designer to the stars. They had now been worn by most of the whores in San Francisco. Unanticipated was the jealousy this innovation provoked in the men's detention area. To quell a serious disturbance it had been necessary for the Mayor to recall the designer to create attractive slippers for male prisoners. Theirs were of black fur, and bore the outline of a bull's head in gold detail.

"I'm Ingrid," said the black girl, "and this is Mantra. It's a fact you don't look like you was working in those clothes."

Penny began to understand. "My name is Penny. I'm charged with murder and other things but not with 'working'."

This news excited the redhead. "Murder! I've never met a murderer before. How did you do it?"

"Well, actually I'm innocent. But my gun went off and killed a man. An accident."

"Was he your man?" Mantra strove to recharge the situation following Penny's excitement-dampening explanation.

"No, it was a real accident. A guy was snatching my purse, and my gun was in it and went off. I'm really innocent."

The redhead, manifestly disenchanted at this news, asked, "How come they got the likes of you in here if it was really an accident?"

"There was a woman, a street person, at the scene, and she accused me of murdering the man. One of the cops who came bought it."

"Well you're a rare bird. Innocent women are pretty scarce around here," said Ingrid. "Your lawyer getting you bail?"

"I couldn't reach him. I got a voice mail."

"What's a voice male?" asked Mantra. "Like phone sex?"

"Not m-a-l-e," Penny spelled the words. "M-a-i-l. Like an answering machine, only more confusing."

Ingrid laughed. "Our lawyer, Mr. Fulmen, he ain't got no machine. He just hangs around the court and finds his clients there, but he's good at getting us bail."

"Could he get bail set for me?" Penny asked.

"I don't know. Mantra, what do you think?"

The redhead pondered the point. "Well, I've never seen him do anything but whores."

"How do I get hold of him?"

Ingrid responded. "You got to go to Sex Court. That's the problem. I don't think they'll take you there. It's really just for working girls and boys. They'll take us there pretty soon."

But Penny was not out of hope. "I heard they do sometimes set bail there for other crimes when there's no other judge around."

"I never heard of no murderer in Sex Court," said Mantra doubtfully.

Ingrid was consoling. "Cheer up. Sometimes they make mistakes with those files. Files are strange things. You could get lucky. And Judge Furplay, he's a good egg. The problem will be with the deputy DA. The murder charge will blow his circuits."

Mantra laughed. She had thought of a joke. "Look, who knows? Maybe you'll be back on the streets tonight."

They were chuckling over this when the deputy sheriff from Department 33 arrived. "Ingrid Ames, Mantra Grant, and Penny Hill. Let's go to court."

"I'll be damned," said Ingrid, "you got lucky!"

DEPARTMENT 33 WAS IN RECESS when they arrived. The room was full of women in white bunny slippers and a few men in black bull ones, the exits loosely guarded by deputy sheriffs. The bench was empty, but two lawyers sat at tables in front of the bench looking over files. A uniformed woman in her fifties approached Penny and took her aside. "I'm Irma Fong, the court's clerk. I put your file in with the others. Counsel are looking at them now. Brutus Fulmen, the guy on the left, will plead your case to be released on bail. He'll want seventy-five dollars, but you don't have to have it now. The judge doesn't usually read the files, but the guy at the other table does." She pointed at a young man in a dark suit. "He's a new assistant DA, and he'll raise a fuss over your case being on this calendar. Don't say anything unless the

judge asks you to."

Penny attempted to thank her, but Ms. Fong had already turned away. Judge Furplay, a tall man with curly gray hair and a tan was entering the courtroom from a door to the right of the bench. "All rise," cried one of the deputies.

Three cases were called before Penny's, two for sentencing and one for entry of a plea, and were disposed of without controversy. Next, Ms. Fong called "The People v. Penny Hill, proceeding to set bail." Brutus Fulmen rose from his seat at the counsel table and turned toward the audience of bunny-slippered women. "Ms. Hill," he inquired, uncertain which of them was his new client. He resembled a film actor she had seen play the role of a dirty old man, and Penny took an instant liking to him.

"That's me," said Penny and stood up.

Penny's appearance got Judge Furplay's attention. "Ms. Hill, you may come forward and join your counsel at the table," he said in a pleasant voice.

"Thank you, Your Honor," said Penny and did so. When she was standing beside him, Fulmen approached the lectern between the defense and prosecution tables and began to address the court.

"Your Honor, I have only had time to glance at Ms. Hill's file, but I urge the court, as I have on many prior occasions, that whenever justice is to be applied to our frailer sisters, it be done with compassion and full consideration of the conditions which have led the poor girl to her present circumstances." He drank from a glass of water and continued.

"Here she stands before you in ... " He looked at Penny and was forced to pause. This was the point in his presentations where he invariably referred to the outfit worn by his client as "this disturbing clothing which cruel circumstances have forced her to wear," but Penny's tailored suit brought him up sharp. He recovered: " ... stands before you in furry white bunny slippers, a prisoner." A giggle ran through the crowd, and Judge Furplay gaveled lightly for silence.

The deputy district attorney, a Mr. Brickett, had now begun to look through Penny's file, and he started to rise, muttering, "Judge, this case — " but the court silenced him. "You will have an opportunity to be heard, Mr. Brickett. Mr. Fulmen has the floor."

"Thank you, Your Honor," declared Fulmen, recovering his rhythm. "So let us take a moment to examine the conditions which have brought Ms. Hill before this court."

This time the judge interrupted Fulmen. "Remember, counselor, this is simply to set bail. I'm not sentencing, so be brief."

"I will, Your Honor, but in any proceeding it is important to keep in mind that no young woman would so prejudice her life and general well-being by taking to the streets were there not background facts, often sordid, over which she had no control. We cannot now fully inquire into the circumstances that led Ms. Hill to attempt to sell her body for a few dollars — "

"I beg your pardon," interjected Penny, startled by Fulmen's commentary, and then quickly recalled Ms. Fong's admonition to keep quiet. "I'm sorry," said Penny, thinking quickly. "I missed what he said."

Judge Furplay smiled at her. She was the best-looking hooker he had seen in his three years on the Sex Court bench. "The court reporter will read it back, Ms. Hill."

The court reporter read, "... the circumstances that led Ms. Hill to attempt to sell her body for a few dollars."

"Thank you," said Penny.

Counselor Fulmen continued. "But we may be sure that inquiry would reveal a home life shattered by misfortune, a hearth from which love had flown and ... " Penny's clothing was the obstacle again. "Despite the remnants she wears of a prior sufficiency, a fall, precipitous, dreadful, into poverty, from which it appeared to her in her bedeviled mental state that the only path of escape was as a lady of the night."

"Right on," cried a voice from the audience. It was Ingrid's. Judge Furplay gaveled, cautioned the audience, and turning to Fulmen asked "have you concluded your remarks?"

"Yes, Your Honor, except to ask that you discharge my client on her own recognizance, or at most on a minimal bail, say, two hundred fifty dollars."

"Thank you, Mr. Fulmen. Mr. Brickett?"

The young prosecutor rose smiling. "Judge, I'm tempted to ask why, if this woman's home life is so awful, she's so anxious to get back to it. But the real problem with this item — "

Judge Furplay, frowning, cut him off. "Young man, this is a court of law and not a place for rude jokes." He was suspicious of youth in general and young lawyers in particular. Besides, he did not like to be called "judge." His rebuke continued. "I will ask the court reporter to note that you have withdrawn your offensive remarks and permit you to begin again, confining yourself to the amount of Ms. Hill's bail."

"But Judge, have you seen this file? This is a murder charge. There's some mistake been made."

Now Judge Furplay was really incensed. This kid kept calling him "judge" instead of "Your Honor," and now he was implying that the court didn't read the files and made mistakes. The details were not important. An example must be made. "Mr. Deputy, give me your figure for bail. I am prepared to rule."

"But Judge, this case shouldn't be on your calendar. It's — "

He got no further. Judge Furplay turned to Fulmen. "How many days do you need before you can enter a plea?"

"Five, if you please, Your Honor."

"Very well. Ms. Hill you are discharged on your own recognizance until — Ms. Fong, when is that?"

"Tuesday, Your Honor."

"Discharged until next Tuesday, 9:00 A.M. On your own recognizance. That means we are trusting you to return to court and plead on Tuesday. And, as I always add in these cases," he added smiling, "keep off the streets. Is that understood?"

"Yes, I will, Your Honor. I will."

THE PROPERTY CUSTODIAN at the Hall of Justice kept Penny's purse, but, except for the weapon, returned its contents, giving her a paper bag to hold them. "What do I do with the slippers?" Penny asked, putting on her shoes.

"Oh, you can keep those."

Penny put them in the bag and headed for home. The cab left her there at 11:45 P.M., following a stop en route for a hamburger to go. April was not at home. Penny took off her shoes and put on the bunny slippers, poured a glass of wine, and began to eat the hamburger. The phone rang; it was April.

"Mother," she shouted. Penny held the phone away from her ear. "We're at the Hall of Justice."

"April, please don't shout. Who are 'we'?"

"The lawyer. BH and T sent one. His name is Mr. Sayer, and I met him here. He says you've been improperly discharged."

"Who cares if it's proper. I didn't have to spend the night in jail."

"He says they'll get your discharge revoked. There has to be bail for what you did."

"Am I paying him for that kind of advice?"

"Mother, don't be difficult. You've put us to a lot of trouble."

This appeared to be true, but Penny was not disposed to confess. "April, this has been a terrible day. I want it to end and I want to go to sleep. I'll explain everything tomorrow."

"Wait! The lawyer wants to talk to you." Penny waited.

"Ms. Hill, I'm Hamilton Sayer, Boyd Evans's partner. I came in response to your daughter's call to the firm. There was a voice mail too. We think it was from you, but — " Penny interrupted.

"Thank you, Mr. Sayer, but I'm too tired now to talk. Could you call me tomorrow after 10:00 A.M.?"

"Ms. Hill, there's the matter of bail. You should not have been discharged without putting up bail. It's all rather complicated.

The Sex Court and all that."

"You mean it can't wait? They're coming for me tonight?"

"No, no. It's just, well, all very irregular."

"If it's just irregular then I can go to bed, can't I?"

"Certainly. I'll call tomorrow. Wait — your daughter wants to talk to you."

April came back on. "Mother, please stay up and tell me about it. You've never done anything exciting before. I'm so excited."

"All right, but don't bring the lawyer."

"I'll be right there."

However, halfway through Penny's account of the day's proceedings, April began to yawn. "It's not really that exciting," she said. "I'm getting tired; I think I'll go to bed. Where did you get those stupid slippers?"

"I was just coming to that."

11. PROBABLE CAUSE

WHILE PENNY SLEPT, OTHERS WERE AT WORK on her case. R. "Doc" Wayward, Mayor Homer's campaign consultant, got both the details of Penny's arrest and of her discharge from custody in the same late-night phone call from District Attorney Frank Lavelle.

"How in hell did she get out without bail on a homicide charge?"

"It's a puzzler, Doc. Somehow she got on the Sex Court calendar, and I guess, Judge Furplay took a liking to her." Lavelle was contrite. "We can get proper bail set tomorrow. Anyway, there's no reason to have her in custody."

"No. But the media may glom onto this and do a 'the rich don't need bail' number." Wayward sighed. He was accustomed to a high incidence of things that did not go right. "Ah, well. It wouldn't be a picnic without ants. I'll work something up for the mayor to give to the media."

"Doc, it ain't going to be a picnic even *with* ants."

"How so, Frank? They're not going to rebook on a lesser offense are they?"

"No. Sonia doesn't think the booking needs changing, except there are resisting and attempt to escape charges we'll probably drop. Anyway, Sonia thinks there's probable cause to file a homicide complaint and to get past a preliminary hearing."

"OK. Just remember, I can't have the mayor going on about homicide and end up with a concealed weapon misdemeanor."

"I know, but the witness to the shooting is kind of flaky. She says she's sure Hill shot the guy, but in the same breath she says she didn't see her with the weapon. Then in the next breath she says Hill had to have shot him because the bullet was smack in the middle of his forehead. Her mantra is, 'The rich bitch must have shot him.' I think, all things considered, there's probable cause, but it won't be an easy case to prove. Another problem is, the witness we have to rely on is a street person herself, like the victim."

"Look, Frank, does it look like this guy was really snatching Ms. Hill's purse?"

"She claims he was, but no one saw it happen. Who knows?"

"Have you checked to see if he had any priors for purse snatching?"

"Yeah. There's nothing on him like that. One drunk-and-disorderly a couple of months ago. He was just a street freak as far as we can tell."

"Then you think it's reasonable to prosecute for homicide?"

Lavelle searched his conscience. It was not a time-consuming process. "Well, Doc, I'd like it better if I had a motive and a better witness to the shooting, but — "

Wayward cut in. "But no case is perfect, and a motive and some other witness may turn up. Isn't that about it?"

"Yeah. That's about it, I guess."

Wayward followed up quickly. "It's like the mayor's going to say: 'We can't have the rich living above the law.' I'm thinking of that girl who's going to be the witness. She may be flaky, but she swears Penny Hill shot the guy. She could raise all kinds of hell with the press if no complaint is filed. The Cock will love it. And there's the Native-American angle. Have you thought about that?"

"Smoking Mother. Yeah. One witness said the victim called himself that. It's an alias, and the corpse is blonde and blue-eyed."

"You can't be sure that won't become an issue, Frank. I'll bet you a hundred dollars that angle will get some play in the media. They'll love the 'Smoking Mother' name."

"His real name's Thorson Grebe. He's from St. Paul, Minnesota. He's a Swede, or something like that."

"That's a detail, Frank. Anyway, this shooting's going to draw the media, and if we don't do the right thing they're going to whip us to death. That's not fair to the mayor."

"Doc, tell him we're going to file a complaint and take it to a preliminary hearing. You better show some restraint, though, till we get a probable-cause ruling."

"We will, Frank. Count on us."

DOC WAYWARD'S PHONE CALL woke the mayor. "Waylon, I'm sorry to trouble you at this hour, but ... " He explained. "You can see the situation's not exactly what we had hoped for, but the way it stands if there's no complaint filed the media will beat us to death. So will Sybil."

"Doc, it sounds to me as if instead of solving a problem, we've had one thrust upon us."

"Yeah. That's about it, Mr. Mayor."

"What if the magistrate doesn't find probable cause?"

"Well, that would solve this problem, but Lavelle thinks he will find probable cause. If he does, they'll take her to trial. She's rich, rides horses, all that stuff; the victim's one of the downtrodden. We can make some hay out of that. For now, I've worked up a press release, and we'll get you on the tube tomorrow morning.

We need to get going before the media start to focus on her release without bail. By the way, you don't know Penny Hill, do you?"

"No. I was going to ask you the same question."

"I don't either, but Lavelle says there's a lot on her in the society-page archives. She's about forty and a real looker. Divorced. Lives in Pacific Heights with her daughter."

"That's not really my idea of a fat cat, Doc."

"No, not the best fit, but we can maybe improve on the situation. I'll come by with the press release."

12. FREEDOM OF THE PRESS

PENNY WOKE TO A POUNDING on her bedroom door. "Mother! Wake up! You're famous!" April came through the doorway waving a copy of *The Cockerel*. "Look. The front page. There's a picture of you!" Penny looked at the paper. A two-column head ran: "Society Matron Nabbed in Street Shooting."

"Matron," said Penny with displeasure. Below the headline was a photograph of her astride Sweetie Pie, a favorite mount of years gone by. "Where did they get that old photo?"

"They have archives, Mother. Never mind. There are two stories; it's fabulous. I never knew you had a thing against street people and Indians. I'll bet it's on TV, too." April ran out of the room leaving Penny with the newspaper.

The Cockerel account included an interview of Wendy Papp, Penny's accuser, at the New Reality Homeless Shelter. In addition, a representative of the mayor was quoted expressing the mayor's outrage. That got Penny's full attention. What the hell was the mayor outraged about? She read:

R. "Doc" Wayward, a representative of Mayor Waylon Homer, said that the mayor had been informed of the shooting soon after the arrest of Ms. Hill. He was outraged. "In this City," the mayor had advised Wayward, "the rich may not go about taking the lives of the poor. The matter will be investigated and followed up with utmost vigor."

Penny read on. It was apparent that her nemesis from the library steps, now identified as Wendy Papp, had exceeded her earlier performance:

The Cockerel interviewed Ms. Wendy Papp, one of the key witnesses to the crime, at the New Reality Homeless Shelter. In tears, the young girl deplored the taking of another young person's life. We asked her what part of the crime most disturbed her. She responded at once that it was the attempt by Ms. Hill to justify the shooting on the grounds that her purse was allegedly being snatched by the victim. We say 'allegedly' because no witness has surfaced to support the suspect's contention. As the tears poured from her eyes, Ms. Papp cited the horror of the victim's being gunned down by an assailant unknown to him simply because he was a street person. Others interviewed seconded Ms. Papp's sentiments. One resident of the shelter said, "These rich people coming down here shooting at us. What next?" We at The Cockerel suggest that this frightful episode betokens the 'class war' which has been smoldering in our fair city since good Mayor Lint's untimely death. As Mr. Wayward, the mayor's representative, commented to us, "Perhaps the commission of this heinous crime and its prompt punishment by the appropriate authorities will serve as a check to further violence and send a message to those more privileged in our city that the poorer citizens have lives as well, lives that Mayor Homer means to see are protected by the law."

Penny's stomach turned over on the main story, but she forced herself to read the companion piece, which was headed, "Senseless Shooting of Native-American." The Cockerel, the article explained, inspired by the victim's name, was investigating the significance of his apparent Native-American lineage. The paper queried "Ms. Hill's evident animosity toward Native-Americans." It noted Smoking

Mother's blonde hair and blue eyes, but concluded that he was at least a "virtual" Native-American. The virtue of awareness vigils or teach-ins on Native-American survival was held out. Neither story referred to Penny's account of the shooting, except to quote Ms. Papp's tearful repudiation of the alleged purse snatching.

A shout came from downstairs. "Mother. Come quick! The TV's even better. There's a lot of old pictures of you. It's terrific."

When Penny got there, the pictures of her were over. They were interviewing Mayor Homer. She arrived as he was saying that he meant to use "the full force of the law to prevent vigilantes of the privileged from imposing their law on our less fortunate. Moreover," he added, turning full face to the video camera, "speaking of the underprivileged, I am today forming a blue-ribbon committee of dedicated citizens to investigate new means of funding Mayor Lint's food and drink stamp program. We mean to directly address all difficulties that life in our city presents for the needy with all the power of our office. Mr. Wayward ... " the mayor turned to a tall, heavily built man with white hair who stood smiling beside him, "... will head the search for members of the stamp funding committee. Meanwhile, I will be personally in touch with the district attorney's office concerning the investigation of this dreadful shooting."

The interviewer broke in, "Mr. Mayor, we understand the suspect was discharged from custody without posting bail. Was that because of her position in society?"

"No. I think Mr. Wayward can speak to that."

The camera shifted to Wayward. "I have spoken to the district attorney, and he advises me that proper bail will be set today. If it is not posted, Ms. Hill will be returned to custody. Her discharge without bail was due to an identification error in which she participated. She represented to the magistrate that she was a prostitute, and got a bail hearing in Sex Court."

"Mother," screamed April, "you're something else!"

"It sounds as if Ms. Hill will stop at nothing," appended the interviewer, and the program went to another story.

April turned off the TV. "What are you going to do, Mother?"

"Get dressed and have breakfast. Is Millie here?"

"Yes. She showed me the paper. She's all excited that maybe the media will be coming here."

"I'm going back up and dress. Please ask her to make me some bacon and eggs. I missed two meals yesterday."

But when April went to the kitchen to place the order, it was empty. Millie, who was twenty-four and a recent immigrant from Scotland, had left a note saying she had gone home to change and would be back before 11:00 A.M. She was back even earlier, her appearance greatly modified. The maid now wore a close-fitting black dress with a string of pearls, her blonde hair piled high on her head, her eyes heavily shadowed. "I apologize for running off, Ms. Hill," she began, "I just thought I ought to look my best if there's to be picture taking. I've often fancied myself being an actress, getting my picture took and the like."

Penny was not prepared to be understanding. "If you let just one of them in the house, you're fired."

"Oh, Ms. Hill, don't be angry. I won't let anyone in, and I understand what happened. I hate those dirty bums. I'm glad you shot one."

"Millie, I didn't shoot the man. The whole story in the paper and on the TV is poppycock. The mayor and these people are behaving like swine."

"It's all right, Ms. Hill. I'll bet you'll be acquitted. There's lots that don't take to having the streets full of filthy bums."

Penny called the garage where she'd left her car. It was ready. Then she called Hamilton Sayer and asked him to come for lunch. He said he would be bringing another lawyer with him. She told Millie there would be two lawyers for lunch at 1:00 P.M., reminded her to keep out the media, and called a cab. As the cab pulled out, Penny noticed two trucks that looked like the kind used by film companies parking across the street from her house.

WHEN PENNY RETURNED an hour later, the street was full of vehicles, many double-parked. A large tent had been erected on her front lawn. The lawn was covered with people and the driveway blocked with cars. Looking up, she saw two men installing something on her roof. She double-parked in the street. Then, as she approached, she saw that a rope fence had been installed around the front of her property. As she started to climb over it, a uniformed guard held his arm toward her, palm up.

"Sorry, lady, only media admitted. You'll need a media badge."

"Officer," Penny said, with grudging patience, "I live here!"

"Well, lady, we can't start carving out exceptions, can we? Where would we stop?"

Penny's patience was short-lived. "You idiot! I'm telling you, that's my house. Get yourself and all these turkeys off my lawn!"

The guard appeared to be weighing this defiant position, judging which side to take in his own interest. Then Penny saw Millie. She had, as instructed, not let anyone in the house. Instead, the girl stood resplendent on the front steps, happily at bay before cameras and microphones.

"Millie," Penny yelled, "tell this man who I am."

"Oh, Ms. Hill!"

The mention of Penny's name by the maid provoked dramatic action among the press, and all in attendance upon Millie left her and rushed toward Penny, brushing aside their security guard in the process. The winner of the race, a middle-aged woman, was not one to get bogged down in preliminaries. She immediately shouted, "Why did you shoot him, Ms. Hill?

Penny's first impulse was to scream and run for her door, but on reflection she concluded it was a chance to tell her side of the story. "All right, I'll tell you exactly what happened." The pack crowded in closer. "I had a gun in my purse when I went to the library yesterday that I carry when I drive out of town — "

The woman who had asked the question interrupted. "Just tell us why you shot him. There won't be room for the details."

But Penny, undeterred from her course, told her story. It was met with disenchantment, if not disbelief. Like the whore in the holding cell, the press wanted something more stimulating than a declaration of innocence. There came from them a low, murmuring sound evincing discontent, wordless, unpleasant.

The woman interrogator took another tack. "What have you got to say regarding the witness who swears you shot the man?"

Penny answered quickly. "That girl called me a rich bitch. Maybe she really believes I'd shoot him, but I think it's more she doesn't like rich bitches."

Another member of the pack cried, "Do you believe in the death penalty for purse snatching?" But even his fellows did not laugh. They were getting restless. Uninterested in defusing explanations, they wanted explosions. Many were moving out of the circle around Penny. She turned to the woman who had first interrogated her.

"What is that thing they put on my roof?"

"It's an aid to satellite reception."

"Well, now that the interview appears to be over they should take it off."

"Oh, not yet. We'll be staying here to catch people coming to your house. Besides, we haven't finished with your maid. She's going to do a human interest spot. What it's like to work for a killer, something like that." She paused, turning to look at Millie, still established on the front steps, some of her earlier attendants again circled around her. "Funny-looking maid; basic black and pearls. Does she always dress like that?"

"Invariably," responded Penny and pointed at the tent. "Does that stay too?"

"Sure. And the portable toilets — this story is going to take awhile."

13. Trouble Across the Water

Tallfellow stood alone in a sanctuary at one end of the long house. It was in this sanctuary that Big Mouth most often manifested Himself to His priest. Tallfellow had risen before dawn with an awareness that Big Mouth wanted to speak with him. He did, and the news was not good. There was trouble across the water that related to the visitor, Peter Walker, and that would, which was Big Mouth's concern, profoundly impact affairs on Nova Cannes. Big Mouth could not or would not be specific, but advised Tallfellow to raise the matter with Peter as soon as possible. "Do You see what it is he should do," asked Tallfellow? But the god was no longer apparent or communicating.

Peter woke to a loud squawking noise. At first he took it for the cry of the parrot-like multicolored birds that abounded on the island. Then he recognized the noise as the sound the radio made when someone was trying to reach them. He jumped up. Ellen was already up and beside the set, a ghost-like presence beneath mosquito netting in the dim, early-morning light. He stumbled to her side, pulling his netting about him.

"It's Farrington," she said. This was immediately confirmed when Farrington's voice came from the speaker.

"Hello, Peter, Ellen! Have I got you there?"

"Yes," said Peter. "What's got you up so early?"

"We got a fax from your employer for you. Thought you'd better hear it ASAP. Not the best news, mate." Ellen remembered Farrington as a connoisseur of things that were not the best news.

"They run out of money?" asked Peter. It had happened to him on an earlier grant-supported project.

"No, not that. It's your leave." He began to read the message:

"URGENT, PETER WALKER, NOVA CANNES
VIA UNTT HQ., PORT MORESBY.
*Necessary you postpone leave two months and report fully soonest on
subjects cannibalism and relation to Big Mouth cult. Do plenty on
this Tallfellow as high priest. Suggest Day in the Life of Tallfellow.
We need to publish here soonest these subjects. Emphasize this essential to obtaining further funds for your work. Also additional
two months' presence Nova Cannes will enhance report credibility.
— B. Salvo, Chairman, Nova Cannes Research Project.*"

Farrington paused. "That's it, mate. Any reply?"

"Yes." Peter looked at Ellen who, to his surprise, had received
the news with no visible sign of distress. Was she determined to
resign and leave Nova Cannes in any event, and this made it easier? "Fax Salvo this: 'Received your direction to delay leave, etc.
and will proceed accordingly. Walker.'"

"Right. Everything else OK up there?"

"Same as usual. We'll need some more food and drink."

"We'll lower into the clearing Saturday afternoon," Farrington
promised.

"Thanks." Peter turned off the radio and turned to Ellen. "You
know, this delay of leave; it really only applies to me."

"I know, but I haven't made up my mind about sticking with
this project or cutting the cord. If I'm on for the duration, there's
no sense in us being on leave at different times, is there?"

"No, no. I just didn't want to press-gang you, knowing how
much you dislike the place."

Ellen smiled. "I'm liking it better." This was true. She had the
feeling that Peter's behavior toward her had been different ever
since the flap over the girl who wanted to wrestle her. She was
sure he didn't really understand why she had gotten upset, but
he had been more attentive; he was definitely looking at her more.
There seemed to be an increasing personal interest on his part,
and two months' delay would provide a better opportunity for
something to develop. A bird screeched in the forest, and Ellen

imitated the sound, moving her arms like wings beneath the mosquito netting.

Peter laughed. He would miss her a lot. His reserve, and the notion not to pressure her, left him. "I hope you stay, Ellen. It would be pretty awful here without you."

"Oh well — " She was delighted by this emphatic plea for her company, but she got no further, for Peter had more to say.

"And I was thinking, Ellen, if you do stay, then maybe when we get our leaves you would like to come to San Francisco for a bit when I visit my sister."

Ellen knew this was a significant revision of his plans. Things were changing; it would be something like meeting the parents. "I'd like that," she said. "I'm going to stay on."

Peter suppressed an urge to embrace her, settling for, "I'm so glad. I would have been miserable here without you." Then they heard and saw Tallfellow hurrying up the path to their camp. He was alone.

"Not like him to hurry," said Ellen, not at all pleased by this interruption of their dialogue.

Tallfellow came to a stop before them. "I do not like to bother you so soon in the morning."

"It is no bother," said Peter. "We were up. The radio woke us."

"Ah. Then you already know," said Tallfellow mournfully.

"Know?"

Tallfellow explained Big Mouth's warning. Peter explained Farrington's message. Both were perplexed. Finally, Tallfellow spoke. "It cannot be that Big Mouth would consider such news to be trouble."

"I would think not," agreed Peter.

"Then there is further news to come, and you must expect the worriest."

"The worst. It's like worry but not exactly."

"I came because Big Mouth said to tell you as soon as possible."

"Well, I wish He had been more informative. Just knowing bad news is coming ... " Peter stopped the thought; he did not want to be upbraiding the deity for his oracular deficiencies. Greek oracles had been similarly capricious. At least Big Mouth did not indulge in riddles. "Big Mouth was sure of this?"

"Very. He was very ... " Tallfellow searched for the word and got it. " ... disturbed. The trouble will bring bad news for all of us, He says."

Ellen asked hopefully "is Big Mouth ever wrong on things like this?"

"There has never been anything like this till now. He has never concerned Himself with ... with matters across the water."

"I mean," said Ellen, "are His prophecies, His warnings, ever erroneous? Is He ever wrong?"

"Ah. I understand. Ellen, Big Mouth is never wrong. There is trouble across the water that concerns Peter and all of us."

"Well," responded Ellen, "please ask Big Mouth to do what he can for us." She had a general belief, though not strongly held or practiced, in the utility of spiritual beings.

"Indeed I shall. I intend at once to organize a war party so that a special feast may be prepared for Him to encourage His help. He is, as you know, most responsive to food."

"Big Mouth eat more," sighed Ellen rather feebly, knowing the special feast would be long pig, the most suitable fare for propitiation of the deity.

Tallfellow nodded affirmatively. "Big Mouth eat more," he declared with devout enthusiasm.

At 5:00 p.m. Farrington left his office in Port Moresby and crossed the street to The Thirsty Crocodile, a public house. With a tall beer and a dish of nuts beside him, he stood at the bar rail savoring the beginning of the best part of the day. The pub door swung in, admitting a bookkeeper who shared office space with Farrington. The newcomer shouted, "David, your fax is going

absolutely ape. There's already at least ten pages. Thought I'd better fetch you." Farrington scowled, set down his glass and re-crossed the street.

In his office he saw that the fax had stopped receiving and that some of the printout had fallen to the floor. One page, displaying what was evidently a newspaper story, caught his eye. "Society Matron Nabbed In Street Shooting," he read. He picked up the page, but the name Penny Hill meant nothing to him. He gathered the other papers. The fax was for Peter, from the Penny Hill who was being held. It was a letter with enclosures. Then Farrington remembered. This was Peter's sister in San Francisco. He stared with displeasure at all those pages. It would be a long radio message with bad news, a tiresome business, and it was after five o'clock. He sighed deeply and after a moment's reflection went back to The Crocodile. Farrington drank down the large beer and ordered two more. Thus armed he returned to his office. After finishing half of one of the new beers he began to twiddle with the radio. In a moment he heard the tone of the incoming message signal sounding on Peter Walker's receiver.

14. Nothing Counts But Appearances

Penny forced her way through the crowd on her front lawn toward her front door. Some of the invaders had now set up tables outside the tent and were selling drinks. She would have liked to overturn them, but the main thing was to get inside the house. Millie was still holding forth on the steps, her face animated with the telling of the promised human interest story to her clustered listeners. Getting through the crowd was heavy going, but Penny managed to get in behind the maid without Millie seeing her and unlocked the door. Leaving it ajar, she turned to the knot around Millie, raised her arms, and formed her fingers into a scratching position. Then she screamed frightfully. The group reacted by breaking apart but retreated in good order firing cameras. The next day, *The Cockerel* carried a front-page photo of Penny, fingernails poised, face ferocious, under the heading, "Suspect Displays Vicious Nature."

Before Millie's audience could reform, Penny seized the girl around the waist and quickly pulled her into the house, slamming the door. "Millie, we have to get lunch made."

"But I was just telling them what a fine mistress you are, Ms. Hill, and now they'll — "

"Yes. They'll report me as a brutal slaver of Scottish girls, but I need your help. If they can get through the gauntlet, the lawyers will be here in five minutes."

The lawyers arrived fifteen minutes later and were intercepted on the lawn. Upon identifying themselves they were provided with cocktails. A press conference ensued. Sayer was unaccustomed to press conferences and had little to say, but his companion, Barton Playchek, who stressed that he had not yet been retained by Ms. Hill, sailed smoothly on familiar seas. Having delivered an array of newsworthy platitudes, mostly connected with Penny's sanctified status as a female of the species, a fragile thing, a mother, and (when all the facts were in) an innocent victim of male assault, he thanked them all and finished his drink. Without waiting for Sayer to finish his, Playchek took him by the arm, announced to the media that he and Sayer must now meet with their client, and marched to the front door, the crowd parting before him and his companion as if to assist their progress. At the door, Sayer knocked, identified himself, and Penny admitted them.

Hamilton Sayer introduced Playchek. "Mr. Playchek is an expert in defending criminal cases, Ms. Hill. I asked him to join us because I think you should retain someone with his expertise."

Penny shook Playchek's hand. Indeed, he looked to her better suited for war than did Sayer. "Well," she said, "I already have another criminal lawyer who works the Sex Court. I owe him seventy-five dollars. This will make it three lawyers. Do you think I will need any more?"

Sayer took her seriously. "Well, we'll also need some young person during the investigation and trial. It's a serious charge. The Sex Court lawyer, Mr. Fulmen, I assume he'll step aside once he's paid."

"He was very effective," said Penny.

Playchek laughed. "Ms. Hill, it's good you have a sense of humor."

"Is that a sign that I'm innocent?"

"We don't need any signs. You are innocent. Isn't that true?"

"I think I am. Let's have lunch, and I'll explain."

Penny explained. Playchek listened, and Sayer took notes. When she had finished her story Playchek sighed. "It's OK, but it needs some tweaking."

"I don't understand," said Penny, who didn't understand.

"What I mean," said Playchek, admiring his prospective client's appearance, "is that, while I think you personally have a great deal of jury appeal, your account of what happened doesn't."

"But it's the truth."

"Yes, but that doesn't mean it has jury appeal."

Hamilton Sayer looked at his watch. "Ms. Hill, I've got another appointment, I'm afraid. May I leave you two alone to talk this over?"

Penny feigned surprise. "Don't you want to hear what has more jury appeal than the truth?"

Sayer reddened slightly. Playchek, noting his colleague's discomfort, said, "Hamilton, she's pulling your leg."

Sayer stood up. "I really must go. I'll call later to see how it went."

Penny went with him to the door. "Mr. Playchek, I take it he's meant to run the defense?"

"Yes, Ms. Hill, his expertise — "

"Do you know how he means to tweak my story?"

"No. He'll get into all that now. Knows his stuff, Playchek. Impressive record. We're fortunate he's available."

"I think it's more that we're unfortunate that we need him."

"Yes, you have a point there. I'll call later."

Penny returned to the dining room. Playchek was finishing Sayer's dessert, which the latter had left untouched. "This is delicious, Ms. Hill. What is it?"

"It's called trifle. It's English." She sat down. "Mr. Sayer feels I should retain you, and I shall, but I want to know how you propose to tweak my story."

"Well, first of all, Ms. Hill, we have to get something clear: we're only going to tell the truth. Your story needs improvement, but it's still going to be the truth. You just don't understand the full truth as yet."

"Obviously, you are going to tell me what the whole truth is."

"Yes. That's my job. Let's get at it this way. You've been under a lot of stress since the shooting, but you probably were long before that — "

"Not in the least. I've been quite free of stress. An easy life most would say, a happy one."

"Your divorce, Ms. Hill, didn't that — "

Penny interrupted. "Create stress? Quite the contrary. It resolved the most stressful situation I had, my marriage."

Playchek rubbed his chin. It was deeply beard-shadowed. He decided on a different tack. "What I said about jury appeal. It's that certain scenarios ring true to jurors, and others don't swing. Outright innocence is never appealing. It turns them right off. On the other hand, there are certain themes that have been really big recently. One of them is called 'diminished capacity'."

"Insanity?" Penny asked this in a half-shrill voice.

Playchek composed his face into a reassuring expression. "No, not really. It's just that because of something the defendant has experienced his or her ability to tell right from wrong has been diminished. It's been a hot item with juries ever since Governor Lovebird brought it back."

"But I didn't shoot the man. What does my capacity to tell right from wrong have to do with it? It was an accident."

"Yes, I can see how you feel. You've pretty much convinced me we should contend it was an accident, even though that will bore the jury, but we mustn't stop there. We should contend that you're not guilty because you didn't shoot the victim, but that even if you did — which you have no present recollection of doing — your capacity was so diminished you could not tell it was wrong to do so."

Penny's voice rose. "It sounds like insanity to me, and I don't like it."

Playchek shook his head. "It's different, and we should have an alternative defense. Juries like them. Gives them a fuller meal."

"Mr. Playchek, for starters there's been nothing to diminish my capacity."

"I was just coming to that. Do you take an interest in politics?"

"Average, I suppose. I've never wanted to enter politics."

"No, I just meant do you follow the campaigns, listen to the speeches and read the blurbs. That sort of thing."

"Sure. How can you help it?"

"Over many years?"

"Well, since I started to vote, I guess. Twenty years."

"Can you tell when something one of the politicians says is not the truth?"

"Not really, I suppose; I mean, sometimes it's so outlandish that it's clear."

"But most of the time you can't tell if what they say is right or wrong?"

"Well, that may be stretching it, although it is a problem at times with politicians and the like."

"Exactly. Now do you realize, Ms. Hill, that years of being exposed to the representations and cant of politicians and spin doctors can diminish a person's ability to distinguish right from wrong?"

"I'd never thought of that. Do you really think so?"

"Absolutely. I've been certain that one day I'd find this to be the case with one of my clients and, lo and behold, it has come to pass. Your capacity to tell right from wrong has been diminished by years of exposure to political rhetoric."

"Mr. Playchek, that's simply ridiculous."

"Ms. Hill, please. I've had numerous diminished capacity cases, and I can recognize one when I see it. In fact, it affects your ability to consider my advice."

Penny stared at the lawyer. "You mean, I can't really disagree with your conclusion that my capacity is diminished because my diminished capacity precludes my being able to properly evaluate your conclusion."

"That's well said."

"That's a neat new species of Catch-22, but I'm going to disagree anyway. Why don't we just tell the jury the truth?"

"Ms. Hill, you're missing the point. This is the truth. You've retained me, and I would be guilty of malpractice if I failed to present a fully truthful defense."

"But I don't feel in the least insane. I simply didn't shoot the man."

"Ms. Hill, that is a simple explanation, and it pinpoints the problem. Jurors do not trust simple explanations. They think they're being gulled by the defense, that there must be more to a case than that. So a simple explanation just won't wash."

Penny groaned. Playchek finished his coffee and held out his cup for more. She filled it. "Look," he said, "I'll explain. What happens is, jurors — most people — watch TV and read newspapers all the time and not much else, and the media always present the simple explanation as the wrong one. So they're conditioned, see, to reject simple explanations. It's like what really happened is sometimes too pat to be believable. Take President Kennedy's assassination. No one wants to believe that one nut with a rifle did it; it's too simple. It's human nature — jury nature — to prefer a conspiracy, a better story. What really happened is beside the point. It's what the jury is most likely to want to believe happened."

Penny's heart was pounding. "This is awful. I didn't shoot him, and you say the jurors won't want to hear that."

"Certainly not. It takes all the suspense out of the case. They'll shut their ears. We've got to give them something more entertaining."

Penny stood up. What particularly bothered her was that Playchek's cynical appraisal had a ring of truth to it. "It's horrible to believe that we're all so ... so stupid and plot hungry that we have to be fed a complicated defense when ... " She paused, searching for some other answer. "Maybe we should get a second opinion?"

Playchek's brow furrowed. "Ms. Hill, this isn't elective surgery. Second opinions are worthless. Lawyers will always disagree as a matter of principle to prove they can form independent opinions."

Penny considered this. It sounded right. The more opinions, the more lawyers, the more confusing it might become. She felt trapped, with the only feasible course depressingly unattractive. "Can you write out just what these alternative defenses boil down to so I can look at it in writing before I decide?"

"Sure. I'll do it right now." He reached for his briefcase.

"One other thing, Mr. Playchek, will I be able to testify?"

Playchek's brow re-furrowed. "I don't know about that. Jurors generally associate that with desperation. You know, they think that only a guilty person would be so desperate as to take the stand. Have you noticed that defendants who are acquitted almost never testify?"

"Neither do the ones who are convicted."

"You have a point there, Ms. Hill, but you have to understand that the jurors will want you to decline to testify. They all know the constitution prevents the prosecution from forcing the defendant to take the stand, and they'll want to see that played out, like it is on TV."

"You make everything sound as if the main thing is not to disappoint the jurors with a story that doesn't live up to their media-inspired expectations."

"I couldn't have said it better. Our story has to fit the myth in their heads as to how this encounter between you and Smoking Mother should have played out."

"And if I take the stand and tell them it was an accident it will make them furious?"

"Very much so."

"Maybe we've all got diminished capacities," Penny said dismally.

"The hole in the ozone layer or something ... "

"You've got a natural flair for this kind of thing, Ms. Hill." He began to write.

Penny rang the bell for Millie to clear the table. "While you're writing the proposed defenses," she said, "I want to write a letter to fax to my half-brother. He's in a place near New Guinea, and I want him to come here if he can. My daughter's only nineteen, and I have no other close relatives to turn to."

Playchek looked up. "Where's your ex-husband?"

"The last I knew, he was living in Norway with a Finnish flight attendant. We don't stay in touch."

"Then your brother would be the main family representative in court?"

"Yes, I hope so."

"Would he make a good appearance? Don't get mad, now. That's important."

"Yes. He's quite handsome. He's a scientist, but how awful he has to pass an appearance test to support me."

Playchek leaned toward her, speaking warmly. "Ms. Hill, in a trial, nothing counts but appearances. The jury can't see what's underneath; all they see are appearances. Whether you're really good or bad underneath is beside the point."

"So if you look bad, you lose whether you're really guilty or not?"

"Most probably. There may be a few exceptions. But think about it. It's not that different from the rest of life; almost all judgments are made on the basis of appearances. It's one of the laws of nature."

"So many of the laws of nature are unpleasant," Penny declared with uncharacteristic gloom.

15. THE LAWS OF NATURE

"LET'S SEE," ELLEN BEGAN. "If we're to report about a day in the life of Tallfellow, I imagine it would begin with him installing his penis promoter, and it would end with him taking it off for bed. I mean, I can't imagine the men can sleep with those things on." She was in a puckish mood. Big Mouth's warning had not dampened her elation over the earlier talk with Peter.

"No," said Peter, "but they're very private about that. I've never seen an adult male without his penis sheath, except, of course, the captives." It had rained most of the day, and they had spent it in Peter's tent going over their notes, marshalling the material needed for the report to the project chairman. "Still, I wouldn't call it a penis promoter, even though I guess from a woman's viewpoint — "

"Peter! From any viewpoint that's what they are, but we'll not say that in the report. In fact, we'd better begin and end Tallfellow's day some other way. He might read the report, and he wouldn't think that emphasis appropriate, would he?"

She laughed, and Peter joined in. He too had been in an upbeat mood, primed by Ellen's decision to stay on the project, and she sensed she was the cause. Her heart had not been lighter since their arrival on the island. They had been working at close quarters in the tent, and she thought she had felt a kind of favorable energy exchange between their mosquito-net-shrouded bodies whenever they had touched. She had read somewhere about personal energy fields. Maybe they were real. In any event, it was a nice thought and it emboldened her. She began to think seriously once again about bedding Peter.

It seemed clear enough now, she mused, that her company was personally important to him and not just useful for the project work. He would not otherwise have asked her to come to San Francisco. Wanting to have sex seemed to her a normal concomitant of wanting her company. They were young, unattached, and Peter was to all appearances a normal male. He was possibly a bit retarded on matters of sex. The males in her profession often were. But she had the laws of nature on her side. It should just be a matter of getting him over the hump, so to speak. The question was how to get things going so nature could take over. She pondered the matter as she worked with the papers.

The tent contained two camp chairs, a small table, and Peter's camp bed, which though narrow was adequate for her purposes. The table had insufficient surface for their work, and the papers were spread out all over the bed. That would not do. The rain, however, was a good thing. Generally, they had their drinks outside, but as long as the rain kept up ... She looked at her watch. The time to make a move was after a couple of drinks, and she wanted to have them inside the tent. It was not quite five o'clock, but there was a risk the rain would stop. It usually did around five. She reached a decision on how to proceed.

"Peter, my eyes are getting tired with all these notes. Let's break and have a drink. I just want to get the paperwork in some sort of order for our start tomorrow. I'll get all this stuff into piles and put it over there." She gestured toward one corner of the tent where there was bare space.

"Fine," said Peter, "but it's still raining."

"We'll have our drinks in here," she responded.

"Sure. Let's do that," said Peter.

Ellen began to clear Peter's bed. She listened with satisfaction to the steady dripping on the tent. Peter returned from the food locker with the vodka bottle and two glasses. "It's really coming down," he said. "Funny, it usually stops by now."

"Yes." She finished piling the papers on the floor. The bed was cleared and ready for occupancy. But there were other problems. As Peter had, she thought about the mosquito netting and the obstructive clothing. In contrast to Peter, however, Ellen faced these matters as obstacles to be overcome rather than justifications for inaction. Besides, in her experience, what one was wearing never seemed to be much of a hindrance once something got going. She thought fleetingly of early struggles with jeans and underwear in parked cars. There would be a few mosquito bites. A small price. She sat down on one of the camp chairs, which she arranged so that it faced the other, and watched Peter pouring. "Does your sister look like you, Peter?"

"Not much. We have different mothers. Besides, she's very good-looking."

"I'm sorry to hear that," Ellen said laughing.

"Oh, she's not at all intimidating. You'll like her." He raised his glass, having handed Ellen hers. "Anyway, here's to our continued partnership."

Ellen liked that. "Yes. To our continued partnership." She raised her glass and drank. Then she moved her chair forward a little, so that the mosquito netting over their knees almost touched. "You say I'll like her, but will she like me, barging in on her only time with her brother?"

"Penny's not like that. She'll be pleased. I'm sure of it."

"Well, I'm pleased," said Ellen. "It'll be nice to be somewhere with you without all the drawbacks of Nova Cannes." She thought of the mosquito netting again. That was going to take some careful handling. Peter thought of the netting too. Her reference to drawbacks brought back his earlier thoughts about having sex with Ellen on the island. This recollection was reinforced by the fact that Ellen was leaning forward toward him quite a bit, one hand holding her glass, the other poised above his left leg, her pretty, veiled face smiling. Ellen was really attractive and had such a good figure. Warmed by the vodka, he felt a little giddy. Her glass was empty.

"Your glass is empty," he declared, and reached for the bottle by his side.

"Good idea," said Ellen. As he poured, their knees began to touch. Ellen believed she felt a proper surge in Peter's energy field. Peter felt something too, but would have described it differently. Ellen drank a healthy belt and, setting down her glass, put both her hands on Peter's knees, pushing the netting up and inward so she could lay them flat on his legs. "You know, Peter," she began, "I'm really happy you said those things to me this morning about wanting my company. I really needed to hear that."

Peter felt no sense of alarm. The situation seemed quite under control. "Well, I meant it. I've really gotten to enjoy being around you."

"Good," said Ellen, and she moved her chair again so that her knees were on either side of one of his. "The problem, Peter, was that I'm very attracted to you, but I didn't know at all how you felt, so I was kind of at sixes and sevens about this job." She looked directly into his screened eyes, her netted hands meanwhile moving a bit further up his legs. "That was the problem," she repeated, feeling a little dizzy from the vodka, the bit between her teeth. "I took this job mainly to be with you."

Under the stimuli of the vodka and Ellen's behavior, Peter began to feel ever more romantic. He started to tell her so. "The fact is, Ellen, I've been attracted to you too. It's just ... " He faltered. How to explain about the mosquitoes, the netting, and the other things that had sapped his sexual courage?

A furry spider the size of Ellen's fist marched into view near her feet. She sent it spinning with a swift kick without loosening her hands from Peter's thighs. She was not about to lose focus. She moved even nearer, her knees now on either side of his thigh. "There doesn't have to be any 'it's just,' Peter." Under ordinary circumstances she would simply have kissed his lips, and was pondering how best to deal with that aspect of the mosquito netting when the radio emitted a loud noise. It was the incoming call signal.

Peter jumped. "Farrington," he said weakly.

"Damn it," said Ellen.

FARRINGTON, SLIGHTLY WHIZZED from his nine-percent beers, got right to the point. "Bit of hard cheese, mate. They've caught your sister red-handed."

"What?" Peter shouted.

"Murder. Shot him dead, she did. Did it from horseback. Picture of her on the horse. Dead man's one of your abos. Think of it. Shot him from a horse. Just like the Wild West." Farrington hiccuped. "Last frontier, America," he added emphatically.

"David! Are you sending me up?"

"No joke, old boy. She's sent you a ten-page letter plus clippings from the Frisco papers. Caught her red-handed. Out on bail she is. Didn't read the letter. Ten pages."

"David, for Heaven's sake, read me the letter!"

"Hold on there. Ten pages. Need a little slosh first. Wet the old whistle." The glugging sound of Farrington wetting his whistle came from the speaker. Then he began to read. The letter contained an account of events: the death of Smoking Mother, the hostile crowd, the strange police, Penny's arrest, her release on bail, the siege of the house, the political angle, her experiences with the lawyers, and ended with an ardent request that Peter come as soon as possible. Farrington punctuated his reading with further sloshes and commentary. At the end he expressed his great disappointment that the killing had not been accomplished from horseback. "Wasn't mounted, after all. Pity. Paper misled us. Good shot anyway."

"David, she says she didn't shoot him."

"Well they all say that, don't they? Specially women. Never plead guilty, the birds. Better prepare for the worst, mate. No sense going back there with your eyes shut."

Peter ignored Farrington's moody assessment. "David, I'll wait on the news stories till I get to Moresby. I want to talk to Ellen about this. Can I get back to you in half an hour?"

"It's been a long day, mate. Don't make it an hour." Farrington stared at the remains of his beer. Peter shut down the radio.

"Peter," Ellen declared, "that man is just horrible. He's already got her in the gas chamber. Don't listen to him."

"I won't, but I have to go to San Francisco. We may just have to put off the report."

"No. We'll lose the grant. I can write it."

"You don't have to do that, and I don't fancy leaving you here all alone."

"I'm not alone. There's Tallfellow."

"I know. It's just — "

"Peter, after all this work, we can't just chuck the whole thing. I can write that report alone. I have all your notes."

"I don't doubt that. It's leaving you alone, Ellen."

"I'm perfectly safe." She was determined to do the right thing, show mettle. "Peter, if you'd feel better, ask Farrington to send someone over here from Moresby."

"Yes, I could." Then with a rush of strong feeling he threw his arms around her as best his wraps permitted, and pressed his netted face against hers. "Ellen, you're wonderful." Ellen pressed back. He wanted to get past the netting and kiss her. Sensing this, she pushed both veils up and pressed her lips onto his with a confidence that surprised her. She could tell at once that it was not misplaced. After a moment they parted. "Ellen — "

— "Go call him. I'll come to San Francisco after I get the report off."

Peter felt joyful over the kiss, and for the moment, that pleasure took precedence in his thoughts over concern for his sister. He got Farrington immediately. "David, Ellen's going to stay on to do the report, but I want someone else to be here with her in case of some emergency."

"That's a tough order, mate," Farrington declared with a pronounced slur. He had been back to the well between radio calls.

"David, there has to be someone. I don't mean another anthropologist. Just a — "

Farrington interrupted. "Wait a minute. There's Dipper Edwards. He's been hanging around Moresby looking to get on somebody's payroll."

"Dipper? That's not an encouraging name. What's his story?"

"Former patrol officer. Sepik River. Some sort of blowup with the natives. Bit rough cut, I suppose, but can't think of anyone else really."

Ellen was dubious. "Peter, I might be better off just with Tallfellow."

"No. Suppose you had an accident? Tallfellow wouldn't know what to do."

"He does drink a bit," put in Farrington. "Can't think of anyone else."

"All right," said Peter, "sign him up. When can I get down there?"

"Send the chopper up tomorrow. Only thing is if Dipper can be ready. He'll need provisioning. Takes a lot of beer to run Dipper Edwards."

"Oh, God," said Ellen, in dismal contemplation of her protector running on beer.

"Usually pretty sober during the day, though," added Farrington.

PETER WENT TO SAY GOODBYE to Tallfellow the next morning, but his war party had not yet returned. Peter and Ellen spotted the helicopter shortly before noon and went with Peter's bags to the clearing. It appeared to be flying erratically but landed without mishap. The pilot got out and greeted them. He looked unhappy. "Rough trip. Way overloaded. Bloke asleep in the cabin came with thirty cases of beer. Should never have let him bring it."

"I see," said Peter, a little gloomily.

"Illegal to sell it to the natives, you know."

Ellen responded. "Oh, no. The bloke who's asleep is going to drink it himself. They tell us he runs on it."

"Sorry to hear that," said the pilot. "I'll rouse him and get him to help lift it off. He ran off somewhere when we were loading his kit."

"Probably to get a beer," offered Ellen.

As she spoke a figure appeared in the door of the helicopter and stuck its head out. Dipper Edwards was a tall, spare man in his forties, with thick, dark hair carefully combed. He had a narrow moustache. It was an almost handsome face, as yet largely unimpaired by his diet. He hailed them. "Hello, I'm Dipper Edwards. Need any help with my kit?" He began to descend, cautiously, exhibiting the practiced drinker's instinct for self-preservation on stairs. On the ground he continued his thought as he walked toward them. "Bit heavy, my kit. May need a couple of abos."

"We don't call the natives 'abos,' and we don't work them," Peter said by way of introduction.

"Steady on, old boy. New to the place. Learn the drill soon. You're Waters?"

"Walker," said Peter, "and this is Ellen Ross."

Edwards turned to look at Ellen. He was pleased. "Hello! It's you I'm to watch over, eh? Well that should go down just fine."

Peter responded sharply. "It's not watching over Ms. Ross that you're here for. It's simply in case of an emergency if she needs your help."

"Sorry. Wrong verb. Saying all the wrong things, I am." Dipper displayed a wronged rather than apologetic look.

Peter ignored it. "Look, we'll help you get your kit out of the helicopter. There are no porters here. You'll have to stockpile the beer in the little shed there. Move it later in smaller loads to the camp."

Edward's face expressed alarm. "But all these ab- natives?"

"They won't go near it. They have their own tipple. They never drink ours. Come on. Let's get moving."

When Dipper's kit was unloaded and his own put on the helicopter, Peter took Ellen aside. "I wish you were coming with me. You can still change your mind."

"No, Peter. I'm going to get that report out." Peter took her hands, and Ellen smiled. "Don't worry about me. I'll see you soon in San Francisco." She began to cry. "I'm sorry, I can't help it."

"I know. It's terrible I have to leave. Just when we ... " But he was unable to complete the thought. They embraced briefly.

Afterward, Ellen stood in the clearing watching the helicopter head toward Port Moresby. Dipper Edwards opened a beer. "Damn hot here. Makes a man thirsty."

The helicopter disappeared. She turned to Dipper. "Yes, it is hot, and you'll need mosquito netting."

"Got all that. Been in this sort of soup before. Sepik River. Plays hell with cassettes."

"Cassettes?"

"Yes." He lifted a boom-box that had been behind his suitcase. "Like a bit of good rock, I do. Like to dance?"

Ellen suppressed any sign of concern at this suggestion. "I hate dancing," she said smoothly, and turning began to walk toward the camp.

Dipper followed, studying Ellen's graceful body. It inspired him. "Hot here but never too hot for dancing," he proclaimed, rallying from her putdown. Then he stopped. "Hold up a minute. I need something from my case."

Ellen stopped and looked back. Dipper had withdrawn a holstered pistol and belt. "You won't need that here. We don't have firearms. The natives hate them."

"I always wear mine in the boondocks. Natives. They'll get used to me wearing it. Never took it off on the Sepik. Abos there are cannibals."

Ellen turned and resumed walking. Dipper had all the makings of a problem.

LATER THAT DAY, while Edwards was off on one of three roundtrips to his stockpiled beer, Ellen sought out Tallfellow. Preparations for the long-pig feast to propitiate Big Mouth were in progress. She explained how Big Mouth's prediction of trouble across the water had been correct, that Peter's sister in San Francisco had been falsely accused of murder, that Peter had gone to be with his sister and was sorry to have been unable to say good-bye. She would have to go to San Francisco too, but they would be back. Until she left, there would be another white man in their camp. He wore a gun, but she did not think he would cause any trouble.

Tallfellow was not as sanguine. "Ellen, remember Big Mouth said the trouble across the water would cause trouble here, too. This new white man with a gun. Might not he be the cause of that trouble?"

Ellen had not thought of that. "Yes," she said, bothered by the thought. "I'll keep a close eye on him. If he gets out of line, I'll radio Moresby to lift him out of here."

"I think it is a bad thing that Peter has had to leave," Tallfellow said solemnly.

THAT SAME EVENING, Tallfellow began to receive the first complaints about the new white man. He had a funny box that made loud, terrible noises. It interfered with the sounds of the long-pig ceremony. Even the dogs were growling at the awful noise. The Ellen woman did not appear to like the man either. Should they not throw this new man and his dreadful box to the crocodiles for the good of all concerned? Tallfellow did not air his own concerns about Dipper. It was essential to prevent violence. He explained that the new man was here at the behest of Peter to be with Ellen during Peter's absence. He would only be here for a short time. They should simply ignore him. There was grumbling, but no further proposals to do away with Dipper.

Soon thereafter Dipper's boom-box fell silent. He was exhausted from his beer hauls, had drunk his measure and fallen asleep on Peter's cot. Ellen had complained to him about the noise, but he had only reduced the volume a little. "Need a few sounds of life when you're out in the boondocks," he responded, dismissing her complaint with a pull on his twelfth and next-to-last bottle of beer for the day. Now in her own tent, Ellen was still awake listening to the sounds of long pig. She welcomed them after the blasts from Dipper's box. It was a curious proof of the principle that nothing is so bad that something else cannot be worse.

THE NEXT DAY, DIPPER AWOKE stiff and sore of limb and body from his beer-hauling trips to the camp. He opened a beer and sat up on Peter's bed, thinking. There had to be a better way. His eye fell on the carriage for Peter's radio. It had two sturdy wheels and a frame handle, which enabled the heavy device to be moved as if on an air-travel wheeler. If he freed the carriage from the radio and extended the frame with a couple of planks, it would make an excellent hand truck. He set about doing so.

After awhile, Ellen came out of her tent to go to the food locker and saw the work in progress. "What are you doing to the radio?"

"Radio doesn't need the wheels. I do. Move my kit." He stopped working to look at Ellen and drank some beer. He had had ample opportunity to observe her while following her to camp the day before. This morning she looked even better. "Smashing figure, you have. Bloody shame you don't like to dance."

The remark maddened Ellen. She spoke sharply. "Look, I don't like personal remarks, either. If you make any more I'm going to radio Farrington to haul you back to Moresby."

"Now, now. No sense getting on the high horse. Just paying a compliment. Can't a man tell a nice bird she looks good?"

Ellen knew it wasn't just that. It was a pass at her, and she felt unprotected. She had to be firm with him. "No, he can't. I don't want any personal remarks from you. I mean what I said about calling Farrington."

"Bloody awful, I say. Just a law of nature, man complimenting a woman."

Ellen did not respond and returned to her tent. When she was inside, Dipper went at once to the radio. Projecting near the dials was the security key. It was a simple mechanism. If turned and removed, messages could not be sent. He turned and removed the key, placing it in his suitcase. "She'll need a loud voice to reach Farrington now," he reasoned. He had decided Ellen was going to dance. There was no bloody sense wasting a figure like that. He would have a nice heart-to-heart with her that evening. Bring her around.

16. What's Reality Got to Do with It?

Tula Fogg became eligible for the San Francisco Police Department when the minimum height requirement was done away with. She was barely five-feet-two, though she had a vertical leap of twenty-nine inches. Then the height barrier was discarded, and the door to a career in law enforcement opened.

During her training, Tula routinely bested taller, male trainees in physical contests. She hopped around them like a boxing kangaroo. This was duly noted and held against her by her male superiors. So, on completion of training she did not receive the street duty she wanted but was assigned instead as an investigator to the district attorney, where her vertical leap would not upstage other officers. Her warmhearted, enthusiastic nature, however, solaced her and helped in her work, which was mainly contacting and interviewing potential witnesses. If she did well at this, perhaps a street assignment would come later.

At the school for police recruits she had undergone an intensive course in sensitivity training. Tula was a sensitive person to begin with, and while she fully concurred with the objectives of the course — her college track coach had called her "the flea" — the details were often bewildering. Was it always improper, for example, to bring up something regularly associated with a particular ethnic group when talking with a person from that group? It seemed to her that in the proper circumstances it should be a useful means of establishing some common ground or interest. Tula was unsure, for example, whether it showed commonality of feeling and friendliness to tell someone of Italian ancestry that she loved pasta, or if it was taboo. She knew from a training video that it was improper to refer to sake in conversations with Japanese Americans. It would make them think you saw them as Japanese, the video related, rather than as ethnically indistinguishable Americans. And that was the problem: she was uncertain why a Japanese American would prefer one point of view to the other.

This was her state of mind as she found herself responsible for contacting Smoking Mother's next of kin who would, of course, be Native-Americans. The deceased's effects had included a wallet containing papers that identified a Mrs. Flora Grebe of St. Paul, Minnesota as his mother and gave a telephone number. Tula read the entire Smoking Mother file thoughtfully before making the call. "Smoking Mother, a.k.a. Thorson Grebe." The significance did not escape her: a Native-American family that had adopted Anglo names to lessen discrimination. Her heart went out to the soon-to-be-grieving mother. After studying the facts of the homicide once again she dialed the number. The phone rang five times; then there was a sound of connection that preceded an ear-shattering crash, as if the phone at the other end of the line had fallen to the floor. This was followed by the voice of a woman cursing and finally by a shouted declaration: "If that's you again, Riley, stop houndin' me about your damn bill."

Tula responded, "This isn't Riley. Is this Mrs. Grebe?"

"Never mind who this is, sister. Who are you?"

It sounded to Tula as if the woman had been drinking. She had read that Native-Americans were often sensitive to alcohol and was immediately sympathetic. "If this is Mrs. Grebe, we're very sorry to bother you. I'm Tula Fogg with the San Francisco Police Department investigative unit. It's about your son. I — "

She was interrupted. "Don't come to me looking for bail money. What's that bum done now?"

Tula kept steady. The poor, distraught woman. It would not be easy to tell her. "He hasn't done anything, but ... " She grasped for a sensitive way to put it. "He's- he's gone to the Happier Hunting Ground."

"Are you crazy?" The woman shouted it.

Tula tried again. "He is now one with The Great Spirit."

"Why are you talkin' like some goddamned Hollywood Indian? Is there something wrong with Thorson?"

Tula gulped. How explain to the poor, anxious mother? "Well, yes, there is something wrong with him."

"What is it, for Christ's sake?"

Tula could think of no way to soften the news. "Mrs. Grebe, he's dead," she said in an anguished voice.

There was a pause. Breathing came down the line from St. Paul. "Did he take anyone with him? He always said he would."

Tula did not understand the question. "Take anyone with him?"

"You know, stupid, kill anybody himself?"

"Oh, no. He was the only one shot."

"Shot, eh?" Mrs. Grebe pondered the matter. "Who shot him?"

Tula's warm heart pounded. What a terrible thing to learn of your son's death by phone from a stranger. "A woman shot him."

"Yeah? That don't surprise me. He liked to beat up on 'em."

Tula was close to tears. The poor woman was truly unbalanced by the news. "Oh, it wasn't that. It was a stranger, a wealthy woman.

She claims it was an accident."

Flora Grebe's voice took on an interested edge. "Can you sue for something like this?"

"I'm sorry, Mrs. Grebe, we cannot give legal advice, but she will be prosecuted. That's why I'm calling. The district attorney might want to call you as a witness at the trial."

"Do they pay for that?'

"Well, there are certain witness fees, and we'll pay travel expenses too."

Mrs. Grebe hiccuped. "How much will you give me? I never been to Frisco before."

Obviously the news had completely overcome the poor mother. It was not vitriol and greed or intoxication that Tula heard. "I'll have to check on that, Mrs. Grebe. Any reasonable expense will be taken care of. But I need to get some other information."

"Not so fast, sister. This woman who shot him, she's got money, eh?"

"That's what the file says. A society woman."

"I was just thinkin' maybe I should get a Frisco lawyer to go after her for me. She might cough up some bucks."

Bucks. The word reminded Tula that she must inquire about other kin in this Native-American family. It would have to be a sensitive, feeling exchange. The mother was already so disturbed. "I really must ask you some personal questions about the family, Mrs. Grebe." Tula heard liquid being poured into a glass.

"Well don't be at it too long, sister." Though separated by thousands of miles and diverse cultures, Flora Grebe and David Farrington shared a common aversion to the interruption of Happy Hours.

"It won't take long. Is Thorson's father a Native-American?"

"Christ, no. He was a goddamn Swede."

Tula noticed the past tense. "You say, 'was'?"

"Yeah. He's been gone since right after Thorson was born."

"Gone?"

"Dead, for Christ's sake. The bastard bit me when he saw the baby. Then the next day we caught him biting the baby. We had to have him put down. My brother's a veterinarian. He arranged it."

Tula wept softly. The distraught mother was literally deranged by the news. She knew she must avoid any challenging questions. Best to just accept the mother's disturbed vision. "You mean you had the father put to sleep?"

"Yeah. Good thing, too. I suppose if we'd been out in the country we could have kept him penned, but here in St. Paul ... "

"I see," said Tula sympathetically. "Are there any siblings?"

"Any what? Look, I'm a Christian."

"Any brothers or sisters?"

"Christ, no! After Thorson, that cooled me on offspring. Probably should have had him put down too. My brother was all for it. Used to bite and kick the other schoolkids. Mean little mother."

Little Smoking Mother, thought Tula. The word "mother" meant something different to her. She must not forget to pin down the Native-American connection. "Smoking Mother's baby and childhood photos, Mrs. Grebe. We might want to use them at the trial."

"What's this 'Smoking Mother' crap?"

"That's Thorson's Native-American name, isn't it?"

"Yeah, and I'm Sitting Bull."

It was terrible. The overwrought woman was in denial of her own heritage. Tula determined not to confront her at this anxious time. "He was known here by that name, Mrs. Grebe. We presumed he was a Native-American."

"That's bullshit. He was a typical worthless Swede, just like his old man. Sad day I ever raised my skirts for that bum."

Tula disregarded the distressed woman's bitter assessment. It would take time for her to recover her senses. Tact was needed. "Well, do you know why he was called Smoking Mother?"

"No, but he lied about everything. An Indian, eh? Prob'ly some scam. Do Indians get more welfare out there than Swedes?"

"I don't know. I'm very sorry to be troubling you with all these questions."

"Well, there aren't going to be any more questions till I see some money."

"Yes," said Tula understandingly, "I understand. We're very sorry about your son."

"Yeah, he made everybody sorry." Mrs. Grebe hung up.

Tula thought. The proper course was clear. A literal account of the interview was out of the question. It would be a betrayal of the poor mother's confidences. Her terrible distress must be given consideration.

Tula turned to her computer and began to type an e-mail to the assistant district attorney in charge of the case, Sonia Taft. Mrs. Grebe had been fully cooperative but might be living at the poverty level. She needed an advance on travel expenses. She was very disturbed by the news and suspicious of contact from the authorities. It had made her reluctant to discuss the Native-American side of her family. Yet she seemed motivated to be a witness. She had wanted to sue Mrs. Hill, for example. Tula decided to stop there. Any other details would be a betrayal of the desperate, grief-deranged mother.

When Sonia Taft read the e-mail she immediately sent through a check requisition for Mrs. Grebe's witness fees and travel expenses. It would be nice to have a weeping mother on the witness stand.

THE MAYOR AND HIS CONSULTANT, Doc Wayward, sat in the mayor's office glumly surveying the latest polls. "Doc, we're still behind Sybil Watch with all groups. We need a shot in the arm."

"It's coming, Waylon. The judge found probable cause in the Hill case this afternoon. We'll get some good stuff to the media right away."

"What judge was it?"

"Perry, but he won't try the case."

"Who will?"

"Well, I wanted to discuss that. Potter Flex would be ideal, but he's sitting on the civil side."

"Why Flex?"

"With him the trial will take a long time, and we want the ball in the air as long as possible. Besides, Flex always commits error and gets reversed, which is good in case she's innocent. A conviction will get overturned."

The mayor pondered the last point. "You're right, Doc. She might be innocent, if what her lawyer has been giving to the media is accurate."

"Exactly, Waylon, but with a probable-cause determination there's got to be prosecution. If she's innocent, the way I see it, with Flex as the judge there'd be an insurance policy that she ultimately walks."

"How do judges get reassigned?"

"Let me look into that."

THE CLERK OF THE Superior Court called the deputy in charge of courtroom assignments. "Flex is being moved to crimes. Where we gonna put him?"

"There's zero space available at the Hall of Justice. He'll just have to try cases at his courtroom here. We've had criminal cases at City Hall before."

"Yeah."

"What's going on, anyway?"

"The mayor started raisin' hell about the backlog of criminal cases. Got on the DA's behind. DA says there's not enough judges to try the old cases, and he's got a big new one, the Hill murder case. So they're movin' Flex for that case."

"Has Judge Flex ever tried a criminal case?"

"Not as far as I know."

THE APPLICATION FOR A SEARCH WARRANT came before Judge Flex on the same day as his reassignment. "Premises of the defendant? Well, I suppose that's the usual thing, eh?"

"Definitely, Your Honor," said Sonia Taft, tucking the signed order into her briefcase. Later she met with her investigators, Tula Fogg and Arnold White. "Tula, I want you to interview Hill's neighbors, particularly the guy across the street who called us. The one who said she tried to run over his kid."

"Yes, Ms. Taft."

"And Arnold, you search the premises. Take another cop. I know what, take that female officer who arrested her. Here's the warrant. Pick up anything that looks interesting."

"You mean that would put her in a bad light?"

"Well, I wouldn't put it that way."

ARNOLD WHITE AND THE FEMALE officer arrived at Penny's house that afternoon. The media, by now showing signs of outpost fatigue, paid them little heed. At the door, they were greeted by Millie. White showed his badge and the warrant.

"Police? Ms. Hill's not at home."

"That don't make any difference. This is a search warrant. You got to let us in."

"Are you sure?"

"Read it, Miss. You read English, don't you?"

"Of course. I'm Scottish."

"Well, you never know these days." He pointed at his companion. "She don't read English."

Millie stared at the document. "I can't understand all this. Let me call Ms. Hill's daughter." Millie departed and reappeared with

April, who was in workout regalia and reading the search warrant.

Arnold White, who pumped iron himself, was moved by her appearance. "Hey, you got some great biceps," he exclaimed.

"Thank you," said April, impressed with his judgment. "I've read the warrant. Come on in. I'll show you around."

"Much obliged," said White.

"Girl disgusting clothes," his companion whispered to him and followed him into the house.

LATER, WHITE STOOD IN Sonia Taft's office, holding the painting of Penny upright for inspection. "She looks mean, don't she?" He spoke with feeling.

"Yes," said Sonia, delighted with the find. "It shows the defendant's true nature, her propensity to violence. Where did you find it?"

"In her bedroom."

"Wow! That's even better."

"I knew you'd like it."

"These tins of caviar, Arnold, what's the point there?"

"See, Ms. Taft, they're from the Russian consulate. Maybe smuggled or contraband or tax dodged. You know."

"How did you find that out?"

"Well, we were in the kitchen, and that woman cop seen them, and she kept saying, 'Russian, Russian' over and over. Then Ms. Hill's daughter said her mother buys them from an old lady at the consulate. I thought there might be an angle there."

"I think you're right. Anything else?"

"She had these books about Indians in her library."

Sonia's face lit up. "Ah. She was planning this shooting for some time."

"Yeah. I thought you'd see it that way. She had a couple of hatchets, too, in the basement. I had to leave those with security down-stairs."

"A tomahawk fetish," Sonia mused, beginning to construct a workable scenario.

TULA FOGG STEPPED OVER the broken red wagon on the doorstep and rang the bell. A small boy opened the door and sized her up. Satisfied with his appraisal, a look of cunning came over his face. "You broke my wagon," he screamed.

"No, no," said Tula, sensitive to the child's despair. "It was that way when I came."

"No it wasn't! You broke it. You threw it down and broke it!"

"Please," said Tula, more moved to sympathy than to anger at the false accusation. "I had nothing to do with it, but I tell you what." She reached into her purse and produced a twenty-dollar bill. "Here, this is for you to buy a new one."

The child grasped the bill and ran back into the house out of sight. Tula pressed the bell again, standing in the open doorway. Presently a man appeared.

"What do you want and how did you get the door open?" he asked angrily.

"A little boy opened it." She showed her badge. "I'm Tula Fogg from the district attorney's office. You called us about Ms. Hill."

"About time one of your people responded. I'm Lambert Crocker. I've got Ms. Hill's number."

"Got her number?" Tula did not like the man at all.

"Yeah, she's a bad actor. Tried to run over my kid. A violent type."

"Well, perhaps it was an accident," Tula offered.

"Listen, lady, are you from the DA's office or from the defense? Never mind about accidents."

"Mr. Crocker, I'm from the district attorney, but I'm only interested in the truth. It seems far-fetched that a woman of her age and background would try to run over a child."

"For Christ's sake! What kind of an investigator are you? Do you want to get the goods on Penny Hill or not?"

"I told you. I just want the truth."

"Well I saw her try to run over him, damn it! Right from that window."

Tula remained suspicious of the man. He didn't look nice, and he had a nasty temper. Nevertheless, she proceeded. "Tell me about it."

He told her. The story, she concluded, was palpably false. Ms. Hill had simply been backing up her car and not seen the child or the wagon. It also revealed that the child was a liar and an extortionist. She wanted her twenty dollars back. "You know, Mr. Crocker, your son accused me of breaking his wagon when he knew it was broken by Ms. Hill's car."

"So what? That's not the point of this interview."

"He accepted twenty dollars from me for a new wagon when he really knew I had nothing to do with breaking it."

"So? He's just a kid. You going to arrest him?"

Tula was disturbed by the father's sarcasm. This was a dreadful family. The district attorney would be better off having nothing further to do with them. She bid Mr. Crocker good day.

Later, she e-mailed Sonia Taft regarding the interviews of the neighbors. Two of them had praised Ms. Hill as a good neighbor. They had nothing bad to say about her. Perhaps, Tula wrote, Ms. Taft would like to talk to these neighbors herself to get a different perspective regarding the defendant. What an odd suggestion, thought Sonia, as she read the e-mail. Then Tula reported upon the man across the street. She went into detail, concluding that both father and son were untrustworthy, that the intentional run-down story was unquestionably contrived, and that the father, and perhaps the son as well, had some irrational prejudice against Ms. Hill. Tula recommended against further contact.

My goodness, Sonia concluded, Tula was not having one of her better days. Then she called a deputy and told him to add Lambert Crocker to the trial subpoena list. It was odd, Sonia thought; Tula had done such a good job with the Indian woman.

APRIL EXPLAINED TO HER MOTHER about the search warrant and what the police had taken. "None of it makes much sense, particularly the portrait," said Penny.

"Well, they left a receipt for everything. Actually, the man was quite nice. He lifts weights." April paused. "I know why they took the painting. It makes you look like you do weird sex."

"What would that have to do with me shooting Indians?"

"It's to prejudice you with the jury. That's how cases are tried. It's all appearances."

"You sound just like my lawyer. I don't mean about the portrait. He hasn't seen it."

"He isn't going to like it, Mother."

"No. I better call Eric and tell him the police have his painting."

BARTON PLAYCHEK AND HAMILTON SAYER were meeting in Playchek's office. "What bothers me a lot, Hamilton, is the media are calling this Nordic purse snatcher an Indian."

"Yes. And there's some group in Berkeley that's been holding 'Awareness Vigils' in his name, awareness of the threat to Native-American survival. It's pernicious."

"Hamilton, we're going to need a real Indian. One who can tell the jury that Smoking Mother was a paleface masquerading as a Native-American. We'll want him to go to the cooler and look at the corpse."

"How does one find a real Indian?"

Playchek picked up the San Francisco *Yellow Pages*. After a moment he looked up. "There's an ad here for a group that sings and does war dances at barbecues, bar mitzvahs, that sort of thing. It's called Native-American Noise." Playchek dialed the number.

A man answered. "Native-American Noise. This is Reginald."

Playchek explained who he was. "Basically, I need a real Native-American to testify that a white guy who called himself 'Smoking Mother' was passing as an Indian; that the guy was a phony." He explained how that would be established.

"Well, Mr. Playchek, we don't generally do morgues."

"I don't mean all of you. I only need one witness."

"I'm sorry, we never do singles. You have to hire the group. Tell you what, though. We've read about this Smoking Mother guy. He was no Indian, and these idiotic awareness vigils in Berkeley are an embarrassment; it's just a bunch of palefaces trivializing tribal dignity. All the tribesmen in northern California are put out. So we'll do this for five hundred dollars an hour. That's a significant discount off our fully costumed war-dance rate."

"The rate's OK, but, look, how big's your group?"

"Seven."

"Well, we can't have seven Indians inspecting the corpse. It'd look overbearing."

"Too much like the day after the Little Big Horn, I suppose."

"Something like that."

"Well, I'll inspect the corpse without the others and be the witness, but if we all come to court that should help you."

In his mind's eye Playchek saw a row of feather-bonneted braves staring truculently at the jurors. "Let me think about it. No native costumes in any event."

"But that would be much more fun. Think of the publicity, Mr. Playchek. And we'd do a war dance for everybody after court."

Playchek experienced a sense of unease, as if he had mounted a restless horse. "Look, come by and we can get acquainted and go over the details." When he had hung up, Playchek sighed. "They're not going to be cheap, Hamilton, but I feel better now that we've got a few Indians in our corner."

"Is this trial really going to turn on which side wraps itself best in an Indian blanket?"

"Not turn on it, but it's a real live issue. Particularly now that we've got Judge Flex. No telling what he'll let into evidence."

"Yes, that's unfortunate. Can't we use a peremptory challenge to get another judge?"

"We don't want to do that. Think about it. He always commits reversible error. Any conviction is bound to be reversed."

"Ah," said Sayer, "I hadn't thought about it that way. Then won't the prosecution challenge him?"

"Not a chance. The DA's office counts success by what happens at the trial. If they win there, that's all they care about. Appeals don't figure in the scoring."

"This is going to be an odd trial, Barton."

"Count on it."

17. BUT WE'RE IN SAN FRANCISCO

PENNY WOKE UP THE NEXT MORNING feeling chipper, despite having had a lot of white wine with Eric Krane the night before. They had concluded that the seizures of his portrait of her and her other belongings were police-state tactics. "It's like we were in Nazi Germany," he suggested, a little uncertain as to whether Nazis would, in fact, have destroyed his painting or exhibited it. "Besides," Eric added with greater certainty, "the portrait doesn't show your sexual interests. It shows mine."

"I know, Eric. We may have to call you as a witness to explain that." Penny spoke half in jest, but knowing it was probably exactly what Playchek would do if the DA used the portrait at the trial.

"You can count on me," said Eric, raising his glass as a pledge, "even if it means coming out of the S-M closet in court." Later, and drunker, he had torn off his shirt and made another failed attempt to interest her in sex. It had been that kind of an evening.

Now she rose and went to feed the birds, noting the portrait's absence from its usual site. This renewed her anger at her tormentors, the civil authorities. "A plague on all those people," she declared in a loud voice. April, who had come to her mother's door, heard the curse.

"Mother! What are you raving about? Look! You're back on the front page. I'm keeping an album of all these items about you. It's wonderful."

"Yes. I can look at it in the gas chamber. They didn't use the portrait did they?"

"No. There's no mention of that or the other stuff they took."

"I've got to tell my lawyer about that search warrant before someone else does. He'll lose confidence in his client."

"He'll lose more than that when he sees the portrait!"

"April, go lift weights."

"Don't get testy, Mother. The worst is yet to come. I'll leave the paper downstairs for you."

At her breakfast table Penny found *The Cockerel* waiting, the front-page heavy with the news: "Hill Case To Get Speedy Trial." The article noted that Judge Flex had been specially assigned to the case and that the trial was expected to commence within three weeks. Then it went on to resound the same themes her case had been linked with from the start. The writer leaned perceptibly toward the conclusion that the "untimely death of the homeless boy, Smoking Mother, was the result of class or Indian hatred, perhaps both." R. "Doc" Wayward, the mayor's representative, commented once again on the mayor's determination to stamp out class and ethnic prejudice and to make serious inroads on poverty itself. He linked that determination to vigorous prosecution of the Hill case and the formation of a committee to find funding for a new Mayor Lint-type food stamp program. He urged all right-minded citizens to rally behind the mayor in this time of municipal crisis.

The article concluded that as part of *The Cockerel's* policy to present the news from a balanced perspective the writer had interviewed Ms. Hill's lawyer, Barton Playchek. Mr. Playchek had denounced the prosecution as a politically oriented attack on an innocent woman, whose well-being and mental state had been sorely compromised by election campaign-driven publicity. Ms. Hill's not-guilty pleas to the charges against her would be forthcoming, Playchek said, and her innocence proved at trial.

Had it not been for the reference to her compromised mental state, which she knew foreshadowed Playchek's diminished-capacity defense, Penny would have welcomed the blast from her lawyer. As it was, it made her feel worse.

The phone rang. It was Peter calling from New Guinea, and he would be arriving in San Francisco late the next day. She resisted the temptation to talk at length. She was doing fine, she said, and would tell him the whole story when he got here. She would meet him at the airport. She ended by asking him what he would like for dinner and hung up feeling better. As she finished her breakfast, she began to plan the dinner for Peter. The bastards had taken the caviar; she would just make another trip to the consulate. Then her earlier concern came back to her that the prosecution was about to leak the results of the search warrant to the media. They might have done so already, and it just hadn't made the morning news. She had better call Playchek right away.

Penny got through to Playchek and described what the DA's investigators had seized. "How bad is the painting?" he asked.

"Well, I'm not naked or anything, but it's a female domination pose, and I look pretty aggressive. I don't do S-M. I was just trying to please the artist; he's a friend of mine, and he wanted to paint me like that. Who would have thought it would get used to prove I committed murder?"

"Yeah, who would have thought it?" mused Playchek. "I'll try to get it kept out of evidence, but this judge we got, Flex, is known for letting everything in as evidence. So we better have some way to explain it. You say you had it in your bedroom?"

"Yes."

"That's not so good. It sounds like you really liked it."

"Well, I couldn't put it anyplace public, like the living room, and Eric insisted I keep it. It would have hurt him if I'd refused. He took some photos of it for himself."

"Let's not get into that. Is there any chance you didn't understand its significance?"

"No way. Wait till you see it."

"Ms. Hill, you're making me feel terrible."

"Yes. My daughter said you wouldn't like it."

"What's with the other stuff, the caviar?"

"There's a kind of market for Russian products at the consulate. You can get chocolates and caviar, other stuff. So I guess they're going to prove I'm a smuggler."

"Sounds like it. The books about Indians and the hatchets, that's easy. That's their Indian-killer theme. The books show you were planning ahead. The hatchets are surrogate tomahawks. I can hear that Welsh prosecutor now, braying about the white man's perfidy."

"So what do we do, Mr. Playchek?"

"I'll make a motion to suppress the whole grab on relevancy grounds, but we're in the arms of Judge Flex. Our chances are poor with him."

"Could we appeal or something if he rules against us?"

"We could do what's called seeking a writ, but I don't want to wear out our welcome at the Court of Appeal. We'll need it later on. Besides, it might be reversible error if Flex lets the jury get that portrait and ... " His voice trailed off.

Penny finished the sentence. "If I'm convicted we need reversible error."

"Precisely, Ms. Hill."

"Is there no balm in Gilead?"

"Maybe in Gilead, but we're in San Francisco."

AT HER HOME IN SAN FRANCISCO, Sybil Watch, who had taken time from her practice as a child psychiatrist to run for mayor, was explaining the centerpiece of her campaign, the New Education Plan (NEP), to her close friend, Wanda Cranberry. Among other features, the NEP would preclude public schools from judging students' abilities or progress. The plan held that such evaluation intrinsically discriminated against students of lesser abilities or ambition, that the aim of education should be to suppress or level ability and ambition, rather than put premiums upon these antisocial characteristics.

Watch's enthusiasm for the NEP was boundless. "Wanda, this may be the only major city in America where a concept like this has a real chance of attracting votes. I'm confident we have a majority of independent thinkers who are not slaves to experience or even common sense when it comes to appraising social programs. They're ready to strike out on their own, guided by hope and good feelings. They'll like the NEP because it's more feeling, caring. No one has to worry about achievement. The plan ensures a desirable, striving-free mediocrity."

"Yes, I suppose mediocrity is rather trendy these days," said Wanda, dipping a cookie in her tea.

"You know, Wanda, history-wise, mediocrity has gotten a lot of unfair press. Look at the root: 'medi' or middle. That's where the focus should be. If everyone's kept in a bunch in the middle, then mediocre becomes the Golden Mean. You see?"

Wanda nodded. She had had an excellent education and was dubious about the NEP. "Well, you're still ahead in the polls, dear. That must prove something."

"I think it does, but I haven't unveiled the full NEP yet. There's the financing to deal with. After I present the whole thing we'll know better. Besides, Waylon Homer is lifting himself out of the 'No Stamps, No Steps' quagmire. His consultant Wayward has shown genius mixing the Hill prosecution and the food stamps funding issues. My consultant is pathetic. I have to give him all his ideas myself. He's like having a husband."

"Get a different one, Sybil. That's what one does with husbands."

"Well, I might just get rid of my consultant and let my husband be chief of staff for the campaign. Actually, Wagner does have some good ideas now and then. One he had was giving those demonstrators portable loudspeakers. Much more noise, and it keeps up their spirits, like fifes and drums with soldiers in combat."

"I think fifes and drums went out with the British Empire, Sybil."

"That's a pity. It was really the only nice thing about war. Anyway, I'm not relying on just the NEP for votes. My fundamental tenet is change, and not just the change of street and park names. But that's important. In fact, changing Golden Gate Park to Golden Change Park is very important. It sets the theme for the other changes."

"Why don't you call it Spare Change Park, dear?"

"Wanda, be serious. Anyway, it's amazing how you can sweep aside opposition by advocating change. It's because there are always so many more dissatisfied people than ones who are. See what's happened the last few years with big businesses. Giving out things like coffee mugs that say, 'Seek Change.' They're scared to death of appearing to stand in the way of change." Sybil crossed the room and drank from a large bottle of flavored mineral water. Her throat refreshed, she began again.

"Another thing, Wanda: as a psychiatrist, I know it's a sound approach to say to people, 'Tell me what you don't like, and I'll change it.' The NEP is just one big change, but other possibilities occur to me hourly. What don't you like, Wanda?"

"You mean, if I tell you you'll change it?"

"Yes."

"It's hard to find a place to park."

"Exactly. I'm going to change all that. To begin with, my plan to rename all the streets after local street people will help, because the drivers who usually hog the spaces will have trouble finding out where they are. But the main thing is to make the big property owners provide free public parking."

"Would I be a big property owner?"

"Oh, no. I don't mean people with big residences. I mean the people who own these big buildings, the corporations and big law firms, those types. We'll make them build garages and parking lots."

"Well, that's solved, but I don't like the demonstrators around City Hall either, particularly since Wagner gave them loudspeakers."

"Wanda, that will all stop once I'm elected."

"You won't permit demonstrations?"

"Well, why should there be demonstrations if I'm in office? Besides, when I'm in charge I'm not going to have people running around shouting like the unruly children parents bring to me. That's going to be an important change. We're going to have peace and freedom from controversy."

"Have you been reading *Mein Kampf?*"

"That book by Hitler. Of course not. Sometimes, Wanda, you say the strangest things."

"Perhaps I should be changed."

AT THE BEGINNING OF HER CAMPAIGN, Sybil Watch had declared that she, not Waylon Homer, was the spiritual heir of good Mayor Lint. Her approach to public funding was, to be sure, vintage Lint: the money was out there; it was just a question of getting it and redirecting its expenditure. She anticipated that her school program would take a lot of money. There would be fifty or more public schools busily molding the student body into a single, unvarying product. They would be "leveling schools," dedicated to achieving perfect social balance. Sybil knew that would be expensive because it was against human nature, but she was determined not to be put off by obstacles of that kind.

The problem, however, was larger than simply the practices of conventional schools. It went to the way parents raised children. Children were constantly being taught to try to improve, to do better. There was this emphasis on excellence, competence, talent. This led to the twin evils: ambition and competition. Life, Sybil felt, should be the leveler, rather than death. No one should be in training to be more competent or talented or to exceed the next person. And school was the best vehicle to propagate this life view. Parents could not be trusted. It would take a lot of retraining of teachers and then a lot of hands-on work with students. That would be expensive but essential to overcome the baleful influence of parents.

Now, her friend Wanda Cranberry having departed, Sybil began to work out loud on a full-scale presentation of her NEP for the media. She stood to do this, pacing to and fro, trying out ideas. "The NEP," she began, "is a real change, and one we shall be proud of. It will create a wholesome educational tradition that fosters and treasures mediocrity." She paused. Perhaps "fostering and treasuring mediocrity" was not the happiest way to put the matter, but she wanted her presentation to be honest, forthright. "Fostering and treasuring mediocrity" would stay in. She continued.

"As a child psychiatrist I know the terrible disappointment a schoolchild feels when it learns that there are other children more gifted in some way. In the NEP leveling schools, gifted children will be spotted and ... well, leveled. Moreover, nothing will be taught that would possibly promote vaulting, elitist ambition. Rather, ambition will be severely discouraged, even penalized." She stopped. A catchy, rhyming slogan had come to her mind:

Slow, slow, slow,
Ambition has to go.

She began to sing it with gusto. She would try it out on Wagner.

Her husband, wearing a white SYBIL LOVES YOU T-shirt, sat in a neighboring parlor, studying the latest issue of *Breastworks*. This magazine described itself as "Dedicated to the Glory of the Feminine Bosom." Sybil entered the room singing, taking in her husband's absorption. In her view, pornography had its place. She had, in fact, subscribed to *Breastworks* for Wagner. Since then he had been better behaved and made fewer unwelcome demands. Her entrance in full cry momentarily transferred his attention.

"Very good, dear. For your leveling-school plan, eh?"

"Yes. I thought of it while working on my speech. I just wish I could come up as easily with an answer to the NEP funding issue. I don't want to make the mistake poor Lint made. He was perfectly forthright about his stamp-funding tax and look where it got him. There can't be a direct tax."

Wagner Watch, anxious to return to the glorious bosoms, agreed without comment.

"The tension," Sybil continued, "is that I want so much to be open and honest. Yet Lint thought taxing business openly and honestly would work. He was far too trusting. I have pretty much concluded we have to be a bit subtler about funding the NEP. Perhaps ..." She then described in some detail an especially onerous form of indirect taxation disguised as a franchise fee. It would be payable by all commercial enterprises employing more than two people. But Wagner's attention had resettled on *Breastworks* before she had concluded. The girl's well-defined nipples projected toward him; her smile was open and honest, like Mayor Lint's business tax.

SYBIL'S NEP SPEECH WAS PRESENTED to the media two days later. The reception by this segment of the electorate was distinctly favorable, and they so reported upon it. This got the attention of Simon Wong, whose family accounting firm had for many generations provided services to small businesses in the City. Wong's ancestors had come from China to lay railroad tracks in California. The family had increased in size and wealth over time, and along the way had founded "Wong's Books and Accounts." He called a meeting of the adult members of the family, most of whom were employed in the family business.

"I confess," he began, "that my thoughts about Sybil Watch have changed since her campaign began. At first I thought she was a harmless nut, which is more than can be said of many of our local politicos. Then, as her ideas became more obvious and she took a lead in the polls, I realized she was extremely dangerous. Now we know all about her principal enormity, the franchise fees to support her New Education Plan. It is essential that she not win the election."

There was a general nodding of heads, heads which, without regard to the prospective franchise fees, held favorable opinions about self-improvement, ambition, competition and talent.

Simon continued. "Our political club can probably ensure that Asians vote against Watch, but there are not enough such voters in the city to defeat her." He paused. "So, I have been thinking about the African-American vote. Blacks will be hardest hit by the NEP. This leveling business will tend to set the status quo in concrete." He turned to his eldest son. "Kevin, James Blake, the black man who is running for mayor, was with you in law school. I think we should sit down with him and exchange views. Here are mine."

THAT EVENING KEVIN WONG MET with James Blake in the latter's law office. Kevin explained what the Wong family thought about the NEP. When he was finished, Blake said, "Sybil Watch will probably win, but I'm not that worried about the NEP thing. It won't hurt because it won't work. You can't level people. As to the franchise fee aspect, how many of my constituents employ more than two people?"

Kevin was disturbed by this response. His voice rose. "Jim, the NEP will hurt blacks the most. They have most to lose from suppressing ambition and a maintenance of the status quo. And with the NEP, that's going to happen. As to the franchise fees, you can't just look at issues from a black-impact viewpoint."

"Why not? I'm black, and my principal issues and constituency are the same color."

"Yes, and you're way behind in the polls because of that approach. You can't get elected as a one race candidate."

"So far, Kevin, no other races have signed up."

"Well, my father thinks the Asian vote would go to you if you attack the NEP. That's why I'm here."

"Kevin, the media are clearly backing the NEP. And the leveling bit. It's got a sugary, populist taste to it. It sounds like eliminating discrimination. I could lose votes in my own backyard."

"I know it sounds that way, but it's a snare and a delusion. If you take the lead and explain what the NEP really means, you won't lose black votes. And my father thinks it will turn the media around too."

"What does the NEP really mean?"

"I want my father to explain that to you."

"Can he actually deliver the Asian vote?"

"I never bet against him."

"Getting the Asian vote, now that would be wild; I might even win."

"Father says you will win."

JAMES BLAKE MET WITH SIMON WONG the next day and thereafter called a press conference. He explained what the NEP really meant. Watch's New Education Plan was part of a white elitist plot to suppress bright minority children. "The idea is, we never get out of the status we're in. They retrain the teachers to keep everybody down. A talented minority kid raises his head, and—

whack — he gets leveled. Meanwhile, the white kids are getting a real education at home on their personal computers and going to private schools. It's up to you guys who control the news to get that message out."

This was the kind of story the media loved: a shocking exposure of one candidate by another. The accusation instantly inflamed the conscience of *The Cockerel*. Wanda Cranberry read the next day's front page with delight: "Watch School Plan Exposed As White Elitist." It was rather her own view of the matter. Besides, Sybil would be such a bore if she became mayor.

A NEW POLL TAKEN FOUR DAYS AFTER Blake's attack on the Watch education plan showed a remarkable shift of votes. A large block of previously "undecided" had joined the Blake camp. Watch had lost votes, and Homer was recovering ground. Blake now had the lead, followed closely by Homer and Watch. Casper Bell had fallen well behind.

His campaign staff felt poorly about it. Mistakes had been made. The proposal to introduce wolves in city parks to help control the homeless population camping there had not been well received. In this case, Bell's basically fascist instincts had betrayed him. The same flaw had led him to accept the support of a local militia group, The Bay Area Aryan Army (BAAA). They had given him money and now behaved as if they owned him. This embrace had cost Bell a lot of votes, and it appeared impossible to break it.

His chief of staff, Waldo Higgins, stared gloomily through the glass-fronted campaign headquarters at the two militiamen stationed at the door. They wore swords, carried long staves, and were dressed to resemble Robin Hood's merry men. They also carried pamphlets promoting the political and social positions of the BAAA. They pressed these on passersby and visitors to the Bell headquarters. Waldo had attempted to have them removed by the police, but the police had declined to take action on the ground that it could lead to the use of force. They cited the Lint Law Enforcement Control Act. Higgins then turned to some neighborhood ruffians, but they had been overmatched by the better-disciplined and equipped merry men. It would take something like the Mafia to get rid of the pests, and Bell had no connection to that kind of aid.

In an effort to rise out of his despondent mood, Waldo turned to the young female campaign worker at the desk behind him, Lydia Grimes. She seemed never to despair. "Lydia, what was that you said earlier about wheelchairs?"

"Not just wheelchairs. Parades of the handicapped. Of course, we'd need plenty of wheelchairs. I think this would get attention. At least, it would create serious traffic problems, and that always gets attention."

"But what would they do?"

"Well, Waldo, I've been thinking. You can always get votes bashing the oil industry. So we have the paraders carry placards saying, like maybe, 'Casper Bell Has Big Oil Scared' or 'Oil Polluters Tremble When Bell Rings,' that sort of thing."

"Yeah, but I don't get the connection to having all these people in wheelchairs carrying on about oil."

"It's easy, Waldo. Voters are sympathetic to the handicapped and are ready to believe the worst about oil companies. You don't need to explain the connection. You just do it that way, and, presto, there's a connection."

"I can see why you never lose heart, Lydia. How do we get all these handicapped to do this?"

"We go to HARP."

"HARP?"

"Handicapped Activists Resource Pool. HARP provides everything: lots of wheelchairs and crutches and angry people with placards, shouting."

"Which oil company do we attack?"

"It doesn't matter. You just go after the oil industry. It's like one big company to the public."

"OK, set it up. We got to do something. I'll tell Casper he'll be coming on big for the disabled and that he's against oil companies. Whoops! I just remembered, we've got some contributions from oil companies."

"No problem. They tried to bribe us to stay off their tails. They failed."

"Grimes, you're going to go far in this business."

18. NEW YORK, NEW YORK GETS INVOLVED

WHILE LYDIA GRIMES WAS PLANNING her "Handicapped Against Big Oil" spectacular, across the continent in Manhattan, Philo Spass, age sixteen, was on his way home from summer school. He began to twitch as he approached the entrance to the Computers Galore store near Columbus Circle. Philo was already on probation, following conviction as a juvenile offender, for breaking into computerized files of the United States government. But inside the store, he knew, would be the underground publication he craved, *Access*. This quarterly provided hackers data from computer technologists and insider informants. Preeminently, it listed assumptions as to access codes for confidential, electronic files. The FBI, CIA and the Republican Party had each sought to suppress the magazine, but it continued to thrive. Philo's heart beat faster. Other boys brought home dirty books, but Philo only wanted *Access*.

For two weeks he had resisted the temptation; today he could not. He entered the store and moments later emerged with the latest issue lodged in his knapsack. He hurried home, sat down before his computer and opened the treasured magazine. He leafed through it and then returned to the page headed "International Organizations." His eye traveled down the page and stopped at the line, "United Nations Tribal Territories." This was the organization under whose auspices the anthropological study of Nova Cannes tribes was proceeding. Indented under the heading were a number of lines. Philo's gaze settled on one reading, "Development Projects." That sounded interesting.

A user name and two passwords were listed. If the informant was correct, Philo could enter the UNTT Development Projects files using these three entry codes. He knew that even if he got into the system he ran the risk of an undisclosed system alarm identifying him. He was willing to take it. Such risks were as exciting as exploring the files themselves.

He put in the codes. A message box came up on his monitor: "Your access to these files is being reviewed by their security system. Will you wait?" Philo clicked the OK button and waited. In a moment a new box appeared: "Thank you for waiting. Access is cleared." He was then offered a menu for specific file selection. Philo clicked on the menu item "File last reviewed," and in a moment the monitor displayed an index to a file on Norwalk Island. Where was that? He moved the cursor to the location line and clicked: In the Pacific, east of Australia. Philo searched neighboring entry lines, picking up more data on the island. It was fairly large, rich in timber suitable for construction, and had excellent harbors. The inhabitants were primarily Melanesian and Polynesian. The economy was in the doldrums, and the island was in the development files for that reason. An ecologist with the UNTT had approved, and the UNTT budget office had seconded, a plan to harvest timber from the island's forests and return the profits to the inhabitants in various forms of economic development.

Philo didn't like the sound of that. He had grown to young manhood in an era suspicious of any form of logging. The trees will just be cut to provide T-shirt shops and boardwalks, he reasoned. But he knew that simply deleting the file would not kill the project. The originators would just start over with the budgeted money. The thing was to consume the funds budgeted by having the project proceed, but at some other site where it was bound to fail. He went back to the file menu and, moving forward alphabetically, immediately hit "Nova Cannes."

He studied the description. An island near New Guinea which had been reviewed for possible development and rejected. There were no harbors; giant hardwood trees predominated, the timber unsuitable for construction or other uses; no other developable resources; an anthropological study of indigenous tribes was underway. It was just what he was looking for. When he was through, the entry indicating that development had been rejected had been deleted, and the description of the project for Norwalk Island had been lifted and moved down into the folder for Nova Cannes. He moved the Nova Cannes material to the Norwalk Island file, leaving the description of the island locations as they were. Now came the tricky part: he had to direct the proper UNTT official to take action pursuant to the ecological and budget approvals. But Philo was equal to the task.

Francis Bowles, Deputy Director for Development, was seated at his desk at the UNTT headquarters on the other side of Manhattan, his feet up, looking out across the East River at the jumbled buildings and billboards of Queens County. His printer began to operate, and several pages came through. The transmission was from the Plans Execution Office and marked "Urgent." The file referenced was "Nova Cannes". Attached was a copy of the file, as recomposed by Philo Spass, and a development directive authored by Spass. It read, "Funds budgeted six months previous for logging and economic development this tribal territory. Urgent project be commenced or re-budgeting process may result in loss of funding."

That got Bowles's attention. The failure to spend budgeted funds was anathema. The directive continued, "Proceed to recruit team for survey Nova Cannes. Evaluation to be completed ASAP. Project execution to commence earliest possible thereafter."

Francis picked up his phone, activated a secure line, and called his brother-in-law, Bernie Cronin, an underemployed lawyer with offices in Jamaica, Queens County. "Bernie," Francis began, "how quickly could you form a lumber company and put together a small team to go to an island near New Guinea?" Francis described the kind of team needed.

"Gimme three days. UNTT Development is footing the bill?"

"Yes, and there's a nice line item for administrative costs, about $150,000 a month. It was my idea to keep as much of that as possible within the family."

"I understand," said Bernie.

Francis then explained the details of the Nova Cannes file.

"Hey," said Bernie, "I think I'll go there myself. Your sister wouldn't mind."

"A separate vacation," inquired Francis?

"Well, we need a break now and then."

"Of course. Head the team. A lawyer can always head anything since there are always legal problems."

"Listen, Francis. A far-off place like that, we might need some muscle, too. Can I take Jumbo Harris?"

"Your cousin? I thought he was still in jail."

"No. He's out."

"That's fine, Bernie. Jumbo should do well in the wild, so to speak."

"The tree expert, the doctor and the photographer, Francis. I'll just have to nose around."

"Right." Francis hung up and sat back contented. It was a happy solution to an urgent problem. The money would be safely spent by and on the right people, and Nova Cannes would get that shot in the arm its economy needed.

BERNIE CRONIN WAS HAPPY TOO. He would be doing good and making a fast buck at it — a combination not characteristic of his practice. It would be nice too to get away from Shirley for a while: her golfing buddies, her videos of professional football games. He got out a world atlas and found Nova Cannes. It was a long way off. Then he called Jumbo Harris.

The call was answered by a woman. "He's not here now. He's at the pet shop."

Bernie called the Corona Pet House, and Jumbo answered. Bernie explained. "I figure, with the budget we got, it'll shake out to about $20,000 a month to key members of the team. Are you able to leave the U.S.?"

"Yeah. I'm off probation. Only thing is, I like this job. The pets are nice, and there's a buck in it, too."

"How so?"

"I can't say on the phone. You got to be careful."

"And that's where you come in?"

"Yeah, sort of. Look, Bernie, I'll take a leave of absence if you can get me $20,000 up front."

"Done."

BERNIE SET ABOUT COMPLETING his team the next morning. He retained a tree expert for $2500 a month. This was Simon Pularski, a botanist with some experience in logging. For lack of botanical employment, he had been working as a bowling instructor, and was happy to return to plants. Next, for $3000 a month, Bernie hired a physician who was also a competent photographer. In this way he killed two salaries with one bird. This individual was Ferdon Clapp, a general practitioner from Teaneck, New Jersey.

It would be a paid vacation to an interesting Pacific island, Bernie advised. But Clapp was primarily enthused by the fact that his services would be paid for without the intervention of insurance carriers or HMOs. "Not to worry," Bernie assured him. "I'll do all the paper work on this trip."

Bernie was pleased with his efforts. He drove to the Corona Pet House to give Jumbo the news. He also brought up Jumbo's remark about there being a buck in the pet business.

"It's the birds, Bernie, exotic birds. They're illegal to bring into the country, but people love to have them."

"You mean, like colored parrots."

"Yeah. Other species, too. But crazy colors. It's a big thing in New York."

LATER, BERNIE REPORTED TO HIS BROTHER-IN-LAW. "We're going to call it 'The Queen's Own Lumber Company.'"

"Sounds Victorian."

"Yeah. I wanted something high-toned for a name, but with 'Queen's' in it."

"I'm faxing you a list of equipment you'll need," said Francis, looking at a map of the subject area. "Your route is via Sydney and Port Moresby. By the way, we have a man in Port Moresby to brief you on Nova Cannes. His name is Farrington, an Australian. Frankly, I'm a bit concerned about him. He was advised about the project and responded that there must be some mistake. No place to dock a boat at Nova Cannes, and some other peculiar objections, like the trees being too hard to cut."

"Probably an environmentalist," said Bernie confidently.

"Yes, exactly."

"Jumbo will keep him in line."

PART III

TRIAL AND ERROR

19. PETER ARRIVES AND CASPER BELL DEPARTS

PENNY BEGAN TO NOTICE the traffic buildup and the balloons while still half a mile from the airport terminals. The balloons were of all colors, basketball-sized, some floating free, some tethered to ground structures. As she got nearer she heard sirens and saw stopped cars. The jam soon forced her to a halt. She locked her car and began walking toward the terminals. Then she saw the first wheelchair, a red balloon bobbing above it. The occupant, a young woman, was slowly propelling the vehicle through the crowd of cars and people while waving a placard that read, "Airlines Are the Running Dogs of Big Oil. Halt Energy Consumption. Vote for Casper Bell."

Just beyond, two men on crutches, standing side by side, blocked Penny's way. Across their backs hung a cloth banner that said: "Oil Company Criminals Fear Bell's Toll." Penny pushed past the pair, drawing their curses. The whole road ahead of her was clogged with people in wheelchairs and on crutches. They appeared to be angry at something. Some supported themselves on one crutch while brandishing the other, weapon-like.

Police were distributing bottled water and health food to the demonstrators. As Penny watched, one protestor smashed a policeman over the head with his crutch, knocking him to the ground. The latter rose, smiling, and offered his assailant a healthy snack. A man in a wheelchair thrust a handbill at Penny, and she took it. "A Vote for Bell Is a Vote for the Handicapped and Against Big Oil," it read.

Penny struggled toward the international terminal, acquiring two balloons en route. Finally she made it to the doors of the baggage claim area — the place appointed for meeting Peter — and pushed inside. An airline security guard spotted the balloons and made for her. "Demonstrators outside only," he shouted, raising his baton.

"I'm not a demonstrator," Penny shouted back.

"You got balloons," he countered.

Penny released the balloons. "Spoilsport," she declared, solemnly watching the freed globes rise to the high ceiling. A man who had been seated on some baggage leapt up and ran toward her. It was Peter. They embraced. The guard, disarmed by this proof of the lawfulness of her embassy to the baggage area, retreated. "Oh, Peter, I'm so glad to see you; everything's crazy here. I had two balloons to welcome you, but the guard — "

"I saw. How are you?"

"I'm fine, but you're so pale."

"I'll explain why on the way home."

"My car's parked out on the road. There's some sort of strange protest going on." But as they emerged with Peter's bags, it was apparent that the energy of the demonstration was mostly spent. A policeman handed them mineral water and health snacks. When they got to her car the way was clear enough to return to the freeway. On the way home, Peter explained that he was pale because the tree cover on Nova Cannes blocked the sun, and Penny explained about her case.

AT PENNY'S HOUSE, the media stopped them and required Peter to identify himself. He was a new face. "You been in the stir, Mr. Walker? You got kind of a jailhouse pallor," one inquired cheerfully.

"No," said Peter, without further explanation.

Penny rounded on the interrogator as if to strike him and he backed away. She pulled Peter through the breech and they escaped into the house. "It's like that all the time, the loathsome toads," she gasped, setting down the suitcase she had been carrying. "Let's have a drink. Then we'll go see April. How old was she when you saw her last?"

"Fourteen, I think. A tall girl. Quite thin."

"She's taller now and not so thin. She lifts weights. Does almost nothing else, really." Penny sized up her brother's heft. "She could probably lift you over her head. Very strong. You like vodka, don't you?"

"Yes." He thought of Ellen, the vodkas in his tent and their interrupted sundown activity.

Penny handed him his drink, and, as if reading his mind, asked, "The girl with you there, has she worked out?"

"Ellen Ross. Yes. She's very good. I was just thinking of her. She likes vodka too." He paused. "Actually, she has to finish some work there, but then she's coming to San Francisco."

Penny went right to the point. "Is this romance?"

"I think so. It's all very sudden."

"It usually is, Peter. How exciting. I'm glad she's coming here." Peter blushed.

She patted his red cheek. "I won't ask any more questions. Bring your glass and greet April."

April was in her fitness room, curling a 110-pound barbell. Peter was unprepared for the change in the girl, despite what Penny had said. She was quite good-looking, but she was almost as tall as he and much more muscular. "You two should remember each other," said Penny. April put down her barbell and extended her hand. Peter shook it and was relieved to find her grip surprisingly gentle.

"You've grown a lot since I saw you last." It was the best he could do, uncertain whether to compliment her astonishing physique.

With April all judgments were instantaneous. It was a critical moment. "Yes, I have," April said, smiling broadly. "I'm glad you're going to be visiting us." He was a handsome man, she thought, but had very white skin. "I don't remember you looking so pale."

"We don't see much sun on Nova Cannes. I'm perfectly all right, though."

"Yes, you look all right, handsomer than I remember."

Penny intervened. "You were only fourteen the last time you saw Peter. Your judgment is better now. By the way, are you going to be here for dinner?"

"Will Peter be?"

"Of course."

"Me too," said April.

Penny was pleased. April's instant judgment had gone in Peter's favor. It would make the visit a lot nicer, she thought. On her part, April was also thinking about how to make the visit a lot nicer. After all, she was adopted; he was not really her uncle, and he was so good-looking.

THE AIRPORT EVENT EFFECTIVELY ENDED Casper Bell's run for the mayor's office. The handicapped demonstration had been gleefully reported by *The Cockerel* and other media, but there had been too much freelance bashing of police and other bystanders. One TV station had taped a wheelchair occupant leaving his seat without apparent handicap and whacking a policeman with a mineral water bottle. It threw doubt on the credibility of the entire assemblage. HARP's response had been ambiguous at best: there were always a lot of volunteers for HARP functions, their spokesman said, and insufficient time to make sure they were really handicapped. Volunteers were sometimes overly enthusiastic.

Against his consultant Waldo Higgins's advice, Bell called a press conference denouncing the airport demonstration. He deplored the sudden fervor with which the protestors had battered the police and public. Bell was at heart opposed to spontaneous exuberance of any sort. The fact that the parade had gotten out of hand confirmed his suspicions about unregulated enthusiasm. This stance, at the end of the day, seemed to leave him on the side of police and oil companies, a perceived alliance reflected in the next poll of voters. He then withdrew from the race, without, however, endorsing any other candidate.

Waldo Higgins found himself unemployed, but his ever upbeat assistant, Lydia Grimes, offered her services to Sybil Watch and was retained. She already had some ideas for strengthening Sybil's campaign and went right to work.

JUDGE FLEX HEARD SOME OF THE PRETRIAL MOTIONS in *People v. Hill* the next day. Sybil took this occasion to put into effect one of Lydia's proposals, which was to share Mayor Homer's embrace of the Hill prosecution. As the media and other spectators left the courtroom, they met Wagner Watch, who was passing out handbills. These announced that if elected, Sybil would rename Market Street, the major east-west thoroughfare in the city, "Smoking Mother Way." This was to be the capstone of Sybil's plan to rename city streets after street people. "The new name," the handbill stated, "will give recognition to downtrodden heroes everywhere who have sacrificed their lives in the struggle with privileged oppressors and the big oil companies." The reference to oil companies had struck Sybil as perhaps excessive, but Lydia had insisted.

20. PREPARATIONS FOR TRIAL

BARTON PLAYCHEK AND HAMILTON SAYER returned to Playchek's office following the hearing in Judge Flex's courtroom. They had lost motions to require the prosecution to disclose its intended witnesses and to exclude the results of the search of Penny's house from admission into evidence at the trial. "Flex," said Playchek, settling in behind his desk, "is a state-of-the-art, family-sized schmuck. That's the first time I've ever had a motion to require disclosure of prosecution witnesses denied."

"I wondered about that," said Sayer, "and his reasoning. The bit about preserving the traditional surprises of litigation. He seemed to be saying the trial will be more fun if the defense doesn't know who the DA's going to call."

"That's what he was saying, all right. And with him thinking like that we're going to have live TV, too."

"That would follow."

"It's the same thing, Hamilton, on the motion to suppress the search results. The trial will be livelier, more exciting, if the DA can put weird portraits, black-market caviar and virtual toma-hawks in the record. Anyway, we need to try to figure out whom they're going to call. We know they'll call that street girl, Wendy Papp, who raised hell at the scene, and the arresting officers."

"Yes, and they'll have to call the investigator who searched the Hill house."

Playchek sighed. "The real problem is not knowing if they've got some eyeball witness other than the street girl. We can figure the rest out."

"Barton, one of my associates had an idea. She thinks we should advertise for an eyeball witness, offer a reward."

"Let's try it. How about something like this?" Playchek began to write. After a moment he read his "Witness Wanted" adver-tisement to Sayer:

Early last month, a man was killed by a bullet on the San Francisco *library steps. This death is the basis of the current prosecution of Ms. Penny Hill. If you witnessed any aspect of this event, please contact the undersigned attorneys for Ms. Hill. We are offering a $1000 reward to any actual witness to the event who is available to testify.*

"That's excellent, Barton. Of course, the DA's people will probably spot it."

"Sure, but under Flex's ruling the DA can't get our witness list either. Have your associate get the ad run in the newspapers. Now, besides people at the scene, who else will they call?"

"Well, with our diminished capacity plea they'll have a psychiatrist, I suppose."

"Yeah. That'll be Max Untergang. The DA always uses him."

"Is he a good witness?"

"It's like this: he's a psychiatrist; they want everyone to love them. He'll agree with Tremorgan Davies, then he'll agree with me."

"What will he say?"

"Well, on direct he'll say her capacity hasn't been diminished, and on cross he'll say maybe it could be."

"Will our expert do the same thing?"

"I never use psychiatrists. I use mental health counselors. They're harder to turn around; they don't care if the other lawyer loves them."

"Who have you in mind?"

"I've used two different experts in the last couple of years. Greta Sweetbacken is technically good, but she often wanders off onto some other topic that has nothing to do with the question. Plus, her bridgework isn't a good fit; sometimes it clacks. Still, I kind of like her for this case. The other is General Sandschloss. He ran a field hospital during the Gulf War. I used him in my last case. Very persuasive, but he likes the girls. I'm worried with our client he might get carried away and lose focus."

"Is there no one available who isn't flawed in some way?"

"Not in the mental health field."

"I suppose General Sandschloss would be more impressive."

"Not if he's drooling over Penny. And you can't tell what he'll do off first acquaintance. In other words, we can't run him by Penny and see what happens. He'd been around my legal assistant, Muriel Fein, for weeks, and no problem. Then, bang, he falls in love with her, and I couldn't get his attention on anything else. Finally she laid him, and that seemed to break the spell, but we can't count on that with Penny."

"Certainly not. It had better be Greta and her bridgework."

"Yeah, I'll call her. We need a weapons expert, too. Modern revolvers won't discharge from being dropped. That old family one Penny's father left her is single action, and a fall can make it fire. We need someone to say that."

"Then they'll have a weapons expert too?"

"Sort of. Not to contradict ours, but someone to say you don't carry concealed weapons unless you mean to shoot them. There's a woman from a group called 'Disarm the U.S. Military' who does that. Tremorgan used her in a homicide case last year. I forget her name."

"You mean the court let her testify that carrying a concealed gun means you shot it?"

"It was in Judge Glowmore's court. She thinks a lot like Flex. They got a conviction, too. It's up on appeal. Say, I just remembered. We got a letter from some guy with Strident Students, Inc. who had a run-in with Smoking Mother the morning of the shooting. He claims Smoking Mother threatened him. Here it is. Martin Blender. Lives here in the city. He writes, 'When I refused to accept him as a demonstrator, he offered violence.' Sounds good. Muriel's going to interview him."

"She didn't leave you for General Sandschloss?"

"No. As an item, they faded."

"Who else do you think the DA will call?"

"It's Tremorgan's practice to interview people in the defendant's neighborhood. You can always find somebody who'll dump on his neighbor. I've got to ask Penny about who might fit the bill. Also, Smoking Mother has a mother living in St. Paul. The DA will probably bring her out to cry in court. I can't think of anybody else."

"I can't, either. Who else do we call?"

"Well, there's Reginald from Native-American Noise. He's going to torpedo the whole Indian issue. We've been to the cooler, and Reginald swears the deceased is a paleface. He made a joke about dead palefaces being the only good ones. I told him not to do that in court. By the way, he keeps pushing me to let them wear their Indian clothes. Flex would love it."

"Do you think it would enhance his strength as a witness?"

"He thinks so. I'm concerned that having what looks like a war party in court may not be the image we want. What do you think?"

"Well, it's carnival to be sure, but the whole trial sounds that way. I guess if he feels more comfortable in native attire it will help his testimony."

"OK, we'll go along. Now, what about Penny's brother — have you met him?"

"No, I didn't know she had one; I thought there was just her daughter."

"He's here. He came back from New Guinea or someplace to see her through the trial, an anthropologist. He's a possibility. I could go into her character and cover the old family pistol issue with him."

"The old family pistol issue?"

"Yeah, we want to emphasize she didn't run out and buy a weapon a week before the shooting. I want the gun to sound like a faithful family dog. But we'll wait on brother Peter till we meet him. How about the daughter?"

"I've only met her once, Barton. Striking girl. What would she testify to?"

"Penny's state of mind. She could help on diminished capacity. Children will usually agree their parents are dotty."

"To be sure."

"Hamilton, one guy we might want to call is Brutus Fulmen."

"The Sex Court lawyer?"

"You don't pretend you're a streetwalker unless you've got a screw loose."

"Penny's not going to like that."

"I know, but I have to do what's right. And if that portrait gets into evidence, we'll have to call the painter, too. The aggressive pose and the flimsy blouse were all his idea. He's got to testify that she's not into turning suitors on and then horsewhipping them."

"You know, Barton, as I listen to this, it's all so ridiculous. These witnesses we're discussing, most of them have no testimony at all relevant to the shooting. It's crazy."

"Hamilton, crazy is normal in this business; it's a fantasy world. In most trials it's simply our fantasy versus theirs."

"And the one who wins is the one with the more appealing fantasy?"

"Well, the evidence might play a role."

"But it's minor?"

"Generally speaking, yes."

THE SAME DAY, LYDIA GRIMES COMPOSED and studied with satisfaction a new Sybil Watch campaign press release. It seemed to her that it set just the right tone. The caption read, "Massive Oil Company Opposition to New Education Plan." The text continued, "In a desperate effort to prevent the election of Sybil Watch, and thereby the adoption of her New Education Plan, the oil cartel, in a last-minute frenzy, is pouring petrodollars into the campaigns of her rivals."

"We expected this," Dr. Watch emphasized in a moving restatement of principles that captured the attention of all present at her morning press conference. "The oil companies will do anything to block my election and improvements in education, so as to advance their secret efforts to destroy the heritage of the common man." Lydia decided there was no need to run the text past Sybil, even though there had been no morning press conference, and Lydia's only knowledge of oil company contributions to candidates had been those to Casper Bell. Sybil had been a bit testy lately about the oil company issue. It was just as well to spare her the details.

THE NEXT DAY Tremorgan Davies and Sonia Taft engaged in their own review of potential trial witnesses. Davies was all smiles. "I signed up the general this morning."

"Sandschloss?"

"The one and only. In this trial we'll have a real counter to Playchek's usual diminished-capacity hokum. I showed the general the file and the photos of Penny Hill, and he really came on strong. Said there was no way her capacity was diminished. Seemed to be quite taken with her appearance, but that won't hurt. Keep him interested in the case."

"I suppose so. He can be very effective. Do I scratch Dr. Untergang?"

"No. With Flex's ruling we don't have to disclose our people to Playchek, but I want to serve him with a request to make Penny available for examination by Untergang. He'll refuse, but that way, he'll think we're putting our money on Max. Besides we might want to call him. How are you coming with the street girl?"

"Wendy Papp. She's still at the New Reality Shelter and as gung-ho as ever. I think she really wants to get Penny Hill ."

"A good girl, Sonia. Fine attitude. She's getting expenses, I assume."

"Yeah. I don't want to take a chance she leaves town, so she's on the dole."

"Does she drink?"

"A bit. She smokes a lot. Probably dope."

"You know, Sonia, we better put her in a hotel the night before she testifies and get her some new clothes."

"I'll take care of it. We'll put her in the same hotel as the victim's mother."

"Perfect. The mother should exert a good influence, keep the girl sober for her testimony."

"Yes, that was my thought too. You know, Tremorgan, none of the other persons at the crime scene who gave statements are any help. No one saw Hill holding the pistol. They all heard the shot, but they'll deny seeing her with the weapon. I'm concerned Playchek will get them to guess. You know, à la, 'As far as you could tell, the gun went off when it hit the ground?' That sort of thing."

"Yes, and they might even speculate that Smoking Mother could have been grabbing her purse. Suppose we just go with Wendy Papp as the death-scene witness?"

"That's got my vote, Tremorgan."

"Of course, Playchek's got the police report. He might call the people who gave statements."

"True, but if they're his witnesses and start speculating, we should be able to jackass their testimony with objections."

"Let's go with the lovely Ms. Papp, Sonia."

"Good, but I think we should definitely call the woman cop who arrested Hill."

"The one who doesn't speak English?"

"She speaks enough to accuse the defendant, and it'll be hard to cross-examine her. She's like Papp: she's decided Hill's guilty and wants to say so. She tried to get her to confess."

"I read that. Sounded a bit heavy-handed according to her colleague, the deaf mute."

"Probably. Her file says that as a kid she was in training to join the Red Guards. Then her father got in trouble with the authorities, and they had to leave China. Went to Taiwan. She's only been in the U.S. a couple of years."

"Still a bit steered by the Great Helmsman?"

"Definitely. Makes for a dedicated cop. Anyway, she'll testify Penny was about to confess when she tried to escape and destroy the evidence."

"What evidence?"

"Her billfold. It was in the purse. Actually, she just wanted her lawyer's phone number."

"Sometimes, Sonia, I get a bit weary of producing these epics."

"Somebody has to, Tremorgan, and Lord knows, the defendant's probably guilty of something."

"Yes, that stands to reason. In the largest sense, aren't we all guilty?"

"And the gun was loaded and concealed."

"I take great comfort in that, Sonia."

"There's other evidence of her general guilt, Tremorgan. Look what the search warrant produced."

"I've been looking at that, particularly at that painting of her, Sonia. She really is an attractive woman and, you know, after awhile the portrait has a strange appeal."

"The defense will be that it was all the artist's feelings. What appealed to him."

"Yes. Playchek said that at the hearing. I suspect him of telling the truth. She doesn't look to me like she does whips and chains."

"Are you saying don't offer it?"

"No, no, Sonia. It's up to the jury to decide its relevance."

"I'm glad to hear that. I was beginning to think you might have looked at that portrait too long. I think we should ring the changes on the Russian caviar too. That's got a real 'wealthy people acting above the law' tone to it."

"Yes, that's a winner. Will we have to call the daughter to get it in?"

"With Flex we might get away with just having the officer who did the search say what the daughter said."

"True. Flex doesn't seem much averse to hearsay."

"Actually, he seems to prefer it. But I'll put the daughter un-der subpoena. Arnold says she's a world-class weightlifter."

"Interesting. Maybe we could raise an issue about power trips running in the family."

"That's more like you, Tremorgan. Stop looking at that painting."

"OK, but you know the Indian books and the hatchets seem pretty far-fetched. In fact, this whole Indian thing bothers me. The black officer at the morgue says Smoking Mother's a honky if he ever saw one."

"Tremorgan, haven't you read Tula Fogg's report on the victim's mother? He may look white, but he's not, or, at least, he's part Native-American. That's good enough."

"But where does it really get us, Sonia?"

"Look, Tremorgan, everybody feels guilty about the massacre of the Indians and isolating them on marginal lands. Now Penny Hill comes along and shoots one who's just panhandling her. You got to keep focus on our story. Now that should make the jury want to punish her. It's a great jury theme."

"You're right, Sonia. I just need a little bolstering from time to time on this case."

"You've got to stop looking at that painting. You're getting attached to her."

"You think that's it?"

"It must be. This case has a lot to it, Tremorgan. And we got a live one in the neighborhood, too. Penny tried to run over a neighbor's child."

"I thought Tula said there was nothing to that."

"Tula dropped the ball on that interview. She took a dislike to the neighbor. I talked to him myself. He's solid."

"Good. Have you contacted the weapons expert at Disarm the U.S. Military? I can never remember that woman's name."

"Neither can I. I wrote it down somewhere — here it is. It's Mary Smith. Yes. She'll testify to the same point she did in the case we had in Libby Glowmore's court. By carrying the concealed weapon, Hill meant to use it and probably shot it."

"That's powerful testimony."

"There you go, Tremorgan. Now remember no more looking at the painting."

THE FINAL PRETRIAL PROCEEDINGS BEFORE Judge Flex included argument on the issue of whether the trial would be televised live. The prosecution and the media presented the case in favor of live TV and were opposed by the defense. Judge Flex appeared to be devoting close attention to the arguments. Finally, having heard each side fully, he announced he was prepared to rule.

He began with a careful reanalysis of the points that had been made, taking them up one by one, lucidly, fairly, putting each point in perspective. His analysis displayed a complete grasp of the tensions, the opposing considerations, and the constitutional and other repercussions of live TV. None of his commentary revealed which way he was disposed to rule. Finally, he paused, and after a drink of water, announced his decision.

"Assuming I receive certain assurances from the media professionals themselves, which need not be a matter of record, I believe live TV of this trial would be particularly appropriate. It boils down to this: the merits of the issue are pretty much in balance, but, from a personal point of view, in thirteen years on the bench I've had a lot of cases and paid a lot of dues, and frankly I don't feel I've received the attention I deserve. So we're going to have live TV. That'll be the order."

AT HER HOME, APRIL WAS PREPARING for a different kind of trial. She set her weight aside and toweled off her perspiration, taking a quick look at herself in the full-length mirror. In the days since Peter's arrival, she had progressed from a state of initial awareness that he was sexually attractive, through a brief, feeble attempt to deny herself a move, to a much more satisfying decision to hit on him. He was, after all, not really her uncle. There would be consequences, but there were always consequences to sex, and April was not, in any event, one to worry much about consequences. Her experience had been that the adverse consequences of improper behavior were generally lighter than advertised.

Mother would, of course, flip when she found out, but that would be half the fun of seducing Peter. She tossed the towel and left the fitness room. Her mother was out, and at last check, Peter had been reading in the living room. He was still there. A good sign. "Hi, Peter, what are you up to?"

"Oh, your mother went to the lawyers, and I'm just getting in a little reading about the art collections in San Francisco."

April sat down opposite him, slouching in an armchair, in gym shorts and tennis shoes, long legs thrust before her. With one hand she toyed with her pony tail. The other lay palm up near the rim of her shorts. She smiled. "I was reading something much more interesting about San Francisco in the paper this morning, about the local sex industry."

The best Peter could manage was a weakly voiced, "The what?"

"Sex industry. They call it an industry. I think it's wonderful that they have an industry for sex. It makes it like mining or automobiles, something to list on the stock exchange. The story wasn't about regular prostitutes. It's about the girly shows and clubs. There are hundreds of girls who are dancers in San Francisco. They call themselves dancers no matter what they do. It says most of them are moonlighting students or housewives. Small salaries, but they get huge tips for exciting the clientele, taking most of their clothes off and getting near the customers, things like that."

Peter was afraid to ask why she was telling him all this, but out of a protective instinct to kill a subject that seemed, at best, inappropriate for discussion with April, he offered, "I guess there's some of that in all the big cities."

April was ready. "Not like here. San Francisco pioneered the sex industry and is still the acknowledged leader in live sex performances." April delivered this in a matter-of-fact manner suggesting that her knowledge of the subject was not limited to the article, was perhaps encyclopedic.

Peter tried another tack. "Well, I'd rather read about art collections than about live sex performances."

But April's retort was swift, sure. "How do you know? You didn't read the article. It's really fascinating, some of the stuff. Have you heard of lap dancing?"

"No." Peter winced, recognizing that April was ratcheting up the discussion. His pale face had visibly reddened.

"It's apparently very popular and quite safe, too. The girls wear scanty clothing, lingerie usually, but sometimes shorts, sort of like mine, and they mostly show their breasts." She paused.

Peter was now distinctly uncomfortable. "Shorts sort of like mine," his mind repeated. Desperately, he avoided focusing on her shorts.

April giggled, noting that his pallid face was reddening, sensing her lecture was getting through to the pupil. "Yes, and then, well, they sort of get on the guy's lap and wiggle." This last was purely April's invention, an improvement on lap-dancing industry practice meant to serve her present purposes. Was she turning him on? He certainly looked uneasy, but what else was not clear. It was time to find out.

Before he could react, she was on his lap. "Please, Peter, I just want to try it for a minute to see what it's like." Her muscular arms surrounded his neck.

Peter struggled ineffectively. "April get up! Please! What if your mother saw this?"

Instead of rising, April began to wiggle. "Oh, Peter, just for a bit. So we can see how it feels." Peter made a determined effort to dislodge the powerful girl but was unsuccessful. He tried to rise. She forced him back. "Peter, stop being such a bore. It's just for a minute so we can see what it's like."

"I don't want to see what it's like."

"Don't you like me?"

"I don't like ... like ... lap dancing."

"How can you tell? You're not giving it a fair shake. Relax a minute, silly. We need your cooperation to really see how it feels."

Peter did not relax. April stepped up the wiggling, and to his dismay he realized he was beginning to see how it felt, and that that might soon become apparent to April. He would feel absurd to have to actually try to throw her off like a mugger, and his lesser efforts to part with her had been useless. In fact, she seemed to have gotten a firmer perch, and her arms held his head tightly against her body. "April, please stop," he groaned. "I hate you doing this."

But April, now quite aware of the results of her wiggling, murmured, "Ah, I think now you see how it feels, and so do I." With that, she kissed his cheek and sprang up. "That was fun, dear. We'll have to do it again," she declared gaily, and adding, "I have to run now," ran off.

21. Dipper's Last Bottle

MEANWHILE, ACROSS THE WATER on Nova Cannes, Dipper Edwards's sundown attempt to have a nice heart-to-heart with Ellen had been a failure. He had removed his pistol and turned off the boom box for the event, but she was impervious to his charms. "Look, Mr. Edwards, I'm not going to dance, as you put it. I'm not even going to sit and drink with you. You're already sloshed." Ellen went to her tent, drawing the netting to after her.

When his beer bottle was empty, Dipper rose from his camp-stool, perplexed and displeased, and went to the river for another beer. He had hit on the idea of stashing bottles in the river to cool once he saw the natives truly took no interest in them. What made the bird so hoity-toity? He'd had better than her often enough. The thought consoled him. He returned to his tent area, put his holster back on, and turned on the boom box. The rock singer's voice, complaining about his failure to get satisfaction, rose through the torpid air. It was almost dark. Dipper lit a lantern and a cigarette, then reseated himself on the campstool and began to sing along with the lyrics. That was when the Trumani dogs began to growl.

There were two of them, slender, dingo-like beasts. They stood side by side about ten feet from him, baring their teeth. It was not Dipper, as such, but the boom box and Dipper's singing that had angered them. The noise hurt their ears. Dipper was indifferent to the cause of their display. It was damned cheek, wog dogs threatening him. He put down his beer and drew the pistol, pointing it unsteadily at his visitors.

"Learn you to flash your gums at me," he declared drunkenly. The dogs remained, stiff-legged, fangs bared, growling louder at his protest. Dipper closed one eye to help steady his vision and pulled the trigger. The round missed both animals, but they ran off, alarmed at the report of the pistol.

The shot brought Ellen out of her tent. "What in hell are you doing?"

Dipper laughed. "Cheeky abo dogs around here growling. Sent them packing. Siddown. Av'a beer," he slurred.

Ellen knew Farrington would be nowhere near the radio at this time of night. "Mr. Edwards I've had enough of your act. I'm radioing Farrington tomorrow to haul you out of here."

"Better sleep on it, birdy. Might need ol' Dipper." He rose unsteadily. "Beautiful little bird, you are. Treat you right, I would. C'mon an' give us a nice hug." He waved his outstretched arms awkwardly.

Ellen was already headed back to her tent. Before she got onto her cot, she put a claw hammer on the floor beside it. There was no way to lock the tent. The idiot might just barge in. With the hammer she could scare him off. But time went by, and Dipper did not appear. The boom box was silent. He was probably passed out with drink. Finally she fell asleep.

Dipper was not asleep. He was sulking over a new beer. What had seemed earlier to be merely perplexing now seemed an outrage.

Here he was the only man on the island — the only proper white one anyway — and the snotty bird was putting him down. It was a matter of pride, a fine-looking man like him. A bloody outrage. She was going to dance, damn it! How? He began to plan, as well as his state of inebriety allowed. Her cot was right inside the mosquito-net door of the tent. If he came up quiet and launched himself fast through the netting, he'd land right on the cot. Once she was good and secured under him she'd have a change of heart. Some birds just needed a little extra push so as not to feel guilty. It seemed a good plan. One more beer ought to top him off right for the plunge, and he'd take it.

IN THE EVENT, DIPPER CARRIED his last beer with him as he launched himself through Ellen's tent door and onto her cot. The beer fell from his hand as he groped to secure her beneath him. His stealth had been surprisingly good for a drunken man, and she had heard nothing until — wham — he landed upon her. He landed right on target, and she soon realized she could not break out from under, but she could squirm.

"Nice little bird," Dipper slurred, dribbling saliva onto her face. "Time to quit your damn squirmin' and dance." She felt him reaching for his fly, but he was having trouble finding it and holding her down too. Beneath the lanky drunken load, she twisted and pushed to no avail, but he was not getting anywhere either. She hit at him to no effect, but she could keep squirming indefinitely.

"Get off me, you creep. You're going to prison for this." Ellen kept her voice down and under control, trying to sound boss of the situation.

"Prison," asked Dipper? He sounded genuinely puzzled.

Ellen hit his face again, again with no visible result. She thought of the hammer beside the cot. Yes, she could reach it, but he was making no progress, and she was afraid hitting him on the head with it might kill him. It was clear to her that if there was a technique to rape, short of knocking the woman out, Dipper did not have it. She also knew intuitively that he was not interested in an unconscious dance partner. He would not try to hurt her, but he had her in a horrible standoff. He was a disgusting and heavy load and seemed determined to spend the night, or until he passed out, on her stomach, dribbling, grunting, and fumbling at his pants. She made another major effort to push him off without success. This drove her to a decision.

She was not about to lie there twisting till the creep gave up or passed out. She would have to try using the hammer. Not on the head, but where? Yes, that would be as good a place as any. In one motion, she gripped the handle and swung the instrument up and down onto what she thought was the middle of Dipper's behind, hoping to dishearten his scrotum. Her strike missed the intended target but hit his thigh hard, and his upper leg muscles cramped painfully in reaction to the blow.

Cursing, Dipper rose, stiff-legged on one side, in an effort to shake off the cramp. He never succeeded. Rather, the foot of his cramped leg came down on his discarded beer bottle, which rolled under his foot, pitching him awkwardly and forcefully backwards. In the fall, the lower back of his skull struck the corner of Ellen's footlocker. Then he came to rest.

Ellen had no idea what had happened, only that she was freed of her loathsome burden. Still holding the hammer, she jumped off the cot and looked down at Dipper, a long heap beside her cot, not moving or talking. "Now get out, you filthy creep," she screamed, brandishing the hammer. There was no response. What the hell was he playing at now? "Edwards," she shouted, "get out of here now, or I'll brain you." But Dipper had already been brained. When there was still no reply, she shoved at him with her foot, causing dipper's limp neck and head to fall away from the footlocker, exposing the sharp, hard corner. In the dim light, Ellen saw that his eyes were open but unfocused. Somehow he'd knocked himself out on the footlocker, or ... She fell on her knees and put her face next to his. There was no breath. She fumbled at his neck and found no pulse. A hand on his chest confirmed the absence of heartbeat.

As a young girl she had had brief training in cardiopulmonary resuscitation. She tried to remember what to do. You had to start the heart by compressing the chest and breathing into the lungs, something like that. She rolled Dipper onto his back, exposed his chest and, as best she could recall, began to employ the procedures. Had she done so perfectly, it would have made no difference. The part of Dipper's brain crucial to respiration and heartbeat no longer functioned. After twenty minutes, exhausted by her effort and seeing it unavailing, she stood up.

Ellen knew she should feel sorry, and she did, but more strongly she felt he had brought it on himself. Not that he deserved to die, but that she deserved not to be blamed for his death. She pictured a Port Moresby court of inquiry peopled by the likes of Farrington. They might even find she'd hit his head with the hammer. She saw no moral obligation to go through that or even to explain what had happened. She stared at the body, trying to come up with a solution. The death would have to appear to have been caused some other way. If she could get the body to the river, the crocodiles would take care of the problem. But she could not carry him, and even if she had the strength to drag him there, his route from the tent to the water would be obvious — there would be a trail showing a body had been dragged there.

As she pondered this, she thought she heard a sound outside the tent, a person moving. Had her shouting at Dipper brought someone from the village? She went outside with a flashlight but saw no one. Then her light fell on the handcart Dipper had made from the pirated radio carriage. That was it! She ran to the device and pulled it back to the tent. Wheels going to the river would not leave a suspicious trail. In fact, Dipper had used the truck to stash beer in the water to cool it.

She pushed the vehicle into the tent. Dipper was long; she would have to pull up his legs and strap him onto the device. Working rapidly she did so, sweating profusely and for the first time fully aware of the feast the mosquitoes were making of her. There was nothing for it, they were everywhere inside the tent. They were on Dipper. She began to sob. What had caused him to fall that way and hit his head? It confirmed her decision to dispose of the body. She would never be able to explain the accident.

Finally, the corpse was trussed to the cart, and Ellen pulled it out of the tent. She had the flashlight, but she felt she could find the path to the river without risking use of it. She began gingerly and then, surprised to find how efficient the cart was, picked up the pace. She had almost reached the river when her foot caught on an exposed tree root, and she fell, striking her head against the trunk. It knocked her out.

She woke up to a familiar voice. "Ellen. Ellen, come back," implored Tallfellow. She came back, looked around. Tallfellow was holding her in his arms, rocking her like a baby. She looked down. Dipper's trussed-up corpse lay as before on the handcart.

"I'm all right now, Tallfellow," she managed. Her head ached.

"That is good. I saw you fall and your head hit the tree. I was very worried." He put her on her feet. "You see, I heard you shouting before. I thought I should come, but when I got to your camp it was all quiet, except I could hear you breathing inside the tent. Then I was afraid to speak. It might have been a bad dream I had had. So when you came out of the tent I said nothing and hid. Still something told me you would need me, that I should stay around, so when you came out again with him like that I followed you."

"Then I fell."

"Yes."

Ellen gathered her senses. The jig was up. "He got onto my cot and tried to rape me. I hit him on the leg with a hammer, and it made him jump off me, but then he fell for some reason and hit his head on my footlocker. It killed him. I don't know what made him fall. I was afraid of having to explain this to the white people across the water. They might think I killed him."

"Yes. The very problem Peter's sister is having."

"Sort of. Anyway, I thought if it looked as if he had fallen in the river and was eaten by the crocodiles there'd be no inquiry."

"Very sensible of you," said Tallfellow. "Let us get him into the river at once. He was a bad man and should not be the cause of any more trouble." Tallfellow untied Dipper's corpse and carried it to the river's edge. He swung the body around him once and released it out over the river. Splashing noises from across the stream informed them that the intended recipients of the meal were aware of its presence.

Tallfellow returned with Ellen and the handcart to her tent. "Tomorrow," he said, "we will find the remnants of his clothing on the bank. He must have been very drunk and ventured too close to the water. The crocodiles are always hungry, and they have very good eyes. With the radio tomorrow you can explain that to Farrington."

"Tallfellow, no one across the water would have the good judgment to solve things this way. I am so lucky."

"Ah, but Ellen, I am guided by Big Mouth."

"Big Mouth eat more," she replied, with increasing reverence.

THE NEXT DAY, ELLEN FOUND THE radio security key among Dipper's effects and called Farrington. She relayed the facts according to Tallfellow's judgment in the matter.

"Funny way for him to cash in. Around crocs all the time up the Sepik. Must have known you can't get too near the water, especially if you're sloshed. Poor old Dipper. Always sloshed at night."

"Yes, he was," said Ellen.

Farrington sighed. "I'll have to make out a form. No next of kin as far as I know. Want to come out? Nobody else to send up there."

"No. I'm still at this report."

"Wait a bit," said Farrington. "I forgot. You might have some visitors. I'm supposed to brief a crew coming out from UNTT headquarters and going to Nova Cannes. Trouble is, there's been some bloody mistake. They want to set up a lumber company and develop the Nova Cannes economy."

"What? They're crazy!"

"I mean to tell them that. Poor old Dipper. The drink'll get you one way or another."

22. TRIALS WITH AND WITHOUT JURY

IT WAS NECESSARY TO REMOVE MOST OF THE MEDIA from the courtroom in order to start the trial. There would otherwise have been no room for the members of the jury panel from whose ranks the jury would be chosen. Judge Flex retained the media dedicated to the live TV presentation and evicted the rest, who snarled and made rude noises as they slunk from the courtroom.

After the panel was seated, the prosecution team affixed their armbands labeled "The People." Judge Flex's offer to the defense lawyers to permit them to wear armbands labeled "The Accused" provoked some giggles from the panel, but a firm look from the jurist, his blue eyes glowing sharply in his makeup-tanned face, silenced them. "We will proceed with selection of the jury," he stated, and the clerk began to call out numbers chosen randomly from a box containing one number for each of the panelists. When twelve persons had been seated in the jury box, Flex called for a brief recess.

During the recess, Playchek examined a list that his legal assistant had prepared of the panelists. It contained brief biographies. "You know, this isn't a bad panel. Of course, Flex will let Davies run wild on *voir dire,* and he may poison all of them."

"What's voir dire?" asked Penny.

"It's asking the jurors questions during selection. You use the chance to talk with them to argue your case. Some judges don't like it and keep the lawyers in bounds, but Potter Flex won't. With him, the wilder, the better."

"Like?"

"Like Davies asking is there any potential juror who is so opposed to criminal punishment that he or she would ignore evidence that the defendant was violent by nature, carried weapons, and thought of the homeless as social inferiors."

"He can do that?" Penny was genuinely surprised.

"You'll hear him do it before you have lunch."

"I won't want lunch. That's disgusting. I had a gun, but the rest is a lie."

"Unfortunately," said Playchek, "the distinction between what's true and what isn't is often ignored on voir dire."

"And will be in other aspects of the trial," added Hamilton Sayer gloomily.

"Look, everybody," said Playchek. They were all gathered around him, including April and Peter. "Don't lose heart. Flex will let Davies get out on some limbs we'll saw off. And we'll get to disturb the peace, too."

The cry of "All rise" heralded the reappearance of Judge Flex, his face visibly freshened. "The Honorable Potter B. Flex, Judge of the Superior Court, presiding," the bailiff shouted. "Be seated."

"Mr. Davies you may proceed with voir dire," declared Flex, and Davies rose to do so.

MEANWHILE, ACROSS THE PACIFIC, The Queen's Own Lumber Company representatives arrived in Port Moresby in good order and were met by David Farrington at the airport. His rugged, tanned face bore a quizzical expression. "Welcome to Moresby," he said heartily, and staring with evident amusement at Bernie

Cronin's blue suit and tie, added, "You'll find that drill a bit stuffy on Nova Cannes. They don't dress for dinner there."

"See here," said Bernie, meaning to take charge of the conversation, "I'm Bernard Cronin. I'm heading this project."

Farrington did not appear to be moved by this news. "You're in charge, eh?"

"Yes. And it's damned hot out here. Are we going to your office?"

"That's the ticket, mate."

On the way to his office, Farrington stopped at The Thirsty Crocodile and picked up several bottles of beer. In his office he offered these to the sweating new arrivals. Jumbo took one; the others declined. Farrington joined Jumbo, and after a lengthy swallow, began, "You know, I tried to save you this trip."

Bernie adopted a firm expression. "Mr. Farrington, the decision to go forward with timber development on Nova Cannes is not yours to make."

"Good thing, too, mate. Wait till you try it."

"I'm not here to debate the issue but to get briefed. That's your charter."

"Look, mate, don't get your prickles up. You'll see what I mean when you go there. That's what I tried to tell them. There's some mistake been made. There's no way to get lumber off Nova Cannes even if you could cut it. And there's no bloody economy to pump up. There's just a bunch of blackfellows who like to eat each other."

Bernie's trial instincts, forged in a hundred petty but bitter disputes in New York courts, came to the fore. "There's trees, aren't there?"

Farrington met him in stride. "There's trees, all right. Bloody big ones, with wood hard as a banker's heart; can't hardly burn it. You'd never use that stuff for lumber. Besides, like I told them, there's no bloody place to pick it up even if the wood was any good."

Bernie produced the file on Nova Cannes, as electronically revised by Philo Spass, with its account of safe harbors, suitable timber and inhabitants eager for development. He read to Farrington. "I know it says that, Mr. Cronin. It's some bloody fuck-up. That's not Nova Cannes. I'm trying to remember. It sounds a bit like another one of our territories."

"Never mind," said Bernie, suspecting a Farrington trick. Just tell us what we should know about Nova Cannes and we'll be on our way."

Farrington told them, including the fact that there were no other whites on the island except a woman anthropologist. "She got there on the chopper. You can charter a boat here in Moresby, like you propose, but you won't be able to land anywhere."

Dr. Clapp was disturbed. "This account certainly doesn't square with the description of the island in the files or with what we were told before we left. I wonder if we're really prepared — "

But Jumbo, the enforcer, was ready. "First things first. We get the boat and go see. Right, Bernie?"

"Right."

"Bon voyage," said Farrington, opening another beer.

A BON VOYAGE WAS OUT OF THE QUESTION, as the charter party soon confirmed. The boat circumnavigated Nova Cannes, taking four days, without observing anything but relentless dense vegetation, the roots of which projected into the surrounding water. There was no harbor, no beach, nor even a dent in this formidable barrier.

When they arrived back at Port Moresby, Farrington greeted them, upbeat with vindication. "I wasn't sending you up about no place to dock, mate, but I could tell you needed to see for yourself."

Bernie was irritable and didn't like to be called "mate." He wiped his sweating face. "You said the others got there by helicopter. How do we arrange that?"

"I do that. But look, mate, you've seen there's no way to get lumber off that dung heap. Why not cut your losses?"

Bernie thought of the unspent budget. It was true prospects were so far unpromising. Yet wasn't he a kind of pioneer? Would Lewis and Clark have turned back at the first sight of desert? Would Napoleon have retreated from Russia at the first sign of snow? The latter was not a particularly happy analogy, but he was convinced anyway. "No. We want to go there. As soon as possible."

"You'll need provisions. The Trumani don't provide shopping or restaurants. Here's what I recommend."

Bernie looked at the list. "This says supplies for only one week."

"I'm erring on the high side," replied Farrington. "You'll probably want out in a day."

"I'm figuring two to three weeks," said Bernie firmly.

"The helicopter can't do that. Too much weight. If you still want to stay after five days, radio me and I'll send the chopper with more beer and tucker. Want me to ask the anthropology woman to see you around?"

The idea of an escort did not appeal to Bernie. "We can make our own investigation. In fact, I think it might be best, Farrington, if you kept our arrival confidential for the time being."

"Whatever you say. Woman's not a bad looker. Bit skittish. Of course, the natives are going to know you're there, and they'll tell her."

"About the natives," Dr. Clapp interjected. "You say they don't eat white people?"

"Not so far. We're told they don't like the smell, and there's no prestige point to killing us either. On the other hand, I wouldn't cross 'em if I were you. They're not tame, and they love a fight. No economic concerns but lots of war games. That's their cup of tea."

Bernie looked at his watch. "When can the helicopter take us there?"

"After you get provisioned, say, noon tomorrow."

APRIL WOKE UP AT 3:00 A.M. and lay in bed pondering the matter of Peter. By about 3:30, she had convinced herself that a direct, forceful approach would carry the day. She rose, removed her nightgown, and quietly made her way to Peter's room. The door was not even shut. An omen.

She entered and spied the prize lying on his back. He was already in the right position, and appeared to be naked under the loosely draped bed covers. Another omen. She shut the door carefully so as to make no noise. Swiftly, she moved to the bed, pulled down the covers and leapt onto Peter. Before he knew what had happened, she was astraddle, her legs braced on either side of his and her arms pinning his to the mattress. When Peter discovered what was going on, he immediately tried to rise, but found himself the captive of April's muscular limbs, her body pressing down on him. "April," he whispered, "this is crazy! Get off me!"

"Just hold still," she whispered back. "I'll take care of everything. I find it's better that way." He struggled unsuccessfully to free himself. This proved to April that she was strong enough to keep him pinned, and she kissed his cheek while improving her position. "Just think about how good it feels," she whispered confidently, beginning to move her lower body against his.

"April! What if your mother saw this? You've got to stop now!"

"We don't want to stop, dear. Let's be honest."

He summoned all his strength, but she felt his muscles tightening and met the challenge. The years of pumping iron were paying off. She smiled as she felt his major effort to dislodge her falter, and this time kissed his lips before he could turn his face aside. Peter felt desperate, sensing control of the situation was entirely in her hands. She was so much stronger, and the power of her body was beginning to tell. "April, we simply can't do this. I'm legally your uncle. Stop now!"

April did not stop. "You're not really my uncle. I looked it up. It's not incest or anything. Just relax. I'll take care of everything."

Peter despaired. Perhaps trickery would work. "April," he whispered, trying to make it sound as if he was giving in, while noticeably easing his resistance to her movements, "you mustn't tell your mother."

April's first reaction was to think, what was the point of seducing Peter if she couldn't tell anyone she wanted to, especially her mother. Then she took comfort in the assumption that Peter's remark indicated an end to his resistance. "Never," she lied softly in his ear, and, sure now of success, relaxed her hold on his arms, sliding one of hers down toward his lower body to prepare the coup de grace. She had not gotten her hand quite in place when he mustered all his remaining strength and, twisting, pushed her off. He jumped from the bed and ran pell-mell for the bathroom, the door of which he bolted.

Shocked by the suddenness of the escape just when he seemed totally in hand, April lay for a moment as if frozen to the bed. Then she got up and tried the bathroom door. "You idiot," she said in a sulky voice. "It was going to be fun. Come out."

Removed from April's body wrap, Peter was back in control of his feelings. "April, you've got to quit trying to lay me. You're a lovely girl, but I'm not interested."

"Yes, you were, I could tell. Come out. We've still got time to do it."

"No chance, April. Besides," he lied, thinking of Ellen, "I'm engaged."

"What's that got to do with it? I don't want to marry you." And she added with emphasis, as if it were a deciding point, "I just want to have sex."

"Then get the boy next door, or something. I'm a poor choice."

"Well, Peter, you're certainly being a poor sport. Come on, open the door. It's going to get light." She had a belief in the power of persistence in sexual matters. "Come on. I could tell you really wanted to," she whispered persuasively at the bathroom door.

The escapee behind it was unconvinced but honest. "April, you are not, as you know, lacking in charms, but I've escaped. Face it, and let's be friends."

"What a dreadful old line. Let's be friends. You're becoming a bore."

"I'm trying to."

"If you don't come out at once, Peter, I'm leaving."

"Now you're talking sense. And I do want to be friends."

April sighed. It had been a near thing, but now, she realized, she was actually losing interest. "Peter, it's OK. We'll just be friends. Come on out."

He remembered how he'd tricked her. It could be tit for tat. "No. I'm going to take a shower."

"Better make it a cold one," said April and departed.

23. THE WORLD OF VOIR DIRE

SONIA'S CONCERN THAT HER LEADER'S prosecutorial zeal might have been diminished by exposure to the portrait of Penny Hill was soon dispelled by his voir dire examination of the potential jurors. Sonia sat delighted as Davies undertook his general questioning in a fashion that presented a litany of prejudicial arguments, and Judge Flex cooperated fully. The result was that even before Davies had begun questioning jurors individually, he had portrayed Penny, among other things, as a vicious, upper-class enemy of the people, the people whose armband he and his colleague wore.

Was there any juror who could not in good conscience convict this woman if the evidence showed a pattern of wanton disregard for the lives of those she deemed lower in the social scale than herself?

"Are there any among you," he asked, "who would feel obliged to acquit even when the proof demonstrates the defendant's unreasoning hatred of two of society's most needful and oppressed segments, the homeless and the Native-American? Will each of you pledge to carefully consider corroborative evidence of defendant's aggressive nature in determining her intent to take the life of this innocent young man?

"The people will show you examples of her aggressive behavior and evidence of her own perception of herself as a person of violence, endowed with the right to punish others. That evidence will include a portrait of the defendant worth, ladies and gentlemen, a thousand words." Here Davies faltered momentarily, and Sonia breathed a sigh of relief when he continued. "Will each of you exercise your sacred duty as jurors and accept the reality of such matters even though they may do violence to your own perception of what a woman of the defendant's appearance, a mother, would do, would be?"

And so it went. Playchek's first objection to Davies's rampant argument disguised as questioning was met with the observation by Judge Flex that he "assumed this was merely preliminary." He went on to say that Mr. Davies was simply exploring the background of the case on voir dire, and that the objection, if Mr. Playchek felt it was necessary, could be made when Mr. Davies offered evidence in support of his statements. The judge cautioned Playchek, however, that he did not favor unnecessary objections. This rebuke in front of the panel kept Playchek in his seat and silent during most of Davies's ensuing voir dire, consoled from time to time by Penny's whispered curses in his ear.

Davies's questioning of individual jurors proceeded smoothly until he reached juror number seven. This was Jack Farnman, a retired San Francisco policeman, whose former employment, Davies assumed, should incline him to favor the prosecution. It was not to be. "It's hard," said Farnman, not responding to a question, but desiring to make his own point, "to get worked up over one of these drunken street bums getting shot. Besides, I read in the paper he was stealing her purse."

Davies's beaked nose quivered, his dark eyes flashed. "Mr. Farnman, you understand the newspaper is not evidence and is often wrong on the facts?"

Before Farnman could answer, there rose a chorus of catcalls from the press. Judge Flex gaveled them down. "Mr. Farnman, you may answer Mr. Davies's question."

"Well," began Farnman, "it's like this. Maybe the paper's wrong, but you lawyers don't know what it's like out there on the streets these days. See, when I was on the beat and these bums got out of line, we gave them a crack on the head to remind them who's boss. Now they give them mineral water and health food, and a cop can't use his magic wand at all. It's that Lint Law Enforcement Control Act."

Davies asked the court to excuse Mr. Farnman for cause, that is, that his remarks showed bias against the people. But Judge Flex, who found Mr. Farnman entertaining, refused to do so. "It seems, counsel, that the juror is merely stating his personal opinion. We may not agree with him, but the court is not here to critique the viewpoints of panel members. Proceed."

Davies abandoned Farnman and completed his individual voir dire of the jurors without further mishap. He had, he stated, one more general question to put. "Has any one of you ever been falsely accused of a crime?" Two hands went up. He turned to the nearest hand, raised by a plump, middle-aged woman wearing a pillbox hat. "Of what crime were you falsely accused, Madame?"

"Well, it wasn't exactly a crime," said the juror. "It was in school. Mrs. Amtrax, the principal, said I was a troublemaker, and that was a lie, but I prayed for her every night, and at the end of the year she was fired. So you see, things work out."

"Thank you, Madame." Davies turned to the other juror who had raised his hand. This was a tanned, thirtyish man with a crewcut and goatee, who looked like the model in a French Foreign Legion recruitment poster. One of his bared forearms was tattooed. "Lower Interest Rates and Your Pants," it read. Davies asked its owner about the false accusation.

"I was charged with assault, first degree, with my motorcycle."

"Tell us about it."

"This guy who'd been coming on to Conrad, my companion, got in front of the bike, and it knocked him down. I was riding it, see, and they said I did it intentionally, because of the sex angle."

"I see. And the charge was false."

"Sure. My brakes were lousy. My lawyer showed that, and the judge let me off."

"So justice was done?"

"You bet. The bike broke a couple of his ribs, too."

"Thank you."

In the course of the next half-hour, Davies exercised peremptory challenges — for which cause need not be shown — and excused the retired policeman and the two falsely accused jurors. Their places were taken by three more panelists.

Playchek commenced his voir dire with the statement, "I want to follow up on a question the prosecution asked, the matter of false accusations." Playchek pointed at the prosecution table. "Is there any one of you who thinks these guys never make mistakes when they bring charges?"

Davies objected that the question was improper, and Flex sustained the objection. "Yes, 'these guys' is improper," he declared. "Particularly with Ms. Taft sitting there. It should be 'these people.' Will you accept that, Mr. Playchek?"

"Certainly, Your Honor. Does anyone think these people never bring charges that should not have been brought?" An elderly woman in the second row raised her hand. Playchek looked at his list of the jurors' names. "Miss Curtin?"

"Yes. It's just a feeling of mine. I've had it since I was a child. About the government being right, I mean."

"Tell us about your feeling, Miss Curtin," said Playchek warmly.

"Well, I grew up when Franklin D. Roosevelt was president, you see. And he always said to trust your government. He had such a fine, large head and a beautiful voice. So I've always felt what the government does is right, more or less. I suppose there are some mistakes."

"Of course there are, Miss Curtin. And, you know, President Roosevelt was with the federal government. This prosecutor is with the state, the city government. That's different, isn't it?"

"Well, I've never really understood about all that. To me the government's the government." She smiled at Playchek. He was a nice-looking man too, even if his head was smaller than Roosevelt's.

And Playchek, sensing the friendliness, decided to keep her. "Well, Miss Curtin, if the evidence showed the pistol went off when it hit the ground, and Ms. Hill didn't shoot it at the victim, then this prosecution would be one of those rare mistakes the government makes, wouldn't it?"

Davies objected on several grounds. Judge Flex, the video cameras recording his absorption, mulled over the matter. Finally, he ruled. "The objection will be sustained. I think the proper question is, taking your own distinction, Mr. Playchek, whether this is one of those mistakes the state or city government makes."

"Exactly. I thank Your Honor for the clarification and so amend my question."

"But Your Honor — " Davies muttered.

"I have ruled," said Judge Flex with godlike simplicity, and his wife beamed at him from the first row of spectator seats.

"You may answer, Miss Curtin," said Playchek.

"Yes. Then it would be a mistake."

"Thank you very much, Miss Curtin. Now, ladies and gentlemen, Mr. Davies referred to a portrait of Ms. Hill. Listening to him you might suppose it was a self-portrait. It isn't. Let me ask you, does anyone believe that a drawing or painting someone else makes of you inevitably shows you the way you really are or want to be?"

One juror, an attractive young woman with a nose ring, asked that the question be repeated, and the reporter read it back. Then she raised her hand. "Ms. Quality?" Playchek asked.

"Yes, Candy Quality. See, I do astral photography."

"And what is astral photography?"

"We take photos of a person's aura. It's like capturing their inner essence. The aura shows up in the photo, like radiation of the soul. So I think, at least what I do, that can reveal what a person's really like."

Playchek decided Candy Quality was not a prosecution juror. "That's astral photography, Ms. Quality, but suppose a male friend of yours, who was an artist and sexually attracted to you, painted you the way he felt about you. That might not look like the real you at all, isn't that so?"

"You mean like he painted me like I was some sex model?"

"Yes. His fantasy of you."

"Well, I shouldn't say this, I suppose. Maybe the judge — "

"No, no," said Judge Flex, fascinated at the turn the examination was taking. "You should explain whatever you want." The judge looked toward his wife to be sure she did not disapprove, and she nodded benignly.

"Well, I like to think of myself as sexy, like everybody wants to be, so maybe the painting would be, you know, accurate." Her nose ring glittered in the video lighting.

Playchek tried again. "But that would only be a part of the real you, wouldn't it?"

"Right. I read lots of metaphysical books too, and I watch PBS television programs."

"Exactly, Ms. Quality. And suppose this hypothetical boyfriend — you know what I mean by 'hypothetical?'"

"Yeah. He isn't real. You're making him up." She giggled.

"That's it." Playchek plowed ahead. "And I'm going to assume that for some reason you don't really understand, he thinks you'd look sexier if he painted you carrying a whip and wearing riding boots. Now you don't associate whips and riding boots with sex do you?"

"No, but some people do. I've seen magazines."

"Yes. But the portrait would not be the real you or the way you wanted to be at all. It would be the boyfriend artist's fantasy?"

Davies rose. "Your Honor, this has gone on far enough. Mr. Playchek is trying to turn this issue into a joke. We're talking about a real portrait of the accused, not a hypothetical one."

Judge Flex was annoyed at the interruption. This interrogation was good stuff. "No, Mr. Davies, I find this line of inquiry interesting, and I think the jury does, too. It's hard enough trying to keep a long trial interesting for the judge and the jury. I'll overrule the objection."

"Do you recall the question, Ms. Quality," Playchek asked?

"I think so. No, I'm broadminded, but I've never used whips or boots with sex. So it wouldn't be the real me. Can I ask you a question?"

"Certainly."

"What's the date of Ms. Hill's birth?"

Davies rose again. "Your Honor, we are really getting far afield."

"Perhaps," Judge Flex responded. "But unless the juror meant to give Ms. Hill a birthday present or something like that, how can it hurt to know? I mean, if Ms. Hill doesn't mind telling us." He turned to Penny.

"Not at all," said Penny brightly. "It's May 5th, 1959."

"Thank you, Ms. Hill," Judge Flex said, and addressing the jury, asked, "Did you all hear that?" Everyone answered "yes." Three jurors, including Ms. Quality, wrote down Penny's birth date on their pads.

When they were through writing, Playchek began again, turning now to the rich-versus-poor issue. "Ladies and gentlemen, do any of you believe that just because someone is well off that that means they hate the poor." A thin, middle-aged man in a brown tweed sport jacket and a tartan tie raised his hand. "Mr. Carruthers?"

"Yes. I am a sociologist, and I think it is well established that there is little love lost between the rich and the poor. Also, I have been poor in the past, and I know how I felt then about the rich."

"Well, sir, did that feeling lead you to go out and shoot one of them?"

"Of course not. I did not want to go to jail."

Playchek had found a bad apple and, moving back to a general question mode, asked, "Does any one of you believe that just because someone is well off, that would lead him or her to want to shoot panhandlers?" No hands rose. "Is there any one of you who doesn't understand that you cannot find Mrs. Hill guilty just because she is rich and the victim was poor?" Carruthers raised his hand again. "Yes, sir?"

"Mr. Playback, I think you are understating the importance of the difference."

This was certainly a bad apple. "It's 'Playchek,' Mr. Carruthers. Are you saying you think you should convict simply because the defendant is wealthy and the victim wasn't?"

"Not entirely, but, of course, that is naturally a consideration."

Playchek asked Judge Flex to discharge Carruthers for cause. The request was denied.

"Again, counsel, as I told Mr. Davies, we are going to hear a lot of different opinions in this case. That's what makes a case interesting. Where would we be if I started discharging jurors just because they were prejudiced against rich people? We'd upset the natural balance of opinions that makes for a good trial. Let's take a recess."

THE DEFENSE GROUP GATHERED about Playchek during the recess. "I'm going to boot this creep Carruthers and turn the voir dire back to Davies," he said. "The rest of the ones in the box are probably as good as we'll get. We'll see what Davies does."

"You know, Barton," said Penny, "there's the nicest-looking man back there in the seats who keeps smiling at me. Is he a juror?"

Playchek looked into the audience. "Is he over in the right-hand seats?"

"Yes. See? He's smiling at me now. What a lovely smile he has."

"He's part of the panel. Don't go near him."

"I won't, but I wish I knew who he was."

"Never mind."

When Judge Flex retook the bench, Playchek rose. "The defendant thanks and excuses Mr. Carruthers."

Judge Flex excused Carruthers, and the clerk drew another number. It belonged to a young woman with a pinkish complexion and curly blonde hair. She wore sliver-rimmed eyeglasses with small oval lenses that barely spanned her eyes. "Mr. Davies, I believe it is your turn," said Judge Flex.

"Thank you, Your Honor." He turned to the newly seated juror. "You are Ms. Frederica Urth?"

"Yes, it's my maiden name. I just got divorced."

Davies beamed. "Good to get your own name back, I'll bet. Now, Ms. Urth, you've heard counsel asking questions of the other jurors. Were there any that you would have responded to had you then been in the box?"

"Yes. Mr. Badcheck asked how jurors felt about rich people. Well, I feel it's the wealthy that are causing real estate developments and destroying the natural habitats, like for the mountain lion. Also, like in this case, they've done things that hurt the Indians."

Playchek stood up. "Your Honor, I submit that Ms. Urth is not responding to any proper question of counsel. She is making a freelance speech. I ask that the court instruct counsel to put specific questions so I can frame objections if necessary."

Davies grunted. "Your Honor, this is an attempt to stifle voir dire."

Judge Flex's face grew serious, and he looked meaningfully at the video cameramen to be sure they were paying attention, then at Playchek. "She did make sort of a speech, counsel, but free speech is important here. I don't want jurors to feel that the First Amendment is not observed in my court." He looked toward his wife. She was nodding her head affirmatively. "The instruction will be that what one juror says is not necessarily binding on the court or the other jurors. Proceed."

"Thank you, Your Honor," said Davies and turned back to Ms. Urth. "You said something about destruction of habitats."

"Yes. It's the wealthy developers. They keep building further and further out into the natural, organic areas. Just the other day in Marin County, a hungry mountain lion ate a jogger, and they shot the lion. It's awful. They were here before we were. It's their habitat, and then we shoot them. It's Vietnam all over again."

"Of course, Ms Urth, but despite your awareness of the depredations of the wealthy on the environment, you could still render a fair and impartial verdict in this case, couldn't you?"

"I could try, but I'm bothered about her shooting the poor Indian."

"Why, of course you are. We all are. Your Honor, the people are satisfied with the jury as constituted."

"Very well. Mr. Playchek?" The cameras swung from Flex to the defense counsel table.

"Your Honor, I ask that the court excuse Ms. Urth for cause. Her opinions clearly show bias."

"Well, Mr. Playchek," Flex responded, "that's your viewpoint. But she says she'll try to be fair and impartial, and I think the court has to assume she knows her own mind better than you do. It's from the horse's mouth, so to speak. Denied."

"Very well, Your Honor, the defendant thanks and excuses Ms. Urth."

"We'll take a recess," said Judge Flex.

"YOU KNOW," SAID PLAYCHEK during the recess, "when dear old Tremorgan goes over the line like he did with that mountain-lion woman, I find myself wishing him into a concrete overcoat. The trouble is, the mob is underrepresented in northern California."

"I have a friend in the business in Boston," said Peter. "I suppose that's too far."

Playchek chuckled. "Not at all. If Tremorgan keeps funning around we'll fly your friend out."

"How did you meet a mobster, Peter?" Penny was surprised.

"It was when I was teaching in Boston. We lived near each other, and I saved his wife from drowning in a swimming-pool accident. He was very grateful. Nice people so far as I could tell, but he was quite frank about his connections."

"We should finish voir dire this afternoon," said Playchek. "That means opening statements tomorrow morning."

"Then come the witnesses?" Penny asked.

"Yes. Probably the street girl will be number one."

"I'll love to hear from her again; she's the one I should have shot."

"Hindsight," said Playchek, as Judge Flex reappeared.

The next panelist seated in the box was a dark-haired man who appeared to be in his early forties. Penny pulled hard at Playchek's coat. "Barton," she whispered, "that's the man who's been smiling at me. Isn't he handsome?"

Judge Flex was speaking at the same time. "Mr. Playchek?"

"Just a moment, please, Your Honor," and whispering to his legal assistant, asked her, "Muriel, what have we got on this guy?"

"Jonathan Barrow, Business Agent Careenists' Union, Local Six — that's here in SF. Single, divorced, BA from the University of California, Berkeley, 1977. Been with the union since graduation. That's about it."

Playchek rose and addressed the court. "May we have a short recess, Your Honor? I need to confer with my client."

"Very well." And a recess was taken.

"Penny," said Playchek, "a lifelong union man is not exactly our cup of tea."

"Please, Barton. Don't excuse him. He likes me."

"You think so, but his natural prejudices are going the other way in my view. Plus, in every trial, Tremorgan does this routine about his ancestors slaving in the Welsh coal mines. It's a very union-y thing."

"Barton, trust me. I can just tell he'll understand what happened. What's his first name?"

"Jonathan. The name's OK."

"So's the man. Please."

"We're back in session. I'll ask some questions." Playchek rose. "Mr. Barrow, you heard Mr. Davies's examination of Ms. Urth?"

"Yes."

"Do you feel you can serve as a juror impartially where the accused is a well-off person and the alleged victim was poor?"

"Yes."

"You're head of the Careenists' Union?"

"Just of Local Six, here in San Francisco."

"Forgive my ignorance, but what do careenists do?"

"It's a nautical term. You careen a boat to do repairs. It means hauling it out of the water and onto land. Into dry dock. We do that."

"And you have disputes with wealthy owners over wages and hours?"

"Rarely in San Francisco. This is a union town." Barrow smiled at Penny.

Playchek continued. "The prosecution and the media have tried to make this into a rich-versus-poor case. Which side are you on?"

"Well, I'm neither rich nor poor, so I guess I'm on the fence. Anyway, I've got nothing against being rich."

"Ms. Urth also talked about Indians. There's a claim here the victim was an Indian. Would that influence your judgment in any way?"

"No. I mean, I think, like most people do, that the Indians have gotten a lot of raw deals from the rest of us, but that doesn't lead me to the conclusion that Ms. Hill goes around shooting them."

"May I confer with my client a moment, Your Honor?"

"Certainly."

Playchek bent down to Penny. "I still don't like the union stripe. This guy is smart and witty. He could be feeding us that good stuff just to stay on the jury."

"No, no, Barton. I'm right about him. He just smiled at me again, and he has such a nice voice."

"This is probably malpractice, letting you call the shot."

"I won't sue."

"I guess not. OK, let's see what Davies does with him." Play-chek stood up and turned to the court. "Your Honor, the defendant is satisfied with the jury as constituted."

There was a conference going on at the prosecution table. Davies asked and was granted time to confer. "I saw the new guy give Penny Hill a big smile," said Sonia.

"But look, Sonia, a lifelong union man and a 1970s U.C. Berkeley graduate. I like that."

"So do I. He was probably just smiling at large. I vote we pass."

"Done." Davies rose. "The people are also satisfied with this jury, Your Honor."

"Very well, counsel," said Judge Flex and recessed court for the day.

AS PENNY AND HER COMPANIONS LEFT the courtroom at the end of the day, they found the hallway filled, not just with the usual media representatives but with men in medieval costume holding up placards that read, "Free Penny Hill." To gain entry to City Hall they had put aside their swords and staves. "Who are these Robin Hood look-alikes who want to free me," asked Penny?

As she spoke, one of the costumed, a large, older man wearing a peaked cap different in color from that of his fellows approached. He had a pastoral face, which was smiling hugely. "Mrs. Hill, I'm Field Marshal Flam of the Bay Area Aryan Army. We support your right to bear arms and your efforts to rid the city of these street scum." He doffed his cap, exposing a head of thick white hair. He looked, thought Playchek, like the veteran of a thousand prayer breakfasts.

"You guys are bad news," said Playchek. "Is the DA paying you to rally around my client?"

Field Marshal Flam laughed, unprovoked by the rebuke. "It is entirely our idea to assist her in her struggle with the authorities."

"Look, Field Marshal, if the jury thinks you and my client are connected, she's a dead duck. Put your Merry Men on someone else's case."

Peter, who was hovering about and confused as to the import of it all, asked Playchek, "Who are these people?"

"The Bay Area Aryan Army is a right-wing militia. They appear to want a publicity ride off your sister's trial. That about it, Marshal?"

The marshal, without responding, handed Playchek some brochures. "Read these, counselor. You'll see we'd naturally consider a case like your client's an important issue."

"We want you to drop it, Marshal," Playchek replied. "I'm going to call a press conference to divorce ourselves from you, and we'll blast you unless you drop it now."

Field Marshal Flam remained cheerful. "This matter is too important to our cause. We can't just let it drop, and we're hard to divorce. We should learn to live together. Read those brochures."

"Barton," Penny asked, "can't we get a court to stop them from supporting me?"

"No. There's nothing a court can do. There's no law against taking sides."

Peter tugged on Playchek's coat. "Barton, you have to prepare for court tomorrow. Let me talk to this guy. Maybe I can get him to back off."

Playchek was surprised at the proposal. "You'll need more than family appeal, Peter. You'll need magic."

"I know, but I want to try."

Peter approached the marshal, who was distributing brochures to others in the crowd. "Marshal, I'm Peter Walker, Ms. Hill's brother. I need to talk to you about her case, but not here. Can I come to your office?"

"To headquarters? Why I suppose so, young man. Maybe we can talk about a photo session with Ms. Hill."

"Marshal, I just want a chance to discuss the problem from

our viewpoint away from this crowd scene."

"Son, we're always ready to discuss important issues. You can come with me in my van. We'll show you around headquarters."

As the van approached BAAA headquarters, Marshal Flam laughed. "It's really our house, Martha's and mine, but now we live in the garage. The house is dedicated to the BAAA as an armory and administrative center." He parked the van, and they and several militiamen entered the building.

The walls were covered with notices and posters. A red flag with a black swastika hung above the fireplace. Nearby, a poster announced the "Second Annual Christian Marksmen's Shootoff." Peter wondered what the Christian marksmen shot at. Another poster announced that Marshal Flam would speak that Saturday at an "Old Fashioned Sod Buster Family Picnic" on "The Slavery Hoax."

"What is the slavery hoax," Peter asked?

"It's this guilt trip that's been laid on the Christian white man in our country, so that we keep on supporting all the nigras who won't work and paying for all the babies they keep having. There never was slavery in this country, Mr. Walker. It's all a hoax."

"How did they get here from Africa if not as slaves?"

"Ever heard of illegal immigration? They've been sneaking in for centuries."

"But we don't have a border with Africa."

"So what? There's always been boats. They go island hopping till they get to Florida. Then they go everywhere, and we pay for it with our tax dollars."

"But there are countless records of the slave trade. I've studied some of them myself."

"What you studied were forgeries. Done by the Jews mostly. The Jews have always been helping the nigras get here, even bringing them in. You see, nigras are the Jews' best customers."

"When did you discover all this, Marshal?"

"We didn't. Other white Christian folk have known about this for generations. Known it was all a hoax. But the big interests, they've covered it up. Look, they even fooled Lincoln. Then, when they could see he was beginning to catch on, that the cover-up conspiracy was breaking down, they killed him. Booth was just a front man for the conspiracy, like Oswald."

"Marshal, we were going to talk about my sister's trial."

"Yeah, but first take some of these pamphlets. They explain all about the slavery hoax. Here's another good one, about the United Nations plot to take over the U.S. See, the UN has put secret coded directions on our highway signs to guide invading international armies. They're out to internationalize the U.S. of A. and take away our national freedoms."

"I really only want to talk about my sister's freedom. Playchek is right. If the jury thinks your people are in her corner they'll convict her, and she's innocent."

"Of course she is, a fine Christian woman like her."

"You keep talking about Christian this and Christian that. Doesn't your Christian conscience bother you that you want to tar my sister with your brush, knowing the jury will hate her for it?"

"We'll pray for your sister that the jury does the right thing."

"I beg you. Reconsider. Find some other cause where you can't do this kind of harm."

"Young man, you should understand something: we're in a war in this country, and in war people get hurt. And like Clausewitz said, the worst mistakes in war result from benevolence. So we can't really focus too much on what effect the war has on your sister."

"Then nothing I can say will change your mind, Marshal?"

"Afraid not, young fella. Too important an issue. Look, I'll square with you. Membership is down. We see this case as a boost to recruitment."

"I see. You say you and your wife live in the garage?"

"Yes. Now you read those pamphlets. You may see things differently. It's no coincidence that the UN and most of the Jews are both in New York City."

"Would you please call me a cab?"

The cab took Peter to Penny's house. He got his address and telephone book from his briefcase and turned to the name Benvenuto Cellini, whose address was listed as Boston, Massachusetts. "Let us pray," thought Peter, "that Ben is still there and in the same business."

A WOMAN ANSWERED PETER'S CALL to Benvenuto Cellini's number. There was the sound of a baby crying. "Mary?" Peter asked.

"Yes."

"This is Peter Walker."

"My God, Peter! Are you back in Boston?"

"No, I'm in San Francisco."

"That's a shame. You want to talk to Ben?"

"Yes, please."

Ben came on the line." Peter, what's up? Long time no hear."

"I know, I've been in the field. I haven't been back to Boston in five years."

"We miss you. Where are you?"

"In San Francisco, where my sister, Penny Hill, lives. We have a problem. She's on trial here for murder."

"Wow! That's no fun."

"Ben, are you still in the same business?"

"Yes, but I don't know how much I can do with a Frisco trial."

"It's not that. There's an organization here of militiamen. You know what I mean?"

"Like the guys in the Midwest that drill in the park and have their own explosives?"

"Exactly. This one is called the Bay Area Aryan Army. They're neo-Nazis, and they want to use my sister's trial to get publicity. See, she's accused of shooting a street person, and today the militiamen were all over the courthouse with posters saying they support her right to bear arms and shoot street people. It'll get worse, and if the jury thinks she's connected to these people they'll want to convict her."

"Peter, this is a thing I can do something about."

"I'd hoped so. I tried to get their leader to back off. No soap. He sees this as a great recruitment opportunity, and I'm not very persuasive."

"We can be more persuasive. Give me his name and address and we'll get on it tonight. It's still early out there."

Peter gave him Marshal Flam's address. "He and his wife are living in the garage; the house is used by the militia. Do you think you can do this without — "

Cellini interrupted. "Peter, the guy's just an amateur. A little talk is all we need."

"Wonderful. We particularly need to keep them away from the courthouse."

"They are not going to have anything further to do with your sister. Nothing at the trial or anywhere else. How are you otherwise?"

"I've been working with some cannibals on an island near New Guinea."

"Well, that's safer than the criminal courts."

"It's much more pleasant too."

"Rest easy. I'll get right on this."

24. Birds of a Feather

At the airport bus terminal, Tula Fogg was holding up a sign identifying herself, and Flora Grebe, newly arrived from St. Paul, spotted her. Tula was expecting someone who looked more like an Indian. Mrs. Grebe's graying blonde hair and florid complexion surprised her, but she at once recognized the voice. "You're kind of little for a cop, aren't you?" Mrs. Grebe's speech was slightly skewed, as it had been when they had talked on the telephone. This time by airline booze. "You smoke a lot when you were a kid?"

Tula had long since ceased to take offense at comments about her stature. Besides, she reminded herself, Mrs. Grebe's terrible loss, as she recalled from their telephone conversation, required an understanding listener. Along with the denial of her Native-American heritage, her bitter account of Smoking Mother and his father, it was only natural, justifiably unhinged as she was, for her to be abrupt with strangers. Tula laughed cheerfully. "No, I never smoked. Our whole family is short."

"Bunch of runts, eh? Well, where we going from here?"

"To the hotel. It's The Bayquake. Quite nice."

"They have a bar?"

"I'm not sure about that."

The Bayquake lacked a bar. "Where's the nearest liquor store?" Mrs. Grebe put the question to the man at the front desk once this deficiency had been determined. And, turning to Tula, held out her hand. "I'll need some more expense money now I'm here."

"Yes, I'm supposed to give you a hundred dollars." She handed her the money.

"That ain't gonna go far. You expect me to live on granola?"

"No, no. If that's not enough for meals I'm sure they'll authorize more."

"Damn well better, rich city like this. You run off now. I got some things to do."

"Well, I have to bring another witness here later, so I'll check by to see if everything's all right."

"Never mind. I'll be OK."

"But I'm supposed to introduce the two of you. It's a young woman. She was there when your son died."

"Yeah? Seems like there were a lot of women around when he got shot. Liked to beat up on 'em, you know. I tell you that? Anyway, I want to meet the one who shot him."

"She'll be in court, but we can't talk to her because she's the defendant. I'll introduce you to the other girl later. Her name's Wendy Papp."

"We'll see. If I've got the 'Do Not Disturb' up, you wait till tomorrow."

"Oh, we won't be late."

"Late, my fanny. I don't like interruptions during the cocktail hours."

"It'll just take a minute, Mrs. Grebe. I'm really supposed to introduce you two tonight."

Flora Grebe grunted rudely.

Tula pondered the matter. The best thing was to explain the situation frankly. "Mrs. Grebe, we think the girl may have a drug and drinking problem. We sort of wanted her under your wing, so to speak, before she testifies."

"Drug and drink problem, eh? Why didn't you say so sooner? We'll take care of that. You bring her around later."

Tula's whole being warmed. Beneath Mrs. Grebe's rough exterior lay true compassion. Here she was, ready to open her heart to a young girl with a drug and drink problem. Perhaps the therapy would be mutual and would help Mrs. Grebe to reassert her denied Native-American heritage. The important thing for now was to be very understanding. Then she left to pick up Wendy Papp and take her shopping for courtroom clothes.

"A DRESS!" WENDY SNORTED. "At The New Reality Shelter they'd think I was on angel dust."

"But, Ms. Papp, Ms. Taft was very explicit. No jeans or poncho in the courtroom."

"She can wear what she wants in court. I'm no frickin' lawyer and I don't wear dresses."

"A skirt and blouse?"

"Forget it! I could use some new jeans. Look, I'll wear a sweater. New jeans and a new sweater. How much have you got for clothes?"

"Seventy five dollars."

"Whoopee! I know where we can get the jeans and the sweater for twenty bucks. We'll split the balance."

"Oh, I couldn't do that."

"Then just you give it to me. I can use the money."

"I suppose that would be all right."

At 7:30 P.M. they arrived at The Bayquake with the new clothes and Wendy Papp's knapsack. She had demanded that they stop en route at a supermarket so she could get cigarettes and a bottle of wine. It was certainly fortunate, thought Tula, that Mrs. Grebe would be there to provide maternal restraint, take the young girl under her wing. After registering, they went to the Grebe room and knocked.

The introduction was accomplished in short order with the room door only half open. Mrs. Grebe was in slippers and a robe, her face a bit more florid than earlier. Tula hoped the room was not overheated. "We won't need you anymore tonight," Mrs. Grebe said firmly, addressing Tula. "You can get back to your stunted family." And addressing Wendy, she said, "We'll see you after you get settled in, honey; have a little nip together."

Tula could see that the two of them had hit it right off and departed with a sense of relief at the mutual support system she had arranged.

EVEN AS FLORA GREBE AND WENDY PAPP settled in for their night's carouse at The Bayquake Hotel, Mayor Waylon Homer and R. "Doc" Wayward were having a belt in the mayor's office. They were celebrating the results of the latest poll, which showed the mayor with a five-point lead over James Blake, and Sybil Watch now trailing both of them badly.

"This is the poll that asked about issues, isn't it?" the mayor inquired of his beaming consultant.

"Yes, and my instincts, Waylon, were right on the money. The main issues they're paying attention to are the conflict, if you will, between rich and poor and, get this, unfair treatment of Indians."

"Ah," said Homer, "the eternal issues, just as you predicted, and they now see me as being on the right side of them, is that it?"

"Yes. I think the Hill trial and the new Welfare Stamp Funding Committee have restored your image as a friend of the man in the street."

"At least of the Indian man in the street." He laughed at his joke.

"Seriously, Waylon, the pollsters find a real mishmash of these issues in the minds of the voters. It's that blend we wanted. There's concern about homelessness, poverty, and Indians, coupled with fear and envy of the rich and powerful. They like your stance that the rich aren't going to get away with anything with you at the helm. And the best thing is that Blake hasn't reacted to that atmosphere so far. He skewered Sybil on the New Education Plan, and that put him ahead, but he hasn't adjusted to our issues."

"Yes, I was worried when Sybil tried to piggy-back on the Hill trial."

"So was I, but what's hurting her, Waylon, is her new total focus on the oil companies. Somehow she caught the same disease Casper Bell developed. It's very peculiar. If we'd had a recent oil spill or a gas price hike, but this is coming out of the blue."

"Well, Doc, candidates have been running against oil companies in this state for years."

"Yes. She seems to be counting on that, but it's not working this time. She's ten points behind Blake now."

"Doc, do you think our lead will hold?"

"I do, unless Blake adjusts to the issues we've created."

SIMON WONG DINED WITH JAMES BLAKE THAT EVENING. "It seems, Jim, we have slain one beast only to have another confront us. I don't like Homer's new popularity or his Welfare Stamp Funding Committee. No telling what that committee will come up with. These recent polls mean we should consider some of the same issues."

"Hold on, Simon. It's the issues the polls show are winners that really upset me, the apparent focus of voters on this cooked-up, claptrap melange of rich against poor and abuse of Indians. That guy who got shot was as much an Indian as I am. Frankly, I could bear the loss of position in the polls a lot more easily if I thought the voters were using decent judgment."

"You're asking too much of them. Anyway, our own polls show us still ahead in the black and Asian communities. It's the rest of the citizenry that's become captive to Doc Wayward's issues."

Blake sighed. "Maybe so, but it's depressing that the white massas actually buy into that crap. I could understand it if some poor brother with no education got snowed."

"It's feeling guilty, Jim. Feeling guilt is a powerful emotion, and Wayward is working it to Waylon's exclusive benefit, a point that suggests the solution."

"It does?"

"Yes. I've been talking to a former associate of Doc Wayward, Michael St. Augustine."

"A new campaign consultant?"

"Yes. More expense, but we need a new approach. Saint Augustine says there's no reason Homer should enjoy exclusive use of his issues."

"Simon, I hate the idea of starting to throw that crap myself."

"Jim, you've got to adjust to the realities of campaigning. But don't worry, I've already discussed some details with St. Augustine. Our approach will be in good taste, at least relatively. You won't, for example, make any direct reference to the Hill prosecution. We'll stress the general propositions. That's what we've got to hit to reach the voters."

Blake sighed. "OK, Simon, you've been right so far."

THE NEXT DAY, BLAKE GAVE A PRIME-TIME TELEVISION ADDRESS. He began by deploring the "shameless attempts" by certain of his opponents "to exploit the homeless and disadvantaged, including the Native-Americans, by playing upon the fears and concerns of those who are better off. Do such political games help the poor?" he asked. By contrast he went on, a vote for Blake would be a vote for a positive program "addressing these issues."

First, Blake explained that he had had funds placed in trust to provide prize money for the best design of an appropriately heroic-sized Smoking Mother Memorial Statue, which would be erected in Civic Center Park following Blake's election. Everyone's heart, he said, was with the impoverished, and all right-thinking people were disturbed by the wrongs done to the underprivileged, including the Native-American. "This memorial will elevate all our spirits and stand as a fitting tribute to the rights of all to a fair shake. And if I am elected, I will set as my primary goal the attainment of conditions under which all citizens will get a fair shake."

The "fair shake" concept had been the idea of Michael St. Augustine. It was, he pointed out, appealing, while being so vague

178

as to be unintelligible, and thus unenforceable — the finest species of political slogan.

In his television address, Blake went on to point out that by "fair shake" he did not mean that he would tolerate lawlessness or misbehavior in the streets. He referred to "aggressive panhandling" and said he was against it. Neither did he like dirty streets. "The streets should be clean for the people who must live on them."

"And yet," he concluded, "we cannot limit our vigilance merely to surveillance and policing of the poor and of the streets." What had been lacking, he said, was adequate vigilance with respect to behavior of the well-to-do. Then, as the capstone of his speech, he announced that if elected he would establish a special committee of qualified citizens, fully staffed for its task, a staff that would include police officers, to "monitor behavior of the fat cats." This was another St. Augustine concept. Blake went on to explain that the committee, in his administration, would be there to keep a close eye on what the privileged were up to. "This essential step will ensure balanced observation of all social ranks. Heretofore," Blake noted, "surveillance of the privileged had been left to other birds of the same feather and to society columnists. Now those less privileged will have a representative body dedicated to adequate monitoring of the activities of the wealthy."

THAT EVENING, SYBIL WATCH STARED at the draft of her next morning press release with growing anger. In it she promised to halt the widespread "vivisection of ethnic minority children by oil company executives." Normally she did not review the press releases, but her friend, Wanda Cranberry, had raised a question about the content of the recent ones. "Sybil," she said, not a little annoyed, "your press releases are depressing my oil company stocks."

Sybil, carrying the release, went to see her husband. She found him comfortably seated in the parlor with a drink and the latest issue of *Breastworks*. "Wagner, put down that tit magazine for a moment and look at this."

"Yes," he said, staring at the press release. "Lydia Grimes does seem to be pushing the envelope."

"How is it she writes all the press releases?"

"She fired the other girls. Said they were soft on oil companies. I didn't think I should interfere. It was some sort of turf battle."

"Wagner, that girl is crazy. Where is she now?"

"I think she's at a bonfire rally at the Anco refinery. It apparently scares hell out of oil companies to have bonfires at the refineries."

"Hire back those girls she fired. I'm getting rid of her tomorrow."

SHORTLY AFTER HER RESIGNATION FROM THE Watch campaign, Lydia Grimes arrived at the campaign headquarters of Waylon Homer, which were presided over by the staff of "Doc" Wayward. She was interviewed by Dolly Wayward, Doc's daughter and chief of staff.

"Quit Sybil's campaign, eh? Any particular reason?"

"Oh, I'd call it a personality thing, really."

"Well, we're getting down to the wire, and we could use another staffer. Can you write copy?"

"Definitely. I prefer that."

"OK. Take that desk. I'll introduce you to my father later. Here's a draft of a Waylon Homer commentary on Custer's last stand. You know, at the Little Big Horn. See if you can liven it up."

"DOC," ASKED WAYLON HOMER, "did you know the oil companies sent Custer and the Seventh Calvary to the Little Big Horn because they'd discovered oil in the Black Hills, and they wanted the Indians out of there?"

"It was gold that was discovered, not oil. I don't think there were any petroleum operations in the west in 1876."

"That's what I thought. But this commentary in *The Cockerel* that I'm supposed to have written has me saying that oil company greed caused the invasion of the Indians' Black Hills and the consequent death of thousands."

"What? Let me see it. I'll be damned! We've caught the virus."

"The virus?"

"The one the Bell and Watch campaigns had. They went haywire. All the issues turned into attacks on the oil industry."

Doc took the matter up with his daughter.

"A girl named Lydia Grimes wrote it. She just came over to us from the Watch campaign."

"Dolly, pay her off with a bonus and encourage her to seek work with the Blake people. Tell her their issues are more compatible with hers. Do this right away."

"Do you want to meet her?"

"Never."

BUT THE GODS OF FORTUNE WERE SMILING on James Blake. In a burst of nepotism he had just hired three of his relatives for the staff. Michael St. Augustine was sorry. "It's a pity we're full up, Ms. Grimes. You certainly have the right credentials."

And with that, Lydia Grimes was at last retired from the campaigns for the office of mayor. Lydia, as usual, did not despair.

There would always be a role for someone who understood what the oil companies were up to.

As the helicopter bearing the Queen's Own Lumber Company representatives approached the landing space on Nova Cannes, a cloud of brightly colored parrot-like birds rose from the surrounding bush. Jumbo Harris, who was looking directly at them, gasped. The birds resettled themselves as the helicopter came to a stop and the pilot shut off its engine. Harris immediately seized his seatmate's arm. "Bernie, did you see those birds?"

"Yeah. Pretty colors."

"Bernie," Harris whispered, "I could get twenty-five hundred apiece for those in New York."

"Interesting. How do we get them there?"

"Cages. We got to get cages."

"Later. Right now we got to get out and look at this place."

They got out, instantly breaking into a sweat, as the torpid Nova Cannes air surrounded them. "Jesus," said Bernie, "this heat is awful." Bernie was wearing a new, short-sleeved khaki outfit he had purchased in Port Moresby, and the mosquitoes were already at work on his forearms. He slapped fitfully at them.

The pilot observed his discomfort calmly. "You'll need a long-sleeved shirt, mate. Got any in your kit?"

"Yes, but I just bought this shirt. They should tell you."

"Shopkeepers in Moresby don't get up to Nova Cannes, mate. Where's the big guy wanderin' off to?" He pointed at Jumbo, who was headed for the edge of the clearing where the birds, now recomposed, were chattering contentedly.

"Jumbo," Bernie shouted to his cousin, "come back here."

"OK, Bernie. These birds are real friendly. Look how they come right up to me."

"He runs a pet shop," said Bernie, anxious to justify his cousin's strange fascination.

The pilot responded, "They're friendly 'cause the natives think they're sacred. Nobody goes after them. Look, pitch your tents right here. Best part of the island. Rest is socked in with trees and creepers."

"Where do we get water?" Dr. Clapp looked about dismally at the site of his paid vacation.

The pilot laughed. "You drink this bottled stuff we brought, mate. And if it's a bath you're thinkin' of, there's a stream right back there." He gestured toward one end of the clearing. "But you best keep an eye out for crocs. They're in all the streams. Nasty buggers. They go twenty feet up here."

Pularski, the botanist, was staring at the tall trees. "I've never seen this species," he offered absently, wiping his forehead and sighing.

The pilot patted him on the back. "Everything's different up here, mate." Turning to Bernie he added, "Before I pull out, be sure your radio is working."

It was working, and the helicopter departed. Despite the enervating heat, Bernie saw the need for exertion to set up camp before dark. He tried to recall the practices of his days as a Boy Scout, but all he could remember distinctly was the procedure for digging latrines. He sent Pularski and Jumbo in pursuit of firewood, while he and Clapp attempted to erect the two tents. It was a fatiguing and confusing process. One tent was partially erected when Pularski and Jumbo returned with a canvas full of wood.

Pularski looked discouraged. "I swung my axe at one of those big trees, and the axe bounced back at me. It's like that Australian in Port Moresby said, it'll be like sawing stone."

"Tomorrow we'll take a good look. There's probably other species."

"There are, Bernie, but they're no good for lumber. All like this firewood or smaller, bush-like stuff." Pularski was emphatic.

Jumbo was carefully sorting the wood into two piles. What with everything else, this seemingly useless process exasperated Bernie. "Jumbo, what the hell are you doing with the wood? Come help with the tents."

Jumbo ceased his sorting. "Yeah. I'll help with the tents." When he was close to his cousin he said softly, "I can make cages with that wood in case we can't get any real cages from Port Moresby."

"Jumbo, you're nuts. Do you expect those birds to walk into the cages?"

"Yeah, more or less. They're real friendly. Listen, Bernie, we could take maybe thirty back to Port Moresby and package them proper there for flying home. That's seventy-five thousand bucks."

"How do we get thirty screeching birds past customs?"

"Bernie, I told you. I know how to get that done in the Port of New York."

"It sounds like trouble to me. Look, where does this orange pole go?"

"Bernie, calm down. I'll fix it." And true to his word, Jumbo soon had both tents standing. Then he returned to his woodpiles. As dusk fell, the two sat covered in mosquito netting, drank some beer and ate. Jumbo completed three cages before going to bed.

He was also the first one to rise the next day. Taking one of the cages and some crackers, he went over to the area where the exotic birds were roosting. They greeted him cheerfully, and, as before, made no attempt to flee. He put the cage on the ground and broke a trail of cracker crumbs from inside it toward the perched birds. Three of them dismounted and began to peck at the crumbs. In due course they were inside the cage, which easily held three birds. He did not shut the cage. The experiment was a success. When the time came, he would put out ten cages at once, with enough crackers in them to keep the occupants engaged while he shut all the cages. That way he would not scare off the rest by caging three of them now. Thirty birds, seventy-five thousand bucks, he mused, his enthusiasm undiminished by the heat and mosquitoes. Nor did he detect the two Trumani tribesmen in the neighboring bush who had witnessed him luring the sacred birds into the cage. These presently departed to report the situation to Tallfellow.

25. OPENING STATEMENTS

THERE WERE NO BAAA MERRY MEN at the courthouse when Penny and her companions arrived the next morning. Playchek patted Peter on the back. "Maybe your friend in Boston can get the case dismissed, too."

"He said he couldn't do anything about that. Just the Aryans."

Inside the courtroom, workers were erecting a massive new array of video cameras. Playchek asked the court clerk about it. "The judge's wife saw some of yesterday's proceedings on the late news and was dissatisfied. We almost didn't have court today, but the media people rushed this new stuff out here. Now the judge is willing to proceed, and they've given Mrs. Flex a monitor."

"What's that other thing she's got?"

"It's a VCR. That way she can tape anything she wants to discuss with the judge or the media."

Later, Judge Flex explained the situation to the jurors. "My wife, Dora, has graciously consented to monitor the televising of the trial. That way, we can correct for any deficiencies as we go along. Innovation, ladies and gentlemen, is as important to the administration of justice as the law itself." He paused, visibly pleased with this observation. "Now, today we are going to have opening statements from the prosecution and the defense. It's important for you to remember that these statements made by the lawyers are not evidence. I used to put it more simply and tell juries that they should not assume that the lawyers will tell them the truth, but I was unfairly criticized for putting it that way, so I don't do it anymore.

"This is not the time when the lawyers argue the case; that comes after we've heard all the witnesses. At this point, they are just supposed to give you an idea of what the evidence will be, a guide to what the case is about." He turned to Tremorgan Davies. "Mr. Davies, are you ready to proceed?"

"Yes, Your Honor." And Davies began, standing by the rail of the jury box and speaking in a soft voice. "On the day of his death, ladies and gentlemen, this gentle soul, called Smoking Mother by his many friends and other homeless persons, whose vile murder brings us here today, this young, innocent victim rose with expectation, with hope. It was to be the last morning of his life." Here Davies's eyes fell, as if he were suddenly overwhelmed by sadness at the thoughts he had expressed.

When he was able to continue he had slightly sharpened the tone of his voice. "As the judge told you, this is not a time for argument, but rather for a calm appraisal of the real issue." Davies laid emphasis on the word "real." "It is my job to provide guidance to help you understand that issue, sort of a roadmap to reach the proper verdict." He paused, and his face took on the look of one who is restraining some deeply felt emotion. "But it is often hard to stifle a voice that wants to cry out in support of the right to life of the homeless, the abused, the American Indian. Especially so here, faced with the wanton execution of an impoverished child of the streets by a member of the perfidious ruling class. So I hope you will forgive me if I raise that voice from time to time.

"It is a great privilege to represent the people, and a great responsibility, too, a responsibility you, as jurors, share. It is your responsibility to see that justice is done; that a crime does not go unpunished which tears at the very fabric of society. We have here the slaughter of a poor beggar, a person whose only crime was being poor, by an idle woman living in luxury, surrounded by servants, closets stuffed with expensive clothes. Ladies and gentlemen, it was that sort of decadent, predatory lifestyle pursued by the upper classes that destroyed the Roman Empire and the Ming Dynasty, and doomed the realm of the Incas.

"Indeed, the issue on which you must focus goes to the very principles on which this country was founded and on which its survival is staked: the protection of the weak from the strong, the poor from the wealthy. The law must redress infamy such as took place on those library steps or our country will fall like Rome, like Ming, like South America. That is our responsibility, yours and mine."

He sipped from a glass of water, re-approached the jury box. "Now," he said confidingly, "during the voir dire, as each of you sat there, I asked myself, is this juror a person who would pledge to fulfill the obligation to right this wrong? Could I be confident that this person would not, under the pressure of conflicting facts, lose focus? Would he or she be able to concentrate throughout the trial on the overriding issue, which is, what are we in this courtroom, who have the responsibility and the opportunity, going to do about the constant oppression of the poor and humble by the rich and powerful?

"What we can do, and I say it is our obligation to do it, is to send a message to the world outside that here in this courtroom we have lifted a hand to help the downtrodden in their unequal struggle with the forces of oppression. You send that message by convicting this representative of oppression, the defendant Penny Hill. That is an obligation you should feel you have, no matter what the facts that may be presented during the trial. For I must warn you that the defense will throw a lot of facts at you. They will seek to confuse you with this and that piece of evidence in an effort to undermine your focus on the issue. But if you keep the issue ever foremost in your minds, concentrating on the proposition that the privileged must be brought to account for what they have done to the poor, you will not be deceived by any facts the defense presents.

"To illustrate how facts may be employed to confuse and to blunt your vision, consider what that woman did" — he pointed fiercely at Penny — "as Smoking Mother lay expiring at her feet. She accused him of purse snatching! So you can expect them to try to make this cold-blooded society matron the victim and the innocent boy the villain. But you know better. You know that that scenario does not fit the issue, and the issue cannot be altered by facts. Facts that would lead you away from the issue, from fulfilling your obligation, should be rejected as untrustworthy.

"I call it the tyranny of facts. You must not submit to such tyranny. Just focus on the issue and the message you want to send."

His voice fell a notch. "Yet such facts do show something consistent with the issue. They show the heartlessness of the accused. Standing there above the dying boy, hurling accusations. Ladies and gentlemen, there are standards of humanity that you, as jurors, must impose on the accused, lest more of her class follow her example, and other humble folk end their days expiring and accused at aristocratic feet."

Playchek rose slowly. "Your Honor, I know the court does not favor interruption of opening statements, and I have held my peace until now, but I must object that what counsel is saying is so improper that it would not even be permitted in closing argument."

"Well," said Judge Flex, shaking his head, "I can't rule now on what is proper for closing argument. This is opening statement, counsel, and this is a highly charged case. There's bound to be some emotion involved. Overruled. Proceed."

"Thank you, Your Honor. Now I was commenting on the victim expiring there at Ms. Hill's expensively shod feet, perhaps the same shoes she wears today — "

Playchek leaped up. "Your Honor, that's so improper he ought to be sanctioned."

"Mr. Playchek, how do we know? They may not be the same shoes. Overruled."

Davies began again. "Exactly, ladies and gentlemen, we may never know if they are the same shoes, any more than we know what led Smoking Mother on his fatal course to the library. But there he crossed the path of the perpetrator of this heinous crime." He pointed at Penny again. "And there she sits, bathed in the blood of his youth." A juror gasped.

"Their paths crossed, the hungry street youth and the well-heeled and well-armed society matron. She had zero tolerance for beggars, and she had the concealed weapon in her purse. It flashed, killing him. The bullet entered the very middle of his forehead. This was no attempt to frighten off a beggar. She meant to reduce the ranks of beggars then and there. He was a social annoyance, expendable, and she exterminated him, as she would grind her sharp heel into a small animal."

Davies took another drink of water. A woman juror was sobbing uncontrollably. "Yes, ladies and gentlemen, it is a cause for tears," said Davies, "but you'll see no tears there." He pointed again at Penny. "There is a kind of heartlessness in so many of the rich and powerful that you and I will never really understand. They see their social inferiors, for that is how they think of us, as not deserving human kindness. We see this callous exercise of power all around us. How many of you have suffered at the hands of the rich and powerful? How many of you have seen those in power at your place of employment promote less able people than yourselves when you deserved promotion but were denied it?

"You know, ladies and gentlemen, I cite these matters that go beyond the immediate facts of this case because in performing your duty as jurors you are entitled, obliged, to consider the overall context in which these crimes and oppressions by the rich and powerful occur. You don't leave your personal experience on the courthouse steps when you come in here. You bring it with you, and you all know and may consider in reaching your verdict the well-known conspiracies of the rich and powerful to exploit and suppress ordinary people. Consider, for example, how people are penniless and reduced to dependence on begging in sections of the world where the international banking cartel has cornered the money market. I don't have to explain. You all know what I mean.

"But the pinnacle of iniquity is reached when the rich and powerful personally take up arms against the less advantaged and take their lives, when in so many cases the victim's labors have been the basis of the criminal's wealth."

Playchek whispered to Penny. "He's getting close to where he talks about his ancestors dying in the Welsh coal mines."

"It seems a pity the mines didn't get all of them," she responded.

A great rumbling noise coming from outside the courtroom was now heard, and of a sudden the large twin doors to the court opened inward and disclosed a man in overalls and a baseball cap. Behind him two other men were maneuvering a giant dolly on which lay two tall and luxuriant palm trees, each in a wooden tub. "Bring 'em right down here," said the man in the baseball cap. "They go up there by the judge's bench."

Dora Flex stood and in an elated voice declared, "Oh look, Potter, the palms are here." She moved into the aisle down which the dolly was being pushed, the palm fronds flapping importantly. "They go on each side of the bench. Right here and there." She gestured, beamed at her husband. "The place looked so bare, and with live TV and everything, I just thought we had to do better."

Judge Flex nodded. "Very nice, dear."

"These will help a lot," added Dora, making way for the tree men, who with much ado succeeded in establishing their cargo on either side of Judge Flex's bench. "Not quite there on that one," cautioned Dora, exhibiting a fine sense of proportion. "It needs to be more to the left."

"I feel just like Cleopatra," said Penny in a low voice to Playchek, as the workmen brought the palms to the vertical.

"Palms do furnish a court," replied Playchek, marveling at their tropical presence. In place on either side of Judge Flex, the palms gave to the bench and its occupant the sense of a movie set for a biblical epic, the jurist seated, Pilate-like, elevated, magnificent, the green fronds arching above him, mysteriously enhancing his cosmetic tan.

"There now, "said Dora Flex, "isn't that lovely?" And addressing the jury she added, "You don't often see palms indoors, do you?"

There was murmured agreement with this proposition. "Lady," said the leader of the tree men, "you better open that skylight." He pointed at the high courtroom ceiling. "These trees are used to bein' outside."

"Oh yes. Potter, can you have them open the skylight?"

The judge's clerk took charge. "I'll call the building engineer." A recess was taken during which the skylight was opened. When court resumed, Davies, now partially shaded by palm trees, continued with his opening statement.

"I have been helping you put this crime in its proper overall context," he began. "I want now to turn to a matter more personal but equally relevant. My ancestors come from Wales, where the men in the family labored in the coal pits for the rich, absentee mine owners. In those days there were no forces to restrain the powerful from exploiting the common man. My great-grandfather died of black lung from the soot in the mines, slaving to make his oppressors wealthy. It was the mine conditions imposed by wealthy and powerful persons like this defendant that killed him." Two more jurors began to sob.

Playchek rose. "I object, Your Honor, to the prosecutor invoking his family history to prejudice my client."

Judge Flex pondered the matter, making some notes on a pad before him, then ruled. "Well, it may be a bit remote, but if it could be shown — I have just kind of thought through it briefly and made some notes — if it could be shown that forefathers of the victim in our case had black lung because of conditions imposed by ancestors of the defendant, then there might be some ancestral tendency that was relevant. Given that, and the fact that we've yet to see what the evidence will be in this case, I'll overrule the objection. You may move to strike counsel's remarks, Mr. Playchek, if he fails to connect it up later. Proceed."

Davies proceeded. "Back in those days in the Welsh mines, there were no unions or jurors to save my great-grandfather or others like him from oppression by the ruling class. But, ladies and gentlemen, a conviction here in this case will be paid attention to in the spacious homes of the wealthy, in the boardrooms of the big corporations, and in every exploitative seat of power. They'll be saying 'a jury held one of us to account. We had best moderate our behavior.' That is the message you must send."

Davies had intended to stop at this point, but he thought of the lucky letter in his breast pocket, the one from his mother. With Flex's rulings today, it seemed likely Flex would not limit him to invoking his great-grandfather, but would let his mother get into the record as well. "You know, ladies and gentlemen, I was just recently talking to my mother about this case."

Playchek began to rise.

"And she said to me, 'Tremmy,'— she always calls me 'Tremmy'—'that woman took another's life—'"

"Objection, Your Honor. He's got his mother telling the jury the ultimate fact in the case. I ask that you instruct the jury to disregard his mother's opinions and that Mr. Davies not give us any more of them."

Judge Flex appeared disturbed. "Well now, counsel, I have always respected the opinions of my mother, so I don't feel at all comfortable telling a jury to disregard the opinions of someone else's mother." He looked at Mrs. Flex, who was nodding emphatically in agreement.

"But, Your Honor," said Playchek, "this is the worst kind of hearsay."

"Nothing of the kind, Your Honor," responded Davies confidently. "Everything my mother said can be corroborated." He drew the letter from his coat pocket. "I have a letter here from my mother corroborating everything she told me verbally. We can read it to the jury."

Judge Flex nodded. "Do you want him to read the letter, Mr. Playchek?"

"Of course not, Your Honor. That would just make it worse."

"Well then, counsel, we have to move along. Justice delayed is justice denied. Overruled. Proceed, Mr. Davies."

"Thank you, Your Honor. I was saying, she told me, 'Tremmy, that woman took another's life as sure as God made green apples.'" A shy smile crossed his underlying, more serious expression. "Mom makes apple pie with green pippins. Well, she told me, 'Tremmy, you must see that justice is done, so other high-society folks won't take example and start reducing their taxes by exterminating the poor.' There were tears in her eyes, ladies and gentlemen. I know my mother, and she meant what she said, and she always tells the truth. So it's up to all of us to join hands, so to speak, and send that message. Just like mother said we should. Thank you."

"We'll take a recess," said Judge Flex.

DURING THE RECESS, PLAYCHEK SOUGHT to cheer up the defense group, which had grown angry and downcast during Davies's opening statement. "That's going to be the high point of the trial for Tremmy," he said brightly.

Sayer was not so sure. "There's still the verdict to come. Three of the jurors are in tears already."

"We'll straighten that out. Listen, did you notice he hardly mentioned Indians? He's leery. That might even keep the Smoking Mother mother out of court."

"But," said Penny, "Davies will bring in his own mother to restate her opinions."

"True," said Playchek, "It's 'Mother Knows Best' in this court. Anyway, we also know he hasn't got an eyeball witness. He waltzed all around the shooting without saying you shot him. All he's got is Wendy Papp's 'she must have shot him.'"

"Barton," said Penny, "I really want to testify. I don't want to have to listen to that populist windbag make a closing argument without having told my story."

"You know how I feel about that."

"I don't care, Barton. I want these people to hear the real facts. All that crap. I don't own any mines. I haven't cornered the money market. I have no idea what shoes I was wearing. Well, yes I do. I remember because they took them away at the Hall of Justice and gave me bunny slippers."

"Penny, you're overreacting to Davies's bullshit. Forget it. And we can't talk rationally about you testifying until we see how the other witnesses go."

The jury returned, all now dry-eyed, followed by the judge, Mrs. Flex, and the court's makeup man. "Mr. Playchek, are you ready to proceed?" Judge Flex inquired.

"Yes, Your Honor." Playchek began with a brief biography of Penny, followed by a linear account of the events on the day of the accident. He explained about the old family pistol and why it was still in her purse when she went to the library. He explained the attempt to snatch her purse, the fall of the purse, and the discharge of the gun. An expert, he said, would explain how the gun could discharge from a fall. As he progressed in his explanation of her innocence, the attention given to it by the jury progressively diminished. Not all jurors, but most, appeared to be bored, and at least two, in Playchek's estimation, showed signs of disbelief. As he had expected, outright innocence was a scenario that simply did not appeal to them.

This was as apparent to Penny as it was to Playchek. At the next recess, she told him gloomily that his prediction before trial looked to be accurate.

"Yeah, they started tuning out as soon as I said you didn't shoot the gun. They simply don't want to hear that all this was just an accident. But we'll get their attention back when I take up the diminished-capacity defense. That's what they want to hear, and they know it's coming."

He began to do so right after the recess.

"Ladies and gentlemen, as you know, we contend Ms. Hill must be acquitted because she did not shoot the decedent. But we also contend that even if she did, which she has, of course, no recollection of doing, her capacity to distinguish right from wrong was so diminished that she could not comprehend it was wrong to do so, and she must be acquitted for that reason.

"She is the real victim at this trial in two senses: First, because the fatal encounter took place when the deceased tried to rob her. Regrettably, she has also been victimized in a more insidious fashion. Your sympathy should be with a woman who may be rich in worldly goods but who is poor in mind, whose reasoning has been impaired by years of exposure to the misleading representations and promises of California politicians, and to the rhetoric of those who campaign for them. Now I don't exempt political figures on the national scene from fault in this process, but their contribution is minor relative to the more-or-less constant drivel of our local people.

"How does this affect a person's capacity to distinguish right from wrong? Consider the endless stream of words and pictures we live under that are dedicated to blurring that distinction, and needless to say, to blurring the distinction between truth and falsehood. We see measures to increase taxes and limit public benefits presented as increases in benefits and reductions in taxes. Propositions whose enactment will result in the loss of thousands of jobs are tendered by groups with names like, 'Citizens for Full Employment'. This fog of campaign mendacity never lifts. We are constantly bombarded by projections of white made to look black, up made to appear down, false made to look true, and wrong made to look right.

"Ms. Hill has been exposed to these influences all her life, during all of which she has lived here in San Francisco, which many consider the epicenter of California humbug. But whether the true epicenter is here, or in Los Angeles or Sacramento, the fact is that for years in this state, truth and falsity, right and wrong, the very meaning of words, have been turned upside-down, distorted and debased until, for some of us, it is impossible to distinguish right from wrong. Not all of us, thank goodness, are so affected. You and I have so far escaped impairment, or so we believe. But the more sensitive souls, like Ms. Hill, who are especially at risk, have had their minds bent by the ubiquitous poppycock of the politicians and the vote grinders. The message this jury should be sending to the world outside the courtroom is not one of class hatred, as you have been invited to do by the prosecution, but one that tells the office seekers and vote doctors to shut up! We don't want to hear any more lies! Cease the kind of mind damaging rhetoric that victimized this poor woman. Acquit Penny Hill and send that message.

"I tell you I was astonished when I first detected the evidence of her impairment. We, her lawyers, were to have dinner with her. At her suggestion we went to a new restaurant south of Market Street, which featured what was called 'authentic California plains cuisine.' Once there, Ms. Hill insisted that we all order the 'wilted buffalo salad with organic prairie grass.' Why this extraordinary demand on her part? She had been exposed to the campaign of a group seeking to convert open space into buffalo pasture. Buffalo would be raised there for consumption. The thrust of this campaign was that the only way to save the buffalo from extinction was to expand the market for its meat. Ms. Hill explained this to me without showing any comprehension that buried under the economic rationale was the terrible premise that the more of these shaggy beasts we butcher and eat, the better for the buffalo.

It set me to thinking about her state of mind at the time that great brute grabbed at her purse. I persuaded her to visit Dr. Greta Sweetbacken, a renowned mental health counselor who will testify in this case — "

There was a shout from behind Playchek's back. "Potter! Something's wrong!" It was the judge's wife. She was standing pointing at her TV monitor.

"What is it, dear?"

"My screen's gone blank, Potter. Make them fix it."

"Yes, of course, dear. We'll take a recess."

DURING THE RECESS, Playchek took Penny aside. "Sayer tells me everyone on the jury is following closely except your beloved Mr. Barrow, the careener."

"I know, Barton. I've been watching too. He doesn't like it because it's bullshit. He looked at me a couple of times, and his face showed that. He doesn't think I'm bonkers, but he doesn't think I shot Smoking Mother, either."

"You put too much faith in men. Anyway, the rest of them are finally getting interested in our case."

There was another shout. It was Dora Flex. "There! It's working. My foot must have caught on the wire. The plug came out." She sat down and began to fiddle with the controls. Satisfied, she turned to the clerk. "All right, tell the judge we can get started."

When court resumed, Playchek returned to Dr. Sweetbacken's examination of Penny. "Dr. Sweetbacken soon suspected the local political environment, with its nonstop bending of the line between right and wrong, truth and falsehood. She had another patient similarly afflicted. She queried Ms. Hill about the history of her exposure to politician and lobbyist cant and found that, while the degree of exposure was not greater than with the rest of us, in Ms. Hill's case the damage had been severe because she had, in Dr. Sweetbacken's words, 'a lower threshold of resistance to humbug.' She was a more sensitive and vulnerable person.

"To test her thesis, Dr. Sweetbacken asked Ms. Hill about selected representations and programs of politicians from our state. She used several drawn from the administration of our former governor, Harry Lovebird, including his program to reduce crime by treating criminals with more respect. She brought up the subject of Lovebird's packing the State Supreme Court with his own appointees by lowering the mandatory retirement age to thirty-five, thus forcing the existing justices off the bench. She asked Ms. Hill for her reaction to the obligatory Lovebird staff mantra, 'Love and Peace in Harry Increase.' She then asked my client about current governor Pelton Throwback's election campaign promises, including the ones to stop 'unwelcome changes' and to improve the physical appearance of voters by providing free, state-run liposuction clinics, the expense to be offset by government sales of bathing apparel. Lamentably, Ms. Hill was unable to see the falsehood, fallacy, or lack of sense in any of the examples Dr. Sweetbacken put to her. My client's capacity to distinguish right from wrong had been completely undermined by the same kind of humbug implicit in the examples.

"Dr. Sweetbacken concluded, as she will testify here, that — "

Davies cut him off. "Objection, Your Honor. Counsel is predicting the opinion of an expert who has yet to be sworn or qualified."

Judge Flex pondered the objection. "It is not," he concluded, "a prediction because Mr. Playchek has evidently already heard the opinion. And it seems to me improper that he should be the only one who knows what it is. We're all interested, so I'll over-rule the objection. Proceed."

"Thank you, Your Honor. Dr. Sweetbacken concluded that even if Smoking Mother was not trying to steal her purse, Ms. Hill certainly believed that he was, and that if she shot the deceased, she lacked the capacity to determine whether her act was right or wrong."

There came a sudden, whirring sound from the upper reaches of the courtroom, and a swarm of middle-sized black birds poured through the skylight and settled into the palms, chittering loudly. Dora Flex leaped to her feet. "Out," she shouted. "Get out!" She waved her arms. The birds, resistant to threatening movements or commands in spoken English, merely fluttered and chittered louder. Judge Flex's gavel was likewise ineffective.

His clerk responded once again. "I'll call the building engineer." In due course, two men arrived bearing long poles.

"Hurry," said Dora, "they're beginning to make droppings." The men poked at the palm fronds, unsettling some of the birds. These squawked and flew about. Then, as suddenly as they had appeared, the flock rose as one and departed through the skylight. A short recess was taken while bird droppings were cleaned from the bench and its surroundings.

"We'll put a screen over the skylight, lady," said the building engineer. "Those birds are starlings, and there's lots of them around City Hall."

"Yes, thank you," said Dora, her own feathers resuming a position of repose. "We can continue, Mr. Playchek." And Playchek continued.

"Now, ladies and gentlemen, this is an important trial, and it is important that it mean something, that its result have some beneficial effect from a public viewpoint. Only then will you, as jurors, feel that your service has been worthwhile. The defense of Penny Hill is not just about Penny Hill. It is about the defense, the protection, of all the people out there who, as Dr. Sweetbacken put it, have 'a lower threshold of resistance to humbug.' And for that matter, for those of us who may have greater resistance to it but are sick of living in a humbug-saturated environment.

"By acquitting Penny Hill, you will be telling the politicians, spin doctors, and other scramblers of right and wrong that you aren't going to take it any more. It is your chance to make a difference. By rallying 'round this woman they have damaged, perhaps for life, you will be showing them that at least in this corner of the state, the public has closed ranks against the pimps of deception, the panderers of confusion. That is the real issue, and that is the message this trial affords you the chance to send. Thank you."

26. Plant and Animal Behavior

Notwithstanding Pularski's discouraging evaluation of the timber on Nova Cannes, Bernie determined that an inspection be made of the local trees. The ones near the campsite responded as had the one Pularski had struck: the axe bounced off the trunk unless the blow was sharply downward, in which case a shallow cut was possible. An attempt to chain saw a trunk ended in despair and perspiration when Jumbo and Pularski's efforts produced only a minor invasion of the tree and damaged the saw's teeth.

Bernie then led the unhappy group into the surrounding jungle in search of more pliable trees. They were soon covered with leeches, and the dim light led to frequent stumbling and falls. In this fashion, Bernie sprained his ankle tripping on a vine. Thereafter, the ankle throbbed painfully, despite a brace applied by Dr. Clapp.

At the end of the day, they returned to camp disheartened and exhausted, having found no trees suitable for lumber. Bernie and Jumbo were nursing beers. "Bernie, that Farrington guy was telling the truth. There's been some mistake. This island doesn't fit the file."

"I know, Jumbo; I just hate to give up so quick."

"Don't. Stay another couple days. That way I can finish these cages and bag some birds."

Bernie's ankle produced a sharp jolt of pain. "Damn the birds!"

"Bernie, I'll split the return with you. And I been thinking. We take thirty out this trip. You stay in Port Moresby, and I'll buy some real cages and make another trip. There's so many birds."

"Farrington isn't going to use the helicopter to ferry birds for you."

"We tell him we're still inspecting. I'll get twenty cages — that's sixty more birds. After taking care of customs, we'll make two hundred thousand."

"You can really get twenty-five hundred apiece for them in the States?"

"At least. Trust me."

Trust was not part of Bernie's nature, but avarice was. "OK, we'll stay two more days, and you can make one more trip. Then, it's back to the Big Apple."

WHEN TALLFELLOW WAS TOLD that newly arrived white men were caging sacred birds, it seemed further fulfillment of Big Mouth's prophecy of trouble. He went at once to the Big Mouth sanctuary and reported the matter to the deity.

Big Mouth's instructions were clear: on no account were the white men to be allowed to capture the birds, but it were better to try to avoid having to kill the intruders. Tallfellow should inform the Ellen woman and enlist her assistance. Then he fell silent, but Tallfellow knew he was still present in the sanctuary. Finally Big Mouth began to speak again.

There had been, Big Mouth declared, nothing but trouble since Peter had been summoned away from the island. He should return here so as to break the bad luck pattern that his departure appeared to have created. Big Mouth understood the problem in San Francisco, but he did not understand it well enough. He must go there to see what he could do to facilitate Peter's return to Nova

Cannes. Tallfellow, on his part, should facilitate the departure of the newly arrived whites.

TALLFELLOW TOLD ELLEN ABOUT his communion with Big Mouth, and of Big Mouth's imminent departure for San Francisco. He explained about the new white men and the sacred birds.

Ellen sighed. It was a matter of some delicacy discussing what a god could or could not do. "I don't think he can stop the trial, and Peter won't come back until it's over."

Tallfellow nodded. "It is not Big Mouth's way to intervene directly in human affairs, but He thought He might be able to facilitate Peter's return if He had more information on the problem across the water. Big Mouth eat more," he added.

"Big Mouth eat more," Ellen repeated. "What's this business about the birds?"

"Big Mouth thought you could help resolve the problem without us having to kill these sacrilegious poachers. He said killing them would just bring more trouble from across the water."

"Yes. How many of them are there?"

"Only four. And only one was disturbing the birds."

"OK," said Ellen, "here's what we'll do."

BERNIE'S PARTY WAS GATHERED AROUND Jumbo and the ten cages. Trails of crackers led to the cages, and they were already beginning to fill with birds. Jumbo clucked excitedly at his colorful prisoners, and knelt to shut the gates to those cages that already held three birds. Suddenly, two Trumani spears were hurled into the ground near his knees, and all four white men looked up from the birds to see the circle of club- and spear-wielding warriors.

"Jesus," said Bernie, "where did these guys come from?" At his words, a chorus of threatening sounds came from the mouths of the savages, whose penis sheaths bobbed as they shook their weapons.

Pularski remembered what the pilot had said about the birds. "Bernie, the pilot said these birds are sacred. These guys with the clarinets on their pricks are unhappy that we're messing with them."

Ellen spoke, emerging for the first time into view of the white men. "It's worse than that. You have already violated the sanctity of the birds and been condemned to death by 'these guys with the clarinets,' the Trumani." Then, pointing at Jumbo, she added, "You with the fat neck. Open the cages and then lie down on your back, or in a second you're going to look like a pincushion."

Jumbo hesitated. Bernie didn't. "Jumbo, do as she says!" Jumbo did. The birds began to wander about, happily hunting down the rest of the crackers, oblivious to the drama surrounding them.

"I don't know if I can do anything to help you," said Ellen. "The Trumani are very serious about religious matters, and they impose the death penalty for just about any sacrilege."

Bernie believed her. "Miss, I guess you're the anthropologist Farrington told us about. We're from The Queen's Own Lumber Company, but we're finished here. There's no suitable lumber. We didn't know the birds were so sacred. Please tell them we will leave the island forever and never bother them again. We just have to radio for the helicopter."

"What is your name?"

"Bernard Cronin. I'm in charge of the expedition."

"And who is the bird-man?"

"Jumbo Harris, but he'll never touch another bird."

"I will speak to them." Ellen began to talk to Tallfellow in Trumani. He appeared to be arguing with her. His men raised their weapons and bellowed. Ellen turned back to Bernie. "He says that if you were the proper color they would roast you and eat you, make what they call 'long pig' of you. They're cannibals. Fortunately, they've already discovered they don't like the way whites turn out when barbecued. They would still like to kill you."

"Miss, please, we can have nice things sent up here for them. I have a budget. I'll send them processed food, potato chips, beer. There must be something they need. Like we're paying a fine. Please tell the big guy that."

Ellen resumed speaking with Tallfellow in Trumani. After a moment she turned back to Bernie. Do you operate the radio?"

"Yes."

"Go call in the helicopter. Don't explain now or when you get back to Moresby what happened. Just say you want out ASAP. All you take with you is the radio. They don't want junk food, but they'll put your gear to use." She pointed to Jumbo. "He stays here on his back until the chopper arrives."

FARRINGTON GREETED THE SOMBER GROUP on its arrival at the Port Moresby heliport. "Good decision you've made to pull out. And you know, mate, I've been thinking; I told you going in that the file description didn't fit Nova Cannes but sounded familiar. Remember?"

Bernie's ankle injury had been aggravated during the escape from the island, and his failure there made him dislike Farrington all the more. "Yes, I remember. What of it?"

"I think it's Norwalk Island. It's one of the Tribal Territories, about nine hundred miles from here. Plenty of harbors and timber for construction. They ran out of potash a bit back and been looking for a leg up. Want me to check with headquarters?"

For a moment, the success or failure of Philo Spass' grand design hung in the balance. There was enough money in the exploratory budget to get to Norwalk and inspect the site, but not enough to finance a new exploratory party from the States. Bernie's companions, their reward based on time served, were still game. But over Bernie and his pulsing ankle there came a sudden nostalgia for the hurly-burly of the Queens County courthouse, the sweating clients, even for Shirley with her golfing buddies and football tapes.

"No, don't bother headquarters. Our authorization was for Nova Cannes, not someplace else. We'll be heading back for Sydney and the States."

And so for Norwalk Island there would be no boardwalks and T-shirt shops. Its economy and forests would continue to languish, unimproved by the modern world.

MICHAEL ST. AUGUSTINE ENTERED James Blake's office wearing a big smile. "We're back in front, Jim. The polls look really good. What's more, the Smoking Mother Memorial design contest is getting a lot of attention. The judges have received over thirty submissions. I released one of the more spectacular to the media."

"What does it look like?"

"Smoking Mother is standing, heroic-sized, in Indian garb, with a big knife in one hand and shading his eyes with the other. He is looking into the distance. There's a Custer-like cavalry officer lying dead at his feet. It's sort of a Little Big Horn tableau. There were, as you might expect, a couple of actual scalping scenes submitted. One was quite shocking."

"To think that blond honky might go down in history as a great Indian warrior — it's enough to make you cry."

"Don't cry, Jim; that's what the people want. These polls show it. They're back on your bandwagon. Of course, the committee to monitor fat cats proposal is pushing up the ratings too. We're getting a lot of letters from people who want a job spying on the rich, especially from police officers who want onto the staff. They want to switch to the program because it gets them out from under the Lint Law Enforcement Control Act."

"They figure they can get back to using force with the fat cats, eh?"

"Something like that."

"My mother thinks I've demeaned myself by carrying on just like the rest of the politicians, but she wants me to be elected."

"Yes, that's the problem. You can't get elected without carrying on like a politician. The public wouldn't take your candidacy seriously if you didn't give them a little song and dance."

"Mike, do you think it's like this everywhere?"

"Well, here in California the essence is perhaps purer. It's like what I just read in *The Cockerel* that the lawyer for Penny Hill told the jury. We've all been raised on humbug."

27. THOUGHTS OF THE GREAT HELMSMAN AND OTHER DISORDERS

SONIA TAFT WAS HAVING TROUBLE seeing eye to eye with Wendy Papp. The latter's did not focus well or for very long. Tula Fogg had brought the girl to City Hall and summoned Sonia to the prosecution's witness room. Over her new sweater and jeans Wendy wore an ancient fur coat dyed to a brownish orange. She smiled a lot, and between puffs on her cigarette tapped ash onto the carpet. Sonia looked at Wendy and the coat. It was not a pleasing prospect.

"You can leave your coat here, Ms. Papp," said Sonia. "You won't need it in court. It's quite warm in there."

"No way! Flo lent it to me. She wants me to look nice in court." She spoke with a pronounced slur and added unresponsively, "That rich bitch shot him." A pause followed, and she repeated the accusation, this time in a louder voice, followed by a hiccup.

"The coat belongs to Flora Grebe," said Tula. "She was wearing it yesterday when I met her."

Sonia took Tula into the hall. "She's stoned, Tula. How in hell did that happen?"

"I don't know, Ms. Taft. She insisted on having breakfast in

Mrs. Grebe's room. They really hit it off, you know. They sent me downstairs to wait."

"She must have had some booze with her in the taxi. The trouble is, we can't really start off with any other witness. Get her some black coffee. I'll tell Davies to try to stall things for a bit."

Davies was told. "How bad is she?"

"Well, her eyes are funny and she talks with a slur, but she keeps saying, 'That rich bitch shot him.'"

"She does, eh?"

"Yes, over and over."

"She's getting coffee now?"

"Tula's doing that. We can't figure out how she got stoned. She had breakfast with Flora Grebe. Wendy must have had a flask or something with her and nipped on the way over here."

"Well, she's got to be the first witness, Sonia."

"Can you stall things for a bit?"

"If it weren't for the judge's wife, we could probably get the morning off, but she's told him to keep the trial moving."

"I know. I heard her say she wants fewer and shorter recesses, too. She doesn't want the trial to run into some vacation she's got planned."

"I can probably get us a half-hour. Go and see how the coffee is working."

When Sonia returned to the witness room, Wendy Papp was slumped in a chair, her eyes closed, the orange fur enveloping her. She looked like a painted bear. "She drank the coffee and fell asleep," said Tula. "I didn't think I should wake her."

"No. We'll let her sleep for half an hour. Did she say anything?"

"She said, 'That rich bitch shot him' a couple more times and then, just before she fell asleep, she wanted to know where Mrs. Grebe was. 'Where's old Flo?' she asked me. I told her, and she wanted to go back to the hotel. They really have hit it off."

"Don't let her out of your sight. I'll be back in half an hour."

A half-hour later Sonia was back. Tula sat beside the still-sleeping Wendy Papp. "Tula, the judge's wife is on a tear about the delay.

We'll have to wake Wendy up and put her on." Sonia approached the sleeping girl and patted her shoulder. "Ms. Papp, it's time to testify."

Wendy awoke blinking and irritable. "Where's ol' Flo?" she asked.

"You can see her later, Ms. Papp. Now we've got to go to court."

"Rich bitch must've shot him," said Wendy, rising unsteadily, assisted by Sonia and Tula. Presently, the three entered the courtroom.

Judge and jury were in their respective chambers, but the other usual inhabitants were present in the courtroom. Dora Flex took charge. "Your witness finally here, Mr. Davies?"

"Yes," he responded, staring unhappily at the luminous coat, the wobbly girl.

The latter, having spotted Penny, suddenly loosed her arms from her supporters and, waving one at Penny, shouted, "That's her. She shot him."

"Tell the judge we're ready to proceed," said Mrs. Flex to the clerk, who departed to do so.

Davies led Wendy Papp to the witness box. "Please don't talk except when I ask questions," he whispered to her.

"Who the fuck are you?" She spoke in a loud voice.

"I'm the chief prosecutor. It's my job to convict the rich bitch, Ms. Papp," he whispered. The jury members were beginning to return to their seats in the jury box.

"What are you whispering for? You 'fraid of wakin' somebody?"

Defeated, Davies raised his voice. "You have to be sworn. Then you can testify when I ask you questions." The jury members were now all in the box and regarding Wendy with great interest.

She waved at them. "Hiya, folks. I'm Wendy Papp." Then she belched energetically. A few jurors returned her wave. Judge Flex reappeared and, all having risen to the bailiff's cry, seated himself.

"Our first witness, ladies and gentlemen, is, I believe, Ms. Wendy Papp."

Wendy's uneven eyes took the measure of Judge Flex. "I sure

am. Everything mellow with you, judge?" She spoke in a tipsy-but-pleasant voice.

Flex's aplomb was undisturbed. "You must stand and be sworn, Ms. Papp."

Ms. Papp rose, smiling broadly. "Hey, this is just like on TV," she declared, steadying herself against the witness box. The oath was administered without mishap, and Davies began his examination by asking her full name and place of residence.

"Wendy P. Papp. New Reality Homeless Shelter. The P is for Portia. You know, maybe my residence now is The Bayquake." She looked into the audience at Tula. "Do I go back there?"

"Your answer is fine, Ms. Papp," said Davies. "Now did you know the victim?"

"Just when he was dead."

"Smoking Mother also lived at The New Reality Shelter, didn't he?"

"The women are in a different section from the men. There'd be trouble otherwise." She snickered and hiccuped.

"I see. So you saw him for the first time there on the library steps?"

"Yeah, and I know that rich bitch must have shot him." She pointed a finger at Penny.

Playchek rose. "Move to strike that remark as non-responsive and as an inadmissible and improper opinion."

"Well," said Judge Flex, "this is our first witness, Mr. Playchek, and I hate to get bogged down so soon in objections. Perhaps, Mr. Davies, you can clear it up."

"Certainly, Your Honor. In your opinion, Ms. Papp, did Ms. Hill shoot the victim?"

Playchek leaped to his feet. "Same objection. Either she saw a shooting or she didn't, and it looks like she didn't, Your Honor. She can't give an opinion that she *thinks* my client shot the man."

"Well, Mr. Playchek, Mr. Davies has done his best to try to clarify the question for you. I understand it, and I think the jury understands it. Overruled."

"You may answer," said Davies in a gentle voice.

Wendy burped. "Sure, she shot him. Who else would?"

Playchek's motion to strike the answer was denied. Davies considered turning the witness over to Playchek, but was bothered by the "Who else would?" part of her answer. "You say 'Who else would?' because it was Ms. Hill who had the gun?"

"No. Because people like her hate street people. Everybody else was like him and me."

"The rest of the crowd there on the steps were street people?"

"Yeah, she's the only one who'd do it. That's why she concealed it."

"Concealed the gun?" asked Davies.

"Yeah." Her voice assumed a cunning tone. "So you couldn't see her shoot him."

Playchek rose again. "Your Honor, this witness now admits she didn't see Ms. Hill shoot the decedent. On that basis I renew my motion to strike her opinion that Ms. Hill shot him."

"But Mr. Playchek," said Judge Flex, appearing a touch vexed, "you heard her say Ms. Hill concealed the shooting from her. Now your client can't have it both ways. Since the actual shooting was concealed from the witness, she's entitled to express an opinion that it occurred. Denied." This breathtaking misapplication of law and logic persuaded Playchek that there was no use pursuing the objection, and he seated himself.

On Davies's part, he was unwilling to take another chance with the witness. "You may examine," he declared.

Playchek rose and introduced himself to Wendy.

"Pleased to meet you," she responded. "You got cute ears."

"Thank you. Now, how much were you paid to testify here?"

"You mean the expense money?"

"How much has the prosecution given you?"

"I don't remember. They wanted me to wear a dress; I remember that. How do you like my coat?"

"It's out of sight," said Playchek. "Did they give you anything to drink this morning?"

"They made me drink coffee." She pointed at Tula. "That little lady cop did it."

"But you've been drinking alcohol, too, haven't you?"

"Just a nip."

"On the library steps, you first saw Ms. Hill after you heard the shot, right?"

"Yeah, that's why I looked. When I heard the shot. You got nice eyes, too."

"Thank you. And the gun was on the ground, wasn't it?"

"Yeah. It was all concealed, the shooting."

"I have no further questions," said Playchek.

"Mr. Davies?"

But Davies had had enough too.

"You are excused, Ms. Papp, and thank you," said Judge Flex.

"Thank you too, Judge. You stay cool, you hear."

WITH WENDY PAPP DEPARTED from the courtroom, Judge Flex called for a recess. Tremorgan Davies began to go over his notes, but Sonia Taft interrupted him. "I'm afraid we may have a problem with Mei Soo von Tirpitz."

"Who's that?"

"The arresting officer. Von Tirpitz is her married name. She just demanded that the judge's wife write a confession. She didn't say to what. We were in the hall, and Dora Flex came by. Mei Soo grabbed her arm and said she looked like a landlord. It was a bit dicey."

"Good grief! What happened?"

"Dora refused to confess, and Mei Soo wanted to take her to the station. Fortunately, the bailiff came up and separated them. Mei Soo's in the witness room now, but she's in a foul mood. Keeps mumbling something like 'destroy all monsters.'"

"Well, it will be difficult to use the other arresting officer, since he's a deaf mute. Besides, wasn't Mei Soo in on the house search?"

"Yes, she spotted the Russian caviar. I've got an interpreter coming over, a young, U.S. born Chinese who's working with us this summer. Maybe he can bring her around."

EDWARD CHUN REPORTED TO SONIA on his meeting with Mei Soo. "Her husband's just run off on her and gone back to Argentina. She's also behind in her rent, and she says a woman who looks like her landlord has followed her to court. She told me to defy all difficulties in the struggle against landlords." He looked at his notes. "Yes, that's what she said, and as I was leaving — I think I got this right — she said 'put up big character posters. Advance wave on wave.'"

"Ed, you should come to court with her. You'll be a calming influence."

DORA FLEX EYED MEI SOO with displeasure as the latter took her place in the witness box, led there by the young interpreter. Tremorgan Davies explained the reason for the interpreter to Judge Flex.

"This is the woman who attacked my wife, isn't it?"

"I believe so, Your Honor, but she seems in control of herself now."

"Very well, proceed."

Mei Soo was sworn and asked to state her name. Simultaneously, she saw Penny seated at the defense table and, instead of responding to the question, began to speak in English in a loud voice. "Criminal woman, try escape, destroy evidence."

Playchek interrupted. "Your Honor, we ought at least to have the name of the witness before the denunciation."

"Quite right, Mr. Playchek. Mr. Davies, what is this woman's name?"

"Mei Soo von Tirpitz, Your Honor." He then spelled the name, but inaccurately.

Mei Soo complained to Judge Flex about the spelling and, suddenly recovering focus, pointed at Penny and declared, "You confess now to judge. Confess crime."

Penny stuck her tongue out, and Playchek rose to object. At the same time, Mei Soo spotted Dora Flex seated behind her monitor. She stood up in the witness box and, now pointing at Mrs. Flex, shouted, "All unite and defeat landlords and their running dogs."

Dora also stood up and shouted, but at her husband. "That's what she called me before, Potter, a landlord. She's crazy. Do something to her." A bailiff blocked Mei Soo's exit from the witness box.

"Make landlord monster work on pig farm. Make confess," Mei Soo continued, warming to her subject while struggling with the bailiff. "Be constantly on guard. Avoid confusion," she added.

The bailiff, however, employing counter-revolutionary trickery, subdued the excited girl, whereupon Judge Flex held her in contempt of court and ordered her into custody. "Maintain constantly correct thoughts," she observed as she was removed from the courtroom. There was a momentary interlude while the prosecution regrouped.

"We'll call the police custodian to identify the material evidence, Your Honor, and dispense with the arresting officer," Davies advised.

"You may as well." said Judge Flex firmly, "That woman's not getting out of the pokey until this trial is over and Dora is safely home."

"Yes, Your Honor. The people call Officer Nina Tarmac." Officer Tarmac took the stand and was sworn. She was carrying a shoebox, and Penny recognized her as the woman who had taken her belongings at the Hall of Justice.

"Officer Tarmac," Davies asked, "what have you brought to court today?"

"Ms. Hill's revolver. It's in this carton."

"And her purse?"

"We couldn't find that. I could swear I saw it just the other day, but it looks like it's gone now."

Davies tried instant rehabilitation of the witness. "And the purse, you believe, is in the custody of someone else in the department?"

Officer Tarmac rejected the suggested answer. "No. I don't know where it is. We misplaced it. That happens sometimes. Heaven knows, I misplace my own purse every so often." She smiled placidly at the jury, most of whom returned her smile.

Playchek rose. "Your Honor, this prosecution cannot proceed without the purse. I move the court to dismiss the charges."

"Well, Mr. Playchek, that would be rather drastic and a great disappointment to everyone who has been watching the case on television. To have it end like that would be terrible. I think we should see if Mr. Davies can proceed without the purse. Do you think you can do that, Mr. Davies?"

"Certainly, Your Honor."

"There, you see, Mr. Playchek? He says he can proceed. Motion denied."

Davies turned back to Officer Tarmac. "Please remove the weapon from the container and tell us how it came into your possession."

The witness produced the weapon. "Officer Flaxseed, one of the arresting officers, gave it to me."

"And what did he tell you when he gave you the weapon?"

Playchek rose again. "It's hearsay, Your Honor."

"But, Mr. Playchek, if the officer isn't here, how else will we find out what he said? Overruled."

"He didn't say anything. He can't talk."

Davies stood firm. "But you are able to identify the weapon as belonging to Ms. Hill in some way, are you not?"

"Well, it was in her purse."

Playchek rose once again. "I renew my motion to dismiss. The prosecution cannot proceed without the purse."

Judge Flex shook his head. "No, counsel. It is the witness, not Mr. Davies, who is relying on the purse. Denied."

The weapon was admitted in evidence, and Davies announced he had no further questions of the witness. Playchek waived cross-examination.

"We'll take a recess. A short one, dear," said Judge Flex, looking fondly at his spouse.

DURING THE RECESS, the fashion editor of a television channel owned by *The Cockerel* came to the defense table accompanied by a video-cameraman. "I'm Glissa Cocoa," said the fashion editor. She wore a large flat hat and dangling earrings that tinkled when her head moved. "We're doing a special on fashions at the trial," she said. "Ms. Hill, do you dress differently now that you're on trial for murder?"

"Hey," said Playchek, "have a heart. We're trying to work here."

"OK," said Glissa, "but I'm not at all happy with this situation. It was bad enough having to look at the judge's wife dressed like she is — that dreadful, baggy old suit. Now we can't interview the killer. And I don't like that outfit the Taft woman is wearing, either. Bargain-basement legal, I'd call it. What a disenchanting trial."

That evening, Penny and her companions watched the fashion report on the TV in Playchek's office: "Hi there, fashion fans. It's your reporter on threads, Glissa Cocoa, this time with a report from the Penny Hill trial." A wide-angle view of the courtroom followed. "It may be a good trial for crime-and-punishment buffs, but believe me, it's a fashion catastrophe. With one exception." A close-up of Penny seated at the defense table was shown. "The lovely defendant, who, really fans, just dresses too well to be executed or go to jail." There followed a detailed description of Penny's attire. "Sad to say, she took the Fifth Amendment when your reporter asked her if she had adjusted fashion-wise for the trial."

"Now let's look at the downside of this trial." There followed video footage of Dora Flex and Sonia Taft. "Really! There should be a law against that sort of assault on the eyes. Let's hope it doesn't reflect the state of justice in our courts. Free Penny Hill! That's all for now. I'm Glissa Cocoa, till we meet again."

"Glissa's kind of funny," said Playchek.

"The judge's wife isn't going to think so," Penny replied.

THE COMMENCEMENT OF TRIAL the next day was delayed while Judge Flex heard argument on the contempt proceedings he had initiated against Glissa Cocoa and her employer. There was the matter of free speech, their lawyer argued. "It is not an available defense," responded Judge Flex, "since all television in this courtroom is within the discretion of the court. Your slanderous presentation has abused the court's indulgence of television. I am thinking," he said, "of some time in the slammer for this Miss Chocolate, or whatever her name is, and a heavy fine for the corporation."

In the event, the matter was settled with agreement to have Glissa go back on the air with a retraction of her critical comments, and a warm appraisal of what the judge's wife was wearing today. It was a dowdy, mouse-colored drape, which particularly set Glissa's nerves on edge. Following the retraction, Glissa's analyst ordered her to take two weeks' complete rest at a nudist colony, where there would be no risk of exposure to offensive apparel.

AS THE MORNING'S FIRST WITNESS, there now entered the courtroom a stocky, middle-aged woman with a big head and thick gray hair cut in a way that made it resemble a football helmet. She carried a white pennant on which in black letters were the words "Disarm U.S. Military." She was accompanied by Sonia

Taft. As they approached the prosecution table, Sonia bent down and, in a low but urgent voice, said to Davies, "Quick! Tell me her name. I've forgotten it."

Davies stared at his next witness, but no name came to him. "I never can remember her name. Didn't you write it down?" he whispered.

"I've forgotten where I wrote it. Please, Tremorgan, ask her her name."

Davies stood up. "Excuse me, Madame, my mind's not working yet today. Your name is?"

"Damn it! You forgot it at the last trial, too. Everybody does. It's Mary Smith."

"Sonia, write that down," said Davies in an authoritative voice.

"Why do you have to write it down," Mrs. Smith demanded? "I'll bet you don't write down other people's names. I'm just sick of people forgetting my name."

"Yes, Mrs. ... " He hesitated, having forgotten her name. Sonia quickly thrust the paper on which she had written the name into his hand, and Davies inspected it furtively. "Mrs. Smith, it must be very frustrating — "

She interrupted. "It sure is."

"I'll keep this paper handy, Mrs. Smith. Count on me."

Sonia gave the witness' name to the clerk as the courtroom awaited the re-emergence of Judge Flex from his chambers. He emerged and, the celebration of that event having ended, he asked the clerk for the name of the next witness. "It's Mary Jones," she replied.

"It's Mary Smith," said Mary Smith vehemently.

"Well, 'Jones' is what Ms. Taft told me," said the clerk.

"I'm sure I said 'Smith,'" said Sonia.

"Please take the stand, Mrs. Jones," said Judge Flex.

Davies, fixedly studying the paper with the name written on it, said, "I think it's Mary Smith, Your Honor."

Dora Flex spoke from her station in the first row behind the bar, "Smith, Jones, what difference does it make? We're wasting time arguing about it, Potter."

"Quite right, my dear. Please swear the witness."

"Mrs. Smith-Jones, please stand and be sworn," said the clerk.

Playchek objected. "Your Honor, this witness should not testify until she is properly identified."

Dora Flex was incensed. "Potter, these objections are slowing down the trial."

"Overruled," said Judge Flex firmly.

Davies, made uneasy by the confusion, began by asking the witness to state her name.

"Damn it! How many times do I have to tell you people?"

"It's just for the record. I know it's Mrs. ... " He looked down at the paper. "Mrs. Smith, Mrs. Mary Smith."

Playchek, sensing an opening, rose. "Your Honor, Mr. Davies appears to be trying to confuse the issue. I thought this was Mary Jones."

"So did I," said Judge Flex angrily. "Mr. Davies, what's going on here?"

"Your Honor, I'm telling the truth," said Davies plaintively. "This is our weapons expert, and her name is Mary Jones." Sonia tugged hard at his coat. "I mean 'Smith,'" he amended anxiously.

"Mr. Davies, if the jury is feeling as I do, they are losing all interest in the testimony of this witness. What is the purpose of calling Mrs. Jones?"

"She's a weapons expert. Highly accredited. The chairperson of Disarm the U.S. Military Now."

Judge Flex turned to the witness. "What does Disarm the U.S. Military Now do, Mrs. Jones?"

"It's Smith, Your Honor, I — "

"Please," said Judge Flex, manifestly annoyed at being corrected, "let's not have any more of these name games, Mrs. Jones. The jury and I have had just about enough."

The witness, intimidated by Flex's pique, gave up the struggle for her name. "Your Honor, Disarm the U.S. Military Now means exactly that: no more military weapons for America."

"And what," asked Judge Flex, momentarily afflicted with an attack of relevancy, "has that to do with this trial?"

Davies responded. "Your Honor, permit me to qualify the witness and I'll demonstrate the relevancy."

"Very well."

"But keep it short," added Dora Flex.

"Yes, Your Honor," said Davies. "Mrs. Jones," he began, "you formed 'Disarm the U.S. Military Now'?"

"Yes, after my husband died. The peace movement was his whole life, and when the Soviet Union broke up that finished him. He had such high hopes for a Soviet liberation of the United States; peacefully, of course."

"I see, and his death led you to form Disarm the U.S. Military Now?"

"Yes, I thought it would be a nice memorial to Melon. That was my husband's name. You see, if the U.S. was disarmed, there was still a chance that some other foreign power would liberate it. The thought of getting rid of our own government has kept me active and my hopes up."

"I'm sure your views are shared by many, Mrs. Jones. Now, focusing on concealed weapons, do you have an opinion whether someone who carries a concealed weapon intends to use it?"

Playchek rose. "Improper opinion evidence, Your Honor. No foundation for such an opinion."

"Sustained. Her expertise appears to be with military weapons, so I think we need to know if the United States is concealing weapons before she can give an opinion on the subject."

"Certainly, Your Honor. Mrs. Jones, your experience with concealed weapons is based in part on the practices of the government in concealing weapons, is it not?"

"Yes, they hide them all over the place, in silos, bunkers. It's dreadful. And they certainly mean to shoot them."

"Your Honor, I believe that lays the foundation," said Davies.

"Your Honor," said Playchek, "there's no connection between concealing ballistic missiles and my client's old family revolver."

"Well, Mr. Playchek, isn't it a matter of degree? Besides, as I've said, I don't want to get bogged down in technicalities. Overruled."

"Do you have an opinion whether a person who carries a concealed weapon intends to use it," Davies asked?

"Yes."

"What is your opinion?"

"Same objection," said Playchek.

"Overruled," said Judge Flex.

"They intend to, and they probably did use it. Conceal a weapon, use a weapon, I always say."

Playchek's motion to strike the answer was denied. "Your witness," said Davies.

Playchek began, "Why do you want to destroy our country, Mrs. Jones?"

"I don't. I want to improve it by getting rid of our government."

"Your opinion that a concealed weapon is always used is not based on any factual proof, is it?"

"I'm an intuitive person. I don't need a lot of factual proof to know something."

"Thank you, Mrs. Smith."

"It's Mrs. Jones," said Judge Flex.

"WHAT AN INTERESTING WOMAN," said Penny during the recess that followed Mary Smith's testimony. "So sure of herself. I wonder what her husband was like."

"He was disappointed," said Playchek, "but never mind. This guy they're warming up now is the one who searched your house."

"The weight lifter that April liked?"

"Yeah. With him they'll be putting in the portrait, the caviar, the Indian books and the tomahawks."

"How dull after the peace lady."

"Tremorgan thinks otherwise. They see this house search stuff as lightning, particularly the portrait and the caviar. There's the portrait now. They've got a cover over it. It's going to be like the climax in *The Picture of Dorian Gray*—a sudden revelation of the evil image, the real Penny Hill."

"You saw it, Barton; it's not that awful."

"It will be when Davies gets through characterizing it."

"What's characterizing it?"

"It's like this: it's not just what the evidence is; it's what the lawyer says it is. That's characterizing. Davies could make a Girl Scout sound like a predator from outer space."

Arnold White, the officer who had conducted the search, took the stand and was identified. April waved at him. He related how he and a fellow officer had arrived at the house, the meeting with Millie and April, and the beginning of the search. It had started in the kitchen, and the first exhibit identified was the caviar.

"How did you come to take possession of these tins of caviar?"

"The policewoman with me, Officer von Tirpitz, started shouting, 'Russian, Russian.'"

"Just a moment," said Judge Flex. "That's that woman I held in contempt. What's she got to do with this?"

"She got all excited, Your Honor, when she saw the Russian label on the caviar. Chinese communists have a thing about Russia."

"I believe," said Judge Flex, "that we've had quite enough to do with foreign powers for one day. Moreover, I don't want to hear a word more about that woman who attacked Mrs. Flex. Go on to something else."

"Yes, Your Honor," said Davies, retrieving the caviar from the witness and handing it to Sonia Taft. "When you left the kitchen, did you then search the library?"

"Yes. She had a lot of books in the library."

"Including these?" Davies held up two books. One was entitled *Better Red than a White Fathead*. The author was Plenty Greengrass of the Benjaminow tribe. The other was *Paleface Go Home*, by Chief Josephus, a Great Lakes Saddoosee.

"Yeah. When I saw they were about Indians, I thought you'd want them."

"Your Honor," said Davies, "the people offer these texts as evidence of the defendant's evil intentions toward Native-Americans."

Playchek objected. "This Indian issue is a red herring, Your Honor. It's totally irrelevant. Besides, these books expose the white man's perfidy toward the Indian. They're not anti-Indian."

"A point of view, Your Honor, which when read by the accused may have provoked her to take violent action against the red man." Davies's rich voice filled the chamber.

"Hogwash," said Penny audibly, and Playchek laid a hand on her shoulder.

Judge Flex, however, had a clear grasp of the issue. "The problems of the Native-American have been treated as irrelevant too often and for too long. That neglect finds no favor in my court. The books will be admitted."

Davies continued. "Now, did you find other evidence of the defendant's preoccupation with Native-American issues?"

"Well, I found an axe and a hatchet in her garage. It's a Boy Scout hatchet."

"Your Honor, we offer these virtual tomahawks on the same grounds that the court admitted the books in evidence."

Playchek's objection was overruled.

"Now, Officer White, did you also visit the bedroom of the accused?"

"Yeah, her daughter took me there." He smiled warmly in the direction of April. "Nice girl. Pumps iron." April giggled, causing a momentary diversion.

"And there in the bedroom, did you take into your possession a portrait of the accused?"

"Yeah, it's there with the cover on it. I can tell by the frame."

"What drew your attention to the portrait as potential evidence?"

Playchek's objection was overruled. "It's preliminary, Mr. Playchek."

"I thought it was pretty wild," said Officer White. "Makes her look really tough."

Playchek's motion to strike the answer was denied. "It's his impression of the portrait, Mr. Playchek. He's not saying that your client herself is really tough. I wouldn't allow that."

"Your Honor, I respectfully submit his impression is irrelevant."

"Now, Mr. Playchek, that's very insensitive of you," said Judge Flex. "I mean calling his impressions irrelevant; after all, a policeman has feelings too. Overruled on sensitivity grounds."

"Your Honor, I don't mean all his impressions are irrelevant; just this one."

"Well, you'll be allowed to cross-examine as to his other impressions. Proceed, Mr. Davies."

Davies walked over to the hidden portrait and placed one hand on the frame; his other hand went to the cloth cover, as if about to expose the image beneath. Then he seemed to freeze. He stood staring at the covering, his hands beginning to tremble. "This portrait, this portrait of the accused ... " He spoke in a halting manner, his usual, powerful voice altogether missing. Then, with difficulty, he steadied his hands and pulled the cover slightly away from the frame. He looked down, the painting still visible only to him. "This portrait of ... " He paused in mid sentence, his face flushed. Davies gulped, then continued speaking. "This portrait of ... of this beautiful woman ... " Sonia gasped. Davies, his hand moving as if directed by some external force, pulled the cover back over the frame so that the portrait was again fully concealed. In a quavering voice he completed the sentence, "... will not be offered by the people." His hands fell. He had broken out in a sweat. He turned to look back at the prosecution table, from which Sonia Taft stared at him icily. "I have no further questions of this witness," Davies said weakly.

Playchek, while perplexed at this fortunate behavior by Davies, was in no doubt as to his own next step. "The defense has no questions of this witness."

"Officer White, you are excused," said Judge Flex, "we'll take a short recess."

SONIA RELEASED HER FURY during the recess. "Men! Men are ridiculous! I told you over and over to stop looking at that portrait."

"I couldn't help it, Sonia. You have to understand. It was there in the office all this time. I had to pass it to get to my desk."

"That's why I put the cover on it! Tremorgan, you've been taking the cover off and looking at it, haven't you?"

"Yes, Sonia. I let you down. And when I peeked at it here in the courtroom, something just came over me. I couldn't bring myself to characterize that portrait the way we meant to. It was like a spell came over me."

"Spell, my behind. You went into a voyeuristic trance all on your own. Anyway, the portrait is gone. I've given it to Playchek along with the caviar. I don't want you mooning over that thing anymore. Are you ready to do Lambert Crocker?"

"Who's that, the neighbor?"

"Yes, he's in the witness room, hot to testify Penny tried to run over his kid. Kind of a smart-ass, but it's good stuff. You all right now?"

"Be kind, Sonia. I should be fine now that we're over the portrait issue."

As he spoke, Sonia was opening a letter-sized envelope. "What's that?"

"I don't know. Tula handed it to me a bit back. I forgot about it." Sonia extracted the single sheet of paper. "Dear Ms. Taft," it began. "I am sorry to trouble you about this, but I am very concerned, having seen that man Mr. Crocker, whom I interviewed, sitting in the witness room. I think he plans to lie that Ms. Hill tried to run over his son. From my own investigation I know he is lying about that. If he testified that way, I would feel, as a matter of conscience, that I should testify too, to explain how he lied. I know you would not want him to lie, but he may do so if he gets the chance, as he did with me. You can count on me, however, to clear the matter up. Faithfully, Tula Fogg."

Sonia handed the note to Davies. "We can scratch Lambert Crocker," she said petulantly.

Davies read Tula's note. "Yeah, he's checkmated. We better fire Tula."

"I've been thinking about that. We can't."

"Oh?"

"We need her to handle Flora Grebe. She's established a close relationship with her."

"This threat to testify. It's rank insubordination, Sonia."

"Yes, but she doesn't see it that way. She thinks she's offering to help us."

"People have the damnedest ideas these days, Sonia. It's getting harder and harder to practice law."

"BARTON, MR. BARROW just did it again, just before the recess."

"Did what?"

"He gave me a thumbs-up sign."

"He's probably going to hit on you after the trial."

"That would be lovely, and he can't do that if I'm in the slammer. He's done it twice; I just didn't mention it the first time. You know, now that the jury will never see my portrait, I'm sort of disappointed. I would have been interested in Barrow's reaction."

"Never mind Barrow; most of that jury would have held the portrait against you. I can't believe that Davies didn't offer it. What got into him?"

"Barton, he looked very strange when he started to take off the cover. Sort of out of control."

"Maybe it's a magic painting. Anyway, tonight it goes home with the caviar. We've had a good day."

"It's not over yet."

But in fact it was, so far as trial was concerned, for Davies, having decided against using Lambert Crocker, had no other witness available that afternoon. He endured a tongue lashing from Dora Flex for wasting available court time. It had been a bad day for Tremorgan Davies.

28. BIG MOUTH AND
MAYOR HOMER COME TO COURT

ELLEN WOKE TO TALLFELLOW'S CALL. "Yes?"

"Ellen, I have interesting news. Big Mouth is in San Francisco."

"How did you find out?"

"In the sanctuary. He can still communicate with me from across the water."

"Is He at the trial?"

"He's going tomorrow. Today He went to a place called 'Alcatraz.'"

"Yes, all the tourists do that. Is He visible?"

"Oh, no, but He could choose to be. Perhaps at the trial it would be appropriate."

"I doubt it. That would be too confined a space to manifest Himself and get away. They'd probably clap Him in irons."

"That is not a problem. Big Mouth cannot be captured by humans. Big Mouth eat more."

"Big Mouth eat more. Well, I'm almost done with this report, so if He manifests Himself, I might see Him there. I'm leaving as soon as it's done."

R. "DOC" WAYWARD STUDIED the poll reports gloomily. Blake's recent moves had had a baleful effect. The embrace by Blake of the Smoking Mother and poor-versus-privileged issues was unexpected and unfair. He, Wayward, had created those issues, and now Blake was taking a free ride on them. Unquestionably, it was the work of Michael St. Augustine. He was clever at whacking you with your own bat. Waylon Homer must recapture center stage on those issues. And some new approach might be in order: women's issues, perhaps. Women's issues were always attention getting. Doc thought about it as he sucked on his plastic bottle of designer water.

THE MORNING NEWS CARRIED THE RESULTS of Doc's self-communion. The mayor would personally attend the Hill trial to "evaluate the proceedings." *The Cockerel* also reported, "the mayor would be particularly observant regarding the extent to which the proceedings confronted important issues of the day, especially those relating to the role and influence of women in American society. The mayor believed, stated his spokesman, R. 'Doc' Wayward, that these issues should be addressed in any major court proceeding." The mayor would also investigate whether "too much emphasis was being placed at the trial on the facts of the case rather than on more important issues."

BARTON PLAYCHEK READ THE NEWS of the mayor's prospective visit to the trial with interest. Then he called Muriel and instructed her to prepare a subpoena for the mayor to testify at the trial and to serve it on him when he arrived in court.

Accompanied by Doc Wayward, Mayor Waylon Homer arrived in court before the commencement of proceedings. Muriel was waiting for him and served the subpoena. It was not welcome. The mayor wanted to be part of the audience, not part of the play. Like most politicians, he had a deep aversion to testifying under oath. Wayward took the matter up with Tremorgan Davies. Could he move Judge Flex to quash the subpoena, thus preventing Playchek from examining the mayor? Davies agreed he would do so. He saw no interest of the people to be served by the mayor as a witness.

Accordingly, before the jury was put in the box, Judge Flex heard argument on the motion to quash the subpoena. As he had on the motion for live televising of the trial, he appeared to give the matter special attention, asking pertinent questions and soliciting applicable law from the parties. Finally, he announced he was prepared to rule, and, with all cameras closely focused on him, he began. It was not, he said, a simple issue. There were many considerations. "On the one hand," he declared, "the defense insists that the mayor has evidence relevant to the case, but Mr. Playchek is understandably reluctant to specify what the evidence is in advance of the actual interrogation. That is quite consistent with my policy of maintaining the sporting element in litigation.

"On the other hand, the mayor contends that subjecting high public figures to unexpected service of subpoenas to testify could intimidate them from performance of their public duties. They could, for example, be deterred from observation of court proceedings were they subject to being made a part of the litigation. The mayor also observes that it was not nice of Mr. Playchek to act without warning, and that, since so much of the former graciousness of life has already been sacrificed to modern attitudes and behavior, we ought to do everything possible to discourage any impolite conduct.

"These are powerful arguments, and we are mindful of them. There is, however," he continued, "an overriding consideration that, in the court's view, is determinative of the issue. That is the fact that in order to testify, the witness must be sworn to tell the truth, the whole truth, and nothing but the truth. Manifestly, to require politicians to tell the truth would set a novel and dangerous precedent. The governance of this state, this country, has been based on a contrary, time-honored principle. Let those of us entrusted with the administration of justice not disturb it. In my view, to require the mayor of a major metropolis to tell nothing but the truth would amount to a civic outrage. The motion to quash is granted."

Big Mouth, who had also come to court for the morning's proceedings, did not understand all of the issue, but He did grasp the point that to require tribal leaders to tell the truth would offend longstanding usage to the contrary. He mused over what He had observed since His arrival in California, both at the trial and otherwise. He had already concluded that Tallfellow's proposed mission to bring the First Principles of Big Mouth to the foreigners would be a waste of time. The objects of the mission were beyond redemption. A trip to Alcatraz, on the other hand, was clearly worth the effort.

TREMORGAN DAVIES'S WITNESS LIST had grown shorter. With Lambert Crocker scratched, there were just Flora Grebe, General Sandschloss, and perhaps Max Untergang. He decided to save Grebe and perhaps Untergang for rebuttal after the defense case and finish his initial presentation of evidence with General Sandschloss. The general had wanted to come to the trial all along. "So I can observe Ms. Hill," he urged Davies. But Davies had concluded it was more important to keep Sandschloss' employment unknown to Playchek until the last minute. General Sandschloss continued to study the file and received regular reports from Sonia Taft on the progress of the case. He had also started, on his own initiative, a collection of photos of Penny obtained from the library and publishers' archives. "She is a very attractive woman," he advised Davies. "A pity she must suffer as a criminal." Davies thought so too and, accordingly, took no notice of his expert's general state of mind regarding Penny. Sandschloss had continued to agree that her capacity appeared to him to be totally undiminished. That was what counted.

On the morning he was to testify, the general arrived at City

Hall dressed in a finely tailored, cream-colored linen suit and carrying a dozen dark-red roses. "What's with the roses?" asked Sonia.

"They come after I testify," he responded obliquely. "I'll just put them here with your briefcases." Sonia took no further heed of the matter, being absorbed with the proceedings on the motion to quash the subpoena. These completed, the jury returned to the box. When they were all seated, Judge Flex reemerged, and Davies announced that General Sandschloss would be the next witness and the last one of the people's initial presentation of evidence.

The general had been kept out of sight in the witness room, so Playchek became aware of his role only as he was about to take the stand. On passing the defense table, Sandschloss paused and, bowing slightly, looked ardently at Penny. While he was being sworn, Muriel whispered to Playchek, "That's the way he used to look at me, how he just looked at Penny."

"Ah." said Playchek, "Interesting."

Davies set about establishing his witness' qualifications as a mental health expert. He was asked how he came to enter the mental health field. The general responded, "When I retired from the army I came to California and took stock of the situation career-wise. I wanted to enter a field that could be expected to grow. This state, it seemed to me, provided excellent growth conditions for computer industries and nuts. I knew nothing about computers, but my years in the military had necessarily provided plenty of contact with nuts. The choice was an obvious one."

"Now, General, you have not had an opportunity to personally examine Ms. Hill, have you?"

"No, and I deeply regret it. I am hopeful the opportunity will arise in the future."

What an odd remark, thought Davies, but plunged ahead. "You have, however, at my request, studied the record in this case and the people's file on Ms. Hill?"

"Yes. And much more. I have a growing collection of photos of Ms. Hill and news articles about her. Did you know that she has received two major awards for her charitable work?"

"No, General. And it's essential, sir, that we stick to the files that are of record. Let me ask you, do those files provide adequate data for you to evaluate the defense presented in this case that the capacity of the accused has been diminished?"

"Yes, they do, and I have studied them over and over. It is such a pity that a person of her quality has to be involved in a prosecution like this."

"General," said Davies, beginning to appreciate the scope of his problem, "please just answer my questions without additional comments."

Playchek rose. "Your Honor, Mr. Davies is trying to impeach his own expert and stifle relevant parts of his opinion. In addition, Your Honor, I am sure his additional comments will be more interesting than dry-bones responses to the prosecution's inquiries. I am mindful that this court has often stressed the importance of keeping the trial interesting."

"Quite so, Mr. Playchek. Mr. Davies, I must caution you not to attempt to confine the witness to less-interesting responses. Proceed."

"Yes, Your Honor. General Sandschloss, have you formed an opinion as to whether the defendant's capacity has been diminished?"

"I have, and I am very happy to — "

Davies interrupted him. "What is your opinion?"

"I was saying, I am very happy to report that her capacity has not been at all diminished. In fact, I feel certain that over time it has been greatly enhanced."

The cryptic conclusion to the answer persuaded Davies that it was time to stop. "You may examine," he said to Playchek, who rose to do so.

"General, you have had an opportunity since you came to court to see my client in person, have you not?"

"Yes, and it has been a great pleasure, Mr. Playchek."

"But apart from that, you have only the cold record of the trial and the collection you have been making of photos and articles as a guide to her capacity?"

"True, and as I look at her now, her vibrant face, her graceful figure, I grieve that I have not had closer contact. Nevertheless, I am absolutely convinced that her capacity is totally undiminished."

Playchek thought about the answer. There was little risk that he would make the testimony worse, and it might be made a lot better. So he put the question. "Her capacity for what, General?"

"For love," said General Sandschloss movingly, looking in Penny's direction.

"Well," said Judge Flex, "this is interesting. Isn't it Dora?" Mrs. Flex grunted affirmatively.

"General," said Playchek, "what about her capacity to distinguish right from wrong?"

"I would consider that to be of little interest in the larger scale of things. It is love that matters."

"And you have not interested yourself in that question since you began to sense her great capacity for love?"

"Precisely, Mr. Playchek. I could not have put it better."

"THESE ARE REALLY VERY LOVELY ROSES the general gave me, Barton."

"Yes, but you'll need an unlisted phone number and a change of residence till his ardor cools."

"Muriel says he's quite nice."

"Don't talk like that. I'll tell your brother."

"I think you're jealous." Penny laughed and waved the roses. "What happens next?"

"Judge Flex will deny our motion to dismiss the charges, and we'll start our case. I'm going to start with a weapons expert that Muriel found. Funny name, Shlomo O'Hara, but she says he knows revolvers."

MICHAEL ST. AUGUSTINE and the James Blake campaign reacted quickly to Mayor Homer's trip to court. The mayor's press conference following his trip had applauded Judge Flex's handling of the trial. It had emphasized Homer's finding that, "These proceedings are addressing important issues of the day, including women's issues, and such issues are not being crowded out by too much attention to the facts of the case."

His assessment was scarcely delivered when the Blake campaign submitted to the media its own press release, concerning the proceedings on the motion to quash the subpoena. The caption ran, "Why Is Mayor Homer Afraid to Testify?" The text emphasized Judge Flex's reasoning on the motion to nullify the subpoena: that it would be improper to put the mayor in a position where he was expected to tell the truth. The release ended with an offer by the Blake spokesman, St. Augustine, to have James Blake appear and testify at the trial regarding important social issues of the day. Doc Wayward was furious at St. Augustine for trumping him with his own cards. There would be one more poll before the election. Doc prayed to the gods of political consultancy that his humbug would, in the aggregate, trump St. Augustine's.

ANOTHER GOD NEAR THE SCENE of this struggle, Big Mouth, communicated the substance of what He had seen at the trial to Tallfellow. "So far," He said, "it does not appear that the trial has had anything to do with the guilt or innocence of Peter's sister. I was, however, sitting quite near to her, and I was able to determine that she is entirely innocent of anything that would be a crime among us. I am troubled, however, that she does not appear to be defending herself. The lawyers and witnesses, not to mention the judge, monopolize the proceedings, and she sits there, innocent but entirely inactive."

"Yes," responded Tallfellow, "that does not sound good. As You have laid it down in the First Principles, the gods help those who help themselves."

"That is exactly so, Tallfellow, and that principle accounts for a large part of my concern."

"Could You not speak to her about this?"

"You know my reluctance to communicate with persons other than yourself, but perhaps this is a special case."

THE NEXT DAY, PENNY APPROACHED Peter during a recess. "Peter, just awhile ago there was a mostly naked man sitting next to you who is about seven feet tall and has a head like a crocodile."

"That's Big Mouth, but He's not here, of course."

"I know who He is. You described Him to me. The god who eats more. I must really be going nuts, but I saw Him right beside you; not clearly, but enough to be sure it was Him. He had one of those things on His penis too."

"Don't worry about it. The trial has your nerves on edge, and your imagination is playing tricks."

"Either that, or Big Mouth is really here, Peter."

29. THE DEFENSE OF THE INNOCENT

PLAYCHEK'S FIRST WITNESS was a trim, neatly dressed man in a dark business suit. "You are Mr. Shlomo O'Hara and are the principal of a weapons distribution firm known as 'Bring 'Em Back Dead?'"

"Yes. Shlomo O'Hara is a fictitious name because of my primary line of work."

"But you go by it?"

"Most of the time. I'm sometimes known as 'Fidel Washington.'"

"Well, we'll call you Shlomo O'Hara here. You are an expert in all kinds of weapons, are you not?"

"Yes. I'm also an international troublemaker. I incite ethnic and national strife, primarily for clients who manufacture weapons. That's why I have to be careful about names. Here, please pass out some of my cards. You never can tell who might be a client one day."

Enchanted by the witness' vocation, Judge Flex wanted to accommodate him. "The clerk can help distribute the cards. Ladies and gentlemen," he continued, addressing the jury, "it's not often we have a witness with such an interesting background. Of course, none of you may need weapons or have use for an international troublemaker at the moment, but you'll have his card."

"Mr. O'Hara," Playchek went on while the clerk passed out the cards, "at my request did you examine the weapon that caused the death in this case?"

"Yes, a single-action revolver. It's an old-timer; they haven't made them for years."

"What else did you conclude?"

"Well, those are dangerous weapons. If you drop a single-action revolver it can go off. A fall won't cause a modern revolver to discharge."

"So, if someone grabbed Ms. Hill's purse, and it fell with this old revolver in it, the weapon could have fired?"

"Yeah. She should get a newer model so it won't happen again."

"Thank you. That's all I have to ask."

Davies took the witness. "As an international troublemaker you would lie, cheat, steal, murder, perhaps even commit rape for a client, right?"

"You can count on it, counselor. Did you get one of my cards?"

"Yes. That's the only question I have."

During the recess, Playchek asked Muriel about the weapons expert. "Where did you get that guy?"

"The Yellow Pages. He sounded good. My uncle's named Shlomo, but now I know he's not a real Shlomo."

"That's how I got our Native-American. I hope he comes across better than Shlomo or whoever he is."

"The judge liked him," said Muriel defensively, "and he made a nice appearance."

THE NEXT DEFENSE WITNESS was the man who had written to Playchek stating that Smoking Mother had "offered violence" to him. This was Martin Blender of Strident Students, Inc. After being identified, he was asked to describe the encounter.

"I heard someone saying, 'Hey! Put me down,' meaning put him on my list of demonstrators for the morning program. I looked up and here was this big blonde man with a feather in his hair. He smelled awful, drink or whatever. I could tell he was a bum."

Davies rose belligerently. "Your Honor, is this would-be perjurer to be allowed to speak ill of a dead man who is unable to reply to these slurs? I object on grounds of human decency."

Judge Flex responded warily. "Mr. Davies, as you know, human decency has been very narrowly confined by the courts. It is scarcely ever observed in modern litigation. Nevertheless, it would be more appropriate if the witness described the deceased with more social correctness. I believe that instead of 'bum' he should call him 'a useful-activity-challenged person.' Proceed, Mr. Playchek."

"So you refused to hire Smoking Mother?"

"Yes, and he bulked up like he was going to hit me. He was a huge man."

"Then what happened?"

"He didn't go through with it. I think because there were a lot of my demonstrators milling around, but he cursed me. It was disgusting."

"Your witness," said Playchek.

Davies rose and, going near to the witness box, bulked up. "Is this what Smoking Mother did?"

"You're smaller and don't smell like he did. Besides, I don't feel threatened here in court."

"Did you consider the hundreds of years of wrongs done to the Native-American population by the white man when you rejected Smoking Mother?"

"Of course not. He was a blond."

"You have no expertise in Native-American hair color, do you?"

"No, but it wasn't just that. Except for the feather, he was pure paleface."

"We'll let the jury decide that, Mr. Blunder."

"It's 'Blender'," said Blender.

"Yes, Your Honor," said Playchek, "it's Blender, and Mr. Davies is just trying to bully and harass him."

"This is cross-examination, Your Honor," said Davies.

But on this occasion, Judge Flex's sense of unfair play was missing. "I am reminded, Mr. Davies, of your argument on the subpoena. You said Mr. Playchek had not been nice in serving the mayor without warning. Now it seems to me that Mr. Playchek's objection boils down to the point that you're not being nice to this witness. What's sauce for the goose ... " He paused in mid-sentence, then added, " ... is sauce for the duck."

"It's 'gander,' Potter," Mrs. Flex interjected. "You never get that right."

"Quite so, dear. Sauce for the gander." And turning back to Davies, added, "So I must instruct you to be nice to the witness."

"Your Honor," Davies urged, "the subpoena was different. I respectfully submit it is reversible error to require a lawyer to be nice during actual trial proceedings."

"Perhaps as a general rule, but this comes under the 'sauce-for-the-duck' exception."

"Then I have no further questions."

MARTIN BLENDER WAS EXCUSED, and a recess was taken so that Judge Flex could hear argument on a motion in a different case. Penny's companions, along with the prosecution team, went to the hallway to wait out the interruption. It was there that Playchek's advertisement for an eyeball witness to the death scene was answered. It was answered because three weeks earlier, Holman Travers had been sober, a condition neither characteristic nor to him desirable.

Holman, a San Francisco street dweller, had retired from employment with *The Cockerel* so as to devote himself to drinking. He obtained the means to acquire drink by panhandling, but there were bad days. On bad days, to fill the boozeless hours, he read parts of *The Cockerel*, chiefly the parts he had worked on while employed.

At the time of his departure from the newspaper, Holman had been responsible for the "Seeking Companion" section of the personals, and it was this he read first. The section was divided into subsections: men seeking women; women seeking men; men seeking men; women seeking women; and a fifth category called, "alternative lifestyles," for any special elaboration of the other four. This last often contained profoundly imaginative specifications. Reading these was not as good as drink, but it was comforting. If Holman was still short of the cash needed for a bottle after finishing the "Companions" section he would read the other personals. In this progress he came upon Playchek's advertisement for a witness. As he read it, he did not at first recall everything that had happened on the library steps, but he remembered being beaten and robbed by Smoking Mother, and the sound of the weapon going off thereafter. He reasoned that these perceptions might qualify for the reward. He tore out the notice and stuck it in his pocket. Then he scored at his panhandling on three successive passes. It would be a two-pint night. It was, and he forgot all about the advertisement.

Holman did not find the crumpled paper until three weeks had passed. He read it with dismay. Perhaps the trial was over, the chance for the money gone. He searched two trash receptacles and, toward the bottom of the second, he found that day's edition of *The Cockerel*. His spirits soared. The trial was still in progress. Holman made at once for City Hall, stopping only briefly to cadge a drink from a fellow street person. He arrived outside Judge Flex's courtroom during the recess and began asking at large among the crowd for Ms. Hill's lawyers. Sonia Taft heard him. His unpromising appearance encouraged her to guide this scruffy bum to the defense team and thus perhaps detract from its trial planning. In such ways do the gods of fortune mock mortal schemes.

Travers waved the scrap of paper at Playchek as he approached, declared his purpose in a semi-intoxicated voice, and was quickly hustled by Playchek and Muriel into the defense witness room. When he emerged from the conference ten minutes later, he had also recalled seeing Smoking Mother grab Penny's purse, and Playchek had decided to put him on no matter how dismal his appearance.

When trial resumed, Playchek announced that he had been approached during the recess by a man answering an advertisement the defense had placed for an eyeball witness to the death scene. With that introduction, Holman Travers took the stand, moving a little unsteadily.

He was sworn in and gave his place of residence as "around

San Francisco" and his occupation as "retired." Playchek then had him relate his reading the notice requesting witnesses. Holman's speech was a bit slurred, which prompted Davies to object. "I object to this witness testifying, Your Honor, on the grounds that he appears to be intoxicated."

Judge Flex overruled the objection on the grounds that it was insensitive. "How would you feel, Mr. Davies, if you were intoxicated and some lawyer made an issue of it in court? Proceed, Mr. Playchek."

Playchek proceeded. He located Travers at the library on the morning of the shooting and asked him if he had seen the deceased on the steps."

"I sure did. Only he wasn't dead yet. He was wearing a feather in his hair. Great big guy." Playchek showed Travers a photo of Smoking Mother. "Yeah, that's him, the bastard."

Davies rose again and asked the court to disqualify Travers as a witness on the ground that calling Smoking Mother a bastard showed the witness was too biased to testify competently.

Playchek countered, "That's not grounds for precluding testimony, Your Honor. Mr. Davies can cross him on bias."

Flex overruled the objection. "I don't find, Mr. Davies, that calling the deceased 'a bastard' necessarily shows bias. Currently, there are countless beloved children born out of wedlock. They are often in court. And historically the bar sinister has been worn by many virtuous souls. Besides, you will have your chance to show that the deceased was not a bastard. Proceed."

"Did you have a conversation with Smoking Mother that morning?" Playchek asked.

"I saw this feather in his blonde hair and said something about Indians, I forget what. He hit me in the gut, knocked me down. Then he robbed me."

Davies roared an objection on relevancy grounds, but Judge Flex observed that the testimony was merely preliminary. "Is that not so, Mr. Playchek?"

"Exactly, Your Honor. After you were beaten and robbed, did

you remain there on the steps?"

"I got out of that bastard's reach, but I stayed there on the steps. I was hurtin.'"

Playchek turned and pointed at Penny. "Did you see Ms. Hill there that morning?"

"Yes," said Travers, blinking in Penny's direction, "I saw her come out with some books."

"What happened next?"

"That bastard grabbed her purse. Just like he robbed me."

Davies rose calmly. "I move to strike the entire answer on the grounds that it mixes apples and oranges. It improperly connects the two events, Your Honor."

Judge Flex was firm. "Overruled. I have never understood that business about not mixing apples and oranges. Why, Dora and I mix them all the time for breakfast, don't we dear?"

"Yes," affirmed Dora Flex, "with bananas and grapes."

"So you see," Judge Flex continued, "it's not like mixing geese and ducks. Proceed, Mr. Playchek."

"Mr. Travers, did you see whether Smoking Mother got possession of the purse?"

"No, I just saw him grab at it and pull."

"Did you see the purse after that?"

"No. When the shot went off I made tracks."

"You could see Ms. Hill before you made tracks?"

"Sure. She screamed when he grabbed the purse."

"Did you see any sign she had or was holding a weapon?"

"No, I didn't see any weapon. I just heard that shot."

"Did you see Smoking Mother after that?"

"Just in the paper. I didn't know till I read it in the paper that the shot had hit him."

"That's all the questions I have, Your Honor," said Playchek.

"Very well, Mr. Davies, you may examine."

Davies was digging into his briefcase for something. When he stood upright again he had a silver flask in his hand. He held it out toward the witness. "You're a drinking man, aren't you, Mr. Travers?"

Playchek's objection was overruled. "It's preliminary, Mr. Play-chek."

Travers said nothing, and Davies repeated the question. Travers licked his lips. "Well, if you're about to offer me a snort, I wouldn't mind that at all."

"I was, sir. Your Honor, may I approach the witness?"

Playchek jumped up. "Your Honor, if Mr. Davies wants to drink with the witness he should do it after court. It's probably even illegal to drink during court session."

"Nonsense, Your Honor," said Davies, and took a pull on the flask. "Why, some of the best judges this city has ever had have taken a nip now and again while sitting. Besides, Your Honor, it will relax the witness. Right now he looks anxious for a snort."

Judge Flex appeared to be giving the matter deep thought. "Well, it is novel. I don't recall any other instance of a cross-examiner providing a witness with alcohol, at least not in this century. But that's in its favor. The courts must continually seek innovative solutions to social problems. Mr. Travers, do you have a drinking problem?"

"I sure do, Your Honor, and I could use a belt right now."

"Very well, the objection is overruled."

Davies passed the flask to Travers who emptied half of it. He smacked his lips. "Now that's good whiskey," he purred, turning and winking at the judge.

"Mr. Travers," Davies continued, "you were offered money to testify weren't you?"

His speech more slurred, Travers said, "Like I just told Mr. Playback. In the paper. There was a reward."

"And except for the money, you wouldn't be here today?"

"Nope." Travers hiccuped loudly. "'Scuse me."

Davies re-offered the flask, and Travers took another deep draft. "From your position you were unable to see Ms. Hill fire the pistol, right?"

Travers blinked and rubbed his face with the back of his hand. "No, I didn't see her. No pistol." He turned to Judge Flex. "Judge,"

Travers mumbled, "why don't we take a little rest?" Then he slumped forward on the witness box asleep.

Davies smiled graciously. "Your Honor, I think I've clearly been denied my right to cross-examine this witness, and I ask on that ground that his testimony go out."

Judge Flex turned to Playchek. "I believe Mr. Davies has a point there."

"But, Your Honor, Mr. Davies got the witness so drunk he can't be cross-examined. He can't take advantage of his own wrongful conduct."

"Well, Mr. Playchek, we can't be sure of that. You called this witness, and Mr. Davies objected that he appeared to be intoxicated, and that was long before he offered him a drink. So it's not all Mr. Davies's fault. I'm afraid I must instruct the jury to disregard Mr. Travers's testimony in its entirety."

The jurors shifted position in their seats, but otherwise appeared generally unmoved by this turn of events. It was 4:00 P.M. "It's a little early," said Judge Flex, "but we'll recess now. That way Mr. Travers can stay here and rest for a while."

"Your Honor," said Playchek, "can't we try to sober up Mr. Travers so Mr. Davies can complete his cross-examination?"

"But to do that, Mr. Playchek, we'd have to wake him up and move him out of the witness box, and I don't want to disturb him. He seems to be at peace. Tomorrow morning, 9:30 A.M., ladies and gentlemen."

TALLFELLOW RELATED BIG MOUTH'S COMMENTS regarding the trial to Ellen. She had completed the report and was packing for the trip to San Francisco. "Usually," she responded, "in our courts the lawyers do all the talking for the clients."

"Big Mouth thinks that is a mistake. I think He means to so advise Peter's sister."

"I didn't think he talked to the likes of us."

"It's a special case."

"Will I be able to see Him there?"

"I doubt it. Probably only Peter's sister will be able to see Him."

"That's too bad. I was hoping I would."

"I'll speak to Him about it. He is grateful to you for your handling of the bird snatchers."

"That would be kind of you. The helicopter's picking me up tomorrow. I should be in San Francisco in a couple of days. I've never been there before."

"Big Mouth recommends a trip to Alcatraz," said Tallfellow.

PETER MET ELLEN at the airport. "I thought you'd never get here," he said as they embraced.

"It wasn't just the report. There were other things: men with New-York-City accents caging the sacred birds. That sort of thing. And Dipper. He raised a lot of hell."

"What happened?"

"He was eaten by crocodiles. I'll explain it all later."

"I'm so glad to see you, Ellen. I missed you a lot."

"I missed you a lot, too. How is the trial going?"

"Penny's lawyer, Barton Playchek, says he can't tell, but he says that if she's convicted, the conviction will be reversed because the judge has made a lot of erroneous rulings."

They drove toward the city. "Peter, I don't have to stay at Penny's, you know. If I got a hotel room it might work out better." Ellen prayed silently for him to get the point.

"You know, Penny said the same thing, but she didn't want to sound as if she didn't want you to stay at her place."

"What did she say?"

"She said we'd have more privacy that way."

"She said 'we'd?' She used the plural?"

"Yes. At first I didn't understand."

"But you do now?"

"Yes, I've made a reservation."

"Peter, is Penny expecting us for dinner?"

"No. She's with her lawyers."

"Then let's go check into this hotel." She squeezed his arm.

Later that night, as they lay together in the hotel room, Ellen told Peter that Big Mouth was in San Francisco. "He went to Alcatraz first. Since then He's been at the trial. Tallfellow hears from Him regularly, and he told me about it."

"Penny says she saw Him sitting next to me at the trial. I told her she was imagining things. I didn't see anything."

"That figures. Tallfellow said she'd probably be the only one He'd manifest Himself to. It's because He wants to tell her something."

"Really? Tell her what?"

"He's concerned she's not personally defending herself. It offends one of His First Principles, the one that the gods help those who help themselves. I explained to Tallfellow that trials are different here. He wasn't impressed. He said the First Principles apply everywhere."

"Ellen, you sound as if you thought Big Mouth was for real."

"I think I do. I guess it's that Big Mouth seems real because Tallfellow is such a sensible person. By the way, the reason Big Mouth came here was to find a way to speed your return to Nova Cannes. Things started going wrong after you left, like Dipper and the bird snatching. Big Mouth thinks the sooner you return, the sooner the bad-luck streak will be broken. He knows you won't stay forever, but He sees your return as a way to break the circuit, so to speak."

"It sounds complicated. What can Big Mouth do to speed up the trial?"

"Tallfellow didn't know. He said Big Mouth would figure out something."

"He should talk to the judge's wife. She wants to speed it up, too."

"Is it dragging?"

"No, actually it's moving faster than Playchek expected."

"You see? Maybe Big Mouth is at work; you just don't see what He's doing."

"Ellen, if Big Mouth is a rational god, and I assume He is, that trial will appall him."

"Yes. He said something to that effect to Tallfellow."

"Ellen, there's something else on my mind besides the trial."

"I'm glad to hear that," she responded, rubbing his chest.

"Will you marry me?"

30. THE RETURN OF LYDIA GRIMES

FOLLOWING HER FAILURE TO FIND employment with the Blake campaign, Lydia Grimes went into self-imposed exile in Berkeley, California, a university town across the bay from San Francisco. While distinguished for its population of scholars, Berkeley had also traditionally served as a home for fanciers of disorder whatever their stripe. In this environment, Lydia knew she would be spiritually renewed. She was. While shopping for designer sandals on Telegraph Avenue, she received a vision so powerful that she left the store without paying for the shoes.

In her vision Lydia saw the entire vast outline of the California coast, and inland from it another meandering line along which lies the major geologic fault where the Pacific and North American tectonic plates meet. Absorbed in her perception, she squatted on the sidewalk in a state of semi-trance. A passerby tried to steal her new sandals, but she clutched them safely to her bosom. Then the complete vision began to emerge with terrific clarity. Lydia saw hundreds of oil company rigs driving giant wedges into the already parting fault line. Powerful drills were at work everywhere, from north to south, prying deep into the earth, severing the lands overlying the Pacific plate from the mainland. A huge portion of California was to be separated, to become one gigantic offshore drilling platform, as the Pacific Ocean filled the cleft made by the oilmen.

Thus freed from the rest of the United States and from existing governmental controls, adrift politically as well as physically, the new island would be open to uncontrolled exploitation by the oil lords, its waters infested with leaking platforms, its inhabitants conscripted into service on the rigs. Her duty was clear. Lydia rose and began to walk north along Telegraph Avenue, all the while receiving further details of the plot as the vision provided them. She stopped when she had reached the southern gateway to the University of California. There, clustered about the gate, some standing, others sprawled upon the pavement, some smoking, some drinking from paper-bag-wrapped bottles, some merely quarreling, shouting, weeping or grinning, was convened a congress of mostly young persons, mostly not students. She approached them. "I am come to lead you out of the aimless dreariness into which you have fallen. I will tell you about what the oil companies are doing and what you can do to help me thwart them. It is important," she said.

Then she explained the situation to them. Not all attended her message, but many did, and of those, several followed her to her residence at the end of the day. They camped at her doorstep, except for two who at her bidding followed her within. These two were later to be known as Priestess Maya and Priest Raymond. By the next morning the gathering at her residence had doubled in size. Lydia emerged radiant into the morning fog to greet them wearing garments suitable to her prophecy: flowing robes of multiple colors and her new sandals. Calling her followers about her, she explained to them how they must carry her message into the streets, and all but a few departed on their mission. Lydia sat curbside with the remainder while she began to reduce the elements of her vision to a simple creed that could be chanted. Within two days her followers numbered in the thousands.

At the end of that first week, Priestess Maya declared Lydia to be divine, the Second Coming of the Great Goddess, embodiment of the nurturing principle, protector of the Earth, Universal Mother. The Great Goddess, who (except for a handful of short-lived Mediterranean manifestations in pre-Christian times) had not been heralded since the last ice age, had recently become a popular icon in Berkeley and many other northern California communities. This absorption was not limited to feminist circles, but extended to those of both sexes who were disenchanted with what the conventional religions provided. It was said that the Great Goddess represented a preferable alternative to the often-warlike male deities who had dominated traditional theologies since Old Testament times. Lydia's apotheosis also provided something for the discontented that transcended the mere desire for social turbulence. Within another week this exaltation had translated into a host of thousands pulsing with satisfaction at following Lydia and her creed. Excitable souls, who had been driven into dormancy by the stultifying eighties, traumatized by the Internet-ness of the nineties, now sprang up and took heart everywhere.

Lydia's creed was simple and easily imparted. It was in essence a three-part plan: preservation of the geological status quo, destruction of the oil companies, and universal adult breast-feeding. The last element had been the inspiration of Priestess Maya, who saw it as "giving demonstrative expression and empowerment to the full meaning of the Great Goddess." Lydia saw that the idea would need some working out but felt that it was socially and politically sound. The details of effecting adult breast-feeding could be left for future experimentation.

Scouts sent to explore the fault line reported no evidence of oil company activity. Thus informed, the Great Goddess announced to her throng that the fossil fuel-men's scheme was more insidious than supposed; they had found some means of concealing their abomination. Her followers roared approval of this conclusion, not the least put off by the apparent absence of the enemy. Lydia then announced her initial tactical objective to be the placement of sentries along the entire length of the fault. The additional recruits and wherewithal needed for such an extensive maneuver would be obtained by a crusade to San Francisco. "When the sun rises tomorrow we shall be on the Bay Bridge headed west," she declared to the cheering assembly.

BRUTUS FULMEN, THE LAWYER who had represented Penny in Sex Court, was apologizing to a client. "Ms. Garter, I've been subpoenaed to testify in the Hill trial today, so we'll have to continue your hearing till tomorrow."

Muffy Garter didn't like the delay. "I'm losing a lot of money, you know, every day, like, I'm off the street. That stupid Hill case," she added, "the dead guy was a, you know, purse snatcher. He snatched mine. I lost a whip and handcuffs, you know, to that thief."

The potential importance of this intelligence to the Hill defense registered at once with Fulmen. "How much are you losing a day?"

"About eight hundred dollars, and it's, you know, tax-free."

Fulmen called Barton Playchek and explained the situation. "She'll need to be compensated for loss of work the day she testifies — about eight hundred dollars. Make the check out to me." Then he explained to Muffy what it was she was going to testify to and that they were going to split the money. It was OK with her; four hundred dollars was better than nothing. She'd set them straight about that feathered purse snatcher.

IN THE EVENT, PLAYCHEK DECIDED against calling Fulmen. General Sandschloss had not at all impaired the diminished-capacity defense, and Playchek concluded that the potential downside of proving that Penny had posed as a prostitute outweighed its upside as evidence that she was loony. But he welcomed the emergence of Muffy Garter and put her on as his next witness.

"You are a professional woman?"

"I try, you know, to be," Muffy responded, smiling at the jury.

Davies asked "can't we have a little more specificity?"

Playchek asked to approach the bench out of earshot of the jury, and Judge Flex agreed. "Your Honor, Ms. Garter is a prostitute. To force her to say so would be to pander to sensationalism, and I know this court would never pander to sensationalism."

"That's quite true, Mr. Playchek. I think 'professional woman' is adequate."

"But Your Honor," complained Davies, "I may want to prejudice the jury against her, and how can I do that if they don't know she's a whore?"

"Well, you have a point too, Mr. Davies. Let me think about it. Meanwhile, Mr. Playchek, you may proceed without further specification of Ms. Garter's vocation."

Playchek turned back to the witness. "Ms. Garter, was your purse stolen not long ago?"

"Yes. The guy, you know, Ms. Hill shot. He snatched it. Good riddance to bad rubbish."

"Ms. Garter, Ms. Hill denies she shot anyone, and we'll get to the identification. Tell the jury what occurred."

"Well, it was around 5 P.M., and I was just getting started for the evening, you know. I had the usual stuff in my purse: some extra panties, you know, rubbers, a whip and some handcuffs. Fortunately, you know, I never keep money there. I have, you know, special bras with money pockets."

Playchek produced a photo of Smoking Mother. "On that evening did you see this man?"

"Yeah, he ripped off, you know, my purse. He ran away. I had on, you know, these real high heels I wear when I'm working, and I can't, you know, run."

"Thank you, Ms. Garter. Your witness."

Davies rose. "Ms. Garter, there are a lot of big blond johns around San Francisco, and you could have mistaken one for the decedent, isn't that so?"

"There aren't, you know, any others wearing feathers."

Davies was undisturbed. "Don't you run into men in your work who like to wear feathers?"

"There was one, you know, come to think of it. But he didn't, you know, want it in his hair. Also he wasn't blond."

"Tell us, Ms. Garter, why you carry a purse with rubbers, a whip and handcuffs."

"You pulling my leg? You're a DA and you don't know?"

"Look, Ms. Garter, I'm asking the questions. Just answer please."

"Come up here and I'll, you know, whisper it to you. I don't want to tell you out loud in front of, you know, the judge."

Playchek rose. "Your Honor, Mr. Davies is blatantly pandering to sensationalism."

"Yes he is, Potter," said Mrs. Flex firmly.

"Go on to something else, Mr. Davies," said Judge Flex. But Davies had no other topics, and Muffy Garter was excused.

LYDIA'S CRUSADE BEGAN THE NEXT MORNING. Once in San Francisco, the host encountered and swept aside a marching, poster-carrying group of Waylon Homer campaign workers. The encounter, however, inspired Lydia. She denounced the mayoral race as a diversionary tactic to take the people's focus off the oil-company menace. She then called for a boycott of the election. Her followers rapidly disseminated news of the boycott. Lydia now fully accepted her divinity and thought of herself as a force of destiny. She was only deterred from declaring a state of divine law by Priest Raymond's advice that events so far would not provoke interest by the federal authorities, being rather the norm for California, but that a declaration of divine law would be another matter.

The hard core of her Berkeley followers converged on and took possession of Civic Center Park. Lydia then entered City Hall. She was not at first certain why destiny led her there, but as she went through the security checkpoint, one of the guards, noting her attire and bemused expression, said, "Hill trial fourth floor. Can't miss it." Then she knew why she had come there. Not only must the election be stopped, but all legal proceedings that might take public focus off the oil company issue.

Accompanied by Priestess Maya and a few other followers, she ascended to the fourth floor and entered Judge Flex's courtroom where trial was in session. She moved with confidence down the middle aisle till just opposite the front-row pew where Dora Flex had the aisle seat. Raising her right arm above her head, Lydia faced Judge Flex and declared, "I am the Great Goddess. This legal proceeding is adjourned until the oil industry plot has been utterly thwarted."

On her feet instantly, Dora Flex cocked her arm and delivered a powerful blow to Lydia's nose. The Great Goddess fell back into the arms of her priestess. "It's bad enough," said Mrs. Flex, "that that crazy woman who wanted to destroy all landlords got in here, but I'm damned if we'll have any goddesses. Bailiff, take this nut out of here."

Big Mouth, who could tell Lydia was not really a goddess and wanted the trial to proceed expeditiously, was cheered by Dora's prompt disposal of the imposter. It was the first positively useful action He had seen at the trial. Penny, to whom Big Mouth was visible, saw His crocodilian smile. "She's not really a goddess, is she?" Penny spoke softly, and Big Mouth, knowing she was addressing Him, shook His head to indicate agreement. It was their first communication. Soon, He thought, I must speak to her about the importance of taking a personal role in her defense.

In the event, the bailiff was not needed, for Priestess Maya and the other disciples dragged the semiconscious Lydia into the hall. When they were safely withdrawn from the premises, Maya spoke soothingly to her goddess. "I think we better concentrate on the fault line and the election boycott and forget about legal proceedings."

"What am I doing here," asked Lydia?

31. FURTHER THE MARCH OF FOLLY

Dr. Greta Sweetbacken took the stand and stated her name and address. "I'm sorry. Dr. what?" asked Judge Flex.

"Your Honor, it's these dentures. They still haven't gotten them right. My name iș Greta Sweetbacken."

"Thank you. Proceed Mr. Playchek."

"Doctor," asked Playchek, "did you prepare a résumé of your accomplishments in the mental health field?"

"Yes." She handed the résumé to Playchek. "Actually, Morris prepared it. My husband. My second husband, actually. My first, Simon, well, that's another story, but, basically he started to — "

Playchek interrupted. "Doctor, I just want to offer the list in evidence, and then I'll ask another question."

"That's all right, Mr. Playchek, take your time. I'll just think back here about Simon, my first husband. Actually, he showed signs of the problem even before we married. The letters to the editor of *Goat Herders Gazette*. That sort of thing — "

"Doctor, forgive me for interrupting, but did you examine Ms. Hill at my request?"

"Why, of course. I thought you knew that. I even sent you a bill. Men are so forgetful. Simon would write those long letters about goats and never remember my birthday."

"Doctor, did your examination of Ms. Hill inquire into her capacity to distinguish right from wrong?"

"Mr. Playchek! That was the whole point. How can you be so forgetful? And you can't even stick with the subject. We were talking about Simon. It wasn't just my birthday he'd forget. Why once he — "

"Doctor, what conclusions did you reach as to Ms. Hill's capacity to distinguish right from wrong? And I assure you I remember what you told me after the examination. It's just that we have to repeat these things for the judge and the jury here in court."

"Could you repeat that, Mr. Playchek? I didn't really follow you there."

The reporter read back the question. "Oh, I see. You want me to repeat my examination but this time with respect to the judge and the jury."

"No, doctor. Let's back up." Playchek explained, and Davies objected to the explanation as leading the witness.

Dora Flex reacted adversely. "It's preliminary, Potter. Wasting time again."

"So it is, dear. Overruled."

But now Dr. Sweetbacken's hand was in her mouth. Her bridgework was out of place. "Tham thing," she managed, finally shutting her mouth with a clacking sound. "There, that's better. Now what was it you wanted, Mr. Playchek?"

"Ms. Hill's capacity to distinguish right from wrong. What were your conclusions?"

"Well, I wish you had come right out and asked me that the first time instead of wandering on about all those other matters. Just like Simon. Only things he could concentrate on were those damn goats. Had little flocks of them all over the state. Dreadful business — ."

"Doctor, your conclusions regarding Ms. Hill. What were they?"

"Ms. Hill. Oh, yes. There she is. Hello Penny." She waved. "Looks good, doesn't she? But inside, upstairs, she's a basket case."

"Can you be a little more specific?"

"About what?"

"About why you think Ms. Hill's a mental basket case."

"Did I say that?"

Davies rose, smelling blood. "Your Honor, Mr. Playchek is trying to impeach his own witness."

Judge Flex shook his head negatively. "No, I think they're just in disagreement about something. Let's let them try to work it out."

"Thank you, Your Honor," said Playchek, truly grateful. "Doctor, did you determine specifically whether Ms. Hill's capacity to distinguish right from wrong had been diminished?"

"Why, of course. I told you, I billed you for it."

"What was your determination?"

"Well, at last we're getting to the point. I was shocked, I'll tell you, at the extent of injury to her capacity. A classic case of what repeated doses of humbug can do to the sensitive mind."

"Tell us how that could happen, Doctor."

"Just a few doses of former Governor Harry Lovebird's thoughts could do it. I tested Penny for that, by the way. I read to her from the governor's memoirs, the parts about his crime reduction program. His proof that, statistically, you can reduce the incidence of crime by making fewer arrests. And, needless to say, his conviction that distinctions between right and wrong should be avoided as being judgmental. But you can't point at just one thing and say that did it. I mean, Governor Throwback and Mayor Lint — she's been exposed to all of them."

"It's cumulative?"

"Yes. It's the year-in, year-out, nonstop bending of the line between right and wrong, truth and falsehood, by our politicians and their campaign people."

"Why isn't everyone's capacity to distinguish right from wrong diminished, Doctor?"

"Some people have a lower threshold of resistance to humbug. Penny is one of them."

"Doctor, if you were trying to increase the probability of someone developing this diminished capacity, what would you do?"

"The most important first step would be to have them move to California. You can't do much about the personal threshold of resistance, so the thing to do is to increase the humbug exposure level."

"And to decrease the probability?"

"Well, short of moving an exposed person out of the state, you would have to get the politicians and their accomplices to shut up."

"Is that a message you believe this jury should send, Doctor?"

Davies rose. "Invades the province of the jury, Your Honor. That's for them to decide."

"But," responded Playchek, "I'm only trying to help them."

Judge Flex nodded. "Mr. Davies, Mr. Playchek says he's just trying to be helpful. I think we should encourage that attitude in counsel. Overruled."

"You may answer, Doctor."

"Oh, yes. Now, actually, where were we? When you lawyers get off on these tangents, I lose my place, so to speak. I think we were talking about Simon's goats. I never did like those animals."

"No, Doctor. The message the jury should send. That's where we were."

"Well, Mr. Playchek, the problem is, no matter what message they send it's not likely to help your client. Once capacity is diminished it's rarely recovered. She probably should stop carrying a pistol."

This answer suggested to Playchek the wisdom of ending his examination, and he did so.

Davies rose. "Doctor, do you think Ms. Hill should be sent to a mental hospital?"

"Wait a minute," said Penny, but Dr. Sweetbacken was already answering the question.

"Certainly not. There she would be exposed to the same sort of thing that damaged her in the first place."

"Now, Doctor, I want to pin you down on something. Are you telling this jury that Ms. Hill could gun down a young Native-American in cold blood and not know it was wrong?"

Playchek rose. "Your Honor, I object. It's argumentative, assumes facts not in evidence, and is not proper conduct for an officer of the court toward a lady. He admits he is trying to pin her down, and that's very improper."

"It certainly is, Potter," said Dora Flex firmly.

"Sustained," said Judge Flex.

"But Your Honor, I respectfully submit I should be allowed to pin her down."

Dora gasped.

"Mr. Davies, the court is disturbed by the very mention of such an act."

"Very well, Your Honor, I'll go on to something else. Doctor, you have a strong prejudice against politicians, is that not so?"

"They cause a lot of trouble. They're like goats. My first husband, Simon, would — "

"Doctor, this jury doesn't want to hear about your first husband."

Playchek rose. "Your Honor, that's objected to as presumptuous. It's very presumptuous of Mr. Davies to conclude the jury doesn't want to hear about Dr. Sweetbacken's first husband."

"Sustained. The witness obviously didn't like her first husband, but that doesn't mean the subject is uninteresting."

"Doctor, you formed these opinions about capacity knowing you would be paid to have them, right?"

"Well, I'd worked with Mr. Playchek before, and he's always paid me. He's not like Simon was. Simon fell behind in his support payments from day one. I had to attach the goat herds. Then the sheriff told me Simon was — "

"Thank you, Doctor, that's all I have."

"BARTON, DR. SWEETBACKEN IS A LOT GOOFIER than I am," said Penny during an ensuing recess.

"Sometimes she kind of gets off the track."

"Mr. Barrow thought the whole thing was ridiculous. I saw him shaking his head."

"Just as long as he doesn't send you a dozen roses."

"He won't send roses, but I know he likes me, and he just seems to get handsomer every day."

"Don't you send him any roses either."

"I'll wait till the trial is over. Are there many more witnesses for us?"

"Just one."

"Me?"

"Sorry. It's going to be Reginald of Native-American Noise."

"Barton, you're not really going to keep me from testifying, are you? I can explain the whole accident. Nobody else can."

"It doesn't matter, Penny. The way the case has gone, it would be malpractice on my part to put you on the stand."

"Damn it! I'm the one at risk, and I'm paying for the whole thing, and I don't even get to talk." She was suddenly aware that Big Mouth was standing beside her, taking in the conversation. He looked upset.

SYBIL WATCH READ THE LEAD ARTICLE in *The Cockerel* on Lydia Grimes's crusade. Then she hooted. "Universal adult breast-feeding! What rot! Why, it's hard enough to get women to suckle their own children, let alone a lot of dippy adults." She said this to her friend Wanda Cranberry, who had become a fan of Lydia's after seeing oil company stocks climb higher and higher.

"Her crusade has had a very good effect on my petroleum stocks. The market seems to believe that the oil companies really have something going. And, Sybil, I would think that you, as a child psychiatrist, would be all for breast-feeding."

"For infants, not adults, Wanda. You have to draw the line somewhere."

"But consider your husband. What's that skin mag you buy for him?"

"*Breastworks*?"

"Yes. You could probably take that out of your budget if the Great Goddess' program takes effect."

"Wanda, I hate this Great Goddess. The girl used to work on my campaign staff, and she kept slipping stupid digs at the oil industry into my press releases. You complained about them yourself. Now she's telling people to boycott the election. The polls were bad enough before she became a goddess, and now she's made it worse."

Wanda, who deplored the idea of her friend becoming the mayor, nevertheless tried to console her. "But if the voters boycott the election, they can't vote for Homer or Blake."

"I'm afraid the ones who favor Blake think Lydia is a kook, just as I do, and they'll stay in town and vote. Waylon Homer and I compete for a lot of the same voting types, and when I think of all those idiots camped out there watching the San Andreas fault it makes me sick."

"But Sybil," said Wanda, "those idiots are your constituency."

"Yes, that's the problem."

"What if you were to become a goddess? Sybil is a lovely name for a goddess. Then you could order everyone to come back and vote for you. A divine commandment."

"I don't think this city can buy into more than one goddess at a time."

"Sybil, this city can buy into anything."

WAYLON HOMER AND HIS CONSULTANT, R. "Doc" Wayward, were addressing the same subject. "I don't like this exodus to the fault line and the election boycott, Waylon. We're losing the white touchy-feely vote, which is one of our strongest suits. The blacks and Asians, who are in Blake's camp, are immune to this 'Great Goddess' crap."

"Doc, why is it that only my partisans are taken in by this crusade?"

"It hurts Sybil, too. Every voting group is susceptible to particular kinds of poppycock. Ours begin to twitch over the Great Goddess kind of thing. It's very Mother Nature, nurturing female goodness. The adult breast-feeding business. That's big with our constituency. I checked it out with your therapist."

"With mine? Don't you have one, Doc?"

"No way. I get paid telling people what to do. A psychiatrist could ruin my edge. Anyway, yours says a lot of our voters will be pickets on the fault line, and others will obey the goddess and boycott the election."

"Doc, after all we've put into this campaign, I hate to lose it because of some phony goddess."

"Wait a minute! Waylon, you've got it! She's a phony. She's misrepresenting herself as divine. That's bound to violate consumer-fraud statutes. Here's what we'll do."

JUDGE FLEX ISSUED AN INJUNCTION against Lydia Grimes the next morning. It prohibited her from further representing herself as divine and "from purporting to enforce a boycott of the mayoral election by divine commandment." The jurist grounded his decision on the strict consumer protection laws of the State of California. Judge Flex rejected protests that the ruling interfered with Lydia's right to practice her religion. "In this State," he declared, "protection of our most valued resource, the consumer, takes precedence over all other considerations." At Wayward's urging, the court's opinion also referred to the persons who had departed the city to guard the San Andreas fault as victims of a hoax.

Wayward hurried copies of the injunction and order to the media. "It's two days until the election," he told his client. "This should repair the damage done by the Goddess' announcement of the boycott. And, since it was you who exposed the attempt to defraud consumers of their votes, that could galvanize support for you that was lukewarm or wavering."

"Doc, you always do the right thing. I'm glad you don't have a therapist."

A poll late the next day, however, showed James Blake still in the lead. "It appears," said Michael St. Augustine to his client, "that the Smoking Mother Memorial and the fat cat monitoring programs are holding their own against Homer's exposure of the Great Goddess."

"You mean our poppycock is more powerful than theirs?"

"Let's not think of it that way, Jim."

"BIG MOUTH EAT MORE," said Ellen, startled when, during a recess in court proceedings, He suddenly became visible to her.

"I need your advice," said Big Mouth. "You were so helpful in the matter of the birds." He paused, turning His massive head toward where Penny sat next to Playchek. "It has been decided that Penny will not testify. She is resigned to that. I should have spoken to her sooner."

"No. It would not have made any difference. The lawyer decided all that, and he was adamant. So don't fault Yourself."

"Ellen, is there any other way for her to involve herself personally in her own defense? As Tallfellow has told you, I feel strongly that that is important."

"I don't know. Well, there's final argument, but the lawyer always does that."

"What is final argument?"

"The lawyers sum up what the trial has proved or not proved. It's the final statement of what each side claims."

"That would be an ideal chance for her to take up her own cause," said Big Mouth, His spirit rising.

"But, Big Mouth, I have never heard of a lawyer letting his client do that."

"Can he stop her from doing it?"

"Probably, if he opposes it with the judge."

"I will talk to her, persuade her to insist upon it to her lawyer."

"MAKE THE FINAL ARGUMENT?" asked Playchek. "We only have to show diminished capacity, not insanity."

"Barton, I've been instructed to make the argument by a god. I have to do it."

"You've been taking me too much to heart. You're sane, perfectly sane. Now no more talk about God telling you to sum up."

"Not our God. This one comes from the island where Peter was working. His name is Big Mouth. He says the gods help those who help themselves. If I don't personally involve myself in my defense, I'll lose. I believe Him."

"Where is He? Is He here in the courtroom?"

"Yes, He's right over there next to Peter and Ellen. But only Ellen and I can see Him."

Playchek turned to look at Peter and Ellen. For the briefest of moments he thought he saw near them someone else, someone big, someone looking at him with huge jaws grimly set, a fortified penis arcing toward the courtroom ceiling. At the same time, Playchek experienced a powerful impulse to let Penny sum up; an intuition that this was essential to victory; that the jury would consider it absolute proof of her diminished capacity. "OK. I'll talk to Flex. I'll tell him it will make the trial more interesting." Playchek had said this before he realized he was speaking.

Penny threw her arms around him. "Barton, I'll do a good job! I'll work on it tonight." She looked over at Big Mouth. He was nodding His head, the fierce visage plainly smiling.

32. THE ONLY GOOD PALEFACE

THE STRETCH LIMOUSINE BEARING REGINALD YOUNG CROW and the other members of Native-American Noise worked its way through the crowd outside City Hall and parked at the foot of the steps. The more aggressive of the mob at once pressed round the vehicle with the intention of harassing the occupants and extorting money from them. They faded, however, when the seven fiercely painted, war-club-armed Native-Americans emerged and presented themselves like disturbed hornets. The mob thus dispersed, Reginald led his group to the security checkpoint where, after a brief contretemps, the attempt to confiscate their weapons was abandoned. They then proceeded to Judge Flex's courtroom. Court was in recess, but the television cameras went to work at once, bringing the arrival of Native-American Noise to the world outside.

Reginald, accompanied by one older Indian, went up to Playchek. "This is Shaman Red Leaf, Mr. Playchek, our spiritual advisor."

Playchek studied the shaman, who was the only Indian he had ever seen with a beard. "Were you ever a rabbi in Brooklyn?" he asked.

"The same. Shimon Rosenblatt."

"Rabbi Rosenblatt. I remember you from my school days."

"It's the beard. It always gives me away."

"What made you become a shaman?"

"The congregation. Easier to please. Also I like the music better."

Playchek turned back to Reginald. "Please ask the group to sit back there and downplay the war clubs."

Penny came up. "Are these real Indians, Barton?"

"Yes. Well, pretty much. This is their leader, Reginald Young Crow."

Penny extended her hand, and Reginald shook it. "Ms. Hill, we'll get you out of this if we have to scalp the DA."

"Wait a minute," said Playchek. "Reginald, that's the wrong attitude. I told you that we need gentle Indians in court, not a war party."

"Mr. Playchek, you're asking a lot. We're no 'loaf about the forts.'"

"That's right, Mr. Playchek," said Shaman Red Leaf, "we're no Uncle Tom red men."

"All rise." It was the bailiff announcing the re-emergence of Judge Flex, and, the ceremony completed, Playchek called Reginald to the stand. He was an impressive figure, tall and slim, chest partly bare, in full headdress, leather pants and moccasins, his war club nicely poised in one hand. Reginald identified himself and his group and explained the services they could perform. "We're musicians and dancers. We're going to put on a show after court. Come see us," he said at large to the occupants of the courtroom.

"Mr. Young Crow," said Playchek, "please tell the jury how you and I became acquainted."

"You called us because you wanted an authentic Indian to check out someone you thought was an imposter."

"And at my request did you examine Smoking Mother's body at the morgue?"

"Yes. A very unpleasant place. Not our usual gig."

"What were your conclusions?"

"He was a hundred percent paleface. Kind of Swede-like. Lots of them up in Minnesota, which is really Indian Territory."

"I didn't quite get that."

"He was a phony. He was no Indian."

"How could you be sure he wasn't part Indian?"

"Because I've seen lots of people who are part Indian, and they've all looked much better than that guy, better complexions, everything."

"Can you assure the jury that no special interest of Native-American tribes is implicated by Smoking Mother's death?"

"Sure. He was a just another son of the Great White Father who bit the dust. No loss at all."

This seemed to Playchek a good place to stop. Davies rose to examine and drew up close to the witness box.

"Keep your distance," said Reginald, fondling his war club.

Davies held his ground. "You're known as 'Redneck Reg,' aren't you?"

"No. You got buffalo chips for brains?"

"You've sold out completely to the white man, haven't you?"

"Watch your step," said Reginald, brandishing his club.

Undeflected, Davies asked, "Aren't you ashamed of yourself for betraying your own people?" His voice thundered majestically.

"Let's find out," said Reginald, rising, his war club drawn back for a blow, "whether it's true that the only good paleface is a dead one."

But before Reginald was able to test his point by slaying Davies, one of his companions stood up and, pointing toward where Peter and Ellen were seated, shouted, "Big Mouth eat more!" He was restrained by Shaman Red Leaf, who did not share his vision.

Judge Flex gaveled for order. "What's going on there," he asked?

"Your Honor," said Shaman Red Leaf, "our brother, Slow Hand, thinks there is a major spiritual entity in the courtroom named 'Big Mouth.' I think I have him calmed down now."

"I don't need calming down," responded Slow Hand. "He's right over there." He pointed at Big Mouth. "Big Mouth eat more," he declared with satisfaction.

"Big Mouth eat more," said Ellen and Penny, almost in unison.

"Your Honor, perhaps if we took a short recess," said Playchek, feeling a loss of control.

"Yes," said Davies, in a voice made uneasy by the posture of Reginald's war club, "I have no further questions."

"Remember," said Reginald, stepping from the witness box, "we dance and sing after court. TV welcome." He rejoined his group, triumphant, the day's clear winner.

33. A Mother's Voice and the Secret of Life

THE PROSECUTION'S REBUTTAL BEGAN the next morning. Flora Grebe arrived in court the worse for early morning gin, accompanied by Tula Fogg and wearing the orange-dyed fur coat she had loaned to Wendy Papp. Tula took Sonia Taft aside. "She's taking it very hard," said Tula. "The loss is just awful. The poor mother."

"She looks smashed to me," replied Sonia dubiously. "And she's walking funny."

"I think it's the coat, Ms. Taft. It drags a little."

"That horrible coat. Get her a cup of coffee, Tula."

"We just had some, but she put some spirits in it. Gin, I think."

"Goddamn it! Something about this trial. The witnesses are always screwed up some way."

"But think of the strain she's been under, losing her son. I just couldn't bring myself to interfere."

"So now she's half bombed."

"Ms. Taft, many Native-Americans have a natural problem with alcohol. We can't really fault her."

"Are you sure she's Indian? She looks pretty florid to be an Indian."

"I think she's denying her Indian heritage because of her great upset over the loss of her son."

"Denying her heritage?"

"Yes. She still insists she's not even part Indian. But she must be, because Smoking Mother's father was a Swede. She's clear on that."

"Tula, why didn't you tell me this?"

"Well, to begin with I felt it would be, well, a betrayal of the poor woman to go into a lot of details with her so upset."

"It sounds like we've got a real crapshoot putting her on the stand. I better explain this to Tremorgan."

But Tremorgan was in the mood for a crapshoot. "Whatever else she is, Sonia, she's the victim's mother. We need her to make this jury think about the impact of the shooting on the family. There's not much to make them sympathize with the victim, but the mother ... "

"I guess you're right. By the way, Tula tried to get her to leave that weird coat at the hotel, but no soap."

"Yes. I don't deserve to have to put on another witness who's wearing that appalling coat."

Dora Flex was somewhat of the same mind. Flora Grebe was no sooner settled in the witness box when the Judge's wife declared, "Potter, we can't be having the same witness twice. I recognize that coat. This one has already testified."

"So do I, dear."

"Your Honor," said Davies, "it's the same coat but a different witness."

Dora was unconvinced. "Potter, I can't believe two different women would have that same dreadful coat. This case will never end if we start recycling witnesses."

"Who the hell are you?" asked Flora Grebe in a husky voice, gleaning that her coat was somehow under attack.

"I'm the judge's wife, whoever you are, and don't you forget it."

"Yeah, and I'm the queen of England. You keep your mouth shut about my coat or I'll give you a fat lip." She hiccuped gently.

"Your Honor," said Davies hurriedly, "this is Flora Grebe, the victim's mother. Forgive her comments. She's overwrought at her loss. She lent her coat to the other witness."

"You want to step outside?" said Flora to Mrs. Flex. "I'll take care of your problems with my coat."

"Potter, this woman is insufferable," Mrs. Flex declared. "Put her in jail or something."

Davies, wringing his hands, began apologizing directly to Dora. "Mrs. Flex, she's lost her son. She's very disturbed. Please let her testify."

"Oh well, I suppose, if she must."

"If I must?" Mrs. Grebe hiccuped in mid-sentence, loudly this time. "Goddamn it, I've been stuck in that Earthquake Hotel for two weeks, and I don't give a damn if I testify. I want to get out of this lousy city."

At a nod from his wife, Judge Flex instructed Davies to proceed.

"Mrs. Grebe, you reside in St. Paul, Minnesota, and came here at our request to give the jury some insight into your terrible loss?"

"Where's the woman who shot him?" responded Flora.

"She sits there, Mrs. Grebe." Davies pointed at Penny.

"Well, a classy looker, eh? Not his type. Liked 'em rough. Beat up on 'em. Just a matter of time till one shot him."

"Mrs. Grebe, tell us what you felt when the police gave you the news about your son."

"How did I feel? I was mad as hell. I thought he'd got the cops to call for bail money. He did that once in St. Paul. She ... " She pointed at Tula. "The little cop that jumps around a lot called me."

"You mean Officer Fogg?"

"Yeah. Then she started in talkin' about him being with the Great Spirit now and all this Smoking Mother crap, askin' about Indians."

"She was thinking of your son's Native-American heritage, Mrs. Grebe. It was important to us."

"Yeah? That crap was important to you, eh? He was prob'ly scamming your welfare people, posin' as an Indian. Was that it?"

"No, no, Mrs. Grebe, it was — "

"Well, never mind that crap. You're not getting a nickel back out of me. But I'll tell you, Thorson was nothing but a goddamn Swede, just like his father. I'm mostly Swede too, but not like them. Say, I'm gettin' thirsty. How long does this go on?"

"Mrs. Grebe, how can a mother's grief ever be assuaged?" Davies's voice trembled with unassuaged grief.

"Well, a drink would go a long way toward assuagin' my thirst. I don't need to assuage any grief." She laughed.

Bleakly, Davies looked at Sonia Taft, who gave him a hook sign. "That's all I have, Your Honor."

Playchek rose. It was already very good, but the temptation to make it better was too much. "Mrs. Grebe, would you say Thorson inherited his criminal tendencies from his father?"

Davies objected. "Not relevant and not the subject of opinion evidence, Your Honor."

"Well, this is a criminal case," Judge Flex observed with confidence, "so it's clearly relevant, and I believe it comes within the 'interesting subject matter' exception to the rule precluding opinions. Overruled."

"You may answer, Mrs. Grebe."

"Yeah. Well, see he was up to no good from the time he could crawl. Bashed a neighbor's kid on the head with a baby bottle. And his old man. We had to have him put to sleep. He started biting. So I say it looks like an inheritance from his goddamn father."

"Thank you, Mrs. Grebe."

This concluded the presentation of evidence. Judge Flex set closing arguments for the next day and recessed. "It's Election Day, ladies and gentlemen," he reminded the jury. "Let us now exercise our right and obligation as citizens and vote."

MAYOR HOMER CONCEDED to James Blake at 9:30 P.M. that night. His consultant, R. "Doc" Wayward, was by his side. Afterward, they had a few minutes alone over drinks. "I'm afraid, Waylon, we were done in by our own issues. Blake got fat on the Smoking Mother thing and on bashing the wealthy."

"Doc," said Homer, laughing, "there must be someone to blame besides ourselves."

"Of course," Wayward replied, joining in his client's laughter. "There's the voters. It's mostly their fault."

"Right you are, Doc. I'll drink to that. By the way, what are you going to do now?"

"It's interesting you ask that, Waylon. Something attractive just popped up: I've been retained to arrange government approvals and stimulate public support to move the Statue of Liberty off the island it's on."

"My God! Where?"

"Anywhere. We just have to get it off that island to be able to get at the Secret of Life."

"Doc, what is this?"

"It's wild. My client's are a very wealthy Hollywood star and her group. They're called the New Vision and Revision Historians. The background is fascinating. In very ancient times, powerful extra-terrestrials, after building the Sphinx, came to New York harbor — of course it wasn't New York yet — and buried the Secret of Life on that island. The facts on all this were received by the historians while they were sleeping in Khufu's sarcophagus in the Great Pyramid. Now we've got to move the statue so the historians can dig up the island in search of the Secret of Life. They've got lots of money."

"Doc," Homer said, taking a deep gulp from his glass of whiskey, "when I hear about things like that, it makes my election loss seem pretty insignificant. It's also good to know there are people out there balmier than we are here."

"Yes, I thought of that when I took the job."

"You know, Doc, I'm thinking of retiring from politics for a spell, sort of regroup, and your kind of work appeals to me. I mean, representing people who hire you so they can excavate the Secret of Life, and paying you well, too."

"It's a good life, Waylon."

"Right. I'm thinking, could they use another consultant? I have powerful friends in the East, right nearby on Staten Island. One of them is with the New York Port Authority."

"A good thought, Waylon. Why break up a losing team, particularly when the Secret of Life is at stake? Besides, it will get this election behind us. Drink up!"

"Right! And fuck Smoking Mother," said the Mayor cheerfully, draining his glass.

PART IV

LAST RITES

34. CLOSING REMARKS

TREMORGAN DAVIES BEGAN HIS CLOSING REMARKS with confidence, his formidable appearance and flair much in evidence despite the discouraging performance of most of his witnesses. He was comforted by the thought that the defense had also put its share of loopy people on the stand. In any event, Davies had decided that the best course was to reprise his opening statement, which in his view had been the high point of the trial, rather than concern himself with the testimony.

He did so with ardor and at length, reminding the jury of their opportunity and obligation to strike back at the upper crust for their centuries-long oppression of the poor, and that this issue was far more important than the facts of the case and the evidence presented at the trial. He concluded, "Only by convicting this shameless representative of the malevolent elite can you make this trial meaningful and send a message to other would-be oppressors that they will be held accountable."

When Davies had finished, Penny left the counsel table and, carrying a single sheet of paper on which she had outlined her closing remarks, went to the lectern. She was wearing a simple white blouse, a string of pearls, a dark pleated skirt and black heels. Glissa Cocoa, fashion editor of The *Cockerel*'s television channel, was revisiting the trial after two weeks' rest in a nudist camp to which her therapist had sent her. She had not entirely recovered from the trauma induced by Dora Flex's attire, but the news that Penny would be making her own summation was an irresistible attraction. What Penny wore could become the fashion statement of the year.

Glissa began to write, "Penny Hill's beautifully fashioned pumps clicked dramatically on the courtroom floor as she moved toward the jury to begin the defense of her freedom."

Penny began that defense by offering to take a lie-detector test on whether she shot Smoking Mother. Davies rose angrily. "This is what comes, Your Honor, of letting non-lawyer defendants argue their own cases. Any lawyer knows it's improper to offer to take a lie-detector test. It suggests to the jury that the accused can scientifically prove she is innocent. Worse, it puts emphasis on the truth rather than on the issues in the decisional process."

Playchek, who had not expected so effective, albeit improper, a move by his client, sat silent. Judge Flex was understanding. "Yes, Ms. Hill, it was improper to offer to prove you were telling the truth. In legal proceedings the truth is almost invariably prejudicial to one of the parties, so even though you are not a lawyer, you can understand why Mr. Davies got so upset."

"Your Honor, I promise not to do it again. It just seemed like a good idea. You know, if the test proved I didn't shoot him, we'd all save a lot of time." Dora Flex smiled approvingly.

Davies was furious. "Your Honor, this clever woman is exploiting her own impropriety by now appealing not only to the truth but to the jurors' desire to save time. I urge the court to condemn this blatant defiance of customary procedures. It is highly prejudicial to the people."

"Your Honor," said Penny, "It is undisputed that Mr. Davies has been trying to win this case by prejudicing the jury against me. I am only trying to prejudice them in my favor."

"Quite so, Ms. Hill, and I am a firm believer in maintaining a balance of prejudice. You may proceed."

"Penny Hill's subdued, professional-appearing outfit," wrote Glissa, "greatly complemented her efforts to prejudice the jury, proving once more how understatement can excel fashion-wise. It also appeared to your reporter that prejudicial remarks from so smashing a mannequin as Penny Hill were particularly infuriating to her opponent. Lesson: Girls, you can be highly prejudicial even when conservatively dressed, but it helps to be very good-looking."

"Ladies and gentlemen," Penny continued, "Mayor Homer came down here and carried on about whether the trial was adequately addressing women's issues. Well, they were staring him in the face, and he never said boo about them. To begin with, there can be no dispute that if I had been a man I would never have been prosecuted. A man would not have been carrying a gun in a purse and would not have had a purse to be snatched. This case reeks of selective, sexist prosecution of women."

"Viewers," wrote Glissa excitedly, "the wrong accessory, as Penny Hill pointed out, can lead to your indictment. Your handbag can make you the target for sexist district attorneys. This was the substance of Penny's blast at male-dominated, fashion-ignorant criminal prosecution."

"On top of that," Penny continued, "there is the serious failure of the government to provide adequate firearm education to its female citizens. Any man would know that that old single-action revolver my father left could go off if it hit the ground, but women do not. We women had to have an international troublemaker come here to court to explain about that weapon. Women are expected to be content learning how to run microwaves and blenders, when our schools should be teaching us to run guns.

"Which brings me to the subject of gun control. Mr. Davies represents the government, and we all know it's up to the government to provide effective gun control. If it had, this death could never have occurred. There would have been no gun in my purse when Smoking Mother grabbed it, and he would be alive today, in the streets, stealing purses, robbing drunks, and beating up on people smaller than he. Ladies and gentlemen, can society afford to lose the likes of Smoking Mother? If your answer is no, then you know where to place the blame: it belongs on the government, whose lax gun-control laws afforded no means of preventing me from having one in my purse."

Davies interrupted. "Your Honor, this argument is unprecedented. The defendant is saying it was up to the people to prevent her from committing the crime."

"Your Honor," responded Penny, "it's not unprecedented at all. It's widely recognized that the primary responsibility for crime lies with the government, either by enacting laws that then are broken or by failing to enact laws that would deter criminal conduct. Either way, crime is clearly referable to government action or inaction, and it ill behooves Mr. Davies to deny his client's role in the commission of crime."

Davies was furious. "Your Honor, that's the most far-fetched, ridiculous argument I have ever heard made in a criminal case."

Penny countered again. "That's what makes it interesting, Your Honor, and the court has enjoined all of us to try to keep the trial interesting."

"Quite so, Ms. Hill. Proceed."

"Ladies and gentlemen, we've pretty much covered the gun control and women's issues that you will want to consider while you deliberate. There are other matters I urge you to consider as well. For example, the actual evidence has been given scant attention during the trial because of the emphasis laid upon socially significant issues that go beyond the facts of the case. But there is no evidence that I shot the deceased. The evidence is, I came down the library steps with a load of books and a dangling purse, and I was well dressed. I emphasize 'well dressed' because that told the purse snatcher that there was probably money in my purse, and he went for me. I was a good mark."

Glissa wrote furiously. "A fashion plus, Penny Hill became a robbery victim because her threads said money. A point Penny failed to make, but we do, is how society must ensure fashion excellence by protecting those who practice it. And, girls, we are all well rid of this vicious mugger who chose his victims from among the better dressed."

"Now," said Penny, "I want to comment on the relevant conspiracy. As we all know from television, films, and other media, most of the tragic events in our nation and in our personal lives are the result of concealed conspiracies. The telephone companies, for example, are still covering up the fact that protracted phone conversations as teenagers can result in enlargement of the ear and mouth later in life. Similarly, until recently exposed by *People Person* magazine, rightist groups had been able to cover up the fact that they are holding former Governor Harry Lovebird and three of his judicial appointees captive in a Tabakistan ashram. And at a personal level, every day of our lives, you and I serve as pawns in a battle between powerful forces known only to the real insiders in Washington. Under the cloak of elaborate deceptions and cover-ups, these massive cartels struggle for power and for their titanic economic prizes, prizes for which our well-being, even our lives, are the price.

"Now, in an effort to get to the heart of the matter that brings us all to court, I had a computer check done on the circumstances surrounding the deaths of any males of Swedish descent that occurred in the United States on the day Smoking Mother died." Penny paused and looked at Playchek. His face shone with admiration. "Ladies and gentlemen, there were six such deaths on the same day: four by gunshot, one by drowning, and one by drug overdose. Moreover, and even more telling, each of the six either lived in or came from Minnesota, where the headquarters of the international grain monopoly is located. Ask yourselves, why this pattern? You and I are not so naive as to believe all this is purely the result of coincidence." Penny drank from her water glass and continued. "Was I a pawn in some master plan of the pan-global grain cartel, the nature of which scheme has been covered up with dollars and deceit? Obviously, these occurrences are not isolated events. Your personal experience, your knowledge gained from films, television, and other media, tells you these events are related. And, ladies and gentlemen, you don't leave your common sense and personal experience on the courthouse steps when you come here to serve as jurors. You can and must bring that knowledge with you when you deliberate."

Davies rose. "Your Honor, I move the court to instruct the jury that there is nothing in the record concerning these dead Swedes that Ms. Hill is going on about."

"Well, Mr. Davies," Judge Flex responded, "it is true there was nothing in the record until Ms. Hill brought up the subject, but if she is able to supply material previously missing from the record, then her argument would qualify as being self-supporting. Motion denied. Proceed."

"Ladies and gentlemen, I have one final point. It's this business about juries sending messages. Now, I know my lawyer told you how you could send a message. It wasn't just Mr. Davies who wanted you to do so. But with all respect to Mr. Playchek, I think it's time juries stopped concerning themselves with what messages their verdicts will send, and focused instead on the facts presented at the trial.

"For years I've been reading in the papers how juries have reached verdicts that were intended to send messages to big corporations, or to the government, or just to the public. But look about you. Have things gotten better? Certainly not. We all know that in the period these juries have been broadcasting messages things have gotten worse. It's time to call a halt and take a new tack. We can't be sure things will get better, but we know that while juries have been sending messages things have gotten worse. The message you should send is 'no more messages from juries.'"

Davies rose. "Your Honor, this argument is making a mockery of the time-honored message sending practice that I invoked."

"Yes," replied Judge Flex, "but Mr. Playchek invoked it too, so it comes under the 'sauce for the duck' rule."

"Gander, Potter," said Mrs. Flex.

"So it is. Gander, what's sauce for the gander is sauce for the duck. Proceed, Ms. Hill."

"Your Honor, I have concluded, except to say thank you, ladies and gentlemen." Penny left the lectern and returned to her seat at the counsel table.

"Concluding her remarks," wrote Glissa Cocoa, "Penny Hill turned on her long legs, her handsome dark pleated skirt twirling before the rapt eyes of the jury, and reseated herself next to her lawyer."

Judge Flex declared a recess.

At the same time, Penny sensed someone behind her and turned to see Big Mouth standing there giving her a thumbs-up sign. "Was I all right," she asked?

"You were extraordinary," said Big Mouth. "You have helped yourself very much."

"It got easier as I went along," said Penny, taking comfort from the approval of the deity. "But I'm afraid the generation of humbug may be habit forming. Now I'll have to break the habit."

Playchek, who could not now see Big Mouth, came up to Penny. "You were wonderful, especially on the conspiracy issue. The jury loved it." He was beaming. "We're going to get an acquittal one way or another."

"You mean, I proved I'm crazy?"

"No. What you really proved is that a great summation need not be captive to the facts of the case. Davies won't be able to top it."

Davies couldn't. His final remarks were little more than a rehash of arguments previously made, which the jury had already grown accustomed to and, accordingly, less interested in.

In due course the jury retired to deliberate Penny's fate. The process took less than three hours.

35. Straight from the Horses' Mouths

THE JURORS FILED BACK INTO THE COURTROOM and took their seats. Their faces and body language appeared lighthearted to Playchek. Penny gripped his arm. "Jonathan Barrow just winked at me. We've won," she whispered.

"It looks good. There's a lot of smiling, but the chickens haven't hatched yet."

They did a few minutes later. Barrow, who had been elected Chairperson, reported the results. The jurors were unanimous for acquittal on the grounds that Penny Hill did not commit the alleged homicide. They were eleven to one for acquittal on the grounds that her diminished capacity precluded her conviction of the crime. Playchek had never seen a verdict like it. Jurors never got to the issue of diminished capacity unless they found that the defendant had committed the offense. But this one had.

Davies had the jury polled. Each endorsed the verdict as reported. The lone dissenter on diminished capacity was Chairperson Barrow. Davies then asked for a conference in chambers. In Judge Flex's chambers he observed persuasively, "Your Honor, there's something very peculiar here. If the jury really believed and understood the defendant had not committed the crime, why did it find she wasn't guilty because of diminished capacity?"

Dora Flex, who had come to chambers with the lawyers, was ready to rule on the issue. "Potter, there is no sense mulling that over. The jury has clearly shown its preference for freeing Ms. Hill. She's got to walk." Penny walked.

MURIEL FEIN, PLAYCHEK'S LEGAL ASSISTANT, commenced interviews of the jurors the afternoon of the day of the verdict and completed them the next day. All the jurors agreed to be interviewed. Their comments were often so similar that Muriel was able to group them and generalize the most frequently encountered conclusions: 1 – Penny did not shoot Smoking Mother, 2 – Smoking Mother was a purse snatcher, 3 – He snatched Penny's purse, 4 – This caused the revolver to fire, 5 – For reasons and by means that have been concealed by the perpetrators, the killing actually was an overt act in furtherance of a conspiracy by the international grain cartel, 6 – Penny's decision to make her own closing argument conclusively established that her capacity was diminished.

Although less often cited, widespread support for the verdicts lay in the jurors' conclusions that 1 – Smoking Mother was not a Native-American, 2 – Penny was too nice a person to have shot anyone, 3 – It would be nicer to have Mr. Playchek in the family than Mr. Davies, and 4 – Penny's offer to take a lie-detector test on the question whether she shot Smoking Mother showed she was innocent.

When Muriel asked the reasons why these conclusions were reached, she got down to the superb chaos underlying the formation of human decisions. Astral photographer Candy Quality, for example, explained how she was able to decide that Penny was innocent: "I don't believe a juror should just sit there like a rock and listen to the evidence. You have to work on the case to do your job right. That's why I asked what Penny's birthday was."

"I remember," said Muriel, "but how did that help you?"

"That was the whole thing, once I ran the horoscope. The stars don't lie you see. It was impossible for Penny to commit a crime on the day of the shooting. It was all there in her horoscope."

"So that way you knew she was innocent?" Muriel was not astonished. She had interviewed other juries.

"Well, I didn't stop there. I looked at the evidence to see what was the most logical explanation for what happened. It seemed to me that it was what Penny told us about the conspiracy the big grain companies have back there in Minnesota. It couldn't just be a coincidence that all those Swedes died that way the same day.

It's like she said, the monopolies try to conceal things from us, but they didn't fool me, and I explained it to the other jurors."

Other jurors also emphasized the importance of Penny's date of birth. Juror Ramon Derecho explained to Muriel, "See, I didn't think she did it for a lot of reasons, like she was probably a little diminished by all that campaign stuff, and I didn't want to be biased just because of her birthday."

"Her birthday?"

"Yeah. May fifth, El Cinco de Mayo. That's important. It's Independence Day in Mexico. Like I say, that wasn't the only evidence, but I just don't believe a nice woman like her born the day she was would be a killer."

Juror Heather Plant had a daughter born on May fifth. "Now, that wasn't the whole story, but naturally I couldn't just block it out. After all, I'll never forget when Marcie was born. She was a whole two weeks early but so cute. So mostly I looked at the evidence that Ms. Hill was innocent and disregarded the stuff about guilt, cause I wasn't really in favor of convicting her."

Another male juror assured Muriel, "Davies had a good point there about this being a chance to make the rich people pay for what they've done to the poor, but so did Mr. Playchek, when he said we had to let these politicians and campaign people know we're fed up with their lies. So I was pulled in both directions. That's why it was good that girl who did the horoscope was on the jury to settle the matter."

A female juror had to resolve a similar quandary. "I'm a real people person, so naturally I don't like to see anyone killed. But I don't like to see anyone arrested for murder either. So it was a hard case for me. Then, Ms. Hill reminded us of the women's issues that were on her side, and that made my mind up that she was innocent."

And so it went. Occasionally, Muriel was told that the juror simply had seen no evidence that Penny shot Smoking Mother, but this unadorned conclusion was rare.

MURIEL FINALLY COMPLETED THE JUROR INTERVIEWS at 7:30 P.M. on the day after the verdict. The process had exhausted her. When she got to her apartment that evening, she collapsed onto her bed and fell asleep. She did not wake until 10 P.M. Then she remembered the message the chairperson of the jury had given her to pass along to Playchek.

Muriel tried Playchek's home number and three restaurants before hitting the right one. He was dining with Penny, Peter, and Ellen in celebration of Peter and Ellen's engagement and the successful outcome of the trial. The headwaiter brought the phone to the table.

"Barton, I should have called earlier, but I just crashed when I got home. Jonathan Barrow, the chairperson, wants to talk to you. He told me he was going to contact Penny, and that it was important, but he didn't know if there was a time period he should hold off. He didn't want to screw up the verdict."

Playchek looked at Penny. This wasn't going to look good, and the media would jump on it. There was, however, no legal prohibition, and he knew Penny would sweep adverse considerations aside. "Muriel, tell Mr. Barrow that Ms. Hill is my girlfriend, and that I don't tolerate competition."

"What?" said Muriel.

"What?" said Penny.

"Did you ask him," Playchek continued, "why he voted against us on diminished capacity?"

"Yes. He was cryptic on that. He said he agrees with General Sandschloss."

"Muriel, tell him it's legally OK to contact Penny, but the publicity is going to curl his hair."

"He needs her phone number. It's unlisted, you know."

"I've got to give him her phone number, too? Now I'm a couples agency."

Penny seized the phone. "Muriel, it's me." Penny carefully recited her phone number. "Tell him I'll be in until noon tomorrow. What did he say?"

"He just said he was going to contact you and asked if there was a waiting period. Oh, yes, he said it was important."

"Muriel, please call him right now. It's important."

36. Endgame

JUDGE AND MRS. FLEX SAT IN THE COMFORT of their home watching television reports on the outcome of the trial, which was still receiving considerable media attention four days after the verdict. "Well, dear," the jurist said, "I think it was a nice trial, and most people seem to have enjoyed the outcome."

"Yes. I just wish that Governor Throwback hadn't been so critical of your instructions to the jury."

"I know. He's been really carrying on about the one I gave that 'You should not find the defendant guilty of murder unless you really don't like her.'"

"Mr. Playchek proposed that, didn't he?"

"Yes, and it seemed quite appropriate. After all, as a juror, I wouldn't want to convict someone I liked, at least not of murder. It was innovative, too. It's never been given in a case until now."

"That's probably what annoyed Throwback, Potter. He's never liked anything new."

"That's quite true, dear. I heard him speak last year at the Statesmen's Club, and I remember exactly how he put it. He said, 'I've seen a lot of changes in my time, and I've been against every damn one of them.' He will never understand how the administration of justice simply cries out for novelty."

"Speaking of novelty, Potter, *The Cockerel* reported today that Penny Hill and the chairperson of the jury, Jonathan Barrow, were seen dining alone together at a south-of-Market restaurant.

Is that allowed?"

"Well, dear, if neither of them is married then I see no objection."

"It doesn't invalidate the verdict or anything?"

"Oh, no. Now if they'd started that before the verdict we'd have to look closely at the situation."

BARTON PLAYCHEK TOOK THE PASS, dribbled directly at the man guarding him, then feinted right and went for the basket. Two points. It was the winning bucket in the Bar Association league game.

Afterward, he sat in the sauna with one of his teammates. "It was unusual letting her sum up, but I had no choice. There was divine intervention." Playchek explained the situation to his friend. "After the verdict, I saw Big Mouth again and heard Him thanking me. His followers all say, 'Big Mouth eat more,' so I said that, and He invited me to visit His island, Nova Cannes."

"I've never heard of it. Must not be on any of the tours."

"Definitely not. The people I'm going with were at the trial, and they say it's a terrible place for whites, that I won't last a week, but I want to see it. They're doing anthropological work there and are going back after their honeymoon."

"Did you hear Davies resigned from the DA's office yesterday? He says he wants to be a defense lawyer."

"He's not likely to receive spiritual assistance, as I do. But then, there's the letters he gets from his mother about his cases. Flex let him present his mother's opinions about our case to the jury."

"Were they helpful?"

BIG MOUTH AND TALLFELLOW WERE COMMUNICATING in the tribal sanctuary. "The high point of the trip, apart from Penny's argument, was the visit to Alcatraz," said Big Mouth. "Although I also enjoyed the Native-American group that came to court. One of them recognized me."

"Would You want to return?"

"Oh, no. It is interesting to observe primitive people, but enough is enough. I attended Peter and Ellen's wedding, a pleasant ceremony, even without any wrestling beforehand. They've gone to some other island before returning here to civilization. By the way, I invited Penny's lawyer, Mr. Playchek, to visit us. He followed my guidance and deserves the trip. He will join Peter and Ellen and arrive with them."

"Should I prepare a celebration for their arrival?"

"A good idea. Prepare our traditional feast, long pig."

"Ah, but You know how Peter and Ellen feel about long pig."

"Yes, but Mr. Playchek is coming, and I believe lawyers may have a different attitude toward eating their fellow man."

WANDA CRANBERRY WAS CONSOLING HER FRIEND, Sybil Watch, who had finished last in the race for the mayor's office. "Really, Sybil, you'll be much happier not having to level all those schoolchildren."

"Wanda, you don't understand. A child psychiatrist can only control things up to a point. But a mayor. It was a chance to do what I know is right, and also to shut up a lot of people whose views I don't like. Now, it's back to Wagner and malfunctioning children."

"I know, dear, it's disappointing. Your plans for stifling dissent down the drain. Having the desire and the qualifications to be a dictator and being denied the chance is very frustrating. But there are real compensations. It could be very frustrating trying to shut people up. It's driven many a despot insane."

"Wanda, has there ever been a coup for the mayor's office?"

"You were thinking of mounting a white horse and riding to City Hall?"

"Too old-fashioned. Maybe something using the Internet."

"Coups are generally reserved for higher office. Why not mount one against Governor Throwback? There are legions of people out there longing for the return of Harry Lovebird or someone like him, but Lovebird's still in some ashram in Tabakistan. That's where you could fit in."

"Well, like Harry Lovebird, I do believe we should show more tolerance for crime. I give similar advice to my patients' parents when a child does something especially vicious or destructive. If people would just be a little more tolerant, they wouldn't get so upset over criminal behavior."

"Exactly, Sybil. Treat criminality as an alternative lifestyle. You could march on our state capital flying a 'Tolerance for Crime' banner and seize control. But a coup now for the mayor's office with you just having lost the election would be thought excessive."

"Wanda, do you think Jim Blake will keep his campaign promises?"

"I certainly hope not, but he might feel a moral obligation to do so. I've heard he's incorruptible and keeps his word, which doesn't give us much to hope for."

"I was thinking mostly about his Smoking Mother Memorial project. He really stole that from my promise to rename Market Street 'Smoking Mother Way.'"

"Yes. All stuff and nonsense too. A real Indian testified at the Hill trial that Smoking Mother was posing as an Indian."

"For Heaven's sake, Wanda, what's that got to do with it? Aren't we all posing?"

"My dear, sometimes you cut right to the chase. You really must take your act to the governor's office."

"I don't know. My concession speech said I was leaving politics to devote more time to my family."

"Sybil, it would be grossly unnatural for a politician to fulfill promises to spend more time with the family. Waylon Homer said the same thing, and his family would never stand for it. No. I'm quite taken with your idea of a coup. It has so much more elegance than running for office. You must do it. Talk to Blake's campaign manager, Michael St. Augustine."

MICHAEL ST. AUGUSTINE and the newly elected mayor were seated with the latter's mother and Simon Wong, enjoying a late dinner at the Fortunate Dynasty restaurant.

"Now that you've won, James," said Blake's mother, "I certainly hope you aren't going to do all those stupid things you said you'd do if elected."

"Mother, I should do what I said I'd do."

"Not if it's in terrible taste, like that spy on the rich folks program."

"Mrs. Blake," said Michael St. Augustine, "according to the exit polls it was our most successful issue. People love the idea of putting the wealthy under surveillance."

"Giving people what they like is not leadership; it's bread and circuses. And another thing: spending a million dollars for a memorial to a purse snatcher who stuck a feather in his hair, that's a fraud on the public till."

Simon Wong sought to comfort her. "None of us was happy with these issues. But polls showed that without embracing them we would lose white votes needed to win. If he doesn't win he can't lead."

"Yes, I must take comfort in that, I suppose, but there ought to be a way to back off honorably from what were lousy ideas to begin with. Politicians do it all the time. Besides the Hill trial proved Smoking Mother was not a Native-American."

"Mother, I made promises, and I'm going to keep them. As to the jury verdict, it makes no difference that twelve people saw through the hoax. There are thousands on thousands out there, still deluded, who love Smoking Mother as an Indian. It's their feelings that count. We're building the future for them, not the jury. I've learned something from this campaign: Politics isn't really concerned with the people who know what's going on. It's for the ones who don't."

Blake's mother sighed audibly.

"Mother, the Smoking Mother memorial is a done deal."

"Then at least don't do that spy on the rich folks thing."

"The fat cat monitor program is different. We'll have to see how it works and what it costs. That's something that might not last forever."

"But," said the winner's mother, "that dingbat purse-snatcher memorial will, and you'll always be associated with it."

"Proudly, mother, proudly," said Blake, opening his fortune cookie. "He who sleeps with his dog must expect to have fleas," read the message on the slip of cookie paper.

PART V

EPILOGUE

THE SMOKING MOTHER MEMORIAL WAS DEDICATED in Civic Center Park six months to the day following the verdict in the Hill case. Mayor Blake presided, flanked by his mother and his new Chief Administrative Officer, Michael St. Augustine. Beside them on the podium was sculptor Eric Krane, erstwhile suitor of Penny and painter of her portrait, who had submitted the winning design for the memorial and supervised its construction.

Penny and Jonathan Barrow, newly returned from a Caribbean honeymoon, were in the audience. Near them sat a newcomer to the Bay Area, Philo Spass. Philo, while not yet graduated from high school, had, with his parents' blessing, entered into a pricey, five-year consulting contract with Macrohard, Ltd., the world's largest computer products company. Macrohard headquarters were located some thirty miles south of San Francisco, which necessitated relocation of the Spass family to the Bay Area. Philo's first act as consultant was to oversee acquisition by Macrohard of Break-in, Inc., publishers of the underground hackers' magazine, *Access*.

Former mayor Homer and R. "Doc" Wayward were unable to be present. They were still in New York, Doc's proposal to move the Statue of Liberty to Fire Island having encountered more opposition than expected.

Mayor Blake's mother pulled the cord unveiling the memorial. A cheer rose from the crowd as the draping fell to the ground. There in heroic dimension stood the representation of Smoking Mother, poised knife in hand, upright feather banded to his head, astride the body of a fallen Seventh Cavalry officer. Eric had meticulously copied the dead soldier's uniform from Hiram Wallis' depiction of Custer's Last Stand, and had thoroughly Indianized the hero's facial features and hair. There could be no mistaking this bold warrior for a Swede. Smoking Mother's left hand shaded his eyes, and his noble face looked into the distance at some point whence the cavalry would never come again, his eyes searching, as if for the Secret of Life.

AT THE SAME TIME, far across the great water on Nova Cannes, it was evening. Rainwater dripped from the lofty trees onto the tribespeople gathered around the big open hearth over which the spitted body of an enemy tribesman was being turned slowly. Tribal elders circled the pit, holding aloft an effigy of Big Mouth and chanting, "Big Mouth eat more." Others sat sipping koda and beating drums. Soon there would be another feast, another long pig.